The Home Scar

KATHLEEN MacMAHON

SANDYCOVE

an imprint of

PENGUIN BOOKS

SANDYCOVE

UK | USA | Canada | Ireland | Australia
India | New Zealand | South Africa

Sandycove is part of the Penguin Random House group of companies
whose addresses can be found at global.penguinrandomhouse.com.

First published 2023

002

Copyright © Kathleen MacMahon, 2023

Set in 12.55/14.88pt Garamond MT Std
Typeset by Jouve (UK), Milton Keynes
Printed and bound in Great Britain by Clays Ltd, Elcograf S.p.A.

The authorized representative in the EEA is Penguin Random House Ireland,
Morrison Chambers, 32 Nassau Street, Dublin D02 YH68

A CIP catalogue record for this book is available from the British Library

ISBN: 978–1–844–88599–2

www.greenpenguin.co.uk

For Kevin and Meg

The storm came in late summer. It swept in off the Atlantic, bringing high seas and gale force winds that battered the whole of the west coast. It was severe enough to earn itself a name, a red warning, a lead slot on the news. People were told to stay away from the sea, but even so some ventured out to observe the spectacle. There were surfers seen riding the waves in Sligo, the occasional swimmer at Salthill. They were endangering the lives of others as well as their own, according to the spokesperson for Water Safety Ireland who went on the radio to warn of the risks. As it happened, there was nobody drowned, leading some to say the dangers had been exaggerated. The storm had not been so dramatic after all. Bearing in mind what was happening in the rest of the world, it seemed blessedly tame.

The TV was at that time broadcasting pictures on a nightly basis of forest fires in Catalonia. Vast tracts of the Amazon were in flames, while in Mexico there were reports of snow. A hellish heatwave raged across Europe, with record-breaking temperatures in France, Germany and Poland. City dwellers took to the fountains to cool down. Ice pops were handed out to the zoo animals.

In North America there was rain, so much of it that in New York City the subway stations flooded. Dive teams had to be called in to evacuate people from their homes in Illinois. There was hail the size of baseballs in Montana, a landslide in Ohio, cyclones over the Atlantic. It was the tail end of one of those storms that had swept across Ireland, ripping the roofs off schools and football stadiums. Trees were uprooted, weather buoys unmoored. But still, we were lucky, people said. It could have been worse.

In the days that followed, the army was called in to help clear the debris from the roads. Electricity repair crews worked night and day to restore power to thousands of homes. Loss adjustors inspected the damage to property, while scientists lined up to blame global warming. Amid all this activity, one thing went unnoticed. It was happened upon purely by chance, by a man out walking his dog on the beach. The man wasn't quite sure what it was that he had found, but he at least had the wit to tell someone about it. Thus was the enormity of his discovery understood and eventually made public. What the storm had exposed was an ancient drowned forest.

The first newspaper to cover the story was the *Connacht Tribune*. A regional paper of long and distinguished standing, the *Tribune*'s newsroom was located in the city of Galway, and it was there that a young reporter took a call about the strange find. Glad of a chance to escape the office, the reporter drove the dozen miles out the coast road to the location described. The dog walker was waiting for him there, with barely contained excitement. It might have been a mutilated body he'd found and not some dead trees. The reporter changed into his wellies, which he kept in the boot of his car, and together they trudged across a muddy field to the beach.

At first it wasn't much to see. The trees were no more than stumps, barely a foot high. The stumps stood knee-deep in the wet sand like a ghostly, decapitated army. It was only when you hunkered down close to the sand that you were taken by the beauty of them. The grain of the wood was clearly visible, tiger-striped in some places, rounding into whorls in others. The reporter had no knowledge of natural history, but he knew that he was in the presence of something marvellous.

Back in the office, he made a few calls and gleaned some facts. His article was filed later that day, in plenty of time for the paper's weekly deadline. The lead story was about a delay to the start of a building project at the local hospital. The second lead was a court case involving a solicitor who'd defrauded his clients of their money. The story about the drowned trees featured prominently on page 3. Occupying more space than the article itself was the photograph the picture editor had commissioned from a local freelance. The photograph showed the dog owner in the background, with his head bent down to look at the ground as he walked. The drowned trees were in the foreground, in all their magnificence.

The ink on the *Tribune* was barely dry before the *Irish Times* picked up on the story. They posted it on their website and from there it travelled far and wide. It was a rare 'good' weather story and, as such, gratefully received by newspapers all over the world. Among those to feature it was the venerable *Guardian* newspaper in Britain. The *Guardian* also ran the story on page 3, under the headline 'Summer storm lays bare ancient forest'. They used the same photograph, diligently credited and paid for. It was a picture story if ever there was one. A quiet miracle, in a world full of noise.

PART ONE

I

Christo might so easily have missed it. He was not in the habit of buying a daily newspaper, although he would sometimes browse the leftovers scattered on a sofa table in the fellows' drawing room after dinner. He liked to start the day with a clear head, cycling into college without listening to the news on the radio. Without speaking to a soul.

This particular day was a Saturday, the last of the summer. It wasn't even ten in the morning, but already the punts were out on the river. The tourists reclined with self-conscious indolence in the dank bellies of the boats, as scruffy youths poled them inexpertly under the low bridges. Among them was one of Christo's more feckless students.

'Hello,' the student called out to him, straightening up from the knees as his punt emerged on the far side of the bridge.

Leaving one hand in sole charge of the handlebars, Christo raised the other hand in the air and gave a hearty wave. The student paused to wave back, rocking his boat as he did so and causing his passengers to collapse into each other in a heap of giggles. Christo cycled on, feeling inordinately pleased to have been greeted in such a manner. A pleasure that had a whoosh to it, it sent him flying along the final stretch of his journey, with his tweed jacket flapping behind him. For a moment, he had the sense that he belonged in the world. A feeling as rare to him as it was precious, he rode it as far as it would go.

Approaching the college, he hopped down off his bicycle without stopping it and ended up running alongside it, as if it were a horse he was trying to restrain. He managed somehow to bring it to heel without catching his ankle on the pedal. Without getting his trouser leg caught in the chain. Master of his environment, he locked the bicycle deftly to the rack and, draping the strap of his satchel across his chest, swung through the college gates. Under the arch and out of the yellow light into the stony gloom of the porter's lodge, where he stopped to peek into his pigeonhole, which was empty as usual.

'Dr Jones,' said the porter, pausing at his tasks. He looked out of his hatch, glaring at Christo over his reading glasses, as if he were the don and Christo the porter. The buoyancy of the bicycle journey was lost, and Christo was reduced to being an impostor again.

'Good morning, Mr King,' said Christo, struggling not to be cowed.

Mr King raised a finger, as if he had just remembered something.

'I have something for you,' he said, looking down at his desk. His tone suggested a rebuke.

'Oh?' said Christo. Aware of some transgression, though what it was that he'd done wrong he could not have said. So many rules here, he was walking on eggshells. Walking on grass that should not be walked on. Wearing a robe he should not have been wearing.

Christo had first come to Cambridge as an undergraduate, but he'd never acquired the ease of the place. Just as he'd never stopped being a new boy at his boarding school, even though he'd spent nearly five years there. He'd been a late arrival, landing like a poor, bruised windfall midway through the autumn term. The headmaster had ushered him into the classroom and the lesson had fallen silent, the boys all turning in their chairs to stare at him with open hostility. Christo felt like he'd been trapped in that moment ever since.

'Dr Singh asked me to pass this on to you,' said Mr King, handing Christo the previous day's copy of the *Guardian*. It had a yellow Post-it on the front with Christo's name on it. A page reference to an article Dr Singh wanted to bring to his attention. 'It wouldn't fit in your pigeonhole.'

'How kind,' said Christo, feeling foolish and relieved in equal measure. 'I'm much obliged.'

He tucked the newspaper under his arm and plunged into the stairwell. Breathing in the smell of dry old wood, he took the narrow, creaking stairs two at a time. Only when he was alone in his study, with the door closed behind him, did he become aware of his own breathing, fast and shallow. The feeling, a familiar one, of having escaped from a barrage of gunfire. It was only when he was alone that Christo ever felt truly safe.

He sat down at his desk. The college buildings were silent around him, but for the summer-weekend sound of tourists wandering in awe through the Old Court. The absence of students was a sorrow to Christo. He missed the youthful shouts that filled the air outside in term time. The rumble of their giddy feet on the staircase as they arrived for supervision. Those were the times when Christo was happiest, with the chairs drawn into a loose circle in his rooms and a pot of tea on the desk. A pack of Walker's shortbread fingers spread out on a plate – Christo liked to think the biscuits would be remembered with fondness long after the mathematics had been forgotten. In the discussions that followed, there was the beauty of a shared interest. An illusion of comradeship that dissolved as soon as the students traipsed back down the stairs. When Christo saw them in the dining hall it was from the high table where he sat with the other fellows, and they seemed so far removed from him as to be not so much the product of a different generation as a different species altogether. Every summer they disappeared, only to be replaced in the autumn by a younger batch, while Christo grew measurably older, year upon year. The effect of this was to make him feel like a rock in the middle of a river, with the water flowing endlessly by him.

The sun fought its way through the wobbly old window-pane, casting dust motes in a stage light as Christo settled down to work. He spent the next hour making notes for a lecture he was preparing on the logarithmic spiral. *Spira mirabilis*, it was also known as, for its miraculous ingenuity. As proof of this miracle, Christo had prepared a slide show depicting the many manifestations of the spiral in the natural world. The images he had chosen were: a cross section of a nautilus shell, the arms of the Milky Way, a cyclone over Cuba and a head of Romanesco broccoli. A final slide showed a photograph of a Danish pastry, which Christo planned to flash up as a joke. He hoped people would laugh. He worried they wouldn't.

'Of course they'll laugh,' he told himself. 'It's funny!'

He stood up and crossed the room to fill the kettle from the tap in the corner. As he waited for it to boil, he took out the day-old copy of the *Guardian* and studied the front-page photograph of forest fires raging in the Amazon. There was a teaser on the masthead for an interview with someone called Taylor Swift. A travel feature on the 'Top 10 breaks in Britain for nature lovers'.

Sitting back down at the desk with his mug of tea, Christo turned the page. It was the headline that caught his attention first, rather than the photograph, although afterwards it would be the photograph that most absorbed him. According to the short, three-column article below the headline, the drowned forest was seven and a half thousand years old, but its existence had only been revealed by the recent storm. The picture showed the trunks rising out of the shallows. The severed stumps had been worn smooth by the water until they were as round as ankle bones. The oily grain of the wood was clearly visible in the picture. Also visible was the figure of a man in the background, walking over a beach of grey stones. Christo checked the caption, but there was no indication of where exactly the beach was located, or what it was called, only the name of the nearest village.

Christo looked up at the clock on the wall to check the time before picking up the phone to call his sister. His blood was bubbling with nerves as he started rehearsing what he would say, but she answered before he'd thought it through.

'Christo?'

Her voice, as rich and deep as a hollow brass instrument. It never failed to sound a long, echoing note in his heart.

'Cassie, did I wake you?'

Like a kidnap victim who's been blindfolded and taken to an unknown location, he leaned his ear into the spaces created by the lag on the line and heard music from what he deduced to be a dance studio near her house. He detected the sound of light traffic and men's laughter, stationary and unhurried. Christo pictured three of them sitting on plastic chairs at a nearby corner. Then came the sound of a street vendor's bicycle horn, parp, parp, parp. A radio pumping out pop music, punctuated by the presenter's voice speaking rapid-fire, excitable Spanish.

'Christo, is everything okay?'

He could hear her breath coming fast and shallow in the expectation of bad news.

'Everything's fine,' he said. 'I just wanted to tell you. They've found Margo's trees.'

2

That was where it all started for Christo. He'd just turned thirteen when Margo took them up the knobbly old mountain beyond the village and told them about the trees. Cassie was with them, and Seamus was there too, but not Jim. In Christo's memory, his mother was also absent, which didn't mean she wasn't there, only that he had no memory of her, and there was nobody he could ask. It was a problem he and Cassie regularly encountered.

'Where did you live in London?'

She was a teenager when she first asked him this, seizing on the sliver of life he'd had before she was born. She was jealous that he'd had their mother all to himself before she arrived.

'I don't know,' he would say.

He'd been a baby then. He had no memory of it.

'How old were you when you moved to the States?'

'I've no idea,' Christo would say. 'One? Maybe two?'

'Where did you live?'

There was no end to her capacity for asking questions. As a child she'd had an endless supply of them. It was exhausting.

'*Cassie Koenig*,' their mother used to say. '*Never in my whole life have I met anyone who asks so many questions. It's enough to drive a person stark-raving mad.*'

Christo was two and a half when she was born, a lone entity until her arrival introduced the concept of relativity. 'You're a big brother now,' he was told. It was only when he was measured against her that he was found to be so. 'Big brother,' he repeated, like a mantra, as if by doing so he could convince himself that this was the case, when the truth was that she took up more space in the world than he did, with her big head and her big eyes and her big demands on everyone's attention. His first memory of her was of a crib that occupied the centre of the living room. Someone must have picked him up and shown her to him. Someone must have explained to him what she was, but he had no memory of it. She was no more than an alien presence, unseen by him and unwanted. Christo couldn't understand why everyone was so pleased by her arrival.

He was three when he discovered he could make her laugh. Up until then Christo had never imagined that he had it within himself to be funny, but that raucous baby laughter of hers cast a bright stage light over him, and he woke up to the comedian inside himself. All he had to do was look at her and she laughed. She laughed until her belly wobbled and her head collapsed on her shoulders. Sometimes she brought on a fit of hiccups from laughing so much. One time she laughed so much that she fell over, right where she was sitting on her play mat. Ever since then, there had been inside Christo a person who could make his sister laugh so hard that she'd fall over. Anytime she was in need of cheering up, he would remind her of it.

'Sometimes you laughed so much the snot came out your nose.'

Cassie would squirm with pleasure. She loved to hear stories about herself.

'Tell me about the time I ate all your Hallowe'en candy,' she might say.

'Well, that wasn't just the one time.'

'Tell me, anyway.'

As a child, Cassie had a great lust for life. Any treat that was going, any opportunity for adventure, she was the girl with her hand up to say, 'Me! Me! Me!' A queue-jumper par excellence, Cassie saw no harm in putting herself to the fore of things. This monstrous capacity for self-advancement was so natural to her that it was somehow endearing. Christo had been saddened in recent years to see it fade, a more subdued sister coming to live in the skin of the old one. This sister was increasingly preoccupied by all the pieces she was missing from the past.

'Do you remember living in the beach house?' she'd asked him recently.

'Not really,' he'd said, which wasn't quite true. He remembered the sandy porch steps that were painted a cheery shade of seaside blue. He remembered the sound of the sea outside the window and the sweet smell of watermelon inside the house. There was no single incident he remembered, only a sense of doors opening and closing. Windows in the walls like square paintings of sea and sky. Voices on the verge of laughter.

By the time he was in elementary school they'd moved to the house in the hills. Christo remembered his first Christmas at the new house – he got a Lego Galaxy Commander – but he couldn't have said how old he was then. He had a memory of losing a tooth at that house – he had a distinct memory of holding the bloody tooth in his hand – but he couldn't pin an age on it. He remembered standing in line for a ride at SeaWorld – '*He's twelve,*' his mother had assured the attendant, but he wasn't. He was only ten. The next date he was sure of was his thirteenth birthday, the summer they were in Ireland.

'A baker's dozen,' he remembered Jim saying, as his mother counted out the candles. Christo had never heard the expression before, but every time he'd heard it since he found himself back in that kitchen in the west of Ireland, with his mother leaning over the big square table, lighter poised to fire up his birthday candles. Cassie kept blowing them out before he had a chance to.

'I wish I could remember where the house was,' he asked her when he called her. 'Do you happen to know?'

He couldn't for the life of him remember the name of the village, only the particulars of it. There was a shop and a pub at the crossroads with some petrol pumps out front. A fork in the road led to a wide white beach, and beyond the beach was the house and beyond the house the pier. That was the route they walked back and forth all summer.

'No clue,' said Cassie. 'Jesus, Christo. I was only ten years old.'

It was early summer when they arrived. This much Christo had been able to calculate from the memory of the yellow flag irises they saw blooming in the ditches. The days were long, light lingering in the westernmost reaches of the sky until nearly midnight as they played down on the pier. By the end of their time there, the berries were ripening to black in the hedgerows. Using empty margarine cartons – or in Cassie's case a blue plastic bucket in the shape of an inverted castle – they combed the back roads trying to find enough of them to make a crumble.

'Always walk on the right-hand side of the road,' Jim had told them. 'That way you can see the cars that are coming to run you down.'

'You'd be amazed how many berries you need to make a crumble,' said Margo, as their enthusiasm for the project began to wane. The ripest blackberries all seemed to grow just out of reach, so you had to battle through brambles to get to them. Cassie and Seamus were both wearing long sleeves, but Christo was in a t-shirt. By the time they got back to the house, his bare arms were torn to shreds.

'*Oh, Christo,*' said his mother, putting a hand over her mouth as a stopper for her laughter. '*You look like you've been mauled by a lion.*'

'That's one brave lad you've got,' said Jim. 'Not a whisper out of him.'

Christo had never forgotten that, just as he had not forgotten the way Margo called him 'love'. The way the woman in the shop said, 'You poor crayturs,' as she held the jar of cola bottles out so they could pick one 'on the house'. A note of pity in her voice that, even as a child, Christo was quick to detect. He heard it without understanding it.

'There's money coming to her from her father.' That was another thing Christo remembered hearing. There was a trip to a lawyer's office in the city. She left them sitting in the car for what seemed like hours. They scrambled into the front, where Cassie sat in the passenger seat and took control of the tape deck. Christo sat in the driver's seat, grabbing the wheel with both hands as he pretended to drive away.

'*Here,*' said their mother, returning to the car with a bag of iced buns that she tossed into the back seat. '*Feeding time at the zoo.*'

She might almost have been a normal mother that summer, getting up in the mornings to make them pancakes, which they ate with lemon and sugar. On sunny days she made Tayto crisp sandwiches that they wrapped in tinfoil and brought down to the beach. She sat on a plaid rug with her book, while they played in the sand dunes, devising ever more elaborate games of make-believe. On rainy days, she made them hot chocolate and let them strip the blankets off the beds to make a den. She would pull the rocking chair up to the kitchen window and sit staring out at the rain, a mug of tea in her hands and the sea on the other side of the glass feeding some need in her. Other times she sat hunched over the kitchen table, humming as she worked away patiently at a huge jigsaw. One of the corner pieces was missing, much to her annoyance. She pulled the dresser away from the wall and searched behind it. Got down on her hands and knees and looked under the chairs, the stove, the radiator.

'*There's a fiver in it for anyone who finds that fucking corner,*' she announced, in that voice of hers that came unsummoned at times. There was no part of her that remained – not her face, nor her smell – so much as her voice. Like a gold filling or a steel pin that's found among the ashes after a body is cremated, her voice was made of some substance that would not be destroyed.

'*Count me out,*' she would have said, the day they set off for the mountain. '*Mountain climbing is for mugs.*'

Christo had no recollection of the actual climb, only the view from the standing stone at the top. He remembered the feeling of being up there. He'd felt like he was standing on top of the world.

'Once upon a time,' Margo told them. 'This whole place would have been covered by trees.'

She produced some wine gums from the pocket of her raincoat. Cassie had to have a red one and Seamus wanted black. Christo wasn't fussy, so he took a green one. The flavour of it was watery and tantalizingly familiar, but he couldn't have said what fruit it was supposed to be.

'Look,' said Margo, hunching down behind him. She wrapped an arm around his shoulders, so the finger she used to point was positioned for his eyeline as well as her own.

'That way is south. That's County Clare.'

Slowly, she turned him from the waist, so they were looking down at the hammerhead formation of the beaches below them. The sea was an impossible shade of turquoise. The sand an unearthly white.

'Now,' she said, continuing the sweep of her arm to the right. 'Out there you have County Mayo.'

He could see a dark headland against the sky.

'Beyond that is Sligo, then Donegal.'

Turning inland, Christo saw great tracts of bog, broken only by the presence of a still, dark lake. In the foreground, nothing but rocks and gorse and tufts of straw-coloured reeds rising out of the soggy ground. He let his eyes roam back and forth, as if he was looking for something, but what that thing might be he did not know.

'Now imagine,' she told him, in that voice of hers that ran clear with wonder. 'A very long time ago, all of this would have been covered in trees. Only the very tops of the mountains would have been visible above the treeline.'

'What happened to them?'

'We did,' she said. 'Human beings. We came along and chopped them all down.'

Christo saw it then, as clear as anything. How the landscape bore the absence of those trees like an old scar.

'The only ones that are left are out there,' said Margo, raising her finger to point at the flat expanse of sea. 'There's a whole forest out there, under the sea. An ancient drowned forest.'

Christo couldn't sleep that night for thinking about those drowned trees. The next day he badgered his mother to drive him to the local library, where he combed the encyclopedias for any mention of them, but there was none. That was before the internet, when the work of finding information was arduous and time-consuming and perhaps even impossible. Christo was forced to abandon his quest, but he never looked at the sea again without wondering was there an ancient forest under the waves? Once you'd heard something like that, you couldn't ever forget it.

He was a postgraduate at Cambridge when he heard that a drowned forest had been exposed on the coast of Wales. He took a series of trains and buses, arriving finally in the village of Borth, where he barely stopped long enough to dump his backpack in the guesthouse before heading to the beach. He walked among hundreds, maybe even thousands, of tree stumps that rose up out of the shallows like shark fins. He could hardly breathe, he was so excited.

Back in the library at Cambridge, Christo found a fifteenth-century travelogue, written in Latin, that attested to the existence of a vast forest stretching all the way from Mont-Saint-Michel to the Scilly Isles. Legend had it that the bells of the city of Is could be heard ringing out from under the waves. He learned there were reports as far back as the late 1700s of a submerged forest near Youghal in County Cork. The Youghal forest was periodically exposed by extreme weather events, only to be covered again by water and sand within a few short months. Tree stumps had also been observed from time to time in south Mayo and Clare, but the forest off the south coast of Connemara had remained sub-merged, until now.

'I need to go there,' he told Cassie. Nothing would do him but to see it for himself. 'I've a few weeks before term starts.'

Already, he was imagining the tides coming in and out, sand deposits building up around the tree stumps. Before long they would be submerged again. Christo couldn't get there soon enough.

'You could come with me,' he said. Gently, gently, gently. He didn't want to scare her off.

'Oh, Christo.'

He could hear her voice falling away from the phone. He imagined her tipping her head back to look up at the ceiling. Deep breath in. Slowly out.

'Wouldn't you like to go back?'

More than a quarter of a century since they'd been there, Christo could still see the low, grey mountains in his mind. He could picture the black slicks of seaweed that littered the coral beach by the road, and the cows that grazed incongruously on its fringes. He could feel the bone shape of the sand when you scooped it up in your hand. He could almost touch the shells of the tiny snails that nestled in the razor-sharp grass of the dunes. The desire in him to go back there was so strong that he felt high on it.

'I'll think about it,' she said. 'That's all I'm promising you. I'll give it some thought.'

After she hung up, Christo closed his eyes and heard the sound of an old cassette deck cranking out the Beatles. He heard the playground calls of seagulls, whirling overhead, and the hiss and suck of the sea. He heard his sister's voice, rippling like a kite through the air of a long-ago summer night, and – in his mind – alongside all of those things, was a feeling of happiness that he had never quite experienced since.

3

Of Ireland, Cassie remembered nothing of any substance. There was no town name that she recalled, no street address, no local landmark. She could not tell you where in the country they'd been, only that they were beside the sea and within a short drive of the school her mother had attended as a girl. The friends they had there were like a family from a picture book. The father was Jim. The mother was Margo. Seamus was the child.

Of the three of them, it was Jim who was clearest in Cassie's mind. 'How's the button?' he used to say to her, and Cassie would clam up, shoulders to her ears and no idea of what to say. 'Is it yourself, Christy?' he would ask, giving Christo a featherweight punch to the shoulder. He was like a wild wind, sweeping them all up with him. Up to the top of the back field at dawn to see a newborn foal, or out on a rowboat in the black of night in search of phosphorescence in the water. He seemed always to be bundling them off on some adventure or other. When they were going to the beach, he let them all ride on the roof rack like monkeys, with their hair blowing across their faces and their legs drawn up to their chests. Their knuckles white from holding on for dear life as the car barrelled along the bumpy country road. The sound of their mother's voice billowed out the open passenger window, ribboned by the wind. They all joined in, singing along with great enthusiasm to 'Penny Lane' and 'Lucy in the Sky with Diamonds' and Cassie's personal favourite, 'Ob-La-Di, Ob-La-Da'.

Margo she remembered as a windblown person, always crumpling into a smile. Always gathering wildflowers from the hedgerow or bending down to pick a shell up off the sand. 'I have no little girl,' she said to Cassie once, as they were setting the table together. 'I'm the only woman in a household of men.' All these years later, Cassie remembered the loneliness with which it was said, and it seemed to her a very adult thing to have told a child. It insisted on being remembered.

In Cassie's memory she and Margo were bent over the kitchen table, where a scattering of wildflowers had been laid out to dry on a sheet of newspaper. Cassie was trying to identify the flowers they'd picked, with the help of Margo's guidebook.

'Look,' Margo said, using the nail of her little finger to spread out the tiny petals of a sea pink. 'See how delicate he is.' Cassie leaned in to see. Her hair, brushing against Margo's hair. Her breath, slow and loud. She felt like a fumbly giant stumbling into a miniature world. 'Now,' said Margo, lifting the flower carefully and setting it onto a sheet of white paper. 'Let's press him.' With extreme care, Cassie laid a second sheet of paper over the first and placed the sandwich they'd made of the flower into the phone book, which was open to F: Foyle to Funcheon.

'Funcheon!' she said. 'That's a funny name.'

The things you remember.

'Don't forget to make him a label,' said Margo.

Cassie chose a purple marker from the jam jar on the table, and in her most meticulous handwriting she wrote out the name of the flower, drawing a curlicue underneath it. She slipped the label into the phone book with the flower and closed the book carefully, replacing the lid on the marker and putting it back into the jar. The markers belonged to Seamus, and she was afraid he'd be angry if he knew she was using them. Even then, she was aware they were trespassing on his life.

Shay-muss, was how they said his name. When Cassie first saw it written down, she wondered why they'd chosen to leave the sea out of it. It seemed a better name to her with the sea in it. Sea-muss the sea monster, with his fishing net in one hand and a plastic bucket in the other, water slopping over the sides and sea creatures in it. In Cassie's memory he was always carrying that bucket around with him, like some kind of trophy. Whatever it was that resided inside the bucket bestowed great importance. A heroic quality to him as he scooped a jellyfish out of the shallows with his net or cleared nettles from his path using a broken branch as a sword. He once licked the palm of his hand and wiped a smear of manure from Cassie's leg. In the pub, he climbed onto a bar stool with a five-pound note in his hand and ordered a red lemonade for himself, 'and one for the lady'. It was the first romantic episode of Cassie's life.

'Who was that on the phone?' Eduardo asked her, sitting up in the bed. She knew he'd been woken by Christo's call, but he'd played at still being asleep. He'd only stirred when she'd finished her conversation.

'Mi hermano,' she said, playing their usual cat-and-mouse game. Eduardo liked to converse with Cassie in his impeccable, graduate-school English. Cassie responded by hiding behind her flawed, self-taught Spanish. When Eduardo told her he loved her, which he had started to do with alarming frequency, she said, 'Yo también.' When he called her 'my love', Cassie reciprocated by calling him 'mi amor'. Spoken in a language other than her own, it seemed to her to mean somehow less.

'Is everything okay?'

'Sure,' said Cassie, pulling her robe from the hook on the back of the bedroom door, while Eduardo watched her from where he was sitting in the bed. 'Why wouldn't it be?'

'It's six in the morning.'

'Not in England it's not,' she said, feeling defensive on behalf of her brother. 'In England it's nearly lunchtime.'

She wrapped herself in the tissue-thin gown, hugging it to her for comfort.

'So, when do I get to meet him?' asked Eduardo. 'This mysterious brother of yours.'

'Yeah, well, it's not like he lives down the road.'

'Maybe he hasn't heard. There's a thing called an airplane?'

Cassie still hadn't figured out whether Eduardo's jokes sounded lame in Spanish too, or was it just in English?

'Time for coffee,' she said, heading for the kitchen. She immersed herself in the task, filling the bottom chamber with water and spooning the ground beans into the top chamber. Tamping it down hard, she screwed the pot tightly shut and set it on the hob. She held a lit match to the burner, savouring the brief, tantalizing smell of gas before the flame took. It was only when she stood waiting for the coffee to percolate that she felt the sadness rising in her. A feeling as familiar to her as breathing, she closed her eyes and clenched her jaw as she tried to force it back down into her gut.

'Are you okay?'

He had come into the room without her noticing, slipping up behind her and making a life ring of his arms. Instead of being grateful that she'd been rescued, Cassie felt like slipping the ring and dipping her head under the waves.

'Wait,' she said, hearing the sound of the pot on the hob geysering. 'The coffee's ready.'

'Forget the damn coffee. Come back to bed.'

'You know the rules,' said Cassie, breaking free of him. 'You go back to bed. I'll bring the coffee.'

The rules were of Cassie's making, established early on and observed without complaint by Eduardo, until recently. They only saw each other at the weekends, alternating between her little house in the city and his holiday home in the mountains. On the nights that she stayed at his house, he would bring her coffee in bed. When he stayed at hers, she returned the favour, pointedly using the old tin coffee pot she'd bought when she first moved to Mexico over the fancy machine Eduardo had given her for Christmas. It sat gathering dust on the counter, a reminder to him not to cross the line she'd drawn around her life, a line that needed constant reinforcing.

'What's this?' she'd asked him recently, holding up an item of clothing she'd found hanging in her closet.

'That's my shirt. I don't want it to get crumpled.'

'No unpacking,' she told him, taking the shirt off the hanger and settling it over the back of a chair.

'Hombre,' said Eduardo, shaking his head in disbelief.

He had insisted on giving Cassie a key to his apartment in the city, on the basis that she might get there before him some day, but she'd only ever used it once, to open the door to a plumber when Eduardo was out of town. She had not given him a key to her place, but she allowed him to leave a toothbrush in the jar by the sink and some shaving foam and a razor in the bathroom cupboard, along with his Clarins-Men Fluido Superhidratante. They did not meet up midweek, except occasionally to attend an exhibition opening or to see a movie. Cassie insisted on sleeping in her own bed, alone, on weeknights.

'Come on,' he might say, leaving the cinema with her on a Tuesday night. 'Let's make an exception for Tuesdays.'

'Tengo que trabajar,' she'd say, which was at least a half-truth. Her work was important to her, no question, but it was the solitude that was sacrosanct. The days spent alone, carving fine lines into stone. Monday to Friday, she survived on a diet of avocados that she plucked from the tree in her garden and ate with oil and salt. She dined on street tacos that she fetched from the stall on the corner. Letting the masonry dust build up day by day under her fingernails until Friday afternoon, when she scrubbed herself clean and washed her hair with her favourite almond-oil shampoo. With her weekend bag waiting at the door, she dressed as she listened for the expensive purr of Eduardo's car pulling up to the kerb outside.

'There must be something wrong with him if she won't introduce him to us,' said the girlfriends she met up with on Thursday nights at a bookstore near her house to drink herbal tea and laugh about life's little absurdities.

'Honestly,' Cassie told them. 'There's nothing wrong with him, I swear.'

'Maybe he doesn't exist. Maybe he's a figment of her imagination.'

Cassie promised to produce him but never did.

'Where did you meet this guy, anyway?'

'Oh, at a work thing.'

A drinks reception hosted by her gallery to bring sculptors into the orbit of architects who might commission their work. Cassie had been led over to him by the gallery owner, and she'd flirted with him, as she was expected to do, in the hope that he might commission her to install a large and expensive piece of stone in front of one of his buildings. Instead, it was Eduardo who had installed himself in her life with what was beginning to take on a feeling of monumental permanence.

'We should move in together,' he'd announced, in the manner of a declaration, on Christmas morning.

'Your apartment's too white for me,' she said, refusing to take the suggestion seriously.

'No problem. I can move in with you.'

She laughed, imagining Eduardo wheeling a rack of designer suits into the casita on the Calle Chihuahua. She saw him fighting through her spider plants to get to the shower. Knocking over her jars of pencils every time he stood up from the table.

'You're an architect,' she said. 'You couldn't handle the clutter.'

Some twenty years her senior, it was Eduardo's age that had first attracted Cassie to him. That and the fact of an ex-wife, three grown daughters and a demanding elderly mother. Cassie had assumed that the presence of all these women in his life would absorb most of his energies, leaving only a small window for a girlfriend, which she could flit in and out of. She had not reckoned with Eduardo's adolescent appetite for love.

'Don't you get lonely without me?' he'd asked her once, as they said their Sunday-evening goodbyes. 'Don't you miss me during the week? Doesn't your bed feel empty?'

'No,' Cassie had said. 'It feels spacious.'

'I'm beginning to think you're not a woman.'

'Oh? What am I then?'

'You're more like a cactus.'

She'd smiled, pleased at the thought of herself as a prickly thing. Something that thrived in arid conditions. It was everything she wanted to be.

'So, what did your brother say?' he asked her now.

'He wants me to go to Ireland with him.'

'Why Ireland?'

'That's where our mother was from. We spent a summer there once, when we were kids. We haven't been back since.'

Cassie raised her coffee cup to her lips before anything else had a chance to come out.

'Interesting,' said Eduardo. It was more than she'd ever told him before.

All she'd told Eduardo was that her parents were both dead. That her father was American, but not who he was. He knew she had a half-brother who was half-English. A sheaf of half-truths that together did not make a whole, but she was not in the habit of telling her life story to some man she'd just met. A reticence that had at first seemed prudent, it was only as time wore on that it began to feel like an injustice to Eduardo not to have levelled with him from the start. So far as she knew, there was nothing about his life that he'd kept from her.

'So, you're both half-Irish?'

'Yes,' she said. 'I suppose we are.'

The Irish in them was silent, like the h in 'helado'. A word Cassie had learned when she first came to Mexico as a child. Un helado por favor. The heat of the coin branding the palm of her hand. The blast of cold air from the freezer as the lid was lifted. The feeling of her sandals falling away from her heels as she rose on the balls of her feet to peer inside. Cassie was just about to turn eleven when she crossed the border with her mother, riding shotgun on a trail of self-destruction that would end within weeks in a cheap guesthouse on the Caribbean coast. Some part of her would forever be in that huge, creaking house, with the rain falling thunderously on the courtyard tiles and the parrot screeching blue murder and the sound of her own voice pleading with her mother to wake up.

Of the return journey from Mexico with her mother's body, Cassie had no memory. It was her mother's friend Bill who came to fetch them – this much she knew – but she remembered nothing until they were safely back in Bill's dilapidated clapboard cottage in the Hollywood Hills. Bill had bought the house in the early sixties after selling his first novel to a movie studio, but he hadn't sold anything since, so the house – and Bill – had entered into decline. The spare rooms were all rented out to students, but Bill created a screened-off boudoir for Cassie in the corner of the living room. She'd no sooner been installed than he put her to work clearing rocks from a patch of ground in the corner of his garden. He wanted to plant a grove of trees there, with a hammock strung between them, so you could lie in the hammock and watch the sun set over the ocean. 'Cassie's Corner', he called it, introducing small improvements over the years. He paved the wall with some broken tiles, added a repurposed wooden cable reel as a low table. He planted some rose bushes. If Cassie had a place in the world, then that corner of Bill's garden was it.

'Is that where your mom is buried?' asked Eduardo. 'In Ireland?'

'Oh no,' said Cassie. 'She doesn't have a grave. She was cremated.'

They drove up to Big Sur to scatter her ashes. The air was thick with the smell of the wild fennel that grew on the side of the highway. The ashes were not dusty, as she had expected, but bone hard, like tiny grains of sand. The wind blew them into their faces. They had to duck to escape them.

'So, do you have family in Ireland?' Eduardo asked. The question seemed so innocent to Cassie that she almost laughed.

'No,' she said, narrowing her eyes against the memory of her grandfather's house. The ominous crunch of gravel on the drive. The hallway with its ticking clock and the piano they were never allowed to play. 'No, my grandfather died a long time ago. There's nobody left. The reason my brother wants to go to Ireland is to see some trees.'

She rolled her eyes, framing the expedition as a daft notion of Christo's, something barely worthy of consideration.

'Some trees?'

'Some trees,' she repeated. 'My brother is more interested in the natural world than the human one.'

She thought of the bird's egg Christo had shown her when she'd visited him in Cambridge. The way he'd wrapped it up so tenderly in his handkerchief, you'd swear it was a live bird and not just its egg. She was struck then by the innocence that he had somehow never lost. Cassie could not help but feel the injustice of it, as if they'd both been in the same road accident, but she alone had been injured. There was something miraculously untouched about Christo.

'My brother is not normal,' she explained to Eduardo.

'Maybe,' said Eduardo, with a shrug. 'But he is your brother.'

'Meaning?'

'Meaning, you should go.'

'Well, you see, that's the thing. I'm not sure I want to.'

It wasn't that she'd never thought of going back. Many times, over the years, she'd promised herself she'd go. She'd even gone so far as to imagine herself sitting at Margo's kitchen table, drinking multiple mugs of tea as they parsed the time that had passed since they'd last met. Hatching and cross-hatching it, the way Margo had once taught her to do with colouring pencils. There were things Cassie wanted to tell Margo – things she'd never told anybody – in the hope that Margo would understand the life she'd lived and the person she had become as a result.

'I'm proud of you,' Margo would say, with shining eyes. 'You're a great girl.'

This was a conversation Cassie longed to have with Margo, but she never felt quite ready. For many years, it seemed that not enough time had gone by, so she waited for some shift to take place in her life before she could go back and present herself to Margo. But the shift she was waiting for never happened, and more years went by, until it began to feel like she'd left it too late to go. It wasn't just the time that had stretched and warped. In Cassie's mind it seemed like the two locations were drifting further and further apart. Like a place that was once one great land mass but had been divided by a rising sea. It was hard to see how you could pass between the two.

'I don't understand you,' said Eduardo, genuinely baffled. 'Why don't you want to go?'

Cassie felt suddenly and unaccountably weary, like she'd been running from something, running and running and running until her last breath was gone and she'd just reached a brick wall.

'Oh, Eduardo,' she said, closing her eyes and despairing of ever explaining it, perhaps even to herself. 'Just because.'

4

In his attic flat in Cambridge, Christo took the giant *Times Atlas of the World* off the shelf and carried it over to the dining table. He had the small, high window open beside him, and through it he could hear the summer-evening sounds of a game of rounders taking place on the common. There was the soft thwack of a tennis ball against a cricket bat. A boy's name was shouted out encouragingly, followed by a little cheer. Listening to the sounds of other people's lives, Christo felt like a passenger on a cruise ship moored in port for the night. He knew there was a real town out there – he could see it and hear it – but it seemed to Christo that he was not a part of it.

'Where's home, Christo?' his landlady had asked him recently, all Cornish and clucky.

'Ah,' he'd replied. 'That's a good question, Sue. I'm not quite sure how to answer it.'

She'd looked at him expectantly, head on a tilt, and Christo found himself under pressure to come up with an answer.

'My father lives in Devon,' he offered, as a starting point. He described the heritage farmhouse. The lavender and roses out front. The river behind.

'It sounds lovely,' said Sue, no doubt imagining Christo's father as a plump country squire. He didn't like to disillusion her.

'Do you visit him often?'

'Not so often,' he said, indulging her curiosity because he liked her very much. He knew she was only being kind.

'He's married again,' he explained. 'His wife isn't exactly my cup of tea.'

He pictured Amanda in her farmhouse kitchen, with the kettle singing away on top of the Aga. She was wearing a sleeveless quilted jacket covered with dog hair, jodhpurs and a pair of muddy Hunter wellies. Her hair bleached blonde and her eyes lined in black kohl, a cigarette always on the go. She didn't use heroin anymore, hadn't done so for years, but that didn't stop the word marking her like a tattoo. Something you could never undo.

'Is that where you grew up – Devon?'

'Oh no. No, I grew up in LA.'

'That must have been nice!'

'Yes,' said Christo, 'it was nice.'

Even though Christo had never really felt at home in LA. He distrusted the strange indoor feel of the place. The trees that looked like film props. The carpet-like lawns. LA was not and never had been Christo's natural habitat, which was unfortunate because his mother loved everything about the place. She loved the sun-baked pavements and the monotony of blue skies and the miracle of citrus fruits growing in the garden. *'I'd like to be reincarnated as a lizard,'* she said once, as she lay on a sun lounger by the pool. Sweat beads gathering in the well between her breasts. In her belly button. On her upper lip. She stuck out her bottom lip and blew to cool herself down. *'Lizards have the fucking life.'*

'So, was that where your mum was from, then?' asked Sue. The word 'mum', so homely in her unsuspecting voice. 'Los Angeles?'

'Oh no,' said Christo. 'She was from Ireland. Originally.'

'I love Ireland!' said Sue. 'We went there a few times with the caravan. We were in Wexford one time and Cork twice. Whereabouts in Ireland was your mum from?'

'County Westmeath,' said Christo, taking on a casual air to cover up the gaps in his knowledge. All he knew was that she was the only child of a country vet. That her own mother had died when she was twelve, prompting her father to pack her off to boarding school. The school was a desolate place – a castle, she'd said – and unmercifully cold. She had described the pervasive damp and the smoking fires and the chilblains she had on her hands and feet from sitting too close to the flames. There was a delivery man who gave them stale cakes from the bakery. A gardener who dealt in contraband cigarettes. A nun who was kind to her. The songs she sang around the house when they were children were the hymns she'd learned at school. The lurid curse words she used and the sudden crushing sorrows that came over her, all part of the baggage she carried from that place.

'If you don't come downstairs right now, I'll murder you,' she would roar. The kids who came to their house were always shocked by the violence of the threats that came out of her. *'If you spill that drink, I'll slaughter you,'* she'd say, or *'I'll skin you alive.'*

There was a little friend of Cassie's who'd cried and wanted to go home.

'She doesn't mean it,' Cassie had to explain. 'She only talks like that because she's from Ireland.'

'I was only there once,' Christo told Sue. 'And that was a long time ago. I can hardly remember it.'

Even as he was saying it, Christo knew this was not quite accurate. He remembered it vividly but incompletely. Like a film reel that had been salvaged from a fire, it was missing whole sections while others were perfectly intact. Snippets of his mother's voice – with her exact turns of phrase – preserved with eerie accuracy. There were entire scenes that had survived – a trek across a dung-pocked field, a night-time drive in relentless rain – but the narrative thread was lost. It was hard to make sense of it.

'*Fasten your seat belts*,' she'd announced, out of the blue. '*Your grandfather's dying, and he wants to see me. Old bastard that he is.*'

That had all been news to Christo. The grandfather, as much as his dying. Most surprising of all was the word his mother had used to describe him. There was money coming to them, she explained, and that was why she had to go back. If she didn't go, there was no knowing what he'd do with it. The dogs' and cats' home was mentioned.

'*He has me over a barrel and he knows it*,' she said. '*God, I hate to give him the satisfaction.*'

Christo opened the atlas to the index at the back, soothed – as always – by the means of finding a way into things by numbers. He found a page reference and followed it to the double-page map of his mother's country.

'*A kip of a country*,' she'd told them. '*Out of there quick enough I could not get.*'

Christo recalled word for word her curiously constructed syntax.

'*There's nothing in Ireland only bog and cow shite*,' she'd warned them.

Christo studied the map, finding place names that he struggled to pronounce, even in the safety of his own mind, names like Ahascragh, and Funshinagh and Monivea. He found place names that made him smile, like Horseleap and Moate. They were none of them familiar to him. Leaning down low and using his middle finger to guide him as he went, Christo moved along the fold in the page, tracing in his mind the journey they must have taken from the airport in Dublin to his grandfather's house in the Midlands.

'*The Midlands,*' she had informed them, '*is the arsehole of the planet. How anyone lives in that place is beyond me.*'

It was night-time when they arrived but still strangely bright in the sky above the trees, like the Magritte painting Christo once saw in a gallery in Venice. They climbed out of the car into a silence like nothing Christo had ever experienced. The world seemed to be holding its breath. From the expanse of overgrown grass in front of the house and the insects in the grass, to the trees that surrounded it and the birds in their branches, there was no sound out of anything.

'Shush,' was all Christo heard, for as long as they stayed in that house. It could have been a week or a month, there was no way now of knowing. 'Shush, your grandfather is sleeping,' said the woman who went around policing any sounds. 'Shush, don't disturb your grandfather now.'

'*Don't worry, kids,*' said Christo's mother. '*The old bugger doesn't have much left in him. We'll be out of here in no time.*'

When they did go, scrunching down the gravel avenue in the dead grandfather's car, she rolled down the driver's window and stuck her head out of it like a dog.

'*FINALLY, I'M FUCKING FREE!*' she roared, pointing the car west. The plan was to spend the summer out there, but whether the summer lasted three weeks or three months, Christo could not have said. All he remembered was the fir-tree air freshener his grandfather had hanging from the rear-view mirror – it created a stale smell of Christmas in the car. He remembered the chewy mints his mother produced from the glove compartment. '*So milky, you can almost hear them moo,*' she said, cackling a laugh as she handed them out. Christo and Cassie sat in the vast back seat, with the armrest acting as a border between them, their elbows battling each other for space as they sucked away happily on the dead grandfather's mints.

They drove for hours, or so it seemed. A smell of rancid pee in the car from Cassie's wet knickers. She had asked to stop, several times, but by the time they did it was too late. '*We have to press on,*' their mother said, nose to the wheel with comic intent, like Penelope Pitstop in *Wacky Races*. Every so often she glanced in the rear-view mirror as if she were expecting to see the Hooded Claw in hot pursuit. The windscreen of the car was streaked with the light of the setting sun. Ahead of them was their destination. The Atlantic Ocean.

Closing the atlas from back to front, Christo sat for a moment with his hand on the cover. The daylight was gone out of the room, night gathering in the recesses, so that all his things took on an unfamiliar appearance. Reluctant to face the glare of the electric light, Christo washed his supper dishes in the gloaming, stacking them in the rack over the sink to dry. He prepared for bed, checking his phone one last time, but there was no message from his sister, a fact that kept him awake for hours. He couldn't settle, turning and turning in the bed as he tried to find a place of comfort. Just before two, exhausted, he fell into a deep sleep and was aware of nothing more until the phone rang.

'I hope I didn't wake you,' she whispered.

'No,' he lied, hard-wired to the defensive, but why that should be he had no idea. 'No, of course not. I was wide awake.'

5

'Okay,' she said, tripping over her breath as she said it. 'I'm in.'

She had a tumbling feeling, like she'd jumped out of a plane. Cassie had done that once, at the suggestion of a college boyfriend, and never again. The jump zone was somewhere in the California desert. They'd started by practising on the ground. 'One thousand, two thousand, three thousand, check canopy, apex, mods.' The routine was drilled into them and remembered ever since. Cassie felt no fear until they were on the plane.

She had expected something larger, with a big hatch they would run out of, but this aircraft was no bigger than her car. They crouched inside, with the door wide open and the air rushing in as they took off. They struggled to gain purchase on the bumpy sky. The landscape below them was suddenly reduced to miniature – toy cars driving along toy roads, a glistening river snaking along the dry ground. Cassie found herself in the grip of a battle between her fear and her pride, but before either side won she was crawling towards the door of the plane on the orders of the instructor. Another moment and she was sitting with her legs dangling out of the fuselage and her fingers gripping the door frame. By the time she got the order to jump, there was nothing that would have stopped her, even if the consequence were death. All that mattered was that she'd beaten her fear.

It was the same impulse that now governed her decision to go to Ireland. Ever since she'd hung up the phone on Christo, she'd been listing all the reasons not to go. There was her work, which she hated to leave. There was an exhibition opening she'd hoped to attend. Yoga classes she didn't like to skip. Plants that would need watering. There was her peace of mind, which had been so hard-earned, and this to Cassie seemed as good a reason as any not to go.

'Those are all good reasons,' Eduardo had said, with his maddening brand of calm.

'Right,' said Cassie, caught off guard. She'd been expecting him to argue against her.

'There's only one bad reason for not doing something,' he said to her, 'and that's because you're afraid to do it.'

Cassie was so irritated she didn't reply. It was only later – awake in the small hours and working with ferocious intensity on a piece of stone that was better left alone – that she realized he was right. There was enough of the old Cassie in her to know this. She was nothing if not brave. Stepping out into the dark garden in her bare feet, she rang her brother and told him she'd decided to go.

'Splendid,' said Eduardo, when she told him her decision. She had slept late and delayed telling him, even when she woke, because it was his birthday. They spent the afternoon reading the newspapers in the garden. Cassie waited to tell him until they were having dinner that evening.

'Let me take you out for dinner,' she'd said. 'My treat.'

Normally Eduardo insisted on paying the bill, which bothered Cassie. It made her feel like a mistress.

'I like to pay my own way,' she'd explained, on many occasions, but Eduardo wouldn't hear of it. He would no sooner allow a woman pick up a restaurant bill than he would let her open the car door for herself or put on her own coat.

'You're a dinosaur,' she'd said to him once, exasperated.

'No,' he'd replied, with one finger raised to correct her, in teacherly fashion. 'I'm a gentleman, there's a difference.'

A man of meticulously disciplined habits, Eduardo was also a devoted son and father. A gourmet cook. A painstakingly attentive lover. And it was no fault of Eduardo's if Cassie sometimes found herself wishing that he would get his lovemaking over with quicker. If she wished that he would, just sometimes, throw a ready meal into the microwave, instead of endlessly marinating meat and chopping fresh herbs for his salsas. That he would occasionally allow himself to express a hint of irritation towards his tyrant of a mother. Cassie could hardly blame him if it was these very virtues – his consideration, his infinite patience, his blind filial loyalty – that brought out the worst in her.

'I want to take you out for dinner for your birthday,' she'd said, digging her heels in.

'If you insist,' he'd said, ceding the point to her with a polite little dip of his head. 'But only this once.'

Wary of sending out the wrong signal by bringing him somewhere too swanky, Cassie had booked a trendy new cantina – celebrity chef, industrial design – midway between his place and hers. They walked there slowly, arm in arm.

'Well,' she said, once they were seated, with drinks in front of them. She raised her glass to him. 'Happy birthday!'

It was his fifty-sixth, or fifty-seventh, Cassie wasn't sure which. He was vain about revealing his age, as he was about his thinning hair. She'd spotted a small bottle of regrowth oil hidden away at the back of his bathroom cabinet, and it had touched her more than any of his words of love.

'Open your present,' she told him, once they'd clinked glasses.

'Should I guess?' he asked, holding the gift-wrapped box in two hands and giving it a shake.

'It's not very original.'

Her initial idea had been a book of poetry. She'd even spent a morning browsing the antiquarian bookshops behind the cathedral, going so far as to stand for many long minutes turning a collection of poems by Maya Angelou over in her hands, before ultimately rejecting it as too personal. She had considered buying him a bird for his balcony, but she was worried the bird would be lonely and to buy two seemed overly romantic. A painting was too permanent, so she'd settled on a shirt.

'A most excellent shirt,' pronounced Eduardo, after removing the ribbon and opening the gift box to reveal it. He could not have known there had ever been the possibility of a carefully selected book of poetry, or a pair of birds in a cage, or perhaps even a painting, and yet it seemed to Cassie as he met her eyes across the table that he had guessed. A recognition between them that the gift was less thoughtful than it should be. Worse still, she saw from the look in Eduardo's eyes that he understood why and was not angry with her, only disappointed. It was the same look her elementary school teacher would give her, when she stuck the point of her compass in Amy Regan's thigh, or when she borrowed Henry Johansson's dictionary and doodled on it.

'Oh, Cassie,' the teacher would say, with a tender, melting look in her eyes. The teacher's pity was the last thing Cassie wanted, but she could see that allowances were being made. Cassie could handle any hard thing that was thrown at her, but softness she could not bear. 'Cassie, Cassie, Cassie. What am I going to do with you?'

The way the teacher peered at her made Cassie feel like a fish in a tank. She wanted to blow out a big cloud of black ink, like the squid she'd seen at the aquarium in Monterey. Cassie took to drawing pictures of that squid all over her copybooks. It became her motif.

'Gracias, mi amor,' said Eduardo at last, bending down to stow the gift box with the shirt in it under his chair.

'Por nada,' said Cassie. For nothing.

There was a man at the next table languorously smoking a cigarette, and Cassie longed to ask him for one. Three years since she'd given up, but she still saw herself as a smoker. Still missed the first cigarette of the morning, every morning. She missed the cigarette with coffee and the cigarette after lunch. The cigarette after sex and the last cigarette in the garden at night. Something she didn't even try to explain to Eduardo because she didn't want to disappoint him. Eduardo stubbornly insisted on believing in Cassie's best self.

'I'm not the person you think I am,' she'd told him, more than once.

'So, tell me. What are you? Are you a spy, perhaps? A fugitive from justice? An alien from outer space?'

How to explain to Eduardo that the answer to all these questions was 'yes'? There was in her the secretive nature of a spy. The restlessness of a fugitive. The loneliness of an alien from outer space. Some days these things formed so small a part of her that she could almost imagine she was a normal person. Other days there was nothing but the loneliness and the secrets and the urge to hide. She had tried on several occasions to explain this to Eduardo, but despite all of Cassie's attempts to disillusion him, he persisted in seeing in her the woman he wanted her to be.

'So, I've decided to go,' she told him, once their plates had been cleared and they were drinking coffee.

'I'll come with you,' he said, without pausing to consider whether he was invited or not. 'We can fly Air France. Stop off in Paris for a few days.'

Cassie tried to imagine herself walking hand in hand with Eduardo along the Seine. She pictured them curling into each other across a small table at an outdoor café. She saw them kissing on a bridge over the river. Those were things any couple would do if they found themselves in Paris, but it seemed to Cassie that she and Eduardo were not any couple. That was the whole point.

'I don't like Paris,' she said, taking advantage of the tangent.

She'd been there once with her mother, and whereas a normal parent might have taken them to sail toy boats on the pond at the Jardin du Luxembourg or ride donkeys in the Bois de Boulogne, their mother took them to see the city's catacombs, where the walls were built not of stone but of dead bones and skulls. In the time they spent in Paris, their mother must surely have taken them to an art gallery. They must have gone to the Louvre to see the *Mona Lisa*, or perhaps to the Musée d'Orsay for the Impressionists. They must have climbed the Eiffel Tower or taken a Bateau Mouche along the Seine. They must have taken a ride on a carousel and bought crêpes from a street vendor, but Cassie had no memory of any of those things. She remembered only the catacombs and the faceless skulls, which lined the walls of her mind even as she slept. To Cassie, Paris would always be a city of the dead.

'What about Rome, then?' suggested Eduardo. 'We could go to Rome. Or Milan. Or even Venice.'

The one thing Cassie remembered of Rome was a hotel with moving staircases, where she and Christo ran up the down escalator and down the up. In Milan there was a man selling violets on a street corner. In Venice there was washing hanging over their heads and the constant threat of falling pot plants. She and Christo were both wearing carnival masks their mother had bought them, in place of Hallowe'en costumes. She kept urging them to knock on people's doors, but there were no doors to knock on, only rows of apartment bells they were too shy to ring. It was only afterwards that somebody told them. They don't have Hallowe'en in Venice.

'It's September,' Cassie told Eduardo. 'Italy will be mobbed with tourists.'

How could she explain to him that she didn't want to go to any of those places? She had been to them all before – sometimes it seemed to Cassie that she'd been to every place in the world – when her dad was on tour. Cassie's mother had refused to be left behind, and she had nobody to mind the kids, so they'd tagged along too, sleeping on mattresses on the floors of hotel suites. Watching TV in languages they didn't understand. Eating room service from large trays with stiff white linen. In Cassie's memory the adults were always either absent or asleep, while the hotel staff did the parenting. There was a chef who showed them how to make ravioli. A chambermaid who braided Cassie's hair into a French plait. Another brought them chicken soup when they were sick.

Helsinki, Stockholm, Copenhagen, Rotterdam. The cities were listed on the back of the tour t-shirts. Tokyo, Kyoto, Osaka, Nagoya. Cassie would have liked to stay in one place for more than a few days, but they'd no sooner arrived some-where than they were packing to leave again. They existed in a state of constant yearning, not for home but for the last place they'd been. Cassie never wanted to feel that way again.

'Look, Eduardo,' she told him. 'This is a trip I have to make by myself. We can go to Puerto Vallarta instead, when I get back.'

They had been to Puerto Vallarta before. It was one of the things they did together. Puerto Vallarta seemed to her in keeping with the part-time, middle-aged romance she had in mind for them.

'Sure,' he said, stiff with resentment. 'As you wish.'

This was a man who was used to women doing his

bidding, from the country girl who was paid to mother him when he was a child, to the mother whose will he alone could bend. His wife deferred to him, even though they were no longer married. His daughters disobeyed him only behind his back. There was nothing in Eduardo's experience that had prepared him for a woman who would not go along with his plans, but this only served to strengthen Cassie's resolve to go.

'So, what's he like,' Eduardo asked her, once he'd stopped sulking. 'This brother of yours?'

'Well, I don't know how to describe him. 'He's like the Tin Man in *The Wizard of Oz*. Or maybe Pinocchio. He's . . .'

She hesitated, unable to find the right word.

'Not quite human?'

She shook her head.

'It's not that. Quite the opposite, in fact. It's like he's *more* human than other people.' She clamped a hand to her heart, to protect it from the sense she had that it might just fall out onto the table. 'You know the way cartoon characters are more human than we are? That's what Christo's like – it's like he's trying really, really hard to be a real person, but he can't because he's made of wood.'

In the week she was in Cambridge, Cassie had encountered many of his acquaintances but nobody Christo described as a friend. In their wanderings around town, he was often greeted by a student – many a young man on a bicycle would raise a hand to wave at him – but none of them ever stopped to talk. Christo took her to his local Thai restaurant for dinner and insisted that she try all his favourite dishes. He gave her a tour of his college and introduced her with undisguised pride to everyone they met. She was his guest at dinner one evening, proceeding on her brother's gowned arm from the sherry reception in the fellows' drawing room to the dining hall,

45

where the students all stood as they arrived. Cassie found herself the focus of polite interest from the other fellows. 'We didn't know he had any family,' one of them told her, in a whisper. 'Your brother's a bit of a mystery man.'

There was no evidence of companionship in his apartment. He had only one bathrobe on the back of the bedroom door, one bedside table with a lamp on it, one dining chair. He took a folding stool out of the cupboard for himself to sit on while she was there, putting it back into the cupboard the morning she was leaving. The crisp white sheets she slept in had been bought especially for her visit – Cassie knew by the factory folds. Also new were the fluffy white towels Christo left out for her. They were so soft they didn't soak up any water, only rolled it around on your skin as you tried to dry yourself. Christo had even thought to buy Cassie a new toothbrush in case she forgot her own. Her heart sagged under the weight of his love.

'Please understand,' she said, to herself as much as to Eduardo, 'I love my brother.'

'Of course you do,' said Eduardo, for whom the love of family was beyond question. He loved his daughters with a ridiculous excess of sentimentality. He adored his mother, even though she was – to Cassie's mind – anything but adorable. Eduardo even revered his ex-wife. As the mother of his children, he included her unquestioningly in his circle of love, but there was nobody he worshipped so much as his brand-new baby granddaughter. Eduardo loved that child to distraction.

'Isn't she a sweetheart?' he would say, to everyone he met, pulling out his phone to show them the latest pictures. 'Here, look at her in this one. How cute she is.'

Everyone agreed, of course.

'She's an angel.'

Eduardo liked to pick the baby up and pepper her with kisses, something Cassie found difficult to watch. In the same way that another person might find it hard to watch someone smack a baby, it was painful to her to see the love that was lavished on Gabriela. Cassie did not begrudge the child her charmed existence, with an adoring circle of aunts and grandparents and great-grandparents all tripping over each other to pave her way in the world by laying down in front of her a red carpet of love. Cassie knew their love was no safeguard against the troubles of life – this child would face her own trials, her own misfortunes – but she would never be alone. That seemed to Cassie the greatest privilege of all.

'She gets more and more cute every day,' Eduardo was telling the waiter. He was scrolling through the million baby pictures on his phone. 'Here. Look at this one.'

'Caray,' said the waiter. 'Que linda.' What a beauty.

'Okay,' said Cassie. 'I'll take the bill when you're ready.'

Normally they wouldn't spend the night together on a Sunday, but because it was Eduardo's birthday Cassie felt obliged to invite him back. They drew two wicker chairs round to face each other in the heady air of the garden and Cassie poured them each a glass of tequila, sipping it slowly the way Eduardo had taught her to do instead of slamming it.

'Slamming tequila is something American college students do at spring break in Cancún. Mexicans drink tequila for *pleasure*, not to get drunk.'

Cassie was tired and longed for sleep, but instead of sending him home she slipped her right foot out of her shoe and slid it along his trouser leg until it was resting on his crotch. He arched his back with feline pleasure, as she used the ball of her foot to rub circles on the hardening mound inside his trousers. Only when she'd finished her tequila and placed the glass on the ground under her chair did she take his hand and lead him into her bedroom, where she took energetic charge of their lovemaking, partly as a birthday present to him, but also in the hope that the quicker it was over, the sooner she could get to sleep. Curled up on her side afterwards, she closed her eyes and waited for Eduardo to fall in behind her. He liked to sleep with his hot, hairy belly nuzzled into the curve at the small of her back. His short, sturdy arms wrapped tight around her waist, as if she might try to escape from him in the night. Cassie lay awake for a long time, fighting off the desire for flight.

6

By the Friday of the following week, the plans for the trip were all in place. Christo tidied up his lecture notes and set off as usual for his weekly squash game with his colleague, Bernard. Bernard was in his fifties but slim and fit as a man half his age. The only giveaway was the antique pair of tennis shorts he insisted on wearing on the squash court. To Christo's horror, they had a tendency to gape at the leg, providing an unavoidable glimpse of the loose swinging bulge in Bernard's distinctly off-white underpants every time he made a dive for the ball.

'Well?' said Bernard, closing the door of the court behind them.

'Well,' said Christo, in reply.

'My ball or yours?'

'Mine,' said Christo, taking one out of his pocket. Once they'd warmed it up, Bernard spun his racket to decide who'd serve.

'Yours,' he said, bending to pick up the racket and ceding the choice of serving box to Christo.

Bernard belonged to the same college as Christo and they enjoyed a mutual disdain for college politics, which drew them to huddle together conspiratorially at the many sherry receptions they were forced to attend. Christo and Bernard had been playing squash together for three years, without ever discussing anything other than squash and their hatred of college politics. Christo knew that Bernard lived in a house on the Huntingdon Road, but whether Bernard shared his house, or indeed his life, with anyone was outside of Christo's knowledge. Christo had never dared to ask, and Bernard had never volunteered any information.

There was one occasion – about a year ago – when Bernard didn't turn up for their game. Christo waited a full hour, but still there was no sign of Bernard. It wasn't until he was at dinner the following evening that he learned Bernard had been suspended from the college, pending an investigation into inappropriate sexual behaviour. From the mutterings at the table, he learned that Bernard had been sending nude photographs of himself to one of his graduate students. The student had confided in the college counsellor. The counsellor had consulted the master of the college.

'And together they mastered our man's disappearance,' said one of the wits at dinner.

Christo lay awake that night, wondering why he hadn't spoken up for Bernard. It was clear from the other fellows' discussion that Bernard's transgression was the source of some amusement to them, if not sympathy. There had been some jokes, of a crude nature, but no one made to defend Bernard. No one expressed concern for him, no one ventured to suggest that he might be innocent of the charges against him. As his friend that was Christo's job, but Christo had said nothing, afraid to set foot on such thin ice. As a single man, flying no obvious flag of sexuality, Christo was aware that he too was an object of suspicion, and he did not want to make things worse for himself. As it happened, Bernard reappeared in college the next week – the word was that he'd received a warning – and he turned up as usual for their squash game the following Friday and neither he nor Christo had mentioned the incident, then or since.

'Good game,' said Bernard, in the changing room afterwards, as he always did when he won.

'Yes, well played,' said Christo.

It was after eight in Cambridge but still warm and bright when they stepped out onto the street. Each plucking a fig from the tree outside, as was their custom at that time of year, they stood for a moment, unpeeling the skin and eating the faintly human flesh.

'Oh, by the way,' Christo added, as if he'd only just remembered. 'I won't be here next week. I'm going to Ireland.'

'Oh, right,' said Bernard, without the slightest hint of curiosity.

'I'll be back the following week.'

'Gotcha,' said Bernard.

He tossed the skin of his fig into a flowerbed, as he always did, while Christo walked with his to the nearest bin. Then, wheeling their bicycles some way together, they parted at the common with barely a word.

'I should mention that I'll be away next week,' Christo told Sue. She was leaving the house as he was locking his bike to the railing. She stopped at the gate to chat, barring his way in her blithely friendly manner.

'Going somewhere nice?'

'Yes,' said Christo. 'I'm going to Ireland with my sister.'

'Oh, that's nice!'

'Yes, it is,' said Christo. 'It *is* nice.'

'Is that the sister who lives in Mexico?' As if there were more than one. 'How long is it since you've seen her then?'

'Oh, a couple of years,' said Christo, deliberately using a broad brushstroke, even though he knew precisely how many. It had been three and a half.

It was April when she came, and the daffodils were in full bloom along the Backs. The rapeseed was in flower in the Fens, slabs of yellow outside the window of the bus as he travelled to meet her at the airport. He'd brought a bunch of yellow tulips with him, and he presented them to her when she emerged. That visit was all yellow in his memory. It was the colour of joy.

He'd been planning the details for months, ever since the moment she'd phoned to tell him that she'd booked her ticket. He had rehearsed in his mind the places he'd bring her, the things he'd show her. There was so much he wanted to say. In the week that Cassie spent in Cambridge, Christo told her about his plans for the book he was hoping to write. He described the nature walks he liked to take on the weekends, showing her a bird's egg that he'd found, with the tiniest hole in it. He told her how amazing it was to him that the baby bird had escaped through a crack so small.

'I find that astounding,' he told her, holding the tiny egg in his open palm. He felt like it was some secret part of himself that he'd revealed to her, and not just an empty egg. A feeling like a ray of sunshine falling across his soul. He felt warmed by the glow of it.

'Oh, Christo,' she said, and to his consternation he saw her eyes well up with tears. 'You haven't changed at all.'

'What do you mean?'

'Just that you're the same person you always were. It's like you're still the exact same person you were when you were a kid.'

Christo studied her face, looking for a clue that would indicate how he should take this. There was a time when he'd known how to interpret every roll of her eyes, every twitch of her mouth, but he no longer had the ability to read her moods. They'd spent too long apart.

'I hardly recognize the person I am now,' she said, shocking him with the sorrow in her voice. 'I'm nothing like the girl I was then. It's like she disappeared.'

In the days that followed, they passed every waking

moment in each other's company, but there remained between them the awkwardness of their long separation. Bumping into each other on their way into the bathroom in the morning – you first, no you first – and again at night, taking turns to brush their teeth, they might have been guests staying in the same house rather than siblings who had once shared a bath. They'd once peeled sunburned skin off each other's backs to see who could get the longest strip. They'd pummelled each other with pillows for the sheer pleasure of physical contact. Now Cassie closed the bedroom door firmly behind her when she went to bed, so when Christo called out good-night, he barely heard her reply, and there was no opportunity for the conversations he had imagined occurring between them as they lay there in the dark. When he walked her to the bus station at the end of the week – she'd insisted on travelling to the airport alone – he had the sense that instead of closing the distance between them, her visit had served to widen it. She waved to him from the window of the bus, and he waved back across the sea of all the things they had somehow managed to leave unsaid.

7

Eduardo had insisted on driving Cassie to the airport. Even though the drive would take two hours each way in rush-hour traffic. Even though she would much rather have said goodbye to him at the house and travelled to the airport alone in a cab, there was no talking him out of it.

'Ready?' he asked her.

'I think so.'

She took one last look around, checking that the shutters were all bolted. The plugs safely out of the wall. The gas cylinder disconnected. A fluttery feeling in her heart, like she'd drunk too much coffee. She'd cleaned out the fridge that morning. She'd filled plastic bottles full of water and planted them neck down into the soil of her pot plants. There were more plants in the kitchen sink and the bath, with an inch of stagnant water to sustain them for the week she'd be gone.

'I hope they survive.'

'The plants will be fine,' said Eduardo. 'It's me you should be worried about.'

'No seas un bebé.' Don't be such a baby.

He looked at her with his bottom lip out, his disconcertingly transparent eyes overacting at being hurt. Cassie made a pretence of showing him pity, when in truth she was irritated by him. Irritated, and guilty for being irritated – with Eduardo there was always the guilt because she couldn't get away from the feeling that she was the one at fault.

'Come on,' she said to him. 'You're too old to sulk.'

'And you, my child, are too young to be so cruel.'

Proof, if proof were needed, that Eduardo misunderstood her entirely. Cassie had not been young since she was eleven years old. If anything, it was Eduardo who was the child in their relationship. Nothing had ever happened to him to make him grow up.

'Bueno,' she said. 'Vamos.'

She was impatient to be gone, a feeling that lasted for the duration of the car journey. It was only when they saw the signs for the airport that she began to feel the first licks of regret. She was sorry he wasn't coming with her, but it was too late for that now. As always with Eduardo, her emotions were either running ahead of her or behind her, never in tandem.

The drop-off area was hot and chaotic after the air-conditioned calm of Eduardo's car. Cassie waited at the kerb while he went to pull her suitcase out of the trunk. Amid all the comings and goings, she felt suddenly and inexplicably desolate, as if the life she had left behind her were about to be swallowed up by some terrible catastrophe. A flood or an earthquake that would sweep away everything she knew. She was seized by the notion that she was abandoning Eduardo.

'Now,' he said, putting her suitcase down at her feet. 'You're all set.'

She stepped towards him, threading her arm through his open suit jacket to grip the back of his waistband. Resting her cheek against the stiff cotton fabric of his shirt, she leaned against the solid mass of him, breathing in his clean smell. In his freshly pressed suit and his professionally starched shirt, he smelled to her like something straight from the shop. Like a pair of expensive shoes you might borrow from a friend, only to discover that they pinch. Like a newborn baby who's been passed to you to be held while its mother eats her lunch, it was the perfection of him that made her uncomfortable.

'Adiós, mi amor,' he said, kissing her tenderly on the forehead. 'Take good care.'

'Adiós,' she said, walking through the sliding doors without looking back.

From the window of the plane the city was a vast coral reef. The many-coloured lights as garish as tropical fish among the dusky buildings. Cassie rested her head against the window, looking down on her adopted home with the sense that she was leaving it behind her for good.

'Were you visiting Mexico on holidays?' her neighbour asked, once the plane had levelled off.

'No. No, I live there, actually.'

'Oh,' said the neighbour, a young woman with a British accent. 'I'm afraid I didn't get to see much of the city. I was only there for three days.'

'Right,' said Cassie, watching as the woman took a small, blue glass bottle out of her handbag and used it to dab the insides of her wrists.

'I'm a bit nervous flying.'

When the drinks trolley came along, the woman ordered two miniature bottles of red wine and suggested Cassie do the same.

'If the plane ends up crashing, we might as well die happy.'

Cassie rejected her advice, ordering only water and declining the meal. Spreading the inadequate airline rug over her knees and plugging her earbuds in to discourage conversation, she settled down to sleep, tumbling straight into a shallow dream. She was aware even as she was dreaming of the roar of the aircraft's engines. The pull of the thin air outside the plane pressing in on them. The forward trajectory of their journey.

In Cassie's dream her mother was still alive. She had aged – her hair was silver, her skin sagging and sweet-smelling – but there was no question that she was Cassie's mother. The whole business of her death appeared to have been no more than a silly misunderstanding.

'*I've always loved air travel,*' she told Cassie, in a neighbourly fashion. She seemed not to know that Cassie was her daughter. She was talking to her like she was a stranger. '*I love the feeling of having no control over my own life. The feeling that someone else is in charge and there's not a thing I can do.*' She was leaning back against the headrest with her face turned to the side. Her honeyed voice little more than a whisper. Her long, grey hair kept falling across Cassie's arm. Cassie kept brushing it away.

'*When my children were small,*' her mother said, '*I used to find myself wishing the plane would crash and we'd all be killed.*' She smiled, and her eyes flared in the darkness of the cabin as she rested a hand on Cassie's arm. '*Wouldn't it be lovely,*' she whispered conspiratorially, '*if the plane were to crash and we were all to be killed. Then our troubles would be well and truly over.*'

Again, her hair fell across Cassie's arm and, again, Cassie tried to throw it off. She opened her eyes and saw that what she was fighting off was not her mother's hair but a scarf that had fallen over her arm from her neighbour's seat. It was the tassels of the scarf that Cassie could feel feathering her arm. Her neighbour was not her mother but the young British woman, who was curled towards Cassie in sleep, as if they were sharing a bed. Her lips were slightly parted, revealing a tongue stud inside her mouth. It took a moment to separate out what was real from what was in the dream. What remained was her mother's murderous death wish, something that seemed to her to belong not to the dream but to reality.

'Do you ever try to picture her?' Cassie had asked her

brother recently on the phone. They'd started to use Whats-App for their calls. The application allowed them the luxury of unlimited time, but there was a change in tempo as a result. Their conversations were slowing down, the pace of them becoming almost lazy. It was a far cry from the days when he would phone her from the call box in the hallway of his school, the two of them babbling down the line until his coins ran out.

'Who?' he asked.

'Her,' she said, using the path of least resistance. They neither of them ever spoke the word 'mother' out loud. 'Mom' was similarly taboo, as was the word she herself had liked to use, a word that held within it – even now, all these years later – a world of pain; she'd never sounded so Irish as when she said 'mum'.

'I sometimes try to imagine how she might look now.'

In Cassie's mind was a bird-boned woman, with tumbling white hair and bright red lipstick. The image had taken on a permanence, supplanting the last memory she had of her mother, stick-thin and puffy from all the drink and drugs. The smell of rotting fruit off her as her liver began to fail. Cassie had never shared that memory with Christo, choosing instead to spare him the details of those last few weeks, when he was at school in England and she alone witnessed their mother's ruinous decline.

'The way I imagine her, she looks a bit like Emmylou Harris,' she said, offering him a glimpse of her salvaged vision.

'I'm afraid I don't know what Emmylou Harris looks like.'

'Of course you don't,' said Cassie, wondering – not for the first time – how he seemed to know so very little about life on earth. 'So, here's the thing. I sometimes think I've seen her.'

The first time it happened was at a wedding in Veracruz.

She was there as Eduardo's date, the only woman wearing black amid the brightly dressed ladies of Eduardo's acquaintance. With their extravagant plumage and their lurid accessories, they gave the cathedral the look of a great, stained-glass aviary. It was only when they were seated in the church that Cassie caught sight of another woman dressed, like her, in the deep, rich black of a crow.

'She was sitting in front of me – maybe three rows ahead – and I don't know why, but I became convinced it was her. There was something about the way she held her head. The way her hair was done. The back of her neck.'

There followed a long silence. Cassie couldn't be sure if it was caused by a lag on the line or a hesitation on Christo's part.

'I went up to take communion – which I never do – because I wanted to see her face, but when I came back down the aisle she was gone.'

She'd wanted to dash out of the church and run through the streets shouting her mother's name, the way people did in the movies, but instead she returned to her seat beside Eduardo. While he prayed – with a blind devotion that was incomprehensible to Cassie – she leaned her head back and stared up into the stone vaults of the ceiling, waiting for the desperate, searching feeling in her to subside.

'Who do you think she was?' asked Christo, sounding confused.

Cassie sighed. Shook her head. Closed her eyes to the utter pointlessness of ever trying to explain anything to him. It was a lonely feeling, because if her brother didn't understand, then who on earth would?

'She was nobody, Christo, that's the whole point.'

Her mother would be sixty-one now if she'd lived. She was thirty-six when she died. Come November, Cassie would be older than her mother ever was, which was quite a thing to wrap your head around. Just thinking about it made Cassie feel like one of those explorers she'd learned about in high school who sailed the world in constant fear of falling off the edge. Like a space traveller encountering the limits of the solar system. She could not imagine what came afterwards, and it frightened her to think of it.

Taking care not to disturb her neighbour, Cassie extricated herself from her seat and wandered the cabin in her stockinged feet. She patrolled the rows of sleeping passengers, feeling like a night nurse in a mental hospital. She leaned for a time on the bulkhead by the toilets, staring out the window at the vast landscape of ice below. It was broad daylight outside, even though the plane's cabin lights were still dimmed in imitation of night. 'That's Greenland down there,' said the flight attendant when Cassie asked. She was forced to bend the flattened map she had in her head into a sphere, to account for the shape of the earth.

8

Christo stepped off the airport bus from Cambridge just as his sister's flight from Mexico was landing. He waited for her at the Arrivals barrier, a wait that took longer than he could feasibly have imagined, even when you factored in a queue for passport control and a delay at the luggage carousel. He was just starting to worry that something had happened to her when she appeared, pulling a small suitcase behind her. His first thought was how short she was compared to him. Every time he saw her, he was surprised by this, as if he'd been expecting her to keep on growing. There was a time when they'd marked each other's heights in crayon on a wall.

'Christo,' she said, smiling as she approached.

'Cassie.' He leaned in to kiss her on both cheeks, when what he really wanted was to wrap her in his arms. Sister of mine, he wanted to say. Dear heart.

'How was your flight?' he asked, in a voice he might just as easily have used with a stranger. 'Not too bad, I hope? It was on time, anyway. Here, give me your suitcase. You packed light, I see.'

He looked about for directions to the Departures area. Two hours to go until their flight to Dublin, but he was anxious to keep moving.

'We may as well go ahead and check in.'

The floor of the terminal building was smooth and glossy, as if a bucket of water had been spilled on it. Christo planted his steps carefully to avoid slipping, while Cassie glided along next to him. She might have been on skates.

'You look well, Christo.'

'Do I?'

It wasn't something he ever thought about. He had no mirrors in his flat except the small one in the bathroom that he used for shaving.

'How about me? How do I look?'

He glanced across at her. She'd put on weight since he saw her last, which he took as a good sign. With Cassie there was always a correlation: fat = happy; thin = sad.

'You look wonderful.'

'Liar,' she said, with a laugh. 'I've just stepped off a long-haul flight. I look like shit.'

Cassie never cared how she looked. Never wore make-up, so far as he could see. Never dyed her hair, which was streaked with single strands of white through the glossy black. She was dressed like a ninja, in a tight black sweater, a pair of plain black trousers and black biker boots. Her one concession to colour was the enormous red embroidered scarf she wore. Watching her march through the airport, it seemed to Christo that his sister looked like a general on the battlefield. She wore the scarf like a military cape, trailing long and loose behind her. Once she was seated on the plane it became a cloak that she wrapped around herself for protection.

'I'll never understand you,' she said to him, as the plane's engines started up.

She'd bought a magazine at the airport stand, and she opened it as they waited for departure. She paid the safety announcements no attention, flicking imperiously through the pages of her magazine. It reminded Christo of those picture books you flick through to create a moving cartoon. The way the women on the pages of her magazine flashed by, all swinging hair and towering heels, created an illusion of motion.

'Why do you say that?'

'Your reading material.' She gestured to the book he'd opened two-thirds of the way through, finding his place by the bookmark he'd put there when he last paused in his reading. The page was composed entirely of numbers that formed a series of equations. 'Most people read books of *words*,' she said. 'You are not normal.'

The insult was a caress to Christo, reminding him of the intimacy they'd once shared as children. They'd spent most of their time taunting each other. Seeking each other out only to escape from each other again. Tumbling on the ground together like bears only to end up drawing blood or tears. It was an endless loop of affection and irritation, love and hate. For years they'd turned those circles, over and over again, until they were separated by their mother's death. Cassie was packed off to live with her grandmother in Oklahoma City. Her grandmother was by then Cassie's only living relative apart from Christo, who remained in school in England under the token care of his father. They begged to be kept together but Christo's father was reluctant to take responsibility for his own child, let alone someone else's, and Cassie's grandmother would not have a boy in the house. She said she'd sooner have a rat.

All the time Christo was at boarding school, Cassie wrote to him in streams of consciousness that relayed the everyday stuff of her life. The envelopes that landed in his pigeonhole with their cheery US stamps were always embellished with intricate illustrations of seahorses and aardvarks and baby elephants. She made her own wax seals for the backs of the envelopes, using lino cuts to produce delicate impressions of a giant squid in various guises. It was 1996 when Cassie got e-mail and the letters abruptly stopped. The new medium brought a different tone to their exchanges – less contemplative, more jaunty – which in turn gave way to the abbreviated and often misspelled language of text messages. They might as well have been communicating in Morse code.

'Let's face it,' said Cassie, as the plane backed away from the stand. 'You're a freak.'

Christo laid the book down on his lap.

'I can lend it to you when I'm finished if you like.'

She rolled her eyes. 'Eh, thanks but no thanks.'

It was an old joke between them – her inability to understand maths, his inability to understand her inability. As a kid he would drill her remorselessly, as if, by sheer force of will, he could transmit his knowledge to her. He would whine with frustration, box his temples, when she still couldn't – or wouldn't – get it. Something he was tempted to do, even now, whenever he encountered a particularly obdurate pupil. Despite everything that had happened to him since, he was still the same person who had subjected his sister to torments because she wouldn't learn from him.

'I only know *some* of the numbers,' she said to him once. 'I don't know *all* of them.'

He remembered gripping her wrists with his crab claws so she couldn't get away. Sitting astride her on the ground, with her belly squidgy under his thighs, her body thrashing around on the carpet. The next thing he knew her hard little head would rear up and her hair would whip him in the eyes. A bite then and he would jump off her, yelping. Afterwards he would sit back against the couch, brooding over the forensics. A row of tiny white teeth marks sunk into the red flesh of his arm.

'It's not that I can't learn how to solve the problems,' she explained to him, another time. 'When someone shows me how, I can do it. I just can't understand how anyone would think up all of that stuff in the first place.'

He had always been good at maths, she was good at art,

but the two were not so very different, as he had often tried to explain to her.

'No,' she'd told him. 'Sorry, Christo, but that makes no sense to me.'

He was in Madrid to see her show. Five years ago, that would have been. She'd flown in from Mexico, he'd come from London. They met up at the hotel in time for a late breakfast. The smell of gas from the buffet was a reminder of the many times they had breakfasted together in similar hotels. Even now, Christo insisted on staying in big ones over small ones for the pleasures of the breakfast buffet. They were the same all the world over.

'Maths is an artistic endeavour,' he said, buttering a cold slice of toast. 'What mathematicians seek is beauty. The beauty is found in the elegance of the solution.'

Cassie put her fingers in her ears and began to hum to herself, loudly, as if she were humming along to music. 'Ta da da da da. Ta da da.'

'What you see inside the stone is what I see inside the numbers,' he told her, once she took her fingers out of her ears to spoon the fruit she had liberally helped herself to into her open mouth. 'It's just a case of releasing it.'

'Michelangelo said he saw the angel inside the marble and carved until he set him free.'

'Okay, so it's not an original thought,' said Christo, slightly put out. A teacher by nature as well as by trade, he was happiest telling people things they didn't know. He didn't like to be told things, especially when the person doing the telling was his little sister.

'Was there someone in your life who inspired you to become a teacher?' the master of his college had asked him once. 'Most teachers have a mentor, someone who lit the flame for them. It's something you never forget.'

'Yes,' Christo had answered, without pausing for thought. 'There was someone called Margo. She opened the door for me.'

It was Margo who first showed him how to look for the geometry in a honeycomb. Once you saw it, you found yourself searching for the maths in everything. Christo couldn't look at a zebra without wondering was there a pattern to its stripes. Couldn't sit watching the waves break on a beach without counting the seconds between them. Couldn't see a rainbow without calculating the bend of its arc.

'None of this is new,' he told Cassie, over their breakfast in the hotel in Madrid. 'There was a German astronomer in the seventeenth century who saw mathematical patterns in the way the seeds grow inside a pomegranate.'

'Wow,' she said, and Christo perked up, thinking for a moment that he had managed to engage her in his subject.

'I can't believe there were pomegranates in Germany in the seventeenth century,' she added, with genuine interest.

After breakfast she walked him through her show dispassionately. Hands deep in the pockets of her long black dress, she was wearing Roman sandals, with her toenails painted pale green to match the overblown green roses on the scarf she had draped over her shoulders.

'Ta-da,' she said, with a joking flourish.

There were twelve pieces in total. A series of granite globes bearing intricate geographies, the gallery had set them on white wooden plinths and placed them at precisely measured intervals along the walls, giving them the appearance of severed heads on a row of stakes. Christo wanted to know how she'd transported them from Mexico. They'd been shipped in wooden crates, she told him. Each one set into its own bed of straw. For some reason the thought of it made Christo feel sick to the stomach. Something about the terrible weight of the stone against the lightness of the straw. The lightness of the straw against the weight of the stone. It frightened him to think of it.

'They're wonderful,' said Christo, stopping in front of one piece to study it more closely. She had carved a network of walls into the stone, working in relief to raise them out of the rock. It was the mark of habitation she had created. The mark of humanity.

'They're so precise,' he said, marvelling at the clean lines she'd carved.

'That's the difficulty,' she said. 'You can take the stone away, but you can't ever put it back. It doesn't allow for mistakes.'

'That's the beauty of mathematics,' said Christo. 'Every problem has a solution.'

She laughed. Not the open-mouthed, showing-all-your-teeth laugh she'd had as a kid, but a closed-mouth version that barely made it out of her throat.

'I'll take your word for it.'

There was a small red sticker on the base of one of the sculptures. The others had so far failed to sell but Cassie didn't seem to mind, something he found hard to understand.

'It doesn't really have anything to do with me anymore,' she explained. 'Once I've finished them, they're of no more interest to me. I don't really care what happens to them.'

They wandered out the door of the gallery and into the Retiro Park. The acacia trees spilled lime-coloured blossoms onto the pavement that ran down the centre of the boule-vard, where Cassie and Christo walked arm in arm. The handsome couple they made was reflected back at them in the eyes of the people they passed on the path. Nobody would have taken them for brother and sister.

Two years between them, two continents, two different

fathers. It was only their mother's curiously dormant genes that bound them together. Cassie had her dad's sallow skin and his coal-black eyes. Choctaw eyes, if you were to believe his account of his own ancestry, which Christo didn't. Not that he would ever have dreamed of telling Cassie this, for fear of pulling on one of the threads that formed the delicate fabric of her identity. Christo's own bloodline had its roots in a Welsh coal mine, which accounted for the blue glare that jumped out of his grandfather's face in photographs. Christo's father had the same seething blue eyes, which in Christo ran still and cool.

A stewardess made her way down the aisle of the plane, still wearing the life vest she'd used for the safety demonstration. She looked right and left as she walked, checking that people's seat belts were fastened. Christo experienced a jolt of fear at the thought that his might not be, but when he looked down it was. He succumbed to the familiar relief of conformity.

'Hey, Christo,' said Cassie, as the plane made a slow, lumbering turn at the bottom of the runway.

'What is it, love?'

'Do you remember "Owls"?'

She had her head turned to face him. Her cheek resting on the seat back. She was so close he could see the gleaming black depths to her eyes. There was an intimacy to it, despite all the people around them. A closeted feeling created by the curtain of sound from the plane's engines. The occasional wail from an unseen child.

'Don't you remember?'

It was their mother who'd taught them that game. You had to touch your noses together and close your eyes. Then you counted down from three, opened your eyes wide and called out the word 'owls' in a long owly hoot as you stared, startled every time, into the other person's eyes.

'Ready?'

The plane had shuddered to a stop. Earthbound and ungainly, it seemed to be mustering its energies for flight. A stillness in the cabin, while they waited for this miracle to occur.

'Right now?' he asked.

'Sure,' she said, leaning closer to rest the tip of her nose, very gently, on his. He might have been touching some creature from another species. That was how odd it felt for him to touch his nose against hers.

She closed her eyes, and he closed his, as the engines roared and the plane moved forwards. Cassie reached her hand out and Christo took it, squeezing it tightly while they hurtled down the runway. He had a giddy feeling of joy, despite the fact that he was propelling them both into a black hole in their lives.

'Three, two, one, OWLS!'

9

That was all it took – their two noses pressed together briefly for departure and the awkwardness between them was gone. They had moved from the formality of their long separation to the practised affection of an old married couple. Cassie wanted to nuzzle into it, but there was in Christo a stiffness that prevented this. No sooner had he taken her hand in his than she sensed his desire to drop it.

'Premature babies don't like to be touched,' Eduardo's daughter, Alejandra, had said, when she brought Gabriela home from the hospital. The baby had been born three months early. She was the size of a kitten, with a ridged forehead and dazed black eyes. They had to tube-feed her for a month.

'She's not ready to be in the world,' said Alejandra. 'Her skin is too thin.'

Christo too had been born prematurely, by as much as six weeks. He had weak lungs as a consequence and had suffered from croup as a child. They'd had to steam up the bathroom some nights so he could breathe. England was the last place he should live, with its long, damp winters.

'I don't know how you can stand the climate here,' Cassie had told him, when she visited him in Cambridge. The air was wet with rain, the college buildings barely visible through it. Christo had been coughing in the night. In the mornings he drank tea with honey to soothe his chest. His bathroom cabinet was stocked with Vicks inhalers and VapoRub. 'You should live somewhere sunny, Christo. At least migrate for the winter. This is no place for you.'

'Oh no,' he'd said. 'I can't stand the sun. I much prefer the rain. I'm quite in my element here.'

Getting off the plane in Dublin, he took his place in the queue with the European passport holders, while Cassie joined the trickle of Asians and Americans at the non-EU booth. Her queue moved faster than his, so she waited for him on the far side. She knew that Immigration was an ordeal for Christo, because of the name on his passport. The officials remarked on it every time. From his face, she could see this occasion was no exception.

'It never fails,' he said, putting his passport back in his pocket with as much dignity as he could muster.

They hired a car at the airport and cleared the city in silence, choosing to forsake the old road for the new motorway that had superseded it. An hour into the journey, Christo pulled into a gas station to buy a road map, emerging with a large bottle of water and a paper bag.

'Do you remember these?' he asked her, producing a plastic pack of candy from the bag.

'What are they?'

'Don't you remember? They're Ritchie's Milky Mints. So milky you can almost hear them moo.'

Cassie had no memory of that, but she opened the pack anyway and helped herself to one before passing them back to him.

'They're pretty good,' she said, as a sop to his feelings. Christo could be very sensitive on matters like this. It was something she'd noticed about him – most recently in Cambridge, when he insisted she order the prawns at the Thai restaurant he'd brought her to, when what she wanted was the chicken. In Madrid he was determined they have an ice-cream cone, for sentimental reasons, even though Cassie had long ago lost her taste for ice cream. The bag of candy was the same thing – it was like he was offering you his heart on a plate. He would take it personally if you didn't like it.

'This sure is a meaty mint,' she said. 'It could double as a dentistry mould.'

'Yes, indeed,' he said, happily. 'Here. Have another.'

A bit further along the road, they spotted an exit for the town their mother was from. This was where she'd spent the first ten years of her life. Somewhere nearby was the house they'd stayed in as children. The graveyard where their grandfather was buried.

'Should we stop?' Christo asked.

'No,' said Cassie. 'Let's keep going.'

They stuck with the motorway all the way to Galway. The road cut a swathe through untidy fields bordered by scrubby hedges. There were trees that were almost human in the way they occupied the landscape. Crows thrown up out of their branches, like flecks of black ash. The occasional farmhouse breathed pale grey smoke out of its chimneys. A lorry had been parked on the ridge of a hill to advertise a carpet showroom. A vapour trail appeared across the sky, like a line of crayon drawn by an invisible hand.

On the far side of Galway city, they took the road that ran west along the coast. Following the road signs to the location that was mentioned in the article, they rolled into the place without any sighting of a beach.

'A drowned forest?' said the first man they asked. He was bending down to peer in through their open passenger window with suspicion. 'I never heard of any drowned forest. Are you sure you're in the right place?'

'It's supposed to be right here,' said Cassie, pointing to the photograph in the newspaper cutting.

The man twisted his head to study the photo.

'Means nothing to me,' he said. 'Sorry I can't help.'

'That's odd,' said Christo, as they pulled away. 'I would have thought everyone around here would know about it.'

'A drowned forest,' said the woman in the crafts shop where they stopped next. She turned her head towards the back of the shop. 'Martha,' she called out. 'Did you ever hear of a drowned forest around here?'

'Oh,' said the woman who responded, emerging from behind a table stacked high with shamrock-motif china. 'Wait a minute, now. I wonder would that be the beach behind Séan Flynn's farm? I've a feeling it might be down there.'

Following her directions, they left the main road and drove down a side road until they reached a solitary and seemingly deserted farmhouse. Stepping out of the car, they climbed over a gate and made their way across a tatty field to where a narrow strip of stony beach was just about visible at the edge of a surging grey sea. The sea was like a full bath lapping over the sides.

'The tides,' said Christo sadly. 'I never thought of that.'

Cassie took his arm and wrapped hers around it as they traipsed back across the field.

'Don't worry,' she told him. 'We can come back another day.'

They drove on into a strangely elemental landscape. The mountains in the distance were as grey as slate; the rolling foreground the colour of rust. The grasses were all copper and gold, the lakes full to the brim with still water as thick and shining as liquid mercury. There was an alien feel to the place. They might have been on another planet.

'Recognize anything?' Christo asked.

Cassie shook her head slowly.

'Not a thing. It might as well be the moon.'

And it was true, the terrain they were passing through was

as bleak and barren as the moon. A place almost bereft of trees, the few there were stood huddled together on small islands in the lakes, as if they were trying to escape some terrible natural disaster.

'I don't know about you,' she said. 'But I could swear I've never been here before in my life.'

It was only when she saw the school that her memory stirred. They had taken a detour to pass it, following a large sign at a fork in the road. They weren't sure which side of the car to look, so they searched out of both and, suddenly, there it was. A picture-postcard castle on the banks of a small, dark lake, with its mirror image reflected in the lake water. Looking at the reeds that wafted this way and that with the breeze, Cassie was aware of something moving inside her head, something so tentative and delicate that she was almost afraid to breathe for fear of blowing it away.

'I remember this,' she said, but no sooner had she said it than the view was lost behind a wall of shrub. They came to the rear entrance, and then a few hundred yards later the front entrance, but the gates were firmly locked.

'She was going to put me into school here,' she said, with surprise. Something she had only just remembered – she remembered having tea with a nun. They were served sugar-sprinkled biscuits with scalloped edges, arranged in a coiled circle on top of a white lace doily. The biscuits were studded with raisins that had been baked until they were as hard as small stones. Cassie ran her tongue along her top lip, working from edge to centre, edge to centre. She was almost expecting to find sugar sprinkles still there.

'She was going to leave me here!'

The feeling of abandonment was fresh and raw.

'No,' said Christo. 'She wasn't going to leave you here. She was going to stay too.'

'Wait,' said Cassie. 'Was that something she talked about?'

'I seem to remember there was talk of buying a house.'

'There was!' she said, pouncing on the memory before it could get away. 'I remember driving around the place, house-hunting. Do you remember that?'

He shook his head slowly, his eyes roving the view as if he were looking for clues in the landscape.

'Definitely,' said Cassie. 'I remember Jim driving us around, looking for houses.'

In her mind was a dappled lane. Trees meeting overhead to form a tunnel, and through the tunnel there was a house. It was all locked up, but they clambered through a gap in the fence and looked in through the windows. They saw a sofa covered in a white sheet. A huge wooden rocking horse. A mountain of old newspapers. Cassie stuck a foot into a clump of nettles and came away with a cluster of stings on her ankle bone. Jim searched the grass until he found a large green leaf that he rubbed against them. He said it would ease the pain, but it didn't.

'I know it's a ridiculous idea,' said Christo. 'But I have this fantasy of her living out her life here. Sometimes I almost believe it's real.'

Cassie was still following the thread of the memory and only half heard him.

She was sitting in the back of a car, whimpering with the pain from her ankle. Her mother was sitting in the front passenger seat wearing a green sundress. Her mother's shoulders were round and bare, the strap marks of her bikini visible as thin white lines around her neck. Jim was in the driver's seat, and her mother was turning to look at him. Some joke passing between them, but Cassie couldn't make out what it was. All she felt was a flash of hatred of the kind you only experience in childhood. Cassie was shocked to remember how

75

she'd hated her mother, at that moment, with a hatred as pungent as love.

'Christo,' she said. 'Can I ask you a question?'

'What's that, love?'

'If we were so happy here, why did we leave?'

The question hung in the air between them, and they both fell quiet as they contemplated it.

'I remember packing up.' She narrowed her eyes against the glare of the memory. 'I remember I was in my pyjamas, and I couldn't find my monkey, but there was no time to look for him.'

It was the middle of the night. Somebody was moving about the house, throwing all the lights on. Then the front door was open, the wet black night blowing in on them. Cassie was barefoot and still half-asleep when they were herded into the back seat of the car.

'I remember how dark it was,' she said. 'It was so dark, and there were all these trees scraping against the window.'

She remembered how frightened she was.

'I don't get it,' she said, turning to look at her brother's profile. 'Why would we have had to leave in a hurry?'

'I don't know,' he said, without turning his face from the road. 'But there must have been a reason.'

A fog had descended on them. The clarity that existed only moments before had all but evaporated. Cassie made one last attempt to chase it down.

'Don't you think it's odd? That we don't know.'

'We were children,' he said in his older-brother voice, the one he once used to lecture her about mathematics. 'You don't think about these things when you're a child. You don't think about why things happen. They just do, and there's not a bloody thing you can do about it.'

Cassie stared out the car window at the strangely empty

landscape. Somewhere out there she and Christo had spent the summer with their mother, but where exactly they'd been she had no idea. Her mother had taken that information with her when she went, along with so much else. What was lost was not only the biographical detail but the substance of the person herself. Cassie would have liked to know all the things her mother loved in life and all the things she hated. All the things she remembered and all the things she'd forgotten. All the thoughts and desires and doubts and regrets, all the fears and thrills, all the hopes and disappointments that made her who she was. Instead, what she was left with was the impossibility of ever knowing the truth of someone else's life, something that is unknowable perhaps even to themselves. Unless – and this was Cassie's hope – unless something remains of a person in the places that were important to them. Unless the air in those places holds some memory of the person they were, the way water is said to retain the memory of a substance that has long since been diluted out of it. If this trace memory were to persist in those places, then it might be possible, even after all this time, to find something of her there.

10

No photograph was ever taken of that summer. Hard to imagine such a thing now, but that was before the age of the selfie, before mobile phones existed and digital technology prevailed. People didn't take photographs with the same abandon. It was customary to ask someone's permission before taking their picture, and those pictures often remained undeveloped on a roll of film that languished for years in the dark drawer of a desk or in the pocket of a seldom-used coat. Even those rolls of film that were lucky enough to be developed didn't always come out right. Often several frames would be obliterated, maybe because the back of the camera had been opened before the film was fully wound on or because the developer had exposed them to light while opening the canister. Sometimes you could make out the top of someone's head at the edge of the frame, just enough to identify the image that had been lost. Other times there was nothing to indicate the moment the photographer had attempted to capture, except for the number that appeared inexplicably off-centre at the top of the frame: 7a.

Without the aid of photographs to freeze time in a series of single frames, all that remained of that summer was a blur of moving images in the memories of those who were there. Christo remembered Margo always packing a picnic basket and hunting down dry towels or roaming the beach for shells. Jim was forever, in Christo's memory, folded in behind the wheel of his old white Citroën. He liked to speed up as he crested the hill, so the wheels lifted off the ground as the children screamed in half-thrilled terror. As for his mother, Christo pictured her always in the act of smoking. He saw her huddled in the cave-like shelter of a sand dune as she tried to spark up the lighter despite the wind. Curled in a childlike hunch over her jigsaw at the kitchen table, with the cigarette in her ashtray sending a snake of smoke into the air. One day he saw her take her shoe off to hammer a stubborn piece into place.

Christo had never forgotten that, just as he never forgot the time he sliced the side of his foot open on the beach by stepping on a discarded tuna can. The sting of a jellyfish that rose in livid bumps on his arm and, even more unforgettably, Jim's offer to pee on it. There was the time that Cassie snagged her blue dress on a coil of barbed wire, and the time Seamus dared her to touch the electric fence with her fishing rod. The time Christo slipped and fell into a cowpat and raged at them all for laughing. All these instances of pain or humiliation stood out in vivid detail, while the many happy moments dissolved into each other to form a blur. As if happiness flowed freely, leaving no evidence of itself behind, while unhappiness scabbed and left a scar.

'Let's stop for an ice cream,' said Christo, spotting the HB sign swinging in the breeze by the side of the road. 'My treat.'

This was one of his favourite indulgences, not just for the pleasure of the ice cream itself but for the sense of agency he had over his own life in buying himself one. His ice cream of choice was a plain chocolate Magnum, but he would occasionally venture into the realm of the almond Magnum. The white chocolate one, under no circumstances.

'I'll have a Cornetto,' said Cassie. 'For old times' sake. Do you remember Jim was always singing the ad?'

She started singing the ridiculous words of the ad, in a heavy Italian accent, to the tune of 'O Sole Mio'. Christo joined in, and the two of them sang it together as they drove away from the shop. They trailed off after a few lines, unable to remember the rest.

'La la la la la LA,' sang Cassie, to round it off. 'La la la la. La LAA la la.'

They barely had time to eat the ice creams before they reached their destination. A town on the westernmost edge of the country, it had two churches, a few small hotels and a wide estuary that breathed water in and out according to the tides. Christo and Cassie drove two loops of the triangle of streets at the centre of town before they parked. Spilling out of the car like sailors making landfall after a long sea journey, they walked up and down the pavement, shaking out their creaking limbs. All around them, people in raingear wandered in and out of the shops. The tourists had come prepared for the weather.

'Busy place,' said Christo to the weary-looking woman in the hotel on the quayside.

'It's either a famine or a feast,' she said. 'If you'd come five years ago, you'd have had it to yourselves.' She looked out of place in the surroundings of her hotel, like a stranded opera singer who had ended up there by some accident of fate. 'Paddy,' she shouted, throwing her eyes to heaven when there was no immediate response. Her next shout was louder, and her intonation had changed, so the stress was on the first syllable. 'Paaa-ddy.'

Still there was no response. Apologizing, she turned to throw her voice behind her. The stress was now on the last syllable.

'Padd-eeeey.'

The man who appeared – with a slightly hammy pretence of rushing – had the fine-boned face of an actor. 'Apologies,' he said, with a touch of *noblesse oblige*. 'I was otherwise engaged.' Bending over almost double, he took Cassie's suit-case by the handle and propelled it up the wide, carpeted stairs, his feet moving as if he were on castors. Cassie followed after him, while Christo drew his passport out of his bag and handed it to the woman, who began to copy his details into a ledger.

'That's quite a name you've got there,' she said. She meant no harm, but Christo had to draw deep nonetheless, to reply with good humour.

'I have my parents to blame for it,' he said, resorting to one of his stock answers.

A name arrived at by them with no thought for the person he would one day become. He divulged it to nobody, choosing instead to use his middle name in all his dealings with the world, along with the deceptively ordinary surname he'd inherited from his father. Christo was at a college table quiz once when it cropped up as a question. By what name is Alistair Jones better known? His teammates were amazed that he knew the answer. Never in a million years would they have imagined him to be the son of someone famous enough to be known by a single word. It was inconceivable that this person could be Christo's dad.

When Christo had first moved to England, his father's celebrity was at its height, rendering Christo's existence tiny by comparison. Everywhere they went people startled at the sight of his dad. They would approach him for an autograph, oblivious to the discourtesy they were showing Christo by interrupting. The pool of light cast by his father's celebrity was small and sharply defined, leaving anybody outside of it in perpetual obscurity.

'You don't mind, do you?' they would ask Christo, handing him a camera and appointing him the photographer.

'No problem,' Christo would say, although of course it

was not quite as simple as that. He wanted nothing to do with his father's celebrity, a commodity that altered Christo in the eyes of anyone who knew of it. None of the boys at school had a parent as famous as his. Some had fathers who were politicians, and one boy had a mother who was a writer, but Christo was the only one with a real-life rock star for a father, and the attention it brought down on him was a source of great discomfort. There were boys who befriended him in the hope of getting free concert tickets. Others asked about his father's famous friends. One boy even went so far as to give him a demo tape to send to his dad, which Christo faithfully did, but no reply was ever forthcoming. The boy pestered Christo about it for three whole terms.

What Christo could not at the time have imagined was that his father's fame would eventually wane. He had imagined it to be for life, like a peerage, but it turned out to be perishable. Middle age made inroads on it, as did the constant influx of new famous people. There seemed to be more and more of them all the time. By the time his dad was getting old and starting to look like any other old person, the whole world had earned the right to be famous. All you had to do was appear on TV or post something on YouTube and you were a star. Celebrity was no longer the preserve just of musicians and actors but of chefs and historians and all manner of nobody. To see his father at last rendered ordinary should have made Christo feel better. Instead, he felt mildly sick to think how much of his life had been lived in the shadow of something that turned out to have no substance.

'How is he?' Cassie asked him, as they headed out of the hotel in search of a place to get some dinner. 'Your dad.'

'Oh, he's fine,' said Christo. 'Same as ever.'

'How old are the kids?' She was referring to the clutch of flaxen-haired children Amanda had produced. Cassie had encountered them only once, when they were babies. It was Christmas Eve and she'd arrived without warning into Heathrow, just as Christo was about to leave for his father's house in Devon. He'd had no choice but to bring her with him, despite his worst misgivings. The visit was not a success – Cassie was in a bad place at the time. Thin and jumpy from subsisting on cigarettes and coffee, sleeping by day, waking by night. She showed no interest in the children, which made her unpopular with Amanda.

'Oh, gosh, how old would they be? I've lost track. Eight, nine, ten, maybe?'

He saw them, at most, once a year. Arriving at their door to be greeted by a barefoot stampede. They liked to scramble all over him, along with their dogs, who were as fair-haired and dishevelled as they were. Making a human climbing frame of his body, they hung about his neck like long-armed monkeys. They wrapped themselves about his ankles and hung on for dear life while he tried to walk. They knocked him down and pinned him to the floor with a web of spidery limbs. Christo always felt like Gulliver in their company.

'They're feral.' He added, for Cassie's amusement, 'Amanda doesn't believe in disciplining children. Or dogs.'

Amanda was a children's TV presenter when his dad met her. Barely three years older than Christo, she was introduced to him with no warning at his school sports day. She was wearing a white fur coat with nothing under it but a Tarzan and Jane minidress. Her legs were bare and sinewy, her toe-nails painted canary yellow to match the Daimler they'd arrived in. Christo tried not to notice the way his dad paraded his tomcat sexuality in front of the teachers. Tried not to notice the panting glances the other boys cast over his father's date. He despised them all for treating him differently at supper that evening.

'Do you see him often?' Cassie asked.

'Almost never.'

Occasionally Christo would suggest to his dad that they might meet up one day in London. He had a vision of them having a civilized lunch together in a hushed restaurant with white tablecloths, somewhere they could talk. Even as he suggested it, he knew his dad would never come. That didn't stop him from wishing he would, and it was the pathetic nature of this wish that saddened him the most. 'We never stir out of the country these days,' his dad liked to say. 'We're quite the country bumpkins.' Even though Christo had seen him photographed out and about in Cannes. On the beach in Barbados. Walking through the East Village in New York.

'I keep track of him through *Hello!* magazine,' he confessed to Cassie.

Not that he ever actually bought it, but he'd been known to flick through the pages in the newsagent's. His father was generally to be found towards the back, where the comings and goings of various minor celebrities were mentioned in brief. With his trademark bandana and his unnaturally robust head of hair, Christo's dad looked like an ageing pirate.

'He's becoming a caricature of himself,' he said, aware that she envied him his father. Inadequate as he was, he must have seemed to Cassie better than no father at all. To Christo, it was a moot point.

'Do you have no memories at all of yours?' Christo asked her now.

'I'm not sure,' she said, tossing her hair. 'I don't have any *specific* memory of him. I just remember him being there. I don't know how I know it was him. I just know it was.'

She was five and a half when he died – of suicide, according to the coroner's verdict. Their mother chose not to believe that, attributing his death instead to an accidental overdose, despite all the evidence to the contrary. There was the testimony of the barman in the hotel, who said Joey had ordered drink after drink, speaking of a need to stoke his courage for what he had to do. The bartender was so alarmed that he stopped serving him, which was quite a turn from a Vegas bartender. There were phone calls from the hotel room to his band members, to his manager, to a former girlfriend, speaking in each case of his despair at the troubles he was having with his record company, of their failure to see what he was trying to achieve with his music, of his rage at being misunderstood by them. They were trying to commercialize him, they were pigeonholing him, they were preventing him from being himself.

'They weren't wrong,' Marty Legge told *Rolling Stone* magazine, many years later. 'That last record was a shit sandwich.'

Marty was the manager of Cassie's dad's band and a constant feature of their lives when Cassie's dad was alive. After his death it was Marty who had handled the press, the record company, the lawyers. Marty was supposed to be the keeper of the flame, which made it all the more sensational when Marty revealed himself to be the poisonous snake Christo had always known him to be.

'You know what?' Marty told the reporter from *Rolling Stone*. 'The suicide was a smart move. If he'd lived, he would have gone down as a second-rate rocker, but by topping himself he managed to get an upgrade for eternity. If it wasn't so sad, it would actually be pretty bloody funny.'

'You remember him,' said Cassie, and Christo knew this was his cue to share his memories with her. She might have been handing him a ball and asking him to serve. It was a game they'd played many times before, and always along the same lines.

'I remember him playing the guitar,' he told her. 'He had

this shiny black guitar, and he would bend down low over it while he was playing.'

She nodded, like a child listening to a bedtime story they've heard a hundred times before. If he got one word wrong, she'd know he was making it up.

'You were wearing nothing but a diaper, and you were dancing round and round in circles.'

'Where were you?' she asked, even though she knew this bit.

'I was on the bongos.'

What he didn't tell her was that Joey, in his memory, had no eyeballs. His eyes had rolled back in his head, but he was still staring out of them, like a zombie in a horror movie. That was something Christo couldn't ever tell Cassie, just like he could never tell her about the time he saw Joey naked in the garden. Joey was covered in warpaint, squatting on all fours by the pool, with the underwater lights making a spectral figure of him. Christo made sure to keep that from Cassie, but the difficulty with keeping something from a person was that you had to keep it from them every time it crossed your mind and tried to escape. It required constant vigilance.

'That's it,' he told her. 'That's all I remember.'

They'd reached the door of the restaurant and Christo pulled it open, standing back to let his sister pass through. She paused as she did so to look up into his face. The low evening sun was refracted through the stained-glass panels of the door, throwing yellow diamonds of light over her. For the first time ever, Christo saw a resemblance in her to their mother. A flicker of a likeness that was no sooner there than it was gone again. It was as if their mother had passed in front of his eyes for a split second before disappearing again. A vision of her so true and yet so gossamer-thin that he didn't even try to explain it to Cassie. By the time they'd stepped inside the resemblance was gone and Cassie was her father's daughter again.

'I've just realized how hungry I am,' she said, as they studied the menu. 'I could eat a farmer's arse through a hedge.'

That was a saying of Jim's.

'Or a nun's bum through a letterbox.'

'Ha,' she said. 'I'd forgotten that one.'

The waitress appeared at their table, with her pen poised to take their order.

'I'll have the pasta,' Cassie told her. 'With a side salad.'

Christo ordered a beef burger, medium-well done, with cheese and bacon.

'Drinks?'

Christo was distracted by the sound of Cassie's phone ringing from her handbag.

'Are you sure you don't need to take that?'

Already that day there had been two calls, which she'd dismissed in a similar manner. It was beginning to make Christo feel anxious.

'No,' she said, 'it's fine. I know who it is. I'll call him back later.'

She ordered a glass of red wine. Christo asked for a pint of Coke.

'Now folks,' said the waitress, materializing at the table with their food only minutes after the order had gone in. She dealt their plates out like a hand of cards. 'Burger, pasta, side salad.'

Cassie reached out to grab a handful of Christo's chips before the waitress had even left the table.

'Oh my God,' she said. 'I will never get over the fact that I'm related to someone who eats a burger with a knife and fork. You probably eat pizza with a knife and fork. You would probably eat a *taco* with a knife and fork.'

'Of course,' he said, to indulge her. 'How else?'

He had his tie thrown over his shoulder to protect it as he ate.

'You're so English it's ridiculous,' she said, speaking even though her mouth was full.

He waited until he'd swallowed before replying.

'And you, my dear, are a consummate Yank, from the parting of your unkempt hair to your unnaturally white teeth.'

She grinned, baring her gums at him in an all-American smile. This was a game they liked to play – the nationality game – to cover up the fact that they were neither of them from anywhere at all.

'Do you know what occurred to me recently?' she asked him, as they stood outside the hotel after dinner. The rain had finally cleared, leaving the pavements shining like they'd been freshly poured.

'I don't know,' he said. 'What's that?'

'I'm going to turn thirty-seven soon.'

'I know that. The first of November.'

How could she think he would forget her birthday?

'I'm going to be thirty-seven,' she said. 'Don't you see?'

Christo felt like he was making his way through a maze. There was a yew tree maze at a castle he'd recently visited in Kent, and he'd spent an hour negotiating his way through it by trial and error. That was what every conversation with his sister felt like to him. He kept coming up against dead ends.

'I'm going to be *thirty-seven*, Christo. Which makes me older than she was when she died. Come November I'll be older than she ever was.'

At that moment, she looked to him more like a little girl.

'I'll have outlived her,' she said, her voice all croaky. 'Isn't that the saddest thing?'

The loneliness of being a survivor. That was something Christo understood only too well. He, at least, had one parent living, whereas Cassie was truly an orphan.

'I feel so old, Christo. I feel like I'm the oldest person in the world.'

'You can't be the oldest person in the world,' he said. 'You see, that's the thing about having a big brother. No matter what happens, I'll always be older than you.'

He saw her eyes fill with tears. He wrapped an arm around her, cupping the back of her head with his hand. Her skull was rock-hard where his fingers slipped through her hair. With his other hand he rubbed her back the way you might wind a baby.

'It's okay,' he said, wondering how long he should hold her. He didn't want to be the one to pull away, but he wasn't sure how long he could sustain the hug. There was only so much rubbing you could do.

'Alright,' she said, straightening up and taking a deep breath. 'I think I'm just tired. It's been a long day.'

'Time for bed,' he said, holding out his arm to steer her towards the door of the hotel.

'I'm just going to make a call before I go in.'

She turned away from him, the phone already in her hand.

'Okay, goodnight.'

'Goodnight, Christo.'

From his bedroom window, Christo watched her standing on the quayside below to place her call. She was bent over, holding the phone to her ear like a seashell as she waited for an answer. Then she straightened up, smiled and began to talk. Christo watched her walk up and down the quay, observing the languid confidence of her movements. The sense she projected of being fully in charge of herself. It was an impression that dissipated as soon as she put the phone back in her pocket. She turned, head lifted with great humility – or maybe despair – to the sky, as if searching it for answers. A thought occurred to Christo: that we are none of us just the one person, but a different person depending on who we're with, and a different person again when we're alone.

It would amuse Christo to know that Cassie had come to think of her life as a Venn diagram. Cassie never could understand maths when it was represented by numbers, but once it was translated into shapes, she had no problem with it. She found bar charts easy to understand, same with pie charts, but it was the Venn diagrams she'd learned about in third grade that made the most sense to her.

She had come to think of her life as a circle, with the people close to her represented by circles that eclipsed hers to a greater or lesser degree. Eduardo's was the one that overlapped with hers the most, creating a shared area the shape of an almond. In that almond-shaped area were the long phone calls Eduardo liked to make to her from his desk when he should have been working. There were the weekends at Eduardo's house in the mountains, the languid evenings spent in his kitchen, where Cassie sat on a high stool by his kitchen island and chopped an onion according to his insanely meticulous instructions, while he butchered a chicken, or skinned a fish, with all the delicacy of a surgeon. Weekend mornings were spent lazing in his bed, with the window open onto the sloping street and the high thread count of Eduardo's cotton sheets lying heavy on her legs as they drank coffee and gossiped about the people they'd been with the night before.

When they were at her house they liked to listen to music: either Bach or Van Morrison or Aretha. They liked to watch the same Hitchcock movies over and over again, marvelling at the use of colour in *Vertigo*. The clothes in *Rear Window*. It was amazing how those movies stood up to repeated viewing. Eduardo would sit at one end of her couch with his legs stretched out and his surprisingly shapely feet resting on the coffee table, while Cassie reclined against a pile of cushions at the opposite end, her bare feet nestled in Eduardo's lap.

'We're a perfect fit,' she'd told him, early on. 'Our proportions are perfect. It's like I had you made to measure.'

In the portion of her life that Cassie shared with Eduardo was the passion they both had for watching tennis on TV. There were art galleries and exhibition openings and long games of backgammon. There were tender nights spent in each other's arms. It was a rich existence and full of beauty, but it occupied only a small part of Cassie's world. Christo's life intersected with hers in a different place, but even that was only a partial eclipse that drew mostly on their shared childhood. There was a part of Cassie that was known only to the owner of the gallery that sold her paintings – he alone knew the bundle of shyness and stubbornness that she was as an artist. Her friends in Mexico had another slice of her, yielded to them in unguarded moments that she would later invariably regret. When Cassie thought of her life, she thought of a campfire in the wilderness, casting a small circle of light over the camp, while a vast dark country lay all around it unexplored. It made her sad to think that we are none of us really known to anyone, except perhaps to ourselves.

'Por fin!' said Eduardo, answering after only one ring. Finally!

Cassie could picture him sitting with his mother at a corner table under the shaded colonnade of the San Angel Inn, as was his habit every Monday afternoon. His mother would be drinking white wine, while he had the house margarita. The two of them conversing without ever taking their eyes off the door, as they monitored the arrival of a stream of people whose history they were familiar with, going back three generations. Some of the people would stop at their table, and Eduardo would stand to greet them, while his mother remained seated. The women bending to kiss Eduardo's mother on the cheek, the men leaning in to hug him, slapping him strenuously on the shoulder as they did so. It was at that point that Eduardo would hear the cell phone ringing in his suit pocket and excuse himself, walking away from the table to take the call.

'Am I disturbing your meal?'

'Yes,' he said, 'but you're a welcome disturbance. My mother was just reminding me of the many links between her people and the Calderón family.'

She saw him standing by the fountain, with one hand in the pocket of his loose linen trousers. The water in the fountain was the exact same green as Eduardo's eyes. He was a man entirely at one with his habitat.

'Ah,' said Cassie. 'Her specialist topic. Family ties to the rich and famous.'

Cassie had met Eduardo's mother on a number of occasions, and watched each time in amusement as she struggled to place Cassie in a category of womanhood that she could understand. Eduardo's mother could see that Cassie was an attractive woman, but she could not fathom the absence of a manicure. The failure to avail herself of even the most elementary cosmetic surgery was a mystery to her, as was the undyed hair. The choice of black clothing.

'You should wear more red,' she told Cassie once, accustomed to airing her opinions as she pleased. Cassie was almost tempted to marry Eduardo, if only for the pleasure of wearing black to the wedding.

'Cómo te vas?' he asked.

'Bien,' she said. 'Todo va bien.'

'I'm curious to know how you're faring in your quest.'

Cassie smiled at how quaint he was when he translated himself into English.

'Good,' she said. 'So far, so good.'

'I'm happy for you,' he said. 'Me alegro mucho.'

Spoken in two languages, his kindness only made her feel doubly bad for avoiding his calls. It was with the greatest reluctance that she'd called him back.

'Describe what you can see from where you're standing.'

'I can see the sea,' she said. 'But it's black. There's a black road in front of me, and a black stone wall with a black boat tied up to it. There are black mountains in the distance, and a big black sky.'

'But how can you tell these things apart if they're all black?'

'Oh, they're all different shades of black.'

'Aren't there any stars where you are?'

Cassie craned her head back to check.

'No stars.'

'No moon?'

'No moon either.' And whereas the tone she had used with her brother over dinner was flighty and excitable, with Eduardo she was the sensible one.

'I'm not sure I approve. What kind of place has no moon and stars?'

'A cloudy one,' said Cassie, determined to be prosaic.

After she and Eduardo had said their goodbyes, she stood at the harbour wall for a moment with the phone in her hand. A strange feeling in her, like she'd just passed through an airport scanner. The sensation you have when you step free of it, as if all the molecules in your body have been rearranged and you need to give them time to settle back into place again. That was how Cassie felt every time she stepped free of Eduardo.

She was still in bed the next morning when Christo knocked on her door. He heard her calling out to him and stepped into the room. She had the curtains open, the morning sun pouring, thick and syrupy, over the huge double bed where she lay sprawled like a movie star in a pool of light.

'I've brought my laptop,' he said, making for the small dressing table between the room's two large windows. Stencils of Virginia creeper danced on the tongue-and-groove panelling of the window casing. Outside, the estuary was at full tide. The fishing boats by the pier were balanced delicately upright. The water mirrored the headland on the far side, with just a faint ripple in the glassy surface.

'I thought we'd do some research before we set off,' said Christo, opening his laptop and tapping into the hotel's wi-fi, with its blessedly simple password. Feeling slightly shabby, he embarked – not for the first time – on a hunt for Seamus. He typed his name into a Google search only to find a multitude of people named Seamus Murphy. There was a photographer who'd worked in Afghanistan. A sculptor best known for engraving headstones. A cinematographer and a used-car dealer. More information would be required, but they didn't have any more information about Seamus, only the memory of a boy with fingernails bitten down to the nail beds and pyjama bottoms cut short by his mother for the summer, giving him the appearance of someone who'd been shipwrecked on a desert island.

The Seamus Christo knew as a child was freckle-faced, with a head of hair as thick and matted as donkey fur. There was a tuft of it at the crown that never would lie down. Margo would sometimes lick her fingers and dab at it, like she was trying to seal an envelope, but Seamus would slip out of her grip.

'Ah, Mam,' he would say. 'Leave me alone.'

Seamus was a shy kid, with grey watchful eyes that took on a pained expression when he was listening. He blushed easily, the blood rising steadily up his pale face, as if someone were standing over him pouring him full of a deep pink liquid. He was also knowledgeable, possessed of a wealth of information and superstition that only a kid who grew up in the countryside would know. Seamus knew that warts could be cured by the rub of a snail. He knew that eels were best gathered at night under a full moon, and that razorfish could be coaxed out of the sand at low tide with salt. He knew it was bad luck for a frog to come into the house – you had to throw it straight on the fire if that happened – and that hares were a bad omen if they appeared too near the door. Anyone who falls over in a graveyard will be dead within the year, he'd told them, with great seriousness.

'That's no lie,' he'd said, crossing his heart to prove it.

Christo could still hear the deathly note of credulity in his voice, could see him standing there crossing his heart with his poor, raw fingers. Margo painted them with Stop'n Grow, but Seamus liked the taste of it, so that was no deterrent.

'He had a school sweater with a crest on it,' said Cassie. 'I thought that was really cool.'

'I'm not sure that's going to help us track him down,' said Christo. 'He probably doesn't wear it anymore.'

They might as well have been trying to find a needle in a haystack. Jim was a better bet, but there was no Wikipedia page for him, only the occasional mention of him as a session musician on other people's albums.

'He was known as Jimmy "Strings" Murphy,' Christo had reminded Marty Legge, when they spoke on the phone. It was only with the greatest of reluctance that Christo had phoned Marty. He was the last person in the world Christo wanted to speak to, but he was also the only person who possessed the information they required for their trip. It was Marty who'd booked their tickets to Ireland when their grandfather was sick, Marty who'd driven them to the airport, and Marty who'd collected them on their return. Marty was their only link to the events of that summer, so Christo tracked down a number for him and forced himself to dial it. The phone rang and rang and rang. Christo was just about to give up when it was unexpectedly answered.

'Christo,' said Marty. 'Where you been, man?'

Twenty-five years since they'd last met, but Marty gave no indication that he'd noticed the passage of time. From the casual tone of his voice, they might have seen each other only last week.

'I need to know where we were,' Christo explained.

'Fucked if I know,' said Marty. 'She went and disappeared. Three months and not a word. The next thing she's on the phone. She's all "Marty, baby. I need you to come and rescue me."'

After forty years in LA, Marty sounded more of a Londoner than ever, which just went to prove that it was all an act. Even as a child, Christo was never convinced by Marty, with his uniform of expensive suits that he wore seven days a week – with a black polo neck instead of a shirt – despite the dry California heat. Christo had never seen Marty wearing anything but a suit and a polo neck, except for that one time when he walked into his mother's bedroom and found

Marty sitting up in her bed, with the covers concealing his bottom half and his top half naked. His bony chest was hairless, and he had a mole in the centre of his ribcage that looked like a third nipple. He was smoking a cigarette and tipping the ash into the lid of a jar of face cream that was balanced on his draped knee.

'Oh!' said Christo's mother, when she emerged naked from the bathroom. Christo turned away in disgust, but not before the image of her luminous body had been stamped on his mind like silver salts on a photographic plate. He ran out into the garden, where he lay face down on the lawn counting the ants between the blades of grass, but still he could not scrub the image from his mind of Marty sitting up in the bed with his three nipples, and his mother without her clothes on. Even at thirteen, Christo knew it was a bad sign for his mother to be sleeping with Marty. It was the clearest indication yet that she was running out of road.

'Guess where I am?' Marty asked Christo.

'I don't have a clue, Marty. Where are you?'

'Come on, Christo, guess.'

It occurred to Christo that Marty might not be entirely aware that he was a grown-up now, or was it Marty who'd never grown up? With his mother and her friends, Christo had always felt like he was in the company of adolescents. A teenage air of delinquency about them – they did not seem to care about the damage they did to things. These were people who trampled on your Lego and never bothered to gather up the pieces they'd scattered. They left cigarettes burning in ashtrays, doors wide open onto the night. As a child Christo would go around the house checking the doors were locked and the candles blown out before he went to bed.

'Come on,' said Marty, as if to prove the point. 'One guess.'

'I don't know, Marty. Barbados?'

'Ha! Not even close. I'm in Uzbekistan, with his nibs.'

That was when Christo remembered how Marty liked to talk in riddles. It was all a part of Marty's act, the way he left gaps in his speech for you to fill in. Even as a child, Christo had found it tedious.

'How are you anyway?' asked Marty. 'How come we never hear from you?'

'Oh, you know how it is.'

'Oh, yeah,' said Marty, with that knowing laugh of his. 'I know how it is.'

In the background Christo could hear the sound of a woman laughing, but he couldn't tell whether the woman was laughing along with Marty or whether she was laughing at something else entirely. There were always people laughing around Marty. Resisting the urge to get off the phone, Christo pressed on.

'I need to know where we went after my grandfather died.'

'Look, all I know is that she rang me from a call box,' said Marty, as casually as if he were describing what he'd eaten for breakfast. 'She wanted me to get her out of there. The way she was talking, you'd swear Saigon was falling down around her ears. She wanted me to organize a fucking airlift. So, of course, I did.'

Christo remembered emerging into the dry heat of LA. He remembered the fuzzy-felt sky over the terminal building and the smell of gas in the pickup bay. His mother settling into the front seat of Marty's car and slipping her feet out of her shoes. Her painted toes perched on the dashboard as they slid onto the freeway. Christo remembered how he'd stared out the window, watching the landscape of his life change and knowing there was nothing he could do about it. That's what he remembered most about being a child. The feeling of being a pawn in a game someone else was playing.

'Can't you remember where she was calling from? It was somewhere in County Galway.'

'Yeah, well,' said Marty. 'You probably had a clearer head than I did back then, so I wouldn't be surprised if you remember more than I do.'

Christo narrowed his eyes as all the old dangers swirled around him. Ashtrays full of half-smoked joints and rows of white powder like snail trails on the glass-topped table in the living room. Christo had a memory of Marty rolling a joint at his mother's memorial service. He remembered how Marty had licked it shut with a flicker of his tongue and passed it to Christo first, out of deference to his bereavement.

'Jeez, Marty,' somebody said. 'The kid's only thirteen.'

'A little bit of recreational drug use never did anyone any harm,' Marty had said, mildly offended.

'Isn't there anything at all you can remember?' Christo asked Marty, on the phone, in a last-ditch attempt to shame him into parting with some information.

'Ha,' said Marty. 'I can hardly remember my own name, son. That's why I got myself a new child bride, to remember these things for me. But give me your number. If I come up with anything, I'll give you a call.'

'Let me guess,' said Cassie. 'He didn't call back?'

She was sitting up in the bed, yawning. Christo took a chair at the dressing table and set his laptop up.

'Of course not.'

He'd expected no more from Marty, but some small part of him had still been hoping against hope that Marty might yet redeem his faith in humanity.

'Well, there's a surprise,' said Cassie, swinging her legs over the side of the bed and pulling on her robe. He watched in the mirror as she raised both arms above her head and stretched, clenching her fists like a baby.

'So, where does that leave us?' she asked, through a yawn.

'Well, I'm afraid we're on our own.'

'And now for something new.'

She came to stand behind him, resting her hands on his shoulders. Christo was just about to speak when she bent down and kissed him, very lightly, on the top of his head. It was a long time since Christo had been kissed by anybody, and he found it overwhelming. He closed his eyes and tried scrunching the moment in his mind to preserve it.

'Don't worry,' he heard her say. 'We'll figure it out for ourselves.'

The next thing, the touch of her hands was gone. His shoulders felt heavier without them, like the weight a branch feels without the bird that a moment ago was perched there. Very reluctantly, Christo opened his eyes.

13

Weather was what Cassie remembered. She remembered endless blue skies and racing clouds and sunshine. She remembered sunburn and the sting of salt water between your legs where you'd peed while you were swimming. She remembered finding filaments of seaweed stuck to the skin of her belly when she peeled her swimsuit off at night.

'What about Space Dust?' she asked Christo. 'Do you remember that? It was banned but they had it in the village shop.'

There were orange ice pops with a seam of vanilla ice cream running through them, and envelopes of lemon sherbet with a liquorice stick to use as a dipper.

'There was an ice lolly called a That-A-Way.'

Cassie grabbed her clothes from the small couch at the foot of the bed, where she'd thrown them the night before. She made for the bathroom, with her brother's voice following her.

'I hope you don't mind me saying so, but all these things you remember are completely useless. What we need is a landmark of some sort. Could you point your memory in that direction, do you think?'

'There was a beach,' she said, speaking to him through the open bathroom door. 'Not a sunbathing kind of a beach. This one was more of a walking beach.'

She loaded her toothbrush with paste and started to brush.

'You could drive across to an island,' she told him, her voice a gargle.

Running the tap, she bent down to gulp a mouthful of water. It was miraculously cold, like it had been poured straight from a cooler.

'What?' he shouted, from the bedroom. 'I can't hear you.'

'Wait.'

She spat the water out, leaned out of the bathroom.

'She let us drive,' she said, certain now that she was on the right track. 'Don't you remember that? We were allowed to drive the car.'

They would take it in turns, pulling the seat of the old Mercedes up close to the wheel so they could reach the pedals. You had to weave in and out of the tidal puddles, your bones rattling as the car bumped its way over the sand. Christo drove slowly and with great caution. Cassie drove fast, with disregard for the consequences. She could barely see over the dashboard.

'*Slow down!*' their mother would shout, grabbing the door handle for dear life. '*You'll have us all killed!*'

Cassie wandered back into the bedroom, rubbing some cream into her face as she went. 'I remember there was horse racing on the beach. Don't you remember?'

Christo entered that into the search engine, but it turned out there were multiple locations where horse racing was held on beaches. It seemed there was hardly a beach in Ireland where horse races were not occasionally held.

'I think there was a graveyard on the island.'

But that too, according to Google, was common enough. Also common were headlands inhabited by surfers in caravans. Cows grazing on beaches. Sunbathing seals. All the things that Cassie remembered – they could have been anywhere.

'There was a house with a lobster on the side of it,' she said. The lobster was emblazoned on the gable wall of a house they drove by every day. They would spot the lobster house and know they were nearly home.

'I don't know a house with a lobster,' said the young woman who served them breakfast. She was from Poland, she explained, directing her attention at Christo in a shy flirt. Cassie saw how handsome he was, through the other woman's eyes. He was so very, very handsome, but the young woman was wasting her time with him. Cassie could no more imagine Christo flirting back than she could imagine him dancing on the table. His reserve was like a straitjacket that he wore by choice.

'Let's just go and drive around.' Cassie crumpled her napkin and tossed it on her side plate. 'See if there's anything we recognize.'

She had the sense they were chasing time. Like they were trying to catch a boat that would not sail again. She was afraid the thing they were looking for would be gone by the time they got there.

'Would you like some more coffee or tea?' asked the Polish woman. 'Some more toast maybe?'

'I'm good,' said Cassie, anxious to get going. The morning was slipping away, and with it the blue sky that only an hour ago had promised to be there for the day. In the time it took for them to have breakfast it had clouded over.

'I wouldn't mind another pot of tea,' said Christo. 'If it's not too much trouble.'

He drank the tea slowly – two cups of it – and afterwards he required half an hour in his room. Cassie imagined him sitting on the toilet, with his trousers down around his ankles and his book of numbers to pore over. The things you know about someone when you've lived with them as a child – Christo had always liked to read on the toilet. He'd liked to collect stones from the beach and swizzle sticks from hotel bars. He'd kept notebooks full of pointless records, tracking the times of the sunset from day to day, the phases of the moon. He'd even tracked the cars that went by on the road below their house, counting how many of them were white. How many were red, blue, black.

'Do you remember that?' she asked him, as they drove. 'God, you were a weird kid.'

'All kids are weird,' he said, in his own defence.

'Really?'

'That's the whole point of being a kid. You have a licence to be weird.'

A few miles out of town they took the turn for Omey Island, driving down a long finger of land with the silvery sea to their left. They rounded the tip of the peninsula and saw the island ahead, separated only from the mainland by a spit of tidal sand. The road brought them sloping down towards sea level, taking them past a church where a funeral was just finishing. A black Ford Scorpio hearse crawled out the church gate and down the lane towards the island. Following after it, a train of people on foot, wielding black umbrellas against the weightless rain. Christo slowed the car down, allowing a respectable distance before he trailed them down the lane. When they reached the car park at the bottom, he cut the engine, and he and Cassie stepped out to watch as the Ford Scorpio crossed the sand towards the island. It was a beautiful sight, with the mourners walking behind it. The graveyard waited for them on the far side.

'Imagine what it would be like,' said Christo. 'To come from somewhere like this. Generations of your family living in the same place. And all your people buried in that graveyard.'

I come from a long line of dead people, Cassie liked to tell people, making light of the fact that there was not a single one of them left. Her grandmother was the last to go, in a cloud of smoke despite her advanced lung cancer. Her bitter take on the world had held fast right to the end.

'I hope you haven't been going through my things,' she'd said, the last time Cassie saw her. She was bedridden by then, the smell off her – of unwashed flesh and bodily fluids – so strong that Cassie asked to open the window.

'Oh no,' her grandmother said. 'Whatever you do, don't open that window. I'm so cold. Here, feel me.'

Cassie reached out with great reluctance to touch her grandmother's mottled old arm. The skin of it was dry and flaky but surprisingly soft, like the skin of the snake Cassie had once touched at a classmate's birthday party. None of the other girls would sit beside her afterwards for fear of touching the hand that had touched the snake. Not that Cassie cared – she was always happier hanging out with the boys, and the snake-toucher title she acquired that day became a source of great pride to her.

'You probably can't wait 'til I die, so you can go through all my things,' said her grandmother.

The drawers of her grandmother's dresser were filled with strange keepsakes. There were baby clothes stuffed into discoloured plastic bags. Threadbare teddy bears and old corsages long decayed. She had balls of wool in there and a million pairs of skin-tone pantyhose. Hair clips and empty perfume bottles and bundles of old mail. Cassie could not think of anything she would like less than to go through her grandmother's things.

'Wait until you see,' her grandmother said, in the same taunting style Cassie remembered the mean girls using at school. 'You can't wait to be rid of me, but you're going to wind up missing me when I'm gone.'

And the funny thing was that it was true. Much as Cassie

had disliked her when she was alive, it was better than having her dead. It was only at the funeral that it dawned on Cassie that, for all her reptilian venom, her grandmother had at least been a living link to her father, and without her there was none. The grief Cassie felt at her going was not a tearful thing as she had imagined grief to be. It was purely physical, manifesting itself as a stabbing pain somewhere between her ribs. She was stunned by the unexpected nature of it. As her grandma's neighbours guided the mourners towards the table of cold cuts, Cassie sank into a chair in the corner of the living room, holding the flat of her hand to the part of her – just under the band of her bra – that hurt. It was like someone had taken a knife and, very tenderly, cut out some small, inessential part of her.

'It's funny to think we're the end of the line.'

'You're assuming neither of us will have children,' said Christo, turning to look at her.

She smiled. 'Well, I don't see you in any rush to procreate.'

'No,' he said, surprising her with the absolute nature of his answer. 'But I'd love to have a dog.'

When he was a kid, he was always asking, 'Can we get a dog, can we get a dog, can we get a dog?'

'Surely there's nothing stopping you getting a dog.'

He seemed surprised that she considered this a possibility.

'I live alone,' he said, definitively. 'In an attic flat. It wouldn't be fair.'

Cassie thought of the two fat golden retrievers in Christo's father's house. The way they spread their golden bodies out on the warm kitchen tiles, waiting for the children to drop scraps of toast or bacon from the breakfast table. The way Christo would sit watching them with a sad half-smile, his sweet face full of nostalgia for something he never had. He was like a salaryman who sits in a railway station watching a rowdy family board a train to the seaside, while he waits for another train to take him to his office in the city.

'What about you?' he asked her. 'Wouldn't you like to have children?'

'Oh, Christo, don't ask me that. Not you too.'

Eduardo was mad to have a baby with her. Despite the fact that he had three grown daughters and a new baby granddaughter, Eduardo saw no reason why he wouldn't start another family with Cassie, as he'd told her on the first morning of their latest trip to Puerto Vallarta. They were sitting on the terrace of their hotel, looking out at a perfect blue sea – a breakfast of coffee and fresh fruit in front of them – when Eduardo went and ruined it all by talking about babies.

'But I love babies,' he said, when she tried to stop him.

'Of course you do,' she said, picturing him raising a naked infant in his soft hands. The child would be a boy, with the same pale European eyes as Eduardo's and the same buttermilk skin. Cassie could see it all so clearly, but it was not a picture she was a part of.

'We're too old,' she told him. 'We're too selfish. We're too busy with our work.'

'There are always reasons not to do things,' said Eduardo, caressing her face with his infinitely patient eyes. 'But that's no way to live your life, mi amor.'

It was that maddening certainty of his that weakened her resolve to be kind to him.

'I'm just not entirely clear why we would want to have a baby,' she told him.

'But that's the difference between us, my love. Because I can't see any reason on God's earth why we wouldn't.'

Eduardo's words sounded in Cassie's head as she looked out over Omey Island. Scanning the wide beach, she saw

108

puddles of water forming here and there as the tide began to creep back in. The low-slung island ahead, with its smattering of cottages. Above the island sat a heavy white sky.

'Why does everyone find it so hard to accept that I don't want to have kids?' she asked Christo.

Down below them on the sand, a woman was walking hand in hand with a tiny girl. The little girl was wearing a yellow raincoat and she had in her free hand a red plastic bucket and a blue spade. She was talking very intently as she walked, and whatever it was that she was saying must have been very sweet, because the woman was smiling down at her.

'You have to be your best person to be a mother, Christo. I'm not sure I can do that. I'm not sure I want to.'

'I think you'd be a great mother!' said Christo, with that cartoon spike of optimism in his voice. It broke Cassie's heart to hear it.

'Oh, Christo.'

How to explain this to him without hurting him? Cassie considered herself to be a damaged person. The tragedy of her mother's life was hardwired into her and there was no ridding herself of it. Like someone carrying a genetic mutation, she had decided it was her duty to draw a line under it by not procreating.

'There's nothing in my experience that qualifies me to be someone's mother. We didn't exactly have a great role model.'

Margo was the closest thing she had, but far from giving her the hope of something she could emulate, her memories of Margo only served to highlight the contrast with her own mother's failings. While Margo prowled the rock pools with them that summer, helping them identify the sea creatures they fished out with a long-handled net, Cassie's mother was huddled in the sand dunes smoking and coming up with new schemes for her own destruction.

'Okay,' said Christo sadly. 'But I see you with children. I see myself as an uncle to your children. It's part of my vision of the future.'

'Right,' she said, feeling her irritation harden into an ice-cold shard of anger. She opened the car door and put one foot inside. 'Well, I'm so sorry I can't oblige.'

14

As a child Cassie could never harbour her anger for long, but the adult she had become was capable of holding it inside her indefinitely. Cassie had been a hot-blooded kid, full of violent passions that drove her to frequent fits of rage. She never cried but she roared. Never smiled when she could cackle with laughter. It was years since Christo had seen her laugh like that. Years since he'd heard her voice raised. What might in another person have amounted to a softening was in Cassie's case a hardening, and with it came a brittle quality. Something easily broken.

'Let's face it, Christo,' she said, once they were sitting in the car. 'She was a terrible mother.'

He sighed.

'That's not how I remember it,' he said, feeling very sad that Cassie's experience was so different to his. 'I wish you could remember her the way I remember her.'

In his memory she was always kissing him, always ruffling his hair. Always calling out his name in a singsong voice. She liked him to climb into her bed to say goodnight. He remembered how she would sometimes lay her head down on his chest, as if she were his wife and not his mother. Christo had never liked the feeling that gave him – it felt somehow upside down – but he'd never thought to blame her for it. All he'd felt was tenderness towards her. She was so vulnerable. So volatile.

'My little old man,' she used to say to him, more like a sibling than a parent in the pleasure she took in teasing him. She was young when she had him, only twenty-two. Seen with the eyes of a child she had seemed unimaginably old, but as he aged himself Christo was increasingly struck by her youth. The older he became the younger she appeared, and this change of perspective was troubling to him.

'The way I remember her, she was a darling person.'

Christo was certain of this above all other things, but of course his sister wanted specifics. A courtroom silence in the air between them as he soldiered on with the defence. Cassie was relentless in maintaining the case for the prosecution.

'When, exactly, was she a darling person? In what way?'

Christo ransacked his brain for an example. He couldn't think of a single one, but that didn't detract from the impression he had – one which he would happily swear on the Bible – that she was a sweet and good person.

'She was so much fun,' he said, remembering how she once woke them from their beds and herded them into the back of the car, twisting up Mulholland Drive with all the windows rolled down and the music blaring – she'd said it was too hot to sleep. On another occasion she called a taxi from their hotel in Barcelona and took them up into the hills overlooking the city. There was an old funfair up there, and they slipped through a gap in the fence and sat in the car of a stationary Ferris wheel, looking out over a city submerged in sleep.

Then there was the day she whisked them out of elementary school, offering the teacher the excuse of a death in the family. It was only when they were sitting in the car that she spun around and laughed. There had been no death, she said. It was just an excuse for an adventure. She drove them through the night to the Grand Canyon, stopping for water and snacks at a 7-Eleven in the desert. They arrived just before sunrise, and she perched for what seemed like hours at the rim, staring out over the ever-changing light while

Cassie dozed in her arms and Christo roamed the car park studying the licence plates. He had set himself the task of finding every state in the union, but he came away without Hawaii and Delaware, something that bothered him all the way back to LA.

'She was a magical mother.'

'I can't believe you're still making excuses for her, Christo. She was a lunatic, plain and simple. It was a miracle she never got us killed.'

'She was so kind to us,' he said. 'She always bought the food we liked.'

Their mother had been forced as a child to eat lumpy porridge. She'd been forced to eat stringy eggs and barely cooked lamb's hearts. Mealtimes in her house were a battlefield, she told them, and no child of hers would ever be subjected to that. The result was that Cassie and Christo ate what they liked, and what they liked was Cheerios at all hours of the day and salted crackers and soda.

'*I don't care what you eat, so long as you eat something,*' she would say.

'She fed us junk, Christo.'

'She was an unconventional parent. But that doesn't mean she was a bad parent.'

'Look at my teeth,' said Cassie, baring them at him in all their imperfection. She could fit a dime through the gap at the front. That was a party trick of hers when they were kids. 'She blew the money she'd saved for my orthodontics.'

'I quite like the gap between your teeth,' said Christo. 'I think it's pretty.'

'She never turned up at any of our parent–teacher meetings,' said Cassie, moving down through the list she had in her head. 'She missed all our school concerts. We didn't even have a family doctor.'

'Well, maybe that's because we were never sick.'

'She went out and left us alone without a sitter. She let us watch TV all the time. She never even told us a bedtime story.'

'Yes, but that hardly amounts to child abuse, does it? I'm not sure people were in the habit of reading to their children back then. Things were different when we were kids. Parenting styles were different.'

'No shit, Sherlock.' That was another one of Jim's sayings. 'I'm not sure parenting was even a thing back then.'

Christo started the engine. Turning the car around, he drove back by the church, arriving at the village of Claddaghduff, where a low-slung pub overlooked the island. The pub had a shop attached, with a single petrol pump out front, along with the ubiquitous HB sign. Christo brought the car to a stop.

'How about an ice cream?' he suggested hopefully.

'Jesus, Christo,' she said, rolling her eyes. 'You can't fix all of life's problems with ice cream.'

'Well, then. A cup of tea?'

'I'll have a coffee,' she said, reluctantly.

Christo took that as the fix that was needed, taking care to get the coffee just the way she liked it, with some hot milk added but not too much.

'We're looking for someone called Seamus Murphy,' he told the woman behind the till. She received him with the poise of a diva, eyes brimming with unspoken passions – the region seemed to specialize in these operatic women. She had homemade brown bread and apple crumble displayed on the counter, along with some professional photographs of the island that had been printed on large greeting cards. Christo selected three of them and added them to his purchases. He had a notion to send one to Bernard. The other two he could keep as souvenirs.

114

'Jimmy's son Seamus?' asked the woman, with a confused expression. 'But Seamus doesn't live here. He lives out beyond Ballyconneely.'

'Oh, I see,' said Christo. 'How do we get there?'

'Go back through town,' she said. 'Follow the sea road until you get to a big grey church. There's a shop and a playground. It's the first turn after that.'

The sea was to the right of them now as they drove. The water a pale teal in places. In others it was darkened purple by the patches of seaweed that lay beneath the surface. They passed through town and out the other side, following a winding coast road with the sea always on their right. They saw seals lounging on the rocks. Houses in various stages of construction and dereliction. They'd been driving for twenty minutes when they came upon the coral strand of Christo's memory. They stopped, getting out of the car to scoop up handfuls of the coral and study the tiny bone-shapes of its grains. A little bit further along the road, they arrived at the large grey church the woman in Claddaghduff had described. There was a shop and a pub and a playground, then a sign-posted crossroads. They took the right-hard turn, but they hadn't gone far when it forked in two.

'Which way?' Christo asked Cassie.

'Hard to know.'

He took the right-hand fork, bringing them down another winding road so narrow that the car scraped against the hedgerows. The bushes that flattened themselves up against the car window had bright pink flowers that dangled from their stems like ballet dancers. Christo had a memory of someone teaching him to suck the honey out of them. It must have been Margo.

'That's fuchsia,' said Cassie.

'How do you know that?'

'Margo taught me. She taught me the names of all the flowers. That one's loosestrife,' she said, pointing to an upright purple flower that grew in abundance in the ditch. It was in the fields too. Great drifts of it, along with a stately, golden grass. There were blackberry brambles ripening to black in some spots. In other places they were still red.

'The orange one is montbretia,' she said. 'And the yellow one's honeysuckle. The blue one is tufted vetch.'

'That's pretty impressive.'

Her capacity to retain these details was amazing to him.

'Hey, Christo.'

'What is it, love?'

'What do you think she looks like now?'

'Wait, who?'

'Margo, of course!'

She seemed in no doubt that they would find her, something that caused a stir of unease in Christo. He suddenly felt the weight of the responsibility he had so heedlessly assumed by bringing her here. The possibility that their trip was a mistake.

'Oh Christo, I can't wait to see her. I hope she doesn't dye her hair. The way I'm imagining her, she looks just the same only with grey hair.'

Her eyes were shining, her face lightened by hope. Not for the first time, Christo saw how vulnerable she was when she opened herself up. Hunkered down, with her scarves wrapped around her for safety, she was protected. It was only when she ventured forth, unleashing all her old enthusiasm for life, that he feared for her. He knew how easily she could come crashing down.

'What about Jim?' she asked him. 'How do you think he's turned out?'

'Gosh,' he said, reluctant to play this game. 'I don't know.'

'I'd say he's thinner. With bad teeth, if he hasn't given up smoking. What's the bet that she's still trying to get him to give up smoking?'

'Most likely,' said Christo.

'Seamus must be around the same age as me,' Cassie was saying. 'At the time I felt so much younger than him. But there was only a year between us. Funny how a year seems like such a long time when you're a kid.'

Seamus was more than a year younger than Christo, but he'd seemed older in some ways. He was the custodian of countless terrifying folk stories, told to him by his twin uncles. The uncles were fishermen, with a rich sideline in the urban myths and legends of the dark hinterland they inhabited. They had showed Seamus the spot on the bog road where a woman met her own ghost on the way back from the fair. It was the uncles who'd told him the story of the fisherman who cast the anchor of his curragh without ever noticing that the belt of his trousers was caught on the tip of it. He went overboard and was missing for three days before it occurred to anyone to raise the anchor. They found his dead body still attached.

'The fish ate his eyeballs,' said Seamus. 'That's what the fish go for first. The eyeballs and the testicles.'

'Tell us another one,' Cassie would say. She couldn't get enough of those terrible stories. She was always begging Seamus for more, but he was more interested in hearing about their life in America, a subject he questioned them about repeatedly. 'Do the cops really carry guns?' he wanted to know. 'Do they really ride motorbikes?'

What knowledge Seamus had of America was television-acquired and existed in a vacuum.

'Is your school mixed? Do you have a school uniform? What's a homeroom? What's a jock?'

Christo had explained as best he could.

'Are all the parents divorced?'

'No.'

'Do you have frozen yoghurt? Jellybeans? Oreo cookies?'

'Yes.'

'Have you ever been to a drive-in movie?'

'No.'

Christo was sorry to disappoint him. He'd never considered America in any way exotic, so it was a surprise to see
it possessed of such valuable currency. He was not above
trading on it to raise his stock with his new friend.

'We've been to the aquarium at Monterey,' he said. 'We
saw a great white shark.'

'That's cool,' said Seamus. 'I'd love to see a shark.'

Many times, over the years, Christo had wondered what
became of Seamus. It was only a single summer they'd spent
together, but to Christo it was the friendship of a lifetime. A
friendship that was sealed by the smell of gunpowder from
the plastic caps they fed into their toy guns, and the taste of
the sour apple drops that fuelled the long walk back from the
shop in the village. The sweets tore the skin off the roofs of
their mouths but that didn't stop them from eating them.
The pain only served to heighten the pleasure.

Their days were spent prowling the pier or trawling the
long grass in the fields behind the house. If they weren't at
the pier or in the fields, they were down on the beach scour-
ing the rock pools or roaming the headland above the sea. In
Christo's mind, he and Seamus were like two medieval knights
adventuring their way around a magical realm. In his memories of that summer, his sister was mostly absent, even
though in reality Cassie must have been mostly present. The
times when he was alone with Seamus were the times Christo
remembered best.

The two of them in Christo's bunk beds. He preferred the

bottom bunk, so Seamus was always up top. Every time Seamus moved, the prison-fence wiring that supported his mattress would sag and creak. Christo remembered the sense of another body up there, and the dislocated voice that seemed to roam free of it in the darkness, the way a soloist fills the space in a concert hall, so that you can close your eyes and lose yourself in the sound, regardless of where it's coming from. That was how Christo remembered those nights they spent in his bunk beds, with a feeling as thick and comforting as home-made soup. Never once in all the time since had he felt so comfortable in the presence of another human being.

'He was a cool kid,' Cassie was saying, but Christo didn't answer. He was preoccupied by the sand dunes he saw appearing on the right-hand side of the car. The next thing, they came upon the beach itself. A beach like a crack in the earth – and, through the crack, the sight of a wild, rolling sea.

'Wait,' said Cassie, sitting up ramrod-straight in her seat, her hands planted by her sides as if she were bracing herself for impact. 'This looks familiar.'

Christo slowed the car as they came to a bridge over the beach. The bridge was only wide enough for one car. Just beyond it, on the left, there was an old stone house. The house was derelict, the roof caved in, the windows boarded up, but Christo saw it as it used to be. In his mind he was seeing canoes out front and surfboards. A dog with its mouth open to bark at a passing car. Small children swirling about the garden.

'Look, Christo,' said Cassie, turning her head as they passed. On the side wall of the house was a giant, painted lobster. The burnt-orange paint of the lobster's shell was worn away in patches, but the wide reach of its claws was the same as ever. It might have been leaping to catch a ball.

'The Lobster House,' he said.

Both of them quiet as mice as the car crept forwards, past a ditch full of grasses. Rising out of the ditch there was a worn old sign standing on two rusty iron legs. The sign itself was made of enamel, with patches of rust blooming over its block capital letters.

YOU ARE NOW ENTERING PARADISE

'I remember that,' she said. 'I remember that sign.'

They topped a small hill and saw the last stretch of road below them, ending at a cluster of fishermen's cottages and a neglected-looking pier.

'Slyne Head to Erris Head,' Jim would announce, imitating the voice of the man on the shipping forecast. 'Rossan Point to Bloody Foreland.'

'*End of the fucking earth*,' their mother would add, in her own voice.

Christo slowed the car, pulling it to a stop at the side of the road.

'Let's get out and walk from here.'

15

The house was still there. Smaller – or so it seemed to Cassie – but otherwise unchanged, it sat halfway down the hill. A balding gravel driveway curved from the front door to the road, where an iron gate was tethered to the fence by a length of rope. Cassie knew the rope was orange before they were close enough to see it, because it had always been her job to hop out of the car and untie it. She had to push the gate open, waiting for the car to pass through before closing it again carefully. If you didn't close it properly the cows would get in.

She and Christo were tumbling down the hill when a white van coming the other way drew level with them and stopped. There were two identical old men inside, each with the same newborn-blue eyes set deep into their furrowed faces.

'Hi there,' said Christo, taking a step towards the van.

There was a crucifix hanging off the rear-view mirror. A smell of stale smoke and brine inside. The driver had his arms folded across the wheel. The other man had his woolly elbow resting on the frame of the open passenger window.

'Grand day,' he said to Christo.

'Lovely day.'

'Are ye staying out here?'

'No,' said Christo. 'No, we're just out for a stroll. We're trying to find a house we stayed in once when we were children.'

The driver peered out at them from the darkened interior.

'It was that house there,' said Cassie, pointing it out to them with her finger.

They all turned to look.

'Oh, right,' said the man in the passenger seat. 'Dympna Conneely's house.'

'That one there now,' said the driver, indicating back the way Christo and Cassie had come. 'Yes, that one there. That's Ballymahon Eggs.'

'That's right,' said the other man, nodding. He had his eyes fixed on Christo, slow and careful. 'The one next to it, that's Doyle's Sports. And do you see the one there with the jetty? He's a doctor up above, in the Blackrock Clinic.'

The driver nodded.

'Mainly bones,' he said solemnly.

'The houses all look empty,' said Cassie. 'Don't any of them ever come down here?'

'Ah they do,' said the driver.

'They do,' said the other one, nodding. 'They come down from time to time.'

'In the summer,' the driver added. 'We wouldn't see much of them after that.'

Cassie straightened up and looked out over the pier at the ominous sky. In the distance were grey clouds, rain hanging down from them like jellyfish trails. A chill in the air even though it was only the middle of September. The summer was already on the run.

'It's not everyone, I suppose, would relish the joys of winter down here.'

'Now you have it,' said the driver, throwing the van into gear. Before there was a chance to ask them anything else they'd rolled off up the road.

They arrived at the door of the house to find it locked, but Cassie located the key under a large rock beside the front door. Knowing how he hated to break the rules, she held it up to Christo as a challenge and waved it in front of him. He looked around, as if he was expecting to see someone, but there was nobody there, only a solitary cow watching them from the next field with mournful eyes.

'Go on,' he said to her. 'You're going to do it anyway, no matter what I say.'

He hung back as she turned the key in the lock. Turning it once, twice, three times until the door fell open. She stepped inside, moving with the slow, heavy tread of an astronaut. The air in the house was thick and still. She could hear her own breath, noisy and deliberate, like she was wearing a helmet.

The living room was in shadow. The couches and the coffee table were no more than dark shapes in the half-light. Two huge picture-windows occupied the exterior wall like great landscape paintings hanging in a darkened gallery. The view they framed was silvered with light. Cassie moved from the living room into the kitchen, where another huge window occupied the exterior wall. A large square table stood by the window. It was the same table that had been there when they were children. The same leather upholstered chairs. The same copper pans hanging on the walls. Everything was exactly the same, down to the supper bell that hung beside the kitchen door. Cassie pulled on its cord, sending a criminal clang through the empty house.

'For God's sake, Cassie,' said Christo, covering his ears with his hands.

'Oh, relax, Christo. There's nobody here.'

She went around the kitchen throwing open the cupboard doors. She recognized the mugs with their cheery blue stripes, the corrugated-glass butter dish, a single surviving egg cup. Every little thing was a miracle to her.

'Nothing's been changed!'

In the louvred cupboard in the bathroom she found stacks

of the same threadbare old towels they had once used for the beach. The curtains on the bathroom window had not been changed in all the years, although the original red cherries of the pattern had been bleached pink by the sun and the linen lining was yellowed in places like old newspaper. The bowl of the toilet was streaked with rust-coloured stains. The same rusty stains marked the inside of the old enamel bath.

'*Oh, don't mind that*,' Cassie remembered her mother saying. '*That's the mark of the bog water. There's nothing better than bog water for your skin.*'

There was a box room opposite the bathroom where some plastic sun loungers were stored along with their mildewy cushions. The room had a small, high window that faced out to sea. Built along the back wall were open shelves that cupped under the weight of hundreds of hardback novels. There were stacks of old board games, their boxes splitting at the corners and held together by yellowing Sellotape. There were jam jars full of coins long past legal tender, and a fish kettle and a battered old panama hat. Cassie was just about to back out of the room when she caught sight of something on the top shelf.

She found a folding footstool behind the door and climbed up on it. By standing on the tips of her toes and gripping the curtain with one hand to steady herself, she could just about reach. Stretching with groping fingers, she grabbed a hold of the thing she'd seen and pulled it out.

'Christo,' she shouted, as the flimsy stool rocked alarmingly under her feet. 'You won't believe it! I've found Honey Monkey!'

16

The smell in the box room took Christo back to a day of summer rain. There was no going to the beach that day, so they were playing hide-and-seek in the house. Christo had squashed himself under the bottom shelf behind the sun loungers when he heard Cassie's voice. At first he thought it was a ploy to draw him out of hiding, so he didn't respond.

'Christo,' he heard her call. 'You have to come. There's a man at the door. He wants to see the TV licence.'

Walking past the open kitchen door, Christo saw the tray on the table with the unfinished jigsaw his mother was working on, along with a steaming mug of tea, but there was no sign of his mother. He opened the front door to find a man with a clipboard standing on the threshold, rain dropping from the hood of his raincoat and a battered blue car parked behind him in the driveway.

'Is your mammy home?' the man asked, peering beyond Christo into the house.

'No,' said Christo.

'Do you know when she might be back?'

'No.'

'Right so,' said the man, and he turned to go. Christo stood in the doorway and watched him reverse his blue car back down the driveway and out into the road. It was only when he saw him disappearing over the hill that Christo went back into the house and closed the door behind him.

'You can come out now,' he shouted, but there was no reply. Christo ducked his head into her bedroom, then looked for her in the adjoining bathroom, but it too was empty of her. He stood out in the hall and called her name again but still there was no answer, only the questioning faces of Cassie and Seamus, who seemed to be awaiting his instructions. Together they checked the house, room by room, lifting bedspreads to look into the dusty spaces under the beds, where balls of hair and discarded sweet wrappers lurked. They opened the press in the hall where the vacuum cleaner and the sweeping brush were kept, making sure there was nowhere in there that a child could hide, let alone a grown woman. They looked inside the suitcases that had been stowed at the back of the cupboard in the spare room, and under the towels in the airing cupboard and behind the shower curtain in the bathroom. They looked inside the fridge and underneath the cushions on the couch, as if their mother had somehow managed to shrink to a tenth of her original size to conceal herself. They became feverish in their hunting, and desperate to find her. They became so hoarse from shouting that they gave up. They gathered in the living room, panting and silent. They were starting to think she might never be found.

'Christo,' said Cassie, her eyes round with fear. 'What if she's gone for good?'

That fear stalked their childhood and would in time be realized, but not quite yet.

'Shush,' said Christo, putting a finger to his lips.

He'd noticed that the curtain was moving ever so slightly, even though the window was closed. Ten toes showed underneath its hem. Christo crept forwards, gesturing to the others to hang back. Hand to the outer edge of the curtain, heart hammering in his chest, he wrenched it away. The curtain flew along its casters, and his mother was revealed, standing with her arms hugging her chest like an upright mummy. Her eyes blazed with triumph as they all fell on her, and she crumpled into them with a cackle of laughter.

'No,' said Cassie, definitively, when he asked did she remember? 'No way did she ever play hide-and-seek with us. You must be imagining it.'

'I'm telling you,' said Christo. 'I remember it very well.'

There was an old pair of binoculars on the windowsill of the box room. Christo picked them up and trained them on the sea outside. Adjusting the focus, he moved his head slowly upwards, seeing only sea and more sea until the horizon line appeared.

'On a clear day, if you're lucky, you can see a ship on the horizon,' Jim had told him. 'It's because of the curvature of the earth. All you can see is the very top of the ship's masts.'

Ever since then, Christo had thought of the sea with a curve to it.

'Look, Christo,' Cassie called, from the bedroom at the end of the corridor. 'Your old bunk bed!'

But Christo had been stopped in his tracks by something he'd seen on the wall outside the bathroom. A series of framed admiralty charts, one for each of the local headlands. The land masses were depicted in mustard yellow and army green, while the shallows around the edges of the land were bright blue, paling to white as the sea deepened. Land and water alike were overlaid with contour lines that were numbered here and there, giving the charts the appearance of a colour-by-numbers painting that had only been partially completed.

Christo stood and stared at the charts, and what amazed him was how he had managed to forget them so entirely. Not once in all the years had he thought of those charts but, looking at them now, he saw they were the source of his desire to map the natural world with numbers. He remembered studying them for hours as a child. He remembered drawing from them the comfort of human order. The sense that no wilderness was uncharted, even out at sea. It made him feel less lonely to think that there was nowhere you could go on the planet that couldn't be described by a set of coordinates. It made him feel like there was nowhere he couldn't belong.

'Do you remember this house having an upstairs?' he asked Cassie.

He could picture it clearly, with its sloping-roof windows and pine-panelled ceiling and the small Alice-in-Wonderland door in the wall. You could crawl through the door into a storage area in the rafters, where sleeping bags were kept along with spare pillows and boxes of Christmas decorations. There was a table-football game up there, which he and Seamus used to play. There was a futon and a wicker armchair and some corduroy beanbags. A trunk full of croquet equipment.

She shook her head.

'It's a bungalow, Christo. There is no upstairs.'

'I remember an upstairs,' he said, unwilling to let go of it. He opened the door of the hot press and peered inside, finding only a stubborn set of shelves and a solid wall behind them. He prowled the corridors, head craned to spot a hatch in the ceiling that might offer access. He opened the back door and stepped out into the neglected space behind the house – it was no more than a patch of weeds edged with a bramble hedge – studying the roof for any sign of a window, but there was none. Even so, Christo could not let go of the idea that the house had an upstairs. He could see it, as clear as anything in his mind. It was hard to accept that it didn't exist.

'Christo,' said Cassie. 'There's no upstairs.'

With the house triple-locked again behind them and the key stashed safely back under the rock, they walked down the last stretch of hill towards the pier. A lump in Cassie's coat, right over her heart, where she had secreted the long-lost monkey. Free to breathe again, Christo threw his head back and took big grateful gulps of the salty Atlantic air. They passed the little jetty first, slimy stone and blistering black seaweed exposed by the receding tide. The pier itself was littered with empty lobster pots and coils of frayed blue twine. One small rowing boat swayed in the shallows, tethered to an iron bollard by a thick rope. In the bottom of the boat was a cool box, just like the one they'd used as children for picnics on the beach. Cans of fizzy drinks inside and KitKat bars, their wrappers wet with condensation. Cassie was a Fanta drinker and Christo was a Coca-Cola man, but Seamus had more exotic tastes. He liked Lilt, or Cidona. Christo remembered the way he would let out a gasp of satisfaction after the first swig of fizz from the can.

'*Aaah.*'

The place where Seamus and his parents had lived was the last in the row of fishermen's cottages. The first cottage was derelict. The middle one had been tastefully restored, with a small white card in the front window advertising the name of a local letting agency. The last one was much as it had been when they were children, with its whitewashed walls flaking and its woodwork shredded by the salt winds. There was a twenty-year-old BMW parked in the space beside the house. It seemed to Christo a clue to the present circumstances of Seamus and his family.

'Looks like there's someone living here,' said Cassie.

She walked up to the small paned window and peered through it, using her hand as a visor.

'I can see a laptop on the kitchen table.'

Come away, thought Christo. It was all he could think. But his sister was over at the door, searching for a knocker or a bell. When she didn't find one, she used her bare hand, rapping out two loud knocks with her determined little knuckles.

'No answer,' she said, but still she stood there. She gave another three raps on the door, in quick succession. Determined to escape before she resorted to breaking and entering again, Christo turned and started walking rapidly back towards the car.

'Chicken,' she said, joining him at last. 'Christo the cowardly chicken.'

She made wings of her arms and flapped them.

'Don't forget to put on your seat belt,' said Christo, starting up the engine.

They drove back to the crossroads, and Christo parked the car outside the shop. They paused on the way in to look at a bunch of handwritten ads in the window. There was a bucket of fishing nets beside the door and a pen of plastic beach balls. Inside the shop they stopped and breathed in the thick, layered smell of factory-baked bread and sugar-encrusted jellies. A smell of fresh newsprint and washing detergent, with a faint suggestion of bleach as a top note. To Christo it was like breathing in the past.

They made their way around the aisles, their eyes full of wonder as they combed the shelves. The shop stocked everything from granny knickers to camping gas. There were woollen walking socks and metal colanders and gingham tea towels and skeins of clothesline. There were industrial-sized cans of peaches and special offers on biscuits they'd forgotten existed, like Jammy Dodgers and Mint Viscounts. There was rat poison in a cardboard carton with a drawing of a charismatic-looking rat on the front. An ice-cream machine beside the counter and, standing beside it, the same woman who'd stood there when they were children. She was strangely unchanged.

'Hi there,' said Christo, as he approached the counter. He was half expecting her to recognize him, although of course she wouldn't. A big woman, red-haired still, she was wearing a sleeveless dress that exposed a pair of mottled pink upper arms as thick as thighs.

'What can I do for you?'

'We're wondering about a house,' he said.

She leaned forwards, resting her hands on the counter.

'Oh?'

'It's the bungalow out by the old pier. We're interested in renting it.'

'We rented it before, years ago,' said Cassie, supplying the information Christo was reluctant to part with. 'When we were children, we lived there for a whole summer.'

The woman straightened up, looking at them intently now, one to the other.

'Hang on a minute. You're not . . .'

'We were here with our mother,' said Christo, preparing himself for a raft of questions that would inevitably be followed by a wave of sympathy. What there was instead was something Christo wasn't expecting. The woman turned suddenly and visibly hostile.

'Of course,' she said. 'I remember you now. It's Dympna Conneely you need to speak to about the house. You'll get her on her mobile.'

She pulled her phone out of her pocket and searched it for a number, which she copied down on one of the brown paper bags she kept in a stack on the counter. Ripping the bag away from the others, she handed it to Christo without a word. As he followed his sister out of the shop, he felt like he'd been tried and found guilty of some dreadful thing, but what that thing might be he could not for the life of him imagine.

PART TWO

17

'You won't believe who I've just had in here,' said Tilly Mannion, when Seamus came into the shop to get his messages.

'Oh?'

'Your woman's children.'

'What woman?' asked Seamus, even though he knew the answer already. He could see it in the sideways shift of Tilly Mannion's lower jaw. The tongue probing her teeth.

'They were looking to rent the same house,' she told him. She had a way of nodding with her eyes, as if to say, what did I tell you?

'And?'

'Well . . .'

This was another of her habits – the dramatic pause.

'Put it this way,' she said, with a sigh. 'Dympna Conneely won't be shy about taking their money. That house has been empty half the summer. She'll take the hand off them.'

'Well,' said Seamus, bending down to get his newspaper. He bought the same one every day, although he liked to have a quick scan of the others. Observing day by day the deepening mess the world was in. The west of Ireland, which had once seemed to him the most God-forsaken place on earth, now felt like the last outpost of sanity in a world gone mad.

'It's getting to the point where I might have to stop buying these things,' he said to Tilly, laying the newspaper down on the counter, along with a twenty-euro note. 'It's not good for my health.'

Accustomed to the choreography, she reached behind her

135

for a pack of fags. Marlboro was his choice of smoke, always had been. He had a soft spot for Americana, and there was nothing more American than Marlboro.

'You wouldn't think of giving these up instead?'

'Are you mad? Sure, the fags are the only thing keeping me going.'

She threw her eyes to heaven with a snort.

'You're a hopeless case,' she said. 'But it's not off the stones you licked it. That's all I can say.'

He folded the newspaper over on itself. Pocketed the fags.

'Well, thanks for the heads-up,' he said, as he turned to go through the doorway at the back of the shop and into the pub, where John Coyne was standing behind the counter polishing a glass.

'There he is now.'

'John. How are we?'

Seamus made his way through to the front room, where his uncles sat side by side at the bar.

'Seamus,' said one of them.

The other gave a little nod of agreement, like the nod you might give when you're watching a pub quiz on the telly and you hear a contestant give the correct answer.

'So,' said John, sliding along the bar with the sly ease of a tiger in a cage. 'The usual?'

He turned and placed the glass he'd polished on a high shelf behind him. Pinned to the shelf was a handwritten sign with the latest winning lotto numbers. The weekly jackpot was 260 euro. John placed a glass at a tilt under the Guinness tap and opened it.

'I see the kids are all on strike up above in Dublin,' he said to Seamus.

'So I hear,' said Seamus.

'Is it the climate change?' asked one of the uncles.

'It's that Swedish girl,' said the other uncle. 'She's the one who started it.'

'Fair play to her,' said Seamus, and the uncles nodded their agreement.

'They'd want to do something soon or we'll all be underwater,' said John, topping up the pint for Seamus.

'Case of the boy who cried wolf,' said one of the uncles, darkly.

'Yeah,' said Seamus. 'But you know what everyone forgets about that story. There's a wolf at the end of it.'

With that, Seamus took his pint and carried it over to his usual table in the lean of a partition. He took his paper out and started work on the crossword as he waited for the pint to settle. He had the crossword finished in the time it took him to drink it. He ordered a second pint and a pack of dry roasted peanuts to stave off the hunger, then took a lift out the road with the uncles. Wedging himself into the front seat with them, he had his shoulder pressed up against the passenger window and his feet stacked one on top of the other in the footwell. There was no space down there to put his two feet flat, what with all the debris.

'Are we right?' asked the uncle at the wheel, sliding the van into first gear and releasing the clutch without waiting for an answer.

The other one fiddled with the radio until he found some class of country and western. The uncles were great fans of Garth Brooks, Declan Nerney, Nathan Carter. They'd even been known to attend a country music festival at Galway Racecourse. Not that they'd ever sing along, they just listened to it knowingly with their heads on a tilt. Their eyes big and sad and watery, like an old cow's.

'I don't know how they listen to that shite,' Seamus's dad had said, more than once.

'Yeah, well, that would be a matter of taste,' Seamus liked to say, in their defence, even though in truth he was inclined to agree. The uncles had shite taste in music, as unsophisticated in this as they were in everything else. That was why Seamus loved them, with a love that seemed to him at times the only uncomplicated thing in his life. He burrowed into it as they drove out the road.

The van smelled of rolling tobacco and sweet lobster shells, as it had done since Seamus was a child. Back then he often spent the day out on the water with his uncles, put-putting round the headland in their little boat while they checked on their pots. When they got hungry, they'd tuck into sandwiches of sliced pan and butter and Calvita cheese, with the smell of diesel from the outboard motor in their throats and the taste of the sea on their lips. A flask of tea to wash down the sandwiches, and maybe a biscuit with it. There were long debates between the uncles about which was the best biscuit – a Kimberley or a Mikado – and it seemed to Seamus a grand way to spend your days, engaged in philosophical discussions with like-minded men on a small boat on the water. He was not expecting his father to laugh him out of it when he mentioned it.

'Sure, that's no life for you, Seamus. Not with your brains. That poor pair of eejits have nothing else to be doing with themselves.'

Seamus was hurt for his uncles that his father would paint them in such a light, but it changed his view of them all the same. When it came time for him to choose a profession, Seamus did not become a fisherman like them, going up to Maynooth instead to study history and geography. He stayed on to do a master's, and then a PhD, a qualification his uncles could not get their heads around, no matter how many times it was explained to them.

'He's a doctor,' they told people, 'but he doesn't make people better.' 'He's a doctor, but he's not a doctor,' they would say, waiting for the idea to take hold. 'Now you have it – a teaching doctor.'

The uncles had never been further than Galway city. Even that was a voyage they undertook seldom and with great reluctance. Their days were spent plying the road between the pier and the village in their battered HiAce van. Getting out to check their pots, then back into the van to eat their sandwiches. By five o'clock they were always in the pub. They kept it to three pints each, because of the drink driving, heading home to a dinner of Knorr instant mashed potato with bacon-flavoured Hula Hoops crumbled on top. The Hula Hoops gave the mash a taste of meat, as they proudly explained to Seamus one night when he was their guest.

'A delicacy,' he proclaimed, and they nodded, pleased.

'Set in their ways' was how people would describe his uncles, but Seamus too had become set in his ways since he came back. He found himself living the same day over and over again. Waking before dawn with the taste of last night's tea and fags in his mouth, his thoughts would come rushing in on him – regrets and recriminations – until the desire for a cigarette mercifully swept everything else away. He smoked his first of the day on the doorstep before going in to make himself a pot of coffee. Sitting at the kitchen table with his laptop, he spent his morning working and drinking coffee, popping out the door at regular intervals for a smoke. Every afternoon he walked the five miles to the village to buy his paper and groceries from Tilly Mannion, stopping off at the pub for two or three pints, depending on the day, before cadging a lift from his uncles back out the road. Dinner was a matter of putting a ready meal in the microwave – generally either a chicken tikka masala or a lamb rogan josh – which he'd have heated and eaten within ten minutes.

'You can't eat Indian food every night, Seamus,' Tilly Mannion would say, as she surveyed his shopping.

'Indian people do.'

'Well, a few vegetables wouldn't kill you.'

The uncles slowed down as they approached the spot where they always left Seamus off. Judging its approach by the fuchsia hedge. The NO DUMPING sign. The mirror on the bend. They pulled to a stop, hazard lights flashing, and Seamus climbed down out of the van.

'Night, now, Seamus,' said one of the uncles.

'Goodnight,' said Seamus, patting the side panel of the van the way you might pat an animal's flank.

'Be good now,' said the other uncle.

Seamus stood and watched as the rear lights moved away from him. Then, one foot in front of the other, he embarked on the last mile of his journey. A journey that took him past low hedgerows, where cows gathered in sober observation. Through reedy hollows and boggy marsh and along a stretch of flat grassland, where drifts of sand blew in from the beach. Up the last low hill towards home – from the top he could see Dympna Conneely's place below him, with a white hire car parked out front and a struggling plume of smoke coming from the chimney. The windows appeared as rectangular blocks of light cut into the dusky stencil shape of the house, giving it the one-dimensional appearance of a stage set.

Through the front window, Seamus saw the dark shape of a woman moving about. As though a stopper had been removed from an old perfume bottle and the scent released into the air, he felt the past all around him. He remembered another woman, moving across the same window in just the same way. In Seamus's memory she was still a stranger to him. The children she had brought with her were only to be guessed at. Potential friends, or they might turn out to be enemies, it was impossible to know. One of them was a year younger than him, he'd been told. The other, a year older. These kids had no dad, or two dads, or a dead dad – there was some confusion around this – but that was neither here nor there. What mattered to Seamus was their domicile, the place he most wanted to go in all the world, and that was California.

The California of his imaginings was a place of towering redwood trees. The tallest trees in the world were to be found there, his mother had told him. There were bears roaming the forests and rattlesnakes in the desert. There were cities built over deep fault lines in the earth and bridges that straddled great stretches of sea. There were motorbike cops patrolling the highways and surfers on the shark-infested beaches. There was Chinese food that came in cardboard cartons – that's what all the cops ate on the TV shows Seamus watched – and giant bags of potato crisps and soda fountains and frozen yoghurt. In Ireland, all you could get was Cadbury's chocolate, but in America they had M&Ms and Oreo cookies and Hershey bars. Seamus wondered would the Americans bring any of these prized items with them when they came?

The day of their arrival, he watched the road for their car like you might watch the horizon for the first sight of a ship's mast. His mother picked montbretia from the roadside and arranged it in a jug on their windowsill. She made fresh brown bread for them, which she carried up to the house in a parcel she'd made of a clean tea towel. She stood at the door half the afternoon, anxiously waiting, and when she saw their car appear she ran outside waving both arms. While his dad settled them into the house and his mam brought up the lamb stew she'd prepared for their supper, Seamus lurked down the pier ignoring her calls to come and meet them. His eleven-year-old heart was bursting with a huge and ill-defined desire to be a part of it all, but his shyness prevented him from doing so.

In no time, of course, he was incorporated into their little circle. Within days he was eating breakfast, lunch and dinner with them. He was going to the beach with them, partaking of their bounty as if he'd been born to it. Plucking a can of Cidona from their cool box and accepting a ham roll from their mother's picnic basket. ('Do you take mayo, Seamus? Mustard?') In the afternoons he would volunteer to cycle with Cassie from the beach to the campsite shop to get the ice creams. With her on his back carrier in charge of the ice creams, he had to pedal furiously to get back to the beach before they melted. On fine evenings, there was always a barbecue out the side of their house, with the table placed to catch the last of the sun. The children would be served first, tucking into charred sausages and burgers with potato salad on the side, as the Beatles' Blue Album streamed out through the open kitchen window. While the adults ate, the children would play tip the can. Seamus saw himself peeping over a low stone wall, with Cassie's voice ringing out through the gradual night. 'Tip the can, tip the can, I see Seamus.' Afterwards he would be invited to sleep in the top bunk of Christo's bed, while the adults carried on with their drinking at the table outside the window. Candles lit against the night, Jim and his mother would both have been chain-smoking cigarettes to keep away the midges. Seamus remembered falling asleep to the sound of their laughter.

18

Cassie stood at the window and watched, mesmerized, as the night fell slowly in a wash of silver light that gradually turned to gold. It was like a movie you'd never tire of seeing. The sky to the west was a vast panorama, the sea like a slick of spilled oil. The grasses in front of the house stirred in the breeze. Mustard-yellow ragwort grew among them, along with the orange flecks of montbretia. To the north were the dreamy mountains, like an illustration protected by a sheet of tracing paper. There was so much beauty it was hard to take it all in. Everywhere you looked there was more of it, so much that it seemed treacherous to turn your back on it. It was a shame to miss a single moment of this passing day, given the possibility that it might be your last and you would never get to see such a thing again.

When Cassie was a child, she would beg not to be sent to bed, desperate to drain every last drop of life from the day. As an adult, she started every day with the same sense of optimism, but by evening it had always dissipated. She found herself longing for sleep, not because she was tired but because she'd exhausted her energy for living. Her battery was easily depleted.

'How hungry are you?' Christo asked her.

'Pretty hungry,' she said, without turning from the window.

It was after eight already. They'd spent the afternoon arranging the rental. 'You'll find the key under a rock to the left of the door,' the owner had told them. Cassie thanked her, all innocence, and they went back to the hotel to pack their things. It was long past the midday deadline for check-out, so Christo offered to pay for a second night, but the hotelier wouldn't hear of it.

'Things would have to be pretty bad before I'd start charging people for beds they're not going to sleep in.'

They thanked her and set off, stopping at the supermarket in town for some groceries. Then they drove all the way back out the road. It was after six by the time they were in the house, and there was a chill in the air they hadn't noticed earlier. A mushroomy feeling of moisture. Even the toilet roll was damp.

'Let's turn on the heating,' said Christo. 'That might warm the place up.'

They lit all the fires too – not just the stove in the kitchen but the open fire in the living room as well. The sight of the flames was as cheering as the heat.

'Do you want cheese in your omelette?' Christo asked.

He had a cotton apron tied around his hips. A whisk in his hand. All he was missing was a chef's hat.

'When did you learn to cook?' she'd asked him when she stayed with him in Cambridge.

'Well, I don't really know how to cook,' he'd told her. 'I only know how to follow instructions.'

He had a solitary cookbook – *The Pleasures of Cooking for One* – with a range of recipes he'd mastered by slavishly following every word. He had a digital weighing-scales that he used with great precision. He doubled the quantities for the duration of Cassie's visit and was inordinately proud of the results.

'Cheese please,' she said, now, in answer to his question.

'Here,' he said, handing her a head of lettuce. 'You can wash the salad.'

He broke six eggs into a bowl and added a handful of the

alarmingly yellow cheese they'd bought ready grated from the shop. A shake of a salt cellar that had more rice in it than salt. Christo delved into the back of a cupboard and found a rusty tin of ground white pepper.

Cassie absorbed herself in the task of washing the salad leaves, patting them dry with a dish towel she'd found under the sink. By the time she'd finished drying the lettuce, Christo had made the omelettes and thrown together a dressing with some more abandoned condiments he'd found in the cupboard. He'd set the table with some cutlery and napkins and opened a bottle of red wine, pouring a single glass for her. For himself, he filled a pint glass with tap water. When he'd served up the omelettes, Cassie tugged on the cord of the old dinner bell. The sound of it was infinitely melancholy, summoning nobody but themselves.

They ate in near silence, both of them tired out by the day.

'I don't know about you,' said Cassie, 'but I'm bushed.'

'*Time to hit the hay,*' their mother used to say.

The bedroom Cassie had chosen was the one her mother had once occupied. She'd selected it because of the sea view from the window, leaving the other double – with a view of the wilderness of weeds behind the house – to Christo. It was only afterwards that it occurred to her this might have been a mistake.

There was a wobble to the air in the room as she moved about taking off her clothes. A sense of the past, butting in, as if the membrane between then and now had somehow thinned. Cassie imagined her mother moving about this room, throwing her clothes over the cane peacock chair in the corner, just as she was doing now. Looking out the window onto the same disappearing light.

Cassie climbed into the cold, damp bed and slid her feet under the covers, scissoring her legs in the hope of working up some warmth. She took her earrings off one by one, noticing as she did so an echo of her mother's movements. Her mother had always waited until she was in bed to take off her earrings, reaching her right arm across her heart to remove the earring from her left ear first. Then the left arm would travel across to remove the earring from the right ear. Transferring the two earrings to one hand, she would spill them out on the bedside table like a throw of dice, just as Cassie was doing now.

Cassie reached for her cleanser and tipped some of it out onto a cotton pad. She pawed at her forehead and her cheeks with impatient strokes, recalling the sticky smell of her mother's skin. She remembered the pale freckles and veins that were exposed when her mother's foundation came off, rendering her skin transparent. Cassie was overcome by a sense of her mother's presence. Not some supernatural thing – it was her mother's physical presence that was in the room with her. Her mother, at more or less the same age Cassie was now, sitting up in this same bed, looking out this same window at the same tumbling night.

Cassie rolled onto her side, pulling the bedclothes into a knot in her fist and clutching them to her throat as she tried to escape the sense of being inside her mother's body. An empathy that was unbearable to her now – she could feel her mother's terrible restlessness as if it were her own, and what she could not bear was the sympathy she felt for her. All her life, Cassie had stood in judgement on her mother and found her wanting. Only now did she find herself imagining what it was like to be her. This glimpse of her mother's life from the inside out was profoundly disturbing. Her brain swelled and swelled until it felt as if it might burst, and there followed a moment of terrible wobbling stillness as Cassie recognized the impossibility of staying in this room with herself for a second longer.

The night outside was almost pitch-dark. The moon only barely visible behind a veil of cloud. Silence except for the churning of the sea. Clenching the soles of her feet against the gravel, Cassie began to mince her way down the driveway. When she reached the road, she walked along the spine of wet grass in the middle, which was wormy but mercifully soft underfoot. The air was colder than she'd expected, and she realized she should have brought a coat. All she was wearing was her nightdress. At some level Cassie knew what she was doing was crazy. That may even have been why she was doing it.

She made her way down the pier, picking her way over empty lobster pots and stray ropes. At the end of the pier was an iron bollard the shape of a toadstool, which she sat on. Aware of the spectral figure she must strike in her white nightdress in the darkness, she had no control over the drama she was creating.

She heard voices over to the left rising out of the water. From the darkness, a small rowing boat emerged with the two old fishermen in it. One of them was sitting down while the other leaned over the side to haul in some lobster pots. The sitting man rowed with one oar, bringing the boat around in a slow circle. The other man raised his hand in greeting.

'Grand night,' he called out, his voice bouncing across the surface of the water.

'Yes,' called Cassie, 'a lovely night.' As if it were entirely normal for her to be sitting in her nightdress at the end of a pier at midnight. The cold, seeping into her bum bones through the iron bollard. Her feet, deathly chill from the damp stone of the pier.

The men brought the boat in alongside the steps and tied it up. Moving like shadows of themselves, they started loading the lobster pots into the back of their van. There was the sound of an engine starting up, and then they were rolling away. Cassie watched their tail lights disappear, and only when she was sure they were gone did she get up and turn away from the sea. As she made her way blindly along the pier towards the road, she noticed that someone was standing there in the shadows. She picked up the earthy smell of dope on the air. The tip of the joint the person was smoking glowed red in the darkness.

'Hiya,' he said, as Cassie came to a stop in front of him.

'Hiya,' said Cassie, wondering if he knew who she was.

'So, you're back.'

'Yes. I suppose I am.'

For a moment it seemed there was no need to say anything else. She stood facing him in the darkness. Her feet smarting from the cold, her nightdress flimsy at best. She was curiously at ease.

'Do you want a blast of this?'

He held the joint out to her and she took it from him with only the slightest hesitation. It was a long time since Cassie had touched any drugs. There was a time in college when she'd smoked a lot of weed, along with everyone else. Then someone gave her a line of cocaine at a party, and she liked it too much. She saw the road ahead – the same road her mother had taken – and resolved to stop right there and then. For a long time, it was her refusal to take drugs that had defined her among her peers, but she felt suddenly and recklessly free of that resolution now. She had the sense that she had stepped out of her life and that this moment, standing here on a pier at the edge of the Atlantic, could be enjoyed without consequence. She took a drag on the joint, feeling the smoke tearing through her lungs as if it had tiny little shards of glass in it. It left a sweaty taste in her mouth. A swirl behind her eyes. She handed it back to him.

'You had me a bit worried there,' he said, as he pulled on the joint. The tip flared in the darkness.

She couldn't see his face. There was only the sound of his voice. The tone of it was deep, the accent pure. There was nothing in it that she remembered, but then why would there be? This was the voice of a man, not a child.

'Don't get me wrong,' he said. 'It wasn't you that I was worried about. It was the thoughts of me, having to go in there after you.'

Cassie felt a rush of pleasure at the notion that he'd been prepared to go in after her.

19

Seamus remembered very well the day he first met her. He remembered it, because she'd made him guess her name. A real-life Rumpelstiltskin, she threw out the challenge with a wicked confidence, certain he'd guess wrong, but Seamus nailed it first time.

'Cassiopeia,' he'd said, just like that. Seamus was a great man for the stars. His mother had bought him a book about the night sky, and they would sit together on the pier at night, with sleeping bags wrapped around them, identifying the constellations. Cassiopeia was the first one they'd found.

'It's ninety-nine light years from earth,' said Seamus, who had all the facts to hand. 'Four of the stars are greater than the third magnitude.'

'Cassiopeia wasn't just a bunch of stars,' said Cassie archly. 'She started out as a queen.'

Christo broke in on them.

'Cassiopeia was so vain that she started a war with Poseidon. Andromeda ended up chained to the rocks because of her. Poseidon banished her to the sky as punishment.'

Seamus could see she'd been backed into a corner.

'Yeah, well at least I'm not named after a stupid planet.'

'What planet are you named after?' Seamus asked, turning to Christo with thinly disguised interest.

Christo lowered his head and whispered the answer into his chest, but Cassie repeated it out loud, just to be sure.

'Jupiter,' she said, whipping it out in front of her like a matador's cape. 'His name is Jupiter Christopher Jones.'

The name hung in the air for what seemed like a long time.

'Just as well they didn't call you after Uranus,' said Seamus, and peeled off towards the pier with Cassie running after him. In the tournament that was childhood, it was clear to everyone that she'd won that round.

She was his first love, no question about that. Whenever he was asked the question – by women, always – he'd happily supply the answer. It was an easy one to impart in all its innocence. A story that was nice and safe for everyone involved. She was only ten at the time – an American girl with long black, crinkly hair and a red swimsuit with a glittering fish on the front. He was madly in love with her, but didn't she go back to America, and he never heard from her again?

'I'm still scarred,' he'd told Rhona, shortly after they'd met. Three dates in, and the time had come to exchange their romantic histories. 'What can I tell you?' he said. 'It's a sad story.'

'Sweet, though.'

'Yeah,' he said, even though in truth it was anything but sweet.

'Turbulent', was a better word for it. A summer of soaring highs, hurtling over the sand dunes and sailing down the far side of them on gusts of joy. Horsing about in the waves, all tumbling limbs and wet whips of hair and breathless near-drownings. They would lie on the sand together coughing up salt water and spent passion. There was laughter, but it was hard to know if they were laughing with or at each other. They made schemes and plans that had them giddy with elation, but there followed dreadful bursts of deflation. Grievous hurts at small slights. Exclusion. Dejection. Her brother was always there, the three of them constantly pushing and pulling at each other. Circling a space that only had room for two, like they were playing musical chairs. By the time they left, Seamus had been knocked about so badly he hardly knew which end was up.

'So, was she your first girlfriend?' asked Rhona.

'Ah, no. It wasn't like that. We were only kids.'

He had to wait a long time for a first girlfriend. All through senior school, there was no progress on the girlfriend front. He did try to make a move on a girl once, charting the long journey across the floor at the disco in the community hall with everyone watching him. The girl he tapped on the shoulder turned to cast a quick glance over him and said, 'Eh, no thanks,' before closing ranks on him again in scorn. He chose in future to hang back, playing a defensive game while better-looking, sportier boys did all the scoring. Seamus resolved to at least avoid injury, which he managed to do, knowing all along that this defence was an injury in itself.

He was a blusher, which didn't help. A girl only had to look at him and he'd blush. He blushed whenever he was asked a question in class, rows and rows of heads turning to look at him. Then he'd burn up even harder, his eyes watering with desperation as he waited for the moment to pass. He blushed when he saw some girl on the street he fancied, or even some girl he didn't fancy. He'd blush for fear she might *think* he fancied her.

'Any ladies in your life?' Tilly Mannion would ask him, ever hopeful.

'Oh, there's quite a few,' he took to saying, 'but no one special.'

By the time he got to college, that was, at least technically, true. There was the girl he lost his virginity to, a Latvian lounge assistant who made a meal of him one night on the beach in Salthill. There were the three wild Kerry women – classmates of his – who shared a flat beside the university. Seamus had already been with one of them, and was about to fall into the hands of a second, when he opened their kitchen press to find the chart they'd taped to the back of the door. All the boys in their class were listed, with ticks next to some of their names, and in some cases – but not his – the abbreviation 'PE'. He had to ask the girls what that stood for. Premature ejaculation, they told him, laughing. The witches.

His first real girlfriend, as in a girl he slept with more than once, was a girl he met in Barcelona. It was the summer of first year and he was there to teach English. He got a job at a language school on the Plaça de Catalunya, where Olga was the administrator. They took to having their morning coffee together across the road at the Café Zurich. For a Spanish affair, it had a curiously Germanic tinge, but apparently Olga was quite a popular name in Spain. She was studying English at night for her Cambridge certificate, and she took Seamus into her bed as an extra resource. She had a steady boyfriend stationed in the Pyrenees on military service, so the arrangement was only a temporary one until the boyfriend came back, which suited Seamus just fine, since he had to be back at college in September. Olga was fascinated by his milky skin and his million and one freckles. 'Muy mono,' she said, which meant 'very cute' in Spanish. It wasn't clear to Seamus if this was a compliment, but it was better than a kick in the arse, as Jim would say. Beggars can't be choosers. All that guff.

'I think you're handsome,' Rhona had assured him. Rhona was his third and most long-standing girlfriend. She was preceded by Susan, who'd said she loved him but didn't stick around. There had been nobody since.

'Get away out of that,' Seamus said to Rhona. 'I've a good face for radio.'

Through no design of his own he had somehow become

153

a regular contributor to a morning current-affairs show. They were always looking for experts to talk about climate change, deforestation, rising sea levels. Seamus liked to point out that these things had all happened before – dramatic and some-times sudden changes in the climate being a phenomenon that could be observed over the millennia. It was a geological perspective he tried to introduce, and not for a moment intended to suggest that everything would be alright. On the contrary, Seamus knew it was all going to end badly – as it had done many times before – but it was not his job to stop it, no more than a homicide detective is expected to prevent a crime. His job was to establish the facts, which he did dis-passionately and without judgement. It was this pragmatic attitude that was misinterpreted in some quarters as climate change denial, but the controversy only made him more attractive to the show's researchers. Rhona liked to tease him about being a media whore.

'Okay, so you're not *obviously* handsome,' she'd said. 'You're not George Clooney kind of handsome. You're more like Russell Crowe, or Ed Norton maybe. If I was casting you in a movie, I'd cast you as the good cop who gets killed.'

'Oh, great,' said Seamus. 'Thanks for that.'

'Come on,' she said. 'You've got a good face. You've got the kind of face that gets better and better as it gets older.'

'Well, that's something to look forward to,' he said. 'By the time I'm a hundred I'll be quite the looker.'

'I'm no oil painting myself,' she said, which wasn't true. Rhona would have been magnificent painted in oils. She had a high forehead, with long red hair that she wore parted in the middle like a pair of curtains. Her eyes were gleaming and round and ever so slightly close-set. Her eyebrows were narrow and fair, her nose bumpy. Her teeth were large and prominent, so that her lips never quite closed over them. She had a knobbly jawline and a long, elegant neck. She was not the kind of woman you'd see in a fashion magazine or on a billboard, but she'd be right at home in an art gallery, swathed in velvet robes with her fair skin gleaming under the lights. Not that Seamus ever told her that. He found her beautiful – more Frances McDormand than Uma Thurman, to use her own yardstick – but never said so. He'd assumed she knew, but it turned out she didn't. Turned out she needed to hear it – all that stuff on the Hallmark cards that Seamus so scrupulously avoided, that was all stuff Rhona wanted to hear, and if Seamus wouldn't tell her then she'd find somebody who would.

'So, it didn't work out between you and the girl up in Maynooth,' Tilly Mannion had said to him, shortly after he and Rhona broke up. Tilly had never met Rhona, so she couldn't put a name to her. Couldn't put a face to the name because Seamus had never brought her home. That was another thing that came up in the final reckoning. How he'd never thought to introduce her to his people.

'No,' said Seamus with a shrug. 'No, sadly. It didn't work out.'

If you'd told Seamus, when he was eighteen, that he would find himself, at thirty-seven, living in the cottage where he grew up, within a few miles of the place where his dad was living and in plain sight of the community who'd known him since the day he was born, he would have thrown himself off a bridge.

Of all the certainties he'd had in mind as a young man, foremost among them was the knowledge that he would leave the west of Ireland as soon as he could, never to return. He saw himself going abroad once he'd graduated, to Canada most likely. He'd spent a summer there on a student visa and liked it very well. He might end up living in Toronto, or

Montreal perhaps. There was plenty of work out there for a geographer, and a vast expanse of land and water to practise his geography on. Canada might well be the place for him.

He postponed the decision for a year to do a master's and then found himself signing up to a PhD. He was doing a line with Susan by then, and they went backpacking together that summer in South America. They discussed heading out there again once he'd handed in his thesis. Seamus had liked Argentina in particular, could imagine himself living out his life on the Pampas, but then a position for a postdoc came free in the geography department in Maynooth and it seemed too good an opportunity to turn down. Susan went back to Buenos Aires without him and married an Argentinian. The last he heard from her she had three boys and a job running a small hotel. He should look her up, she said, if he was ever passing through. She made it sound like she was just down the road.

There was some talk, when Seamus was living with Rhona, of moving to Australia. Rhona was a marine biologist by trade and there was a lab in Sydney whose work she admired. They talked about going out there for a year, on a trial basis, but the trial year kept being postponed for one reason or another. One year there was a wedding they had to go to, another year Rhona had to have her wisdom teeth out. Those seemed to Seamus like daft reasons not to go, but what did Seamus know? When Rhona's mum died, she abandoned any notion of moving to Australia. She only had the one brother, and he was already living abroad. She couldn't countenance the idea of leaving her father home alone.

In this way the years passed, and while Seamus did get to do some travelling for work – he went to Iceland one year for a conference, and Costa Rica another time on a research project – he was never away for more than a few weeks. Bar those summers he'd spent abroad as a student, he had never lived off the island for any significant length of time. 'A home bird' was how Rhona had described herself when she was rationalizing her decision to stay, and Seamus was eventually forced to the conclusion that he too had become a home bird. Like a bloody homing pigeon, he'd arrived back at the very place he'd started. It was embarrassing to him that Cassie had found him there. It was as if he'd never left.

'You're a hard guy to track down,' she said. 'We looked for you on the internet, but we couldn't find you.'

He had the advantage over her, so. He'd looked her up many times, finding her first on Artnet and tracking her to her gallery's website, where her photo was accompanied by a short bio. From there he'd followed her to Madrid, snooping on the coverage of her exhibition in the Spanish arts pages. He'd seen the giant stone globe she'd installed in the sculpture garden of an American collector in St Louis, Missouri. A similar one had ended up outside a bank in Veracruz. She was pictured standing beside it, looking much the same as she always had. He was amazed to see how little she'd changed.

'Wanna hear a dirty joke?' she said, and Seamus was reminded of how unpredictable she was. That hadn't changed either.

'Sure,' he said, smiling already.

20

Christo heard their laughter bouncing off the water and, at first, he thought they were out in a boat. Making his way down the driveway in the dark, he strained to separate out the land from the sea. There was a difference in texture but not in shade. The sky was matt and still. The sea rippled and seething. The ground beneath him was dense and squirming with life. He scanned the water, seeing only its crawling black surface, empty of anything but itself. He followed the sound of their voices, which now seemed to be coming from the base of the pier. It was only when his eyes adjusted to the darkness that he made them out. The white fabric of Cassie's nightdress made a cookie-cutter shape of a girl in the night.

He'd been woken by a sound, but it had taken him a moment to understand what it was that he'd heard. It was the thump and click of the front door closing as his sister let herself out of the house. The lurch of fear in his heart reminded him that he was never not worried about her. No matter how strong she seemed at times, Christo knew there existed within her deep cracks that she could at any moment fall into.

The first time he saw it happen was at an exhibition of her work in Santa Fe, New Mexico. Christo had flown in especially – a journey that required three flights – but she didn't turn up for the opening. He searched for her for hours, and found her at last on the roof of her hotel. She was sitting on the ground in her party dress, arms wrapped around her knees, looking up at the stars. He tried talking to her, but she looked back at him with great confusion, as if he were speaking a language she didn't understand. Christo put her to bed and kept vigil in a chair while she slept. She woke after fourteen hours, refreshed and ravenously hungry, but she offered no explanation for what had happened, only that she was sorry for the trouble she'd caused.

Then there was the time they went to Florida together to avoid Christmas. Cassie's grandmother had just died, and Christo was concerned about her. She seemed distracted every time he rang her, as if she had one eye on the TV. But even in person, the distractedness persisted. She spent her days swimming laps of the hotel pool. Up and down, up and down, like the senile polar bear they once saw at the zoo in San Diego. On Christmas night she stayed in the pool so long the doctor had to be called. Another Christmas he brought her to stay at his father's house in Devon, and she went out walking the cliffs in a storm. 'Who the fuck does she think she is?' said Amanda. 'Kate Bush in Wuthering Fucking Heights?'

'Cassie,' he called out. He didn't want them to think he was sneaking up on them. His voice was swallowed by the night. 'Cassie,' he said again, and this time they turned.

'Christo! I've found Seamus!' she announced, triumphantly.

The clouds thinned to reveal a gauzy moon. Like a dim bulb behind a silk shade, it was enough to light Christo's way along the pier.

'Hello, Seamus,' he said, offering his hand as he stepped towards him, just as he would do if they were meeting at a sherry reception in college.

'Good to see you.'

Seamus gave Christo's hand a firm shake. He had the same hangdog posture he'd always had, the same wary eyes looking up out of his terminally serious face.

Christo turned to his sister.

'We had better get you in out of the cold.'

His relief at finding her on dry land was tempered by a desire to bring this escapade to a safe conclusion. He knew she needed to warm up. She needed to rest.

'Why don't we all go up to the house and have some tea?' Cassie suggested, hopping from one foot to the other to keep herself warm.

'It's pretty late,' said Christo, dubiously, glancing up at the moon as if it were a clock.

'Oh, come on,' she said, and Christo was reminded of how as a child she would repeat this plea as often as necessary. 'Come on, come on, come on, come on, come on,' she would say, jigging up and down with impatience until, finally, she had her way.

'COME ON, guys,' she said, turning to climb the road towards the house, with a single overhead stroke of her arm to indicate they should follow. Christo glanced at Seamus, and Seamus glanced back at him with raised eyebrows as if to say, what the hell.

Stepping into the lighted kitchen, the first thing Christo noticed about Seamus was that his freckles were gone. As a child you could hardly see his face for them, but the adult Seamus had become was surprisingly freckle-free. His eyes were the same eyes that he'd looked out of as a child, but Christo saw there was a touch of amusement in them now – maybe even cynicism – where before they were wide and shy. He had the same hide-textured hair he had then, but it was cut tight to his head where once it stood on end. His face had broadened and there were wrinkles around his eye sockets, but he was nonetheless himself. Like an image produced by age-progression software, he carried unmistakable traces of the child he once was.

The clock on the wall said ten to two as the teapot hit the

table. Using the last remaining firelighters, Christo had revived the fire in the kitchen stove, managing to coax flames out of it but, so far, no heat. Cassie poured the tea into three mismatched mugs and passed them out. She was wearing a sweater over her nightdress, with a plaid rug doubled over her shoulders. She was still in the throes of violent shudders, which she blithely ignored.

'Isn't this something?' she said, looking from one to the other of them with undisguised delight. 'The three of us sitting here again after all this time!'

Christo nodded, but he felt uneasy. It was the same feeling he'd had yesterday when Cassie took the key from under the rock and let herself into the house. He'd had to suppress the urge to call her back.

'You know, I wondered if I'd recognize you? But now that I see you, I don't know why I wondered. You couldn't have turned out any other way.'

Seamus gave a little shrug, a sceptical expression in his eyes. There was a reserve to him, or so it appeared to Christo – something Cassie seemed determined not to pick up on.

'What about us?' she asked, pulling herself up tall and rearranging her rug across her shoulders. She angled her head to one side to offer her profile, like a model posing for a portrait. 'Do you find us much changed?'

Seamus studied Cassie's face for a long moment, then turned his attention to Christo.

'You're both exactly how I remember you,' he said, and Cassie beamed. 'I'd know you anywhere.'

'How long has it been?'

'Twenty-six years,' said Seamus, without hesitation. He was squinting against the glare of the light. The bulb that had been fitted into the ceiling fixture was far too bright.

Christo stood up to turn on a lamp in the corner of the room, turning off the overhead.

'That's better,' said Seamus. 'I felt a bit like I was under police interrogation.'

His eyes were still squinting, and Christo wondered was this just his way? There was a defensiveness to him that hadn't been there when they were children, but then why wouldn't there be? This was something of an invasion after all. No wonder he felt like he was being interrogated.

'Have a biscuit,' said Christo, passing him the pack of chocolate fingers they'd bought earlier. Seamus raised a hand to decline, but Christo insisted. 'Go on. Please do.'

Cassie was dunking hers into her tea, leaving the finger in there just long enough for the chocolate to start melting before she drew it out again and sucked the chocolate off, leaving only a soggy stick of biscuit that she then bit off.

'We weren't sure we'd be able to find you,' she said, giving too much away, or so it seemed to Christo.

'You were looking for me?' asked Seamus, with an edge to his voice.

'Not for you so much as the place.' Christo treated each word carefully, as if he was crossing a swollen river using stepping stones. He was glancing a warning at Cassie as he was saying this. 'We were keen to come back here. We have such happy memories of the time we spent here with you and your family.'

Seamus locked eyes with him but said nothing. Even when Cassie started talking again, Seamus kept his eyes resting on Christo's for a moment before turning his attention to her. A lingering watchfulness to him.

'Do you remember the way your dad used to pluck ice creams for us out of the sky? He'd be driving along, and he'd open up the sunroof and stick his arm out and magic an ice cream out of the sky.' Cassie's eyes were shining as she remembered it. 'It was years before I figured out how he did it. He must have stopped off at the shop and stashed the ice creams on the roof.'

Seamus crinkled his eyes. 'That was a good trick he had. That was one of his better tricks.'

'How is he?' she asked, abruptly. 'How is your dad?'

Christo held his breath as he waited for the answer, afraid of what might be coming next, but Seamus seemed untroubled by the question.

'Oh, he's grand,' he said, huffing a kind of laugh out through his nose. 'He's alive, anyway, despite all his best efforts.'

'And your mom?' asked Cassie, her face softening as she said it.

'My mam?' said Seamus, looking puzzled. He leaned in closer to the table, as if he was having trouble hearing.

'Your mother,' said Christo gently, and in the silence that followed there was everything he had feared from this conversation.

'I assumed you knew,' said Seamus, and the strange thing was that Christo did know. He could not have said how, but he had somehow known all along. 'My mother's dead.'

'Oh my God, no,' said Cassie, cupping a hand over her mouth.

'I'm so sorry,' said Christo, bowing his head, but whether he was offering Seamus his sympathy or an apology was not clear to him. 'I'm so very, very sorry.'

21

Seamus had in his possession an old Jacob's biscuit tin that contained his mother's birth certificate, yellowed with age and perished along the creases of its folds. Her baptismal cert was in there as well, with the details of her christening filled out by the local parish priest in ink that pooled in a blue blot over her Christian names, Margaret Mary. Her marriage certificate completed the official record of her life, her surname making the short leap from McLoughlin to Murphy. There were some slides of her wedding in the tin too. A scattering of Kodachrome transparencies encased in grubby card. When held up to the light they showed herself and Jim wearing their wedding clothes. Even within the miniature frame of the slide there was, in the tilt of her head and the sideways pull of her eyes towards Jim's, the unmistakable evidence of her love.

'Oh, she was mad for him,' Tilly Mannion had told Seamus, more than once. 'There was no talking to her. As soon as she clapped eyes on Jimmy Murphy there was only ever going to be the one man for her.'

Tilly Mannion was Margo's best friend. She and Margo had started junior infants together on the same day. The class was seated in alphabetical order, so they were literally joined at the hip – two to a desk – for eight years. They were only separated when Margo was sent over to the Abbey as a day girl, while Tilly went to the school in town.

'Notions,' Tilly's mother said, contemptuously.

When Margo left for the teacher training college in

Dublin, Tilly went in behind the counter of her father's shop. Margo wrote to Tilly from Cologne, where she had a summer job working in a canning factory. It was in Cologne that she met Jim Murphy, and there followed a stream of breathlessly happy letters as she traipsed around Germany after him. She brought Jim home with her that winter, by which time Tilly was engaged to be married to Margo's second cousin, John Coyne. She and Tilly were bridesmaids at each other's weddings the next summer, and they stood godmother to each other's babies in the spring of the following year.

Thanks to Tilly, Seamus knew that his mother wrote with her left hand until the nuns forced her to write with her right. That she had a weak bladder as a child and sometimes laughed so much that she wet her pants. That she was thrown out of Irish dancing class for messing. 'They kept her in the choir,' she told him, 'but she was told to mime the words instead of singing, so she wouldn't ruin the whole thing. She didn't have a note in her head.'

Margo was the first of her family to receive a third-level education, and she realized the great dream of her life in becoming a teacher. She got a job teaching low babies at the girls' school in the village. A store of clean cotton knickers always in her handbag in case of accidents, she kept plasters in there too and individually wrapped barley-sugar sweets she dispensed as treats. She had a nature table at the back of her classroom where they displayed seaweed specimens and shells they'd found. Sometimes tiny creatures crawled out of the shells and there would be great squealing and general excitement, which Margo would laughingly recount to Seamus and Jim over supper. On sunny days she always made a point of taking her class outside, because the sunny days were so few and far between they were not to be wasted.

Once Seamus started school, he and she would walk home together. 'You were such a pair,' said Tilly. And it was true, they were more like siblings than mother and son. They roamed the back roads together, she using a broken branch as a stick to wave around in the manner of a small boy. He with his tracksuit bottoms ballooning over his wellington boots and his wool sweater worn long as a woman's dress. They picked elderflower from the ditches to make cordial, and blackberries to make crumble. If it was a fine day, they might go down to the beach to build a car in the sand, climbing into it and pretending to drive away. She would grip her hands around an imaginary steering wheel and shout into the wind. 'So, where will we go? New York?' Seamus would roar back at her: 'Helsinki! Timbuktu!' On other days they might comb the headland in search of mushrooms or roam the rock pools looking for crabs. Whenever it rained, Margo would devise an indoor task for them, making play dough out of flour and water and food colouring, or tracing maps out on grease-proof paper and filling in the names of all the rivers and mountains of Ireland. In the evenings the two of them would curl up on the couch and eat their dinner in front of the TV.

Jim would have been off on some tour or other. That was how he earned his crust back then, as a jobbing musician on someone else's tour. He would disappear for months on end, the only reminder of his existence the long-distance phone calls that would interrupt their TV viewing from time to time while he was gone. He might have been calling from Vancouver or Miami. He might have been calling from Cape Town. A distance measured in the long, laden seconds of delay on the line. Seamus was as shy of his dad on those long-distance phone calls as he would have been of a stranger. He heard the same shyness in his mother's faltering attempts at conversation.

'We're grand,' she would say. 'No news, really.'

She would lapse into silence as she listened to Jim's stories – stories Seamus would later hear her recounting around the village, whenever people asked after him. 'Oh, he's grand,' she'd say. 'He's in South Africa. He swam in two seas on the one day.' Or, 'He's in Australia. It's a hundred and ten degrees over there. It's so hot his sunglasses melted.'

When he reappeared – often without warning – Seamus would rush out to the taxi to take his duffel bag from him and carry it into the house with great ceremony. Margo would wait for him at the door, leaning against the frame with her arms folded. Seamus had the feeling there was some test his father had to pass – something his mother could tell just by looking him in the eyes – and only when he'd passed the test would he be allowed back in. It always took a day or two for the stranger-ness of him to wear off. For the glow of his tan to fade and the stories of the tour to subside. By the time the exotic chocolate bars he'd brought back with him had been eaten and his clothes had gone through the wash and been hung out to dry, Seamus would feel less shy of him again. An equilibrium developing between the three of them, as Jim's life fell in with theirs, until it was time for him to leave again. For years their lives followed these migratory patterns, and Seamus was happy when his dad was there, happier still when he wasn't.

'Were you not lonely, growing up an only child?' Rhona asked him, shortly after they met.

'Not lonely, exactly,' said Seamus. 'But I'd have loved to have had a sibling.'

There was a time when he'd wished for one. He even wrote the wish on his Santa Claus list one year, but his mam's eyes filled with tears when she read it, so he ripped the list up and wrote a new one. It was never mentioned again.

'She wanted more children,' Tilly told him, recently. 'It just didn't happen. She had herself tested, but they couldn't find anything wrong. Your dad was away a lot, which didn't help.'

'Do you reckon there were other women?' Seamus asked Tilly. Knowing his father as he did, it was hard to see how there wouldn't have been. Jim was a great man for the ladies, by his own admission.

'That was something that was never discussed,' said Tilly. 'Your mother made a point of never asking him. As far as she was concerned, her life with him was here, and anything that happened while he was away belonged to another world altogether.'

'Do you think she really believed that?'

Tilly shrugged. 'She thought her marriage was safe. And it was, until your ladyship rocked up for the summer, with those kids in tow, and ruined everything.'

'You say it like he had no hand or part in it.'

'Oh, believe you me, he hadn't. I warned your mother, but of course she wouldn't listen. Poor eejit that she was, she wouldn't hear a bad word about anybody.'

When Seamus pictured his mam, what he saw was a hologram. A shaky montage of a person in perpetual motion. He saw wisps of her curly hair always blowing across her face, and her crooked teeth biting down on her bottom lip. He saw her gathering up a picnic rug in the wind, and superimposed on that image was another one of her running out of the waves. He saw her smiling one second, but no sooner did he have this image of her in his sights than it was gone, replaced by another of her turning her head to talk to him as she drove, with her mouth open to say something that in his memory was never said. What he wanted more than anything was to make her stay still for a moment, so he could look at her. But the harder he tried, the harder she was to see. Like someone glimpsed for a fraction of a second from a moving carousel, she was little more than a blur that was seen for a second and then gone, seen again and gone.

'Oh my God, no!' Cassie said, when he told them she was dead. Her eyes welled up instantly, and Seamus saw how her brother's head turned to look at her with concern before moving his attention back to Seamus.

'Yeah,' said Seamus, feeling no emotion. This must be what it feels like to be a killer, he thought. The way the blood slows in the veins. The way it cools the heart.

'She's dead alright. She's been dead this long time now.'

They were looking at him like frightened animals.

'I'm so sorry,' said Christo, shaking his head very slowly. 'I'm so very, very sorry.'

'Wait,' said Cassie. 'When did she die?'

There was no way of protecting them from it. Even if he'd wanted to protect them, which he didn't. Spare them nothing, he decided.

'She died the night you left,' Seamus told them, in a rush of unaccountable cruelty. 'The fifteenth of September 1993.'

'I don't understand,' said Cassie.

She'd made a shell of her spine, hunching her shoulders forward and hugging her rug around her chest. Her face was crumpled, her black eyes full of shining tears that hung there without falling.

'What happened to her?'

Seamus noticed how her brother laid a hand on her arm, but whether he meant to comfort her or quiet her he couldn't tell.

'There was a row,' he said, trying to use as few words as possible to tell it. He knew from experience that whatever words he used to describe what had happened would rattle around in his head for days, giving him no peace.

'She was upset. She went out on the headland. She had an asthma attack out there.' He shrugged. 'That's it, basically.'

'Wait. She had an asthma attack and *died*?'

'She didn't have her inhaler with her.'

Cassie gasped, with one hand to her chest and the other covering her mouth, and Seamus couldn't help but regret the way he'd chosen to tell it. There was no need for him to tell it like that, but he'd chosen to do so all the same out of a desire to inflict pain. Or was he just unwilling to shield them from the horror of it? Well, why should he? It was no more or less than what had happened. Let them live with it too. Seamus had to live with the memory of walking the back roads in the black of night looking for her. He remembered and could not forget the way the sound of the rain surrounded them so they could hear nothing else. There was not a whisper to be heard from the horses in the fields, or the waves on the shore, or the wind in the trees, because of that maddening rain. Alongside this memory was the thought of his mother, huddled in the shelterless lean of a stone wall, fighting desperately for her last breath.

'My uncles found her there the next morning.'

They'd loaded her into the back of the van, along with the lobster pots and the fragments of shells. She was all wet, like a mermaid washed ashore. Her lips and eyelids, as blue and cold as the sea.

'Oh!' said Cassie again, and the tears started sliding out of her.

Christo was rubbing his sister's arm. Rubbing the flat of his hand up and down her arm in sympathy, prompting Seamus to think, hang on a second, this is my mother we're talking about, not yours.

'How absolutely dreadful,' said Christo, and he too looked shook. His face was drained and blotchy, his expression unutterably sad. 'She was so kind to us, you know. Cassie and I had hoped to thank her for all her kindnesses to us.'

'She was a *beautiful* person,' said Cassie, vehemently. 'She was everything a mother should be.'

'She was, yeah,' said Seamus, even though there was nothing he could call up as an example of this. A panicky feeling in him, like he'd turned up for an exam only for his mind to go blank. That had happened to him once – in an economics exam – and he remembered still with horror the rows and rows of students all around him filling their scripts like seamstresses bent over purring sewing machines, while he could think of nothing at all to write. He had the same feeling now, trying to think of something to say about his mother. It seemed to him in that moment that his memory had been wiped clean of her.

22

'I can't believe it,' said Cassie. They were standing in a puddle of light in the open doorway watching Seamus disappear into a patch of darkness at the bottom of the driveway. They could hear a creak as he opened the gate and another as he closed it behind him. Once he was out on the road he reappeared, and they were able to follow the dark, moving shape of him to his door. They watched him turning in.

'I've thought about her so many times. I thought about coming to see her.'

She could hear the confusion in her own voice.

'She's been gone all this time,' she said, as if by saying it she could somehow absorb it. She had a strange feeling of jet lag, her mind struggling with the shift from past to present. Cassie had once left a pair of earrings she was fond of in the bedside drawer of a hotel room in Madrid. It was only when she got off the plane in Mexico City that she realized she'd left them behind. For one crazy minute it occurred to her to fly straight back to Madrid and get them. The journey seemed easily reversible to her, like a pancake you could just flip over. In the same way, her mind was playing with the notion that she could just as easily travel back in time to see Margo.

'Oh, Christo,' she said. 'I was counting on her being here!'

Ever since her mother died, Cassie had been aware of a handful of people holding her in place, like pegs pinning down a flimsy little tent. There was Christo, more valuable to her in recent years as an absence than a presence, but nonetheless crucial. There was Bill, the friend in LA who had, on many occasions, provided her with a port in a storm. It was Bill, with his monk's hair and his smoker's teeth and his endless capacity for kindness, who Cassie had gone to when she dropped out of college. When her grandmother died. When she lost faith in life for no reason at all. On each of these occasions Bill took her in without asking a single question, carving out a space for her in his falling-down house, where beauty resided amid the chaos. He would set her up in the corner of his garden that was named for her, with a hammock slung between two trees and a clear view of the sea. Her memory of Bill's house – with the voice of Anna Moffo singing 'O Patria Mia' from *Aida* on a mangled cassette tape – was one of the things that had sustained Cassie's faith in life.

There was a teacher called Nesta who took an interest in Cassie when she was at art college. Nesta saw in her something that Cassie could not at the time see in herself. She encouraged Cassie, cajoling her gently to embrace her talent until she lost patience with her and, finally, resorted to bullying her into action. It was Nesta who organized Cassie's first show after she graduated, at a small gallery owned by a friend of hers in Santa Fe. Cassie went and blew that opportunity, disappointing Nesta in the process, and they hadn't been in touch since. Nesta was nonetheless one of the key people of Cassie's life.

There was also the gardener they'd had in LA. Rigoberto came mainly to water the plants, turning the hose on Christo and Cassie from time to time to squeals of laughter. He brought them candy and taught them elementary words of Spanish – words like 'manzana' and 'piscina' – and, with their mother's permission, he once even took them on a visit to his house, where his girlfriend Daniela served them pork tamales with mole she'd prepared especially for them.

'Hey Christo,' she said. 'Do you remember Rigo?'

'Of course I remember Rigo.'

Rigo was only seventeen then, but he had a black moustache already, and a baby boy called Sebastián back in Mexico in the care of Daniela's mother. Rigo spoke to them often of how very much he missed Sebastián – he would hug himself to illustrate this and say 'mucho, mucho, mucho' – and how sad he was to think of his little boy growing up without a dad. Rigo longed to teach Sebastián how to kick a football, how to tie his own shoelaces. How to ride a bike without stabilizers.

'But Sebastián's only two,' said Cassie. 'I'm eight and I still don't know how to ride a bike.'

'Why not?' asked Rigo, to which there was no answer.

It had never occurred to anybody to teach her, just like it had never occurred to anybody to teach her or Christo to play an instrument – something Cassie would in later years find deeply weird, considering the fact that both their fathers were musicians. It just never seemed to enter anyone's mind, just like it never occurred to anyone to teach them to swim – they had to figure it out for themselves. There was a pool at the house, so it was either swim or drown.

Christo did own a bicycle, but he couldn't ride it himself, let alone teach Cassie. It was Rigoberto who made it his business to teach her. He promised he'd hold on tight to the rear carrier and run along behind her. Cassie pedalled and pedalled, secure in the knowledge that Rigo had a hold of her, but then she reached the turning circle at the end of the road and saw him standing all the way back by the gate. She'd been doing fine when she thought Rigoberto was there to steady her. It was only when she saw he wasn't that she lost her balance and fell.

'It's the same with Margo,' she told Christo. 'I always felt like she was there in the background, cheering me on. Anytime I felt sad, anytime I thought about giving up, I would think of her and feel better.'

It was in Margo's quiet presence that Cassie had first felt herself to be worthy of attention. Through Margo's shining eyes she first came to see herself as a person of consequence in the world, someone with the potential to do wonderful things. Cassie only had to think of Margo to feel her best self rising up inside of her, and there had always in her mind existed the certainty that she would someday see Margo again. To learn that this would not now be possible – had never in fact been possible – took some absorbing.

'She was a *beautiful* person,' said Cassie, clinging to that one thought for ballast.

She could feel the grief rising in her like vomit. It wasn't just the news of Margo's death. It was all the other griefs too, surfacing from the depths. First her father, then her mother. Even her grandmother. They'd all been disturbed from the seabed of her heart.

'Hang on,' said Christo. 'Let's get you into bed. You're as white as a sheet.'

Cassie did suddenly feel overcome by exhaustion.

'Now,' said Christo, leading her into her room and draw-ing the covers back on her bed. 'Sit down there.'

He took the rug from her shoulders and tossed it on the chair.

'Hands up,' he said, and drew her sweater over her head.

Bending down, he swept her feet up off the ground and lifted them into the bed. Cassie allowed herself to tip over, her head dropping to the pillow. Very gently, Christo drew the covers over her and sat down at her feet. The heft of his weight on the mattress was a sweet comfort to her.

'Will you stay until I'm asleep?' she asked him, closing her eyes against the full force of her grief.

She felt him patting her hip with the flat of his hand.

'Of course, love. I'm not going anywhere.'

She closed her eyes, undecided whether she wanted to cry or sleep, but exhaustion took over and she felt herself sinking into oblivion. The last thing she was aware of was the weight of her brother's hand on her hip. The sound of his voice falling over her in soft flakes, like snowfall. She might have been a small woodland animal settling into a bed of leaves for a long winter sleep.

23

Seamus was sitting in front of his computer screen the next morning when a knock sounded on the front door. Not so much a knock as a double tap, it was so gentle as to go almost unheard. He got up to answer it and found Christo standing there.

'I hope I'm not disturbing you.'

Christo was angling himself away from the open door, prepared to retreat.

'Not at all, no. Come on in.'

Seamus led him into the kitchen, where his laptop sat open on the table. A stack of handwritten notes next to it in a scrawl that even he had trouble reading.

'I've disturbed you. You were working.'

'Well, to be accurate, I was trying to work and failing. You've saved me from myself.'

Christo pulled out the chair Seamus had indicated and sat down on it. Something of the marionette about his movements, as though his limbs were being operated from above by invisible strings. The way he dangled one knee over the other as he looked hungrily around the kitchen.

'It hasn't changed much,' said Seamus, apologetically.

The curtains on the window were the same curtains Margo had made as a new bride. The pine dresser was a cast-off from her parents, with its display of clutter that had been there for so long that Seamus didn't even notice it anymore. There was the clay pot Seamus had made in art class when he was six. He'd painted it with poster paints but never got around to the glazing. There were postcards his father had sent from his travels, their golden beaches and blue skies bleached by time to pastels. There were Guinness-branded pint glasses filched from the pub, and old crystal liqueur glasses that nobody ever used, and china cups turned upside down on their saucers. There were various ceramic jars and bowls stuffed full of rubber bands and pencils and plastic straws and paintbrushes and hotel shoehorns and swizzle sticks. On the top shelf was the skull of a sheep that his mother had found on the headland and soaked in bleach to kill the germs.

'Coffee?'

Seamus moved across the kitchen to put on the kettle.

'Please.'

'How's your sister this morning?'

'She's still sleeping.'

'At first, I thought she was sleepwalking, when I saw her out on the pier. I wasn't sure whether to approach her or not.'

Christo winced. 'That's something she does from time to time. I'm not sure if it's designed to attract attention or escape from it. Either way, I don't like it.'

'No, it's a bit mad alright.'

Christo frowned, and Seamus wondered had he said too much?

'I remember her very well,' he said, smiling at the picture he had in his mind, of the child Cassie used to be. 'She was forever telling us what to do. Do you remember? She always had the pair of us marching to her tune.'

Wearing her red swimming togs that formed a neat package of her firm little body, she would have been directing operations down on the beach. You do this, Christo. And Seamus, you do that. At the age of ten, she'd had the natural command of an empress. There was no wobble to her then, no hint of the fragility Seamus had observed in her last night.

He took a carton of milk from the fridge and set it straight on the table, no jug.

'What are you working on?' Christo asked, politely.

'I'm writing a book. For my sins.'

The book had been three summers in the making and he was still nowhere near finishing it. That was the idea of the sabbatical, so he could finish the book. But it was like climbing a mountain range – no sooner did he think the end was in sight than another peak appeared ahead.

'A sabbatical,' Jim had said, when he told him. 'And do they pay you for that?'

They were sitting at the bar. A pint of Guinness for Seamus and a Carlsberg for his dad. A pack of fags each – also of different brands – sitting on the counter, all primed for a quick draw.

'They keep my job for me. The publishers paid me a small advance and I've some money from a bursary.'

'A bursary,' said Jim, with both eyebrows raised. 'Isn't it well for you? Being paid to sit on your arse.'

Seamus laughed. He took no offence because he knew Jim was proud of him. The slagging was the only way he had of showing it. That and an appreciation of his son's intelligence as a commodity. A lifetime of scrabbling for a living had engendered in Jim a whistling respect for what he saw as easy money.

'You've your mother's brains,' he told Seamus once. 'I'm only a tradesman, I'm only a guy who knows how to pick out a tune on a guitar. But you – what you've got . . .' He tapped his temple with a nicotine-stained finger. 'Intellectual capital, you can't beat it.'

Jim never had an education. Never once as a child did

Seamus see him pick up a newspaper. Any forms that had to be filled out, or official documents that needed attention, his father would pass on to him. 'I'm no good with paperwork,' he would say. 'Bores me to tears.' He never used sheet music either. When he was composing songs, he played around with them on his guitar, using a tape recorder to lay them down. Addresses, dates of forthcoming gigs – he never once took note of them. 'Sure, can't I keep them just as well in my head?' He had a prodigious memory, though. You only had to tell him something once and he would remember it. It was years before Seamus figured out that his dad couldn't read. Once you knew, a lot of things fell into place. The disdain for maps, for example. The singing birthday cards he recorded onto cassettes when Seamus was a child. The refusal to vote.

'Illiterate present!' the garda on duty had to shout. They had to clear the polling station, and the returning officer would read down the ballot paper once and only once before recording the voter's preferences in declining order. No wonder Jim said he had no time for politics. So many of the shapes he threw were no more than subterfuge. An attempt to disguise the fact that he couldn't read.

'I could teach you,' Seamus had suggested, the summer he came home to write up his PhD. He'd been tutoring undergraduates for years, and while at first it was only to pay his bills that he did it, he found to his surprise that he liked helping people learn. He was good at it.

'Ah, look,' said Jim. 'I reckon I'd have to be an absolute glutton for punishment to take reading lessons from my own son. I reckon I'd have to be well and truly screwed before I'd sink to that.'

'You're forgetting,' said Seamus, carefully. 'I'm a teacher. This is what I do.'

Every morning, once they'd cleared away the breakfast

things, they would sit down at the kitchen table. An ashtray between them and a pack of fags each, with a lighter perched on top. Seamus had bought a tub of plastic letters at the newsagent in town. They were designed to be used as fridge magnets, but he laid them out on the surface of the table, moving them about with his middle finger as he tried to imagine what it was like not to know them. He taught Jim to sound them out. Buh, Ah, Tuh. BAT. Cuh, Ah, Tuh, CAT.

'Good,' said Seamus, patiently. 'That's good.'

'Cuh,' said Jim, moving the letters about with grim determination, the way you might move the planchette on a Ouija board. Seamus and his friends had done that as teenagers many the night, scaring themselves stupid in the process. 'Uh. Nuh. Tuh. CUNT.'

Seamus threw his head back and laughed out loud.

'Alright. Now try Fuh, Uh, Cuh, Ing yourself.'

In the years that followed, Jim dedicated himself with great tenacity to improving his reading. His interests were at first more sophisticated than his facility, his intelligence greater than his ability, so Seamus bought him a box set of abridged classics. In the set were *Robinson Crusoe* and *Dracula* and *Gulliver's Travels* and *Oliver Twist*. It seemed to Seamus that they would satisfy Jim's desire to catch up on all the things he'd been missing, while staying within the range of his reading skill. He had not anticipated his dad's reaction.

'But these are for kids,' said Jim, after studying both sides of the box. He seemed uncharacteristically quiet. A dull expression in his eyes which Seamus saw was shame. For the first time in his life he felt tender towards his father, and it shook him no end. He'd been so angry with Jim for so long. He wasn't ready to go soft on him yet.

'So, what's your book about?' asked Christo. He seemed genuinely interested, which was a new one on Seamus. At the university, everyone he knew was writing a book, so their interest in anyone else's was purely combative. At home, a book was an alien concept, something to be treated with great suspicion. Whenever he mentioned it in passing to Tilly or John Coyne, he provoked a rustle of discomfort in them as they tried to handle this unfamiliar thing he'd introduced into their midst. They were as awkward around books as they were around dancing. Anything that involved opening yourself up for others to see.

'There's a question,' said Seamus, as he poured the boiling water into the cafetière. 'I'm not sure I know the answer to it myself. It's a book about trees, basically.'

The book was, in theory, a geography. It was also a history – the story of another time, when life was lived under a canopy of trees. It was a ghost story – a requiem for the dominion the forest had once held over the earth and how it was lost. Most of all it was a love song – a romance about trees and all the people who loved them, not least his mother. She was the one who'd taught Seamus their names. Using a field guide, they would traipse the back roads together, searching out the sycamores that huddled around the edges of old farmhouses. In the crook of country lanes – spilling over the ramshackle walls of long-abandoned estates – they found the aspen and the willow and the homely holly. They climbed through brambles to find the poetic hazel, with its catkins in spring and its autumn nuts. The greatest prize of all was the mighty oak. It was the oak that Margo loved best.

'My mother was mad for the trees.'

Seamus put the cafetière on the table and drove the plunger all the way down. He poured two mugs of the scalding black coffee and set one in front of Christo before finally sitting down with his own.

'Yes,' said Christo. 'That's why we came.'

'Oh?'

'The drowned forest,' he explained. 'I saw it in the paper.'

'Ah,' said Seamus, remembering the night of the storm. He'd been expecting to be disappointed by it, long accustomed as he was to life in a place of constant disappointments. From the bags of hand-me-down clothes that had come to him as a child from his mother's cousin in Oughterard, to the power that went down whenever there was a movie on TV, and the rain that fell on every nice thing that was ever planned. Every birthday party, every sports day, every Paddy's Day parade. Even storms tended to wear themselves out over the Atlantic, but this one didn't. Seamus had been woken in the night by a whirling, howling sound above the house. By dawn the next morning the road outside was strewn with debris – wooden pallets and lobster pots and old shoes and oil drums and, bizarrely, the severed headrest from a car. The wind had died down, but the sea was up. Great boulders of waves rolling in from the west. Seamus sat by the window and watched them break like windscreen glass over the pier as he listened to the latest reports on the radio.

The river in town had broken its banks. The roads were impassable. Houses and shops inundated. High tide came and went – the water drained away from the pier, exposing the rocks in the foreground – while Seamus hunkered down for the evening, heating a meal for himself in the microwave and settling into the wingback chair by the open fire with nothing but a book for company, unaware that the drowned trees his mother had planted in his mind all those years ago had been unearthed by the storm only a few miles from where he sat.

It was the next day before he heard about it. A reporter from the *Tribune* rang him asking for some information. Talking on his mobile as he went, Seamus grabbed his keys and headed straight for the door. His heart was racing as he pushed the car out the road, pumping the accelerator hard, the way you might kick the flank of a horse to make it go faster. He was afraid the world and his wife would be there before him, but there were no cars parked along the road when he got there. No TV cameras or satellite vans. He had overestimated the level of interest in his own subject. He didn't know whether to be offended or relieved.

'It was your mum who told me there were trees out there under the sea,' said Christo. 'I've been thinking about them ever since.'

'Right,' said Seamus, as a small tendril of jealousy wrapped itself around his heart. It was no less painful to him now than when he was eleven years old. Bad enough to see the affection she poured on the kids she taught, without watching her wrap her arms around two more kids as if they were her own.

'My poor, jealous little scrap,' she'd said, grabbing him in her arms and squeezing him tight as she covered his head with kisses. 'I know you look at those kids, and you see all the stuff they have. But they've none of the things that you have, Seamus. They've none of the things that normal kids take for granted. The least we can do is offer the poor wee things a bit of normality.'

That summer, Seamus had watched with a hot, angry heart as she plaited daisies into Cassie's hair. She taught Christo how to tuck baby potatoes into egg boxes and stow them away in the hot press, so they would sprout. She made paper cones out of newspaper and filled the cones with salty home-made chips for them to take down onto the pier. It was no wonder they loved her. No wonder they remembered her still.

'So, what is it you do?' he asked Christo.

'I'm a university lecturer. I teach maths at Cambridge.'

Seamus was not surprised. The Christo he'd known as a child was always methodical. It made sense that he'd become a mathematician.

'I'm in the throes of writing a book too, actually.'

'Oh?'

'Have you ever heard of Fibonacci numbers?'

'Sure. But don't test me on what they actually are.'

'They appear in nature,' said Christo. 'Sunflowers, pineapples, pine cones – they all use the Fibonacci sequence to maximize their efficiency. They do it without even knowing about the number sequence. They do it because it's the best way.'

'Intuitive knowledge,' said Seamus, thinking of his mother, who understood that this was something that existed in the natural world but ally too rarely in the human one.

'Yes,' said Christo, his eyes lighting up with the surprise of being understood. 'Exactly.'

'There's no end to the wonders and marvels of the world,' Margo would say to Seamus. She was not a religious woman – he'd never known her to go to Mass, except once a year at Christmas – but she spoke with religious zeal on the subject of nature. A light in her eyes, like the light of God depicted by Renaissance painters in the eyes of the saints. 'It's an endless source of magic.'

Among the things Margo knew were the ways of the weather and the behaviour of the winds and the language of the rain and the strange and often contradictory moods of the sea. She knew the names of all the wildflowers that grew on the headland. She knew all the different types of seaweed – which to eat and which to use to condition your hair. She knew all the stars in the sky above her head as well as she knew the names of the children who sat in rows before her desk in the schoolroom. She knew the cries of the seabirds and the migratory patterns of the swallows. She would stand still on the beach and watch with wide eyes their flight lines.

'She wasn't even aware of all the things she knew,' Seamus told Christo. 'She just knew them.'

They sipped at their coffee and Seamus had the sense that Christo wanted to broach something with him but didn't dare. He sensed an invisible wall between them, created by the friendship they'd once shared. Neither of them knew what the other remembered, but there was in each of them the knowledge of some past intimacy. The possibility that the other person held some vital and private piece of information about you, something you yourself had long since lost sight of.

'Look, I hope you don't mind, but I'd like to dedicate the book to your mother. She was the one who taught me to pay attention to the world around me. I owe her a great debt, and this is the only way I can think of thanking her.'

'The dedication is a nice idea,' he told Christo. 'She'd be very honoured.'

'That means a lot to me,' said Christo, with great solemnity. 'Thank you.'

'You're welcome,' said Seamus, even if he didn't mean it.

They drank their coffee for a moment in silence. Again, there was that hesitancy. It seemed to Seamus that Christo was debating whether to say more. Seamus thought of all those nights he'd spent in Christo's room, with the talk flowing between them in the darkness and their voices layered by the bunk beds. How they'd traded morsels of themselves, in the same way that they bartered marbles by daylight. Seamus remembered the marbles well – the chill, watery feel of them in your hand – but not the morsels of confidence.

'Seamus,' said Christo, at last. 'I feel we owe you an apology.'

'Oh?'

'I'm afraid we've stirred things up for you by coming down here.'

And, of course, it was true, but Seamus didn't like to say so. He shifted in his chair, leaning in over his coffee cup. He narrowed his eyes, trying to focus on something to say, but nothing came to him. For a moment he felt nothing but his breath expanding in his chest. He became aware of a thumping sensation in his ribcage and realized to his horror that what he felt was his own heart, beating in rapid time. It was only with this awareness that he finally came to understand that he was upset.

'We had such a happy summer here,' Christo told him, holding his attention with a gaze that Seamus found hard to maintain but impossible to break. 'We remembered it as an idyllic time in our lives.'

'Of course,' said Seamus. He himself could hardly bear to think of that last summer. He was haunted by the thought of all the time he'd spent with Christo and Cassie, time he could have spent with his mother in what would prove to be her final weeks and days. To Seamus, that summer was nothing but wasted time.

'It's a matter of great regret to us,' Christo was saying, speaking slowly and deliberately, as if he were delivering a eulogy, 'that the reality was so very different.'

24

Of the night they left, Christo remembered only a scattering of peripheral details. He remembered the front door was wide open, even though it was raining outside and the floor of the hallway was getting wet. He remembered the sound of the cassette that was playing in the kitchen coming to an end with a click and automatically ejecting itself. He remembered very clearly the high-necked green satin blouse his mother was wearing, with its billowing sleeves – the blouse was tied, pirate-style, exposing her brown belly above the waistband of her jeans. There was a milk spill on the wooden surface of the table that nobody had bothered to wipe up. Three feet of cold water in the bath.

'It was just a case of joining the dots,' he told Cassie. Like the stars in the sky, the shape they formed only emerged when you connected them. Christo had received a telescope from Santa Claus one Christmas, but he'd never much liked using it. He'd preferred to study the stars in his atlas, where nice straight lines had been drawn to connect them and make sense of them. The stars were too chaotic without the lines.

'It's so obvious once you see it,' he told Cassie. 'That's why we had to leave in a hurry. That's why we couldn't go back for the monkey.'

They were sitting in the shelter of a sandy bluff overlooking the surfing beach. Knees to their chests, arms wrapped tight around their shins, they might have been two soldiers huddled together in a dugout.

'Did you know?' he asked her.

'No,' she said. 'But it's not like it's a big surprise.'

The sky was troubled by clouds, like someone had dipped a paintbrush into a glass of water.

'I'm not sure how I knew, but I did. It's like *Peter and the Wolf*.'

Below them, another wave broke and fell.

'Christo, what are you talking about?'

'I went to see *Peter and the Wolf* in Cambridge a few years ago.'

A colleague of his had been performing in the orchestra. They were raising money for charity, so Christo couldn't not buy a ticket, which was why he found himself sitting in the concert hall in Cambridge on a Tuesday lunchtime, listening to a symphony for children. Christo was not familiar with the story, but he was fascinated to find that he could follow it through the music. It was the same with his mother and Jim, as he explained to Cassie. You didn't need the words to figure it out.

'Margo always let her sit up front with Jim. Anytime we went anywhere in the car, Margo sat in the back with us.'

He was sorting through it all in his mind, tidying up the cluttered pieces of the past with an operating-theatre calm.

'Margo wasn't a smoker,' he said. 'She wasn't into music. She wasn't a night owl.'

A memory came to him – cinematic in its clarity – of his mother and Jim sitting at the table outside the rental house. They were arguing about music, rewinding the tape to play particular bits back to each other, while Margo was in the kitchen washing the dishes. Cassie wasn't there – playing solitaire inside, maybe? Seamus and Christo were clearing the table, ferrying plates and cutlery from the table outside into the kitchen and returning for more. Moving from the yellow light of the kitchen into the starry darkness, where the tape recorder drowned out all the noises of the night. Christo remembered his mother's face flickering in the candlelight. She had a rug wrapped about her shoulders, with a hand emerging from the rug and a bottle of beer in the hand. Jim was sitting at right angles to her, with his head thrown back, blowing sweet-smelling cigarette smoke up into the sky. Christo saw that his mother had her bare foot propped up on the seat of Jim's chair, with her toes tucked in under his thigh, but he thought nothing of it at the time, no more than he thought of the salt that had spilled out of the salt cellar onto the tablecloth or the wax that was dripping down the side of the candle, forming stalactites that his mother leaned in to pick at with the nail of her index finger. None of these things seemed significant to him, then, but of course they were, and it was for that reason that he had stored them away in his memory.

'It was happening right before our eyes,' he said. 'I just wasn't paying attention. Or maybe I was paying attention to the wrong things.'

At the time, Christo was preoccupied by the problem of his schooling. He and Cassie should have been back at school, but there was no talk of them leaving. Seamus had started secondary school in town at the beginning of September. He had a new uniform – a new school jumper with a crest on it and a smart, striped tie and new grey slacks with a knife-edge crease. He had a new schoolbag full of new books, which had been covered by Margo with remnants of wallpaper. Christo saw him heading off every morning with her in the car. You could time your watch by their return at 4.25 every afternoon. Christo would be waiting by the window for the first sight of them. Seamus had homework to do, but he had Margo persuaded that he should be allowed to play outside while there was daylight. The homework could wait until after supper, when he'd lay his books out on the kitchen table. She would sit down with him and do her corrections. 'Pair of swots,' Jim said to Christo, arriving up at the rental house one night with a six-pack of beer. Christo sensed that Jim was trying to forge an alliance with him, but he wanted no part of it.

'I felt like a traitor,' he told Cassie. 'I wanted to tell him I was a swot too.'

'I don't see what difference it makes now,' she said. Their two brains as different as could be. To Christo, the past was a puzzle he was trying to solve. Cassie couldn't see why you'd bother.

'All that matters is they're gone.'

Down below them, three slick, black-suited surfers were bobbing about on the surface of the sea like corks. Allowing wave after wave to slide under them while they waited for a bigger one to come along. Waiting, waiting, waiting, until the right wave came. When it did, they scrambled to climb on board it, riding it all the way into the shallows.

'We should do that,' said Cassie.

She was sitting bolt upright, with her eyes feasting greedily on the surfers, who were lying flat on their boards, paddling their way back out to sea.

'I'm sure we could hire boards some place.'

Cassie was always up for trying things.

'Oh, no,' said Christo. 'Not a chance.'

He was afraid of the sea. He feared the bottomless depths of it, the thought of all the fish in it. He feared the pitiless waves that would not hesitate to throw you down onto the hard sand and hold you there until you began to think you'd never breathe the air again. That had happened to him once, on this very beach, and he'd never been able to forget it. Christo remembered how Seamus and Cassie would spend hours in the waves, using kitchen trays as makeshift surf-boards, while Christo watched them from the dry heights of the beach. After his near-drowning experience, nothing would induce him to go back into the water.

'Okay,' said Cassie. 'Let's get going.'

They crossed the headland and climbed down onto the beach. As they walked, the shadow of a cloud moved across the sand, like the fingers of a giant hand moving across the surface of a lamp.

'We need to get back to the house quick,' she said, looking up at the sky. 'It's about to rain.'

Christo watched as she strode ahead of him – the child she once was, and the woman she had since become, for now one and the same. It seemed to him that he'd spent his whole childhood trying to catch up with her. 'Wait for me,' he would shout, uselessly, while she ran ahead of him.

He bent his head to look at the ground as he walked, study-ing the ridges that had been left behind by the sea on the sand. It soothed him to think that their shape was determined not by some random act but by the direction and velocity of the waves. Some speeds and directions would produce long ridges, running in parallel. Others would produce branched ones, like a cactus. There were even studies of ancient, petrified seabeds that had identified storms that happened hundreds of millions of years ago from the ripple patterns in the sand.

Straightening up, he felt suddenly dizzy. The water was moving in fast over the strand. The sky, as heavy as a blank page above him. He sat down on a rock for a second to steady himself, looking at the water that pooled in the hollows it made in the sand. It was the most wonderful shade of green. Barely a colour at all, it was more like the memory of colour. It occurred to Christo that there was no need to understand why, only to appreciate its beauty.

For the first time he caught a glimmer of what his sister's work might mean to her. For the first time, the possibility occurred to him that hers might be capable of solving something that his couldn't – of finding some meaning in the things that eluded him. He had never really understood the purpose of art. He never could figure out the point of traipsing around galleries looking at things that weren't real, only somebody else's impression of reality. 'Why is nobody wearing any clothes?' he'd asked his mother once, when she brought them to see the nudes in the Uffizi. '*Christo,*' she said, '*I swear, you don't have an artistic bone in your body.*' At the time, this had pleased him no end. Now he found himself wondering, was that the problem with him?

'Christo!' Cassie's voice reached him, thrown about by the wind. She was standing at the bridge, waving her arms in the air. 'Come on. We'll be *drenched.*'

That was one of their mother's words – part of her endless vocabulary for rain. '*I got drowned,*' she'd say, with her usual taste for the dramatic. '*It's pelting out there. It's pissing down. Cats and dogs isn't in it!*'

'It's down for the day,' pronounced Jim, one particular morning. There was no going to the beach, so someone suggested a trip to a nearby waterpark. Just the mention of it was like a lit match to a pile of tinder. The household picked up quickly in a burst of energy. Suddenly there was coffee brewing, eggs boiling for sandwiches, crisps thrown into a bag. Raincoats were located, togs and towels packed.

Christo was in the hallway, anxious to get going. Cassie and Seamus were already in the car, sitting still for once with their swimming bags on their laps. Margo had gone back down to the cottage for something she'd forgotten. Through the open living-room door, Christo could hear his mother and Jim locked in urgent whispering, but he couldn't hear what they were saying. He couldn't see them from where he was standing. He was like a camera on a tripod, his view limited to a single, fixed frame. It was this frame that was captured in his memory, and there was no changing it now. It was maddening to Christo to come up against the limitations of his own brain. He felt like beating himself about the head to somehow shake it loose.

The same thing had happened to him once with a Beatles song. He'd woken one morning with it in his head, nameless and wordless but as real to him as anything he'd ever heard. The song was short and sweet, like 'Blackbird', but it had the melancholy of 'Yesterday'. Christo set out to find it, listening in vain to all the Beatles' albums in the hope of hearing it. He trawled iTunes for it, ploughed through the entire Beatles catalogue on Wikipedia, but nowhere could he find the song. It continued to play in his head, tugging at his consciousness while he was lying in bed at night. It hung around the edges of his mind, taunting him with wisps of music that were thick with feeling but maddeningly intangible. Like the attic room in the rental house – like the memories he had of his mother – there was no way of knowing if he'd imagined it or not.

25

It was Seamus who suggested they speak to Tilly Mannion. Apart from Jim, Tilly was the only surviving adult to have witnessed the events of that summer. A highly partisan witness, as she explained straight off.

'What you have to understand,' said Tilly, 'is that Margo was my friend.'

They were sitting in the coffee shop in the village, their voices raised to make themselves heard over the hiss and splutter of the cappuccino machine. There was the ping of the microwave and the sound of sausages splitting under the grill. Rasher fumes, as pungent as farts.

'Margo was *my* friend,' she repeated, thumping her heart, hard, with her fist. She seemed to have no regard for the drama of the gesture. She might have been on the stage at La Scala.

'I thought you were all friends,' said Cassie, confused.

Tilly sucked a breath in through her teeth.

'Oh no,' she said, shaking her head with a dry little laugh. She wagged her finger. 'No, no, no, no, no. Your mother was Margo's friend from the Abbey. I was Margo's friend from the village.' She made a clicking sound in her throat. 'Never the twain shall meet.'

The waiter appeared with a tray and served up coffees for Cassie and Tilly, a fluffy hot chocolate for Christo. What kind of adult drinks hot chocolate? There were times when Cassie despaired of her brother.

'You have to understand what it was like then,' Tilly

Mannion was saying. 'This was the *seventies*, for God's sake. We were all poor meek little creatures. We were so drab, all dressed in brown corduroy with our frizzy hair and our corned-beef legs. Your mother was different – I don't know where she got it from, but she had such *sass*.'

She smiled, remembering.

'Margo used to bring her home for the weekend. I can still see her sashaying around town in her miniskirt, hips swinging, hair flying. She had this red Rimmel lipstick that she wore morning, noon and night. Nobody around here had ever seen anything like it. She had so much confidence, it was like a red rag to a bull. The girls in town used to hiss at her in the street.'

'And you?' Christo ventured to ask.

'It wasn't that I didn't like her. She was great fun to be around.'

Tilly smiled, clucked her tongue three times.

'Look,' she said. 'Your mother was a nice girl when there wasn't a man around. She was really smart. She could be very funny. The thing is, the second a fella appeared she lost the plot. Nothing would do her but to reel him in. And, of course, she could do it with her little finger.'

Cassie might have been sitting in her grandmother's kitchen in Oklahoma City, listening to this exact same speech. 'Your mom changed the moment a man walked in the room,' her grandmother always said, clicking her nicotine-stained fingers to illustrate her point. 'She was one of those women who cannot be without a man. She had to go to bed with every man she met.'

Cassie's grandmother had been without a man since she was twenty-two, and the truth was that she was happier without one. All she needed in life was an endless supply of Newport 100s and an audience for her bitter musings. 'Your mother had no capacity for solitude,' she liked to say, sparking up another cigarette while her last one was burning itself down in the ashtray. 'She needed a man around to give her a reason to *breathe.*

'The mistake your mom made,' she would say, drawing yet another cigarette out of the pack before delivering her verdict, 'was to rely on her looks to get her places instead of plain, old-fashioned hard work.'

Cassie's grandma had worked the same job all her life, as a toll operator for the Oklahoma Turnpike Authority. It was a stick she liked to beat her daughter-in-law with. She had no use for the idle variety, as she often said.

'Your mom was a pretty girl, I'll give you that. But a girl should be more than just a pretty face.'

Of her mother's face, Cassie had no reliable memory. There was only what she'd borrowed from photographs. The Z-card from her mother's days as a fashion model in London showed a baby face obscured by a mess of wild, dark hair and smudged black eyeliner. In the photos of that time, she was pictured wearing a huge Afghan coat with a minidress underneath it, her pale bare legs disappearing into thigh-high boots. Outdoors or indoors, she was always wearing that ridiculous coat.

It was in London that she met Christo's dad and married him. There was in existence a picture of her there with Christo when he was a baby. The photographer had since become famous, with the result that the image often reappeared in magazine features on his work. Most recently, Cassie had come across it in a copy of *Vanity Fair* that she'd picked up at a friend's house in Oaxaca. In the picture, Christo was sitting on the floor, stark naked, while their mother sat behind him in a low armchair. She was dressed in a black polo neck, white A-line skirt, black knee-high boots, and the smoke from the cigarette she was holding rose like a flare from her upturned hand. There was a faraway look in her eyes, as if she was already contemplating the escape she was about to make. Most famous of all was the image of her – iconic, as the cliché goes – that appeared on the cover of Christo's father's second album. It was that image that earned her the name of 'muse'. 'Groupie' was another word Cassie had heard – from her grandmother's mouth.

'Let's face it,' she'd said. 'Your mom was nothing but a pretty little groupie.'

'She had trouble written all over her,' said Tilly Mannion. 'My mother said she'd lock her up if she was her daughter. But, of course, she had no mother to lock her up, only that awful father of hers. It's no wonder she went off the rails.'

'What do you mean by that?'

'Oh,' said Tilly. 'How to put this? Christmas of sixth year, she takes off with a guy from the reform school in Letterfrack. There may have been the small matter of a pregnancy. So, of course, it had to be London. She went off with all Margo's confirmation money, and that was the last we saw of her until she turned up nearly twenty years later, with you two in tow.'

So, there it was, a piece of their mother's life story. Cassie felt like she'd opened a dusty old trunk and a bird had flown out. Her mother's life had for so long been locked away that Cassie had begun to think it was lost forever. To hear Tilly Mannion release it now, without so much as blinking an eye, was a shock to her.

'Of course, Margo, being who she was, welcomed her back with open arms. I had a bad feeling about it – I tried to warn her, but she wouldn't hear a word of it. Gobshite that she was, Margo was only too delighted to have her back. Believe you me, it gives me no pleasure to say that things worked out exactly as I predicted.'

'Margo *trusted* her,' said Cassie.

'Margo wasn't stupid,' Tilly Mannion was saying. 'She saw what was happening. She tried her best to stop it. She even went into Galway to buy herself some fancy new underwear. As if there was any amount of underwear was going to help her. She was no match for your mother, that was the long and short of it. Your mother was a hellcat once she got her claws into a man. And Margo was not up to fighting her off.'

'I wonder how long it was going on,' said Cassie. She was casting her mind back over that summer, recalibrating everything in light of what they now knew. All those car trips they took to look at vacant houses now seemed no more than an excuse for her mother and Jim to be alone together. For him to stretch a hand across to where she sat in the passenger seat and lay it on her bare thigh. They always took Cassie with them, leaving the boys behind at the house with Margo. Cassie remembered riding around like a queen in the back of the car. She remembered the pleasure of being the chosen one.

'Oh God,' she said, recalling how they plied her with candy and left her in the car to eat it. 'I was their decoy!'

Jim was a handsome man, back then. He had black hair and blue eyes and smile lines like rays of sunshine that lit up his face. Cassie remembered the warm glow of that smile coming to rest on her. She remembered the feeling of her bare legs on the rough denim fabric of his shirt when he carried her on his back. Her fingers clutching his thick hair, like someone bareback horse-riding, as he galloped her up and down a sand dune. He once wound a piece of thread round her loose back tooth and tied the other end to the doorknob, slamming the door shut on the count of three. The tooth that dangled from the end of the piece of string was streaked with blood. The hole it left in her gum, deep and raw when she probed it with the tip of her tongue. Jim handed the tooth back to her and shook her hand solemnly as he congratulated her on her bravery. Forever afterwards, Cassie would consider the courage he saw in her that day an important part of who she was. He became – in Cassie's mind – one of the people of her life. To learn that he was not hers after all but just another person who belonged to her mother felt like a betrayal. What had seemed, in Cassie's memory, to be a happy family summer had turned out in retrospect to be, as everything always was, a drama that revolved around her mother.

'I'm not sure it's fair to blame her entirely,' Christo was saying to Tilly Mannion.

'Oh, come on, Christo,' said Cassie, pulling herself away from the thoughts that were running away with her. 'Let's face it. She brought a trail of destruction with her everywhere she went.'

Cassie heard her own voice forming in her mouth. She had perforated an eardrum once, while scuba diving, and it was the same sensation she had now. She felt like she was hearing herself from the inside out.

'What I'm hearing in your voice is bitterness,' a therapist once said to her. It hardly seemed worth the hundred bucks she was paying him to listen to her. Cassie knew she could spend every last cent she had talking to therapists about her mother until the end of time without ever getting to the bottom of her feelings.

'I don't want to talk about her,' Cassie had told the therapist. Insistent first, then pleading. 'I want to talk about *me*, about *my* life. I'm tired of talking about her.'

But it was always about *her*. Her ups and downs. Her desires and disappointments. Her constantly changing moods. Her mother's history was one of operatic sorrows, from her unhappy childhood with a loveless father to her lonely incarceration in that dark castle of a school. Her modelling days as a young woman in London were cloaked in high glamour, her relationship with Christo's father one of violent passions. The love affair with Cassie's dad was an epic, ending in a front-page tragedy, but the same momentous quality applied to everything that was hers. Her finances and her personal belongings, her drinking and her drug-taking, even her chaotic sleep patterns. Every little thing that was hers was conducted in the major key.

The things of Cassie's life were, by comparison, all minor. The little routines of childhood, from homework to birthday parties, were of less importance than whatever daily drama was unfolding in her mother's world. Cassie's teeth fell out without anyone remembering to supply money from the tooth fairy. Cassie's first period came and went without any help from her mother, who was too hungover to drive to the shop for pads. The loss of Cassie's father was incidental to the great trauma of her mother's bereavement, the separation from her brother nothing compared to the hurt that was caused to her mother by his abandonment. There was never a moment when Cassie got top billing.

'*Now, Miss Cass,*' her mother would say. '*How will we amuse ourselves today?*'

One of the things Cassie liked to do as a child was to play shop with her mother's clothes. Her mother had at one point in her life owned no end of designer clothing, filched from various photo shoots and shows. Anyone else would have made a collection of them – they could one day have been auctioned for charity – but Cassie's mother had no regard for the many beautiful belongings that came her way, casting them off with all the carelessness of a princess. Among the treasures in her mother's closet was a La Perla nightgown of the finest eau-de-Nil satin. There was a mother-of-pearl ring box and a tortoiseshell hair clip and a silk Hermès scarf with racehorses on it. There were black lace gloves and blue glass earrings. A pile of fancy shoes heaped like builder's rubble at the bottom of her closet. Cassie would take them out and display them on a velvet ottoman, while her mother lay in bed and smoked.

'It just so happens that we have your size, Mrs Koenig,' Cassie would say, using the name that appeared in print on the bills that began to gather, unopened, on the table in the hallway after her father died. A name Cassie had never heard anyone use to address her mother, except the teachers at school. She was hardly recognizable as a Mrs Koenig.

'*You see, that's what I love about this shop,*' her mother would say. '*You always seem to have my exact size.*'

Other times they would play nail salon or massage parlour. Her mother's feet were wrecked from all the tight-fitting shoes she'd worn as a young woman. She liked to have someone rub them for her while she sat on the couch and watched TV.

'So you were, essentially, your mother's handmaiden?' said one therapist.

'More like a stagehand,' said Cassie. 'Or a roadie. She liked to have me on hand to fetch stuff for her.'

'Do you think your mother loved you?' he asked.

Cassie had been turning that question over in her mind ever since.

'I'm not sure she was capable of love,' she said. 'Not in the way normal people understand it. There was love, for sure, but even the love was all about her.'

She was always looking for kisses. Always asking them to climb into the bed with her, so she wouldn't be alone. Anytime she took a bath she liked Cassie to be there so she would have someone to chat to. There was a special chair in the corner of the bathroom for this express purpose, but Cassie didn't like to sit there. She didn't like the sight of her mother's pale, round breasts. The large nipples, so dark and flat compared to Cassie's own, and between her legs the mound of smooth, plucked skin where Cassie herself had acquired some alarmingly long black hairs. It made Cassie uncomfortable to see her mother naked, but whether she was ashamed of her mother's body or her own, she could not have said.

What Cassie wanted, more than anything, was one true memory of her mother's love. Cassie knew her mother must have held her as a baby. She must have nuzzled the back of her neck to breathe in the sweet, baby smell of her. Must have pinched the flesh of her cheek between her finger and thumb to see it dimple. Her mother must have brushed her hair from her face as she tucked her into bed at night. She must have told her she loved her – surely, she would have told her she loved her, even if Cassie had no memory of it?

26

Nothing would do Cassie but to visit Margo's grave.

'This is something I have to do,' she told Christo, over breakfast the following morning. 'I have to go and pay my respects to her. After all she did for us, the very least I can do is lay some flowers on her grave.'

The tide was almost out as they drove across to the island, following the road signs that were planted in the sand. Christo felt a wild fairground thrill as he rolled the hire car across the bumpy strand, steering his way around the tide pools. On either side of them was the receding sea, its shallow waters both transparent and not, like an old glass bottle. The island up ahead of them was a low slick of green. The sky above it blue and free of clouds, for once.

They parked the car at the lip of the island. Seamus led them through a gate and up the hill into the graveyard, where he stopped at an unremarkable grave. Edged by an overgrown granite kerb, the plot itself was covered by nothing but grass, where some of its neighbours had been lovingly decorated with rocks and shells. The headstone was made of simple black marble and low-standing, by comparison with the various Celtic crosses and holy statues that imposed themselves as shadows on the postcard-blue sky.

Christo stood to one side of the grave, taking his sunglasses off and slipping them into his pocket out of respect. Cassie had brought a bunch of flowers that she'd bought in the filling station, and she laid them down at the foot of the headstone with all the care of someone settling a sleeping baby into a crib. She took several small steps backwards, coming to stand beside Christo. Christo was aware of Seamus facing him from the other side of the grave, but he didn't like to look at him for fear of intruding. It took him a moment to settle on reading the headstone.

MARGARET MARY
b. 6th January 1957, d. 15th September 1993

From the inscriptions below, he saw that Margo's parents had followed quickly after her into the grave. Her father by just three months and her mother six months later. Three times, the Ford Scorpio must have inched its way across the sands with a line of mourners walking behind it. He imagined Seamus as he was when they last saw him, an eleven-year-old boy with a wild thatch of hay for hair and a face with more freckles on it than there was space between them. He pictured him with his hair plastered down over his forehead and a jacket bought especially for the occasion, following first his mother, then his grandfather and finally his grandmother across the strand to deposit them in this seaside grave, with the tides sweeping in and out twice a day over the white sand and the clouds forming and dispersing in the sky above them, while they lay there oblivious to it all.

'Well,' said Seamus. 'There you have it.'

Christo looked up and saw that he was standing with one foot propped on the lip of the grave.

'I'm so sorry,' Christo said. It had dawned on him that he was not alone in his experience of losing a mother. All his life, Christo had understood the loss of her to be something that set him and his sister apart from the rest of the world, but now he saw that it was not unique. It occurred to him, for the first time, that their grief was just like anyone else's. That it might even be lesser than some.

'You lost your grandparents too,' he said, still shocked by the enormity of it.

'They couldn't handle it.'

Hands in the pockets of his jacket, Seamus took a swing at a stone with his boot, sending it scuttling off onto another grave.

'It must be nice to have a place to visit,' said Cassie, talking across the grave the way a hospital visitor might talk across a patient's bed.

Seamus narrowed his eyes. 'Doesn't your mother have a grave?'

'Oh no,' said Cassie cheerfully. 'She was cremated.'

'And your dad?'

'My dad always wanted to be buried in the Choctaw tradition.'

Seamus took a pack of cigarettes out of his pocket.

'Hey,' said Cassie, 'can I have one of those?'

Christo hadn't seen her smoke for years. He was almost tempted to join her, rather than be left out, but of course he'd never in his life smoked a cigarette. It had never even occurred to him to try.

'The Choctaw leave their dead out in the open to decompose,' she was saying, as she bent to take a light from Seamus. Her hair fell down over her face and she brushed it away with the back of her hand. 'They wait until there's nothing left of them and then they gather up the bones and bury them.'

'Jesus,' said Seamus, looking impressed. He paused in the lighting of his own cigarette, letting it dangle for a moment off his bottom lip.

'The way my dad died, they had to do an autopsy.' Cassie stopped talking briefly to blow the smoke out one side of her mouth. 'I don't think there was much left of him by the time they were finished. So, in a way, he got what he wanted.' She took another pull on the cigarette. 'My grandma ended up taking him back to Oklahoma. She buried him in the local cemetery, but the fans started climbing over the wall to hang out on his grave, so she had him dug up again.'

Christo had met Cassie's grandmother only a handful of times. A woman with long, greasy hair and impossibly long front teeth, she chain-smoked menthol cigarettes, lighting them one after the other with a small plastic lighter she stored inside the cuff of her shirt. She had never in her life been outside the state of Oklahoma, a word Cassie was in the habit of pronouncing as four distinct syllables, to make it sound like a horror show in four acts. Oh-kla-hoe-mah.

'So, where is he now?' asked Seamus, holding what was left of his cigarette between his thumb and forefinger as he took a final drag on it. Christo was reminded of those boys who were always smoking at boarding school. Christo had never been one of those boys – they would barely have acknowledged his existence – but he could see it in Seamus. He had that schoolboy defiance about him still.

'Oh, she died without telling anyone.'

Seamus smiled at that and tossed his fag butt sideways into the hedgerow.

'Alright,' he said, with a jerk of his head and a change of tone that suggested he had thought of a solution. 'Will we crack on?'

Without waiting for an answer, he set off on a diagonal towards the far corner of the graveyard, trampling across a number of graves as he went. Cassie followed in his footsteps, but Christo didn't dare. He weaved his way round the edges of the plots, feeling at odds with the others as he did so.

He was wearing his standard everyday outfit of a tweed jacket, corduroy trousers and brogues. The smooth leather soles of the brogues slid around on the damp grass. His tweed jacket provided him with no protection against the wind. The thin cotton of his shirt might as well have been paper. He found himself thinking longingly of the North Face anorak he had in his suitcase back at the house. His hiking boots, which he'd made a neat square of at the bottom of the case. He was filled with regret at the mistake he'd made in his choice of outfit.

Cassie was wearing the same clothes she always wore. She had on a chunky black knitted sweater that reached halfway down the thighs of her tight black trousers. On her feet she wore her big black biker boots. This outfit had seemed perfectly chosen for the car journey, but it had adapted effortlessly to the outdoors. The scarf that had, in the car, hung loose over her shoulders was now deployed as a wrap to cover her entire head, the way desert explorers wrap themselves up in a sandstorm. With her outsized sunglasses spanning most of her face, all you could see of her was her neat little nose.

Seamus too seemed perfectly adapted to the elements. He was wearing jeans and boots, with a roll-neck jumper that he'd drawn right up to his chin. He was walking, without any apparent difficulty, into the full force of the wind. Cassie was only a few steps behind him.

'Wait for me,' said Christo, rushing to catch up.

Seamus turned to help Cassie down a steep path that led to the beach. She held a limp hand out to him as if for a kiss. Watching them, Christo felt an infantile pang of jealousy, followed quickly by a lurch of loathing for himself at being so foolish as to feel this way. Instead of following the path, he decided to take a short cut by jumping off a small verge. The jump was higher than he'd expected, and he landed hard on the sand with his two feet, shock waves passing through his spine.

'Okay?' asked Seamus, and Christo said yes out of pure bravado.

'Absolutely,' he said, rubbing the small of his back as he walked.

The beach that edged the island was the colour of bleached bone. Where the tide had gone out, the strand lay speckled with bog-black seaweed and seaweed-strewn rocks. The sun was behind them as they walked, casting their three shadows ahead of them on the sand. Cassie made a hop to try to escape hers, but it hopped to the side with her. She took her phone out of her pocket and ran ahead of the others, whipping back to photograph them as they walked towards her. Christo was aware of how very adult he and Seamus had become, walking in a sober line along the beach with their hands in their pockets, where once they would have been zigzagging wildly in search of some adventure or other.

'My father wants his body to go to medical science,' said Christo, with the sense that he was trying to outdo his sister. Just like when they were children, they were each of them vying for Seamus's attention. 'He says he likes the idea of his skeleton sitting around for eternity, playing poker with a bunch of medical students.'

Seamus laughed at that, and Christo swelled up with a ridiculous feeling of pride at having made him laugh.

'His body is a miracle of nature,' said Christo. 'The miracle is that he's still alive, after all the drugs he took.'

It was Christo's dad who'd first introduced his mother to drugs, handing her the seeds of her own destruction, while he himself walked clear of the wreckage. He was over thirty when he met her and living with his childhood sweetheart in a council house in the suburbs. He was working as a carpenter during the day and gigging in pubs at night, which was where they ran into each other. She was only twenty, a fledgling model living on her wits in London. There was a career as an independent woman in front of her for the asking. Instead, she found herself cast in the role of sidekick to his sudden rock stardom. The only modelling she did after that – a job that was unpaid – was to pose for the cover of his next album. She was pictured at the wheel of an open-top car, wearing a white dress and a slash of glossy red lipstick. Her long white head scarf ran like a ribbon in the breeze behind her as she drove. Christo's father was sitting in the back seat, all dressed in black.

The black clothing was his signature, an important part of his carefully curated image. He had occasionally been known to wear a white t-shirt when he was on holiday, but otherwise he stuck to a uniform of black shirt, black waistcoat and black denim jeans. A bandana around his neck which he would, in festive mood, push up over his forehead as a headband. He might have a go of Amanda's kohl eyeliner in the event of a party. There was a time when partying was all they did.

Christo was at boarding school in England by then, obliged to spend his school holidays with them in Devon. That was before the babies arrived, when the house was open to all comers, day and night. He arrived one Christmas Eve to find a rave in full flight. The doors were all flung open, lights on in every room, people dancing with unnatural energy in the sunken living room and spilling out the French doors onto the terrace, where a rig of disco lights had been set up. Christo took one look at the scene and made straight for his bedroom, where he rolled up a bath towel and placed it on the ground against the door to keep the sound out. He stuffed his ears with toilet paper and spent the next few hours sitting up in bed reading his book. He didn't even venture down for food, choosing instead to hunger it out until morning.

'Christo,' said his dad, when finally he appeared downstairs. 'Where did you spring from, man? I'd forgotten you were coming.'

He was standing at the counter grinding coffee. A motley assortment of guests sat around the table, still in their clothes from the night before. Christo had been hoping they wouldn't have heard about the incident in his room in the small hours – how a naked man tried to get into his bed, blind drunk and oblivious to Christo's presence – but it turned out the story had already been shared to widespread amusement.

'Poor Simon,' Amanda said. 'He's very hurt you threw him out. He was hoping it might be the start of something.'

They were all choking with laughter over their coffee and fags.

'Seems a shame to shut yourself off from new experiences at such a tender age,' said a woman Christo had never seen before. She was sitting barefoot at the table, wearing a sequined minidress and an ostrich-feather jacket.

'You never know,' said Christo's dad. 'You might even have learned a thing or two.'

It was that remark, more than anything else that did or didn't pass between them, that clouded Christo's relationship with his father. In the school holidays that followed, he always found an excuse not to go home, choosing instead to remain at school under the pretence that his people were away. He couldn't bear the thought of going back to that house, not because of the constant parties – those he could avoid – but because of the sad joke he was in their eyes. It was only when the parties eventually stopped and the children arrived that Christo had resumed, very reluctantly, his occasional visits to the house in Devon.

'I wouldn't be surprised if my father lives forever,' he told Seamus.

A man with an insatiable lust for self-preservation, his dad had in recent years been following a keto diet. Under Amanda's influence, he'd taken to drinking green vegetable juice every morning. He didn't smoke cigarettes anymore, only the occasional touch of pot that he ingested by way of a water pipe. He'd started practising Pilates on a daily basis, and he took human growth hormone, which he swore explained his youthful appearance. Christo suspected that plastic surgery had more to do with it, but he had no proof, and his father would never say.

'Tell me, do you see yours much?' he asked Seamus.

'As little as possible,' was the reply.

They'd reached the far side of the island, where a small crescent-shaped beach faced out to sea.

'I suppose you'd like to see him?' Seamus asked.

'We'd love to see him!' said Cassie, looking from one to the other of them. 'Where does he live?'

'Right there,' said Seamus, pointing to a white caravan stationed in a field beyond the beach. 'What you're looking at is Jim's permanent residence.'

27

Jim wasn't from Omey. It was Margo's people who were from the island. Her ancestors were among the nearly four hundred people registered as living there back in the nineteenth century. When Margo's father was born in 1935 there were fewer than seventy people in residence, and by the time of Margo's birth in 1957 that number had dwindled further to fifty. There was still a school, but it closed the year Seamus was born. After that, the last of the island's families gave up the ghost. Most of the dwelling places fell into dereliction, their stone walls sinking deeper and deeper into the undergrowth until they were barely distinguishable from the lichen-covered rocks that littered the ground. Those houses that were still habitable were rented out to holidaymakers during the summer, but they lay empty all winter. The only remaining year-round resident of Omey Island was Jim.

'Don't you want to take anything with you?' Seamus had asked, when Jim took it upon himself to move into the caravan. It was bought second-hand on DoneDeal and delivered by truck to the island. By then the house of Margo's ancestors was no more than a pile of stones they used for picnics in summertime.

'That's the thing about a caravan,' said Jim. 'There's no space in it for anything, only yourself.'

Ten years he'd been there, and in that time he'd gone from being a working man in his fifties – robust still, despite all his bad habits – to an old man of nearly seventy, retired and in ill health. The years of smoking and drinking had finally caught up with him. Not slowly, as you might expect, but all at once, the way a house of cards remains standing longer than is feasible and then collapses for no apparent reason. Along with the high blood pressure and the rheumatism and the bloated drinker's belly, he'd developed a cough like an outboard engine running out of juice.

'You should get that checked out,' Seamus ventured to say once.

'Ah, they'd only be at me to mend my ways. It's too late for that now. I'll die with my boots on, thanks.'

For several years, he'd been refusing the offer of a council house in Galway. He insisted on staying in the caravan out on Omey despite the cold and damp, which were a concern to the public health nurse, who traipsed out there every few weeks to check on him. There was no talking sense into him.

'Don't worry,' said Mary Quigley, who ran the pub that sat looking out over the tidal bridge of sand towards the island. 'I'll keep an eye on him. If ever he doesn't make it over for his pint, I'll be sure to ring you.'

Seamus was fully expecting to get the call any day now. Every time he drove over to the island, he was wondering would he find Jim dead and what kind of dead would he be? Knocking on the door of the caravan, he'd be asking himself would Jim be dead in the bed, or maybe lying on his side on the floor, wedged between the table and the bed? It was a surprise to Seamus every time he popped his mad head up alive.

'I'm going to need you to go to the library for me,' Jim had told him, six months back.

It was a grey afternoon in March and Seamus had parked his car out front, coming in the side door of the pub to find Jim already sitting up at the bar wearing his usual uniform of a V-necked lambswool sweater – sleeves pushed up to the elbows – and grey tracksuit bottoms. He had a pint of lager in front of him, as he always did. The only part that was surprising was the wellies he had on. They had a suspiciously clean look about them, like they'd been newly purchased. Come to think of it, it was that precise brand of welly that Mary sold in the shop beside the pub – an olive-green variety with a buckle on the side.

'Been shopping?' Seamus asked.

'I'm on Shanks's mare,' said Jim, which was how Seamus found out that he'd lost his licence. The visit to the Garda station he had somehow neglected to mention. Likewise, the plastic stitches that were required for the deep cut to his forehead. He only came clean with Seamus bit by bit, and most reluctantly.

'A small scrape,' he said, dismissing both the injury and the accident with the one word.

'Right,' said Seamus, waiting for more information.

'Ah, it was unfortunate.'

Three times over the limit, he'd clipped a squad car on his way into the library in town. There were two young guards in the car but, miraculously, neither of them was injured. Jim was lucky to get away with a disqualification.

'That's unfortunate alright,' said Seamus. 'Well, the walk is good exercise, at least.'

'Don't you start, now. That nosey-body of a nurse is at me to do yoga.'

He batted at the air around his ear with his right hand, as if he was batting away a buzzing fly.

'It's all about the flexibility of the spine,' said Seamus. 'The yogis believe that's what determines a person's age.' This he knew from Rhona, who was a great advocate of the yoga. 'I could get you a mat. You could set it up outside the caravan and do your sun salutations there every morning. You'd be standing on your head in no time.'

'Son?' said Jim, cocking his head to one side.

'Yeah?'

'Would you ever fuck off.'

In fairness, they did have a laugh together. It was usually at the expense of one or the other of them, but nonetheless funny for that. They were both of them able to take a joke.

'Seriously, though. Is there anything you want me to get for you? I could do some shopping for you in town. Stop by the chemist if there's anything you need.'

That was how the future would be – Seamus saw it in an instant. In refusing the offer of the council house, Jim was under the illusion that he was guarding his own independence, but there would be a cost for it and Seamus would be the one to pay. He'd start by doing the odd errand to the chemist's, but as sure as night follows day he'd end up wiping Jim's arse. In moving back here – in falling into the habit of regular contact with his dad – he'd walked into a trap he never even saw was there.

'Ah no,' said Jim. 'Sure, I can get everything I need here, except for the library books. I'll get you to bring them back for me and pick up some more.'

Jim had become a voracious reader in recent years, ploughing his way through the shelves of the library in town. Under the guidance of the local librarian, he'd been on a crime spree of late. Starting with Agatha Christie, who was a bit old-fashioned for Jim's liking. P. D. James was more like it, as was Ruth Rendell. Since then, he'd devoured Ian Rankin, Val McDermid and Michael Connelly in short order.

'That Harry Bosch knows his music,' he'd told Seamus. He wanted Seamus to contact Connelly to suggest some rare recordings of Art Pepper that Harry might enjoy.

'He doesn't exist, Jim. He's a fictional character.'

'Sure, that's neither here nor there,' said Jim.

'There is also the fact that I'm not your fucking secretary,' said Seamus, but he tracked down Michael Connelly's contact details anyway and sent him an e-mail. A week later he received a very courteous reply, which he printed and hand-delivered to Jim the next week in the pub. Jim took the e-mail from him and stuffed it in his pocket with all the ceremony of someone who'd been handed a pizza flyer.

'So, what's next?' Seamus asked. 'How about some Scandi noir? That was all the rage, a while back.'

'No, I've had enough of crime. If I read any more of that stuff, I'll end up killing someone myself. Better take a break from it.'

'Do you want me to choose something for you?'

'Laura knows what I like to read,' said Jim, referring to the librarian in town. 'She can choose something for me.'

Laura was from Manchester, originally. A river child, as she explained to Seamus, she'd grown up with an unexplained longing for the sea. Ireland was an accident in her life – ten years back, she came over with a friend for a weekend and never left. Unusually for a Mancunian lass, she didn't have a drop of Irish blood in her. You only had to look at her to see she was all Saxon, but she fell in love with the west of Ireland the moment she arrived. She stepped off the train in Galway, walked down to the quay, took a gulp of Atlantic air and knew she'd found her place in the world.

'Sir is tiring of crime fiction,' Seamus told her, as he returned his father's books.

Her eyes flared with interest.

'Right,' she said. 'Let's try him with something entirely different, then.'

Hovering at the library counter – and then, in time, over a meal in the pub across the road – she and Seamus had conspired to map out his father's reading. Like a doctor and nurse – she was the doctor, he the nurse – meeting to discuss a tricky patient's care arrangements, they deliberated on his vagaries. Taking pleasure in guessing what he might and might not like, Seamus always reported back to her what Jim had said, and they laughed at how wrong they often were.

'So, he hated the Updike. Boring, he said.'

Laura was delighted. Better to her than an appreciative reader was a reader who was hard to please. She took it as a personal challenge.

'Okay,' she said, reaching for a Philip Roth someone had just returned. 'Let's hit him with this.'

'That fella has his foot to the floor,' was the word that came back. Jim devoured the Carver stories she gave him next – 'mad head on him' – and he loved Flannery O'Connor. He didn't like Mailer, but Steinbeck was 'bloody magnificent'.

'Let's try him with Gore Vidal. The history novels should keep him quiet for a while.'

And if he annoys me, I'll bring him some Henry James, thought Seamus. It was nice to think he had that in his back pocket.

Laura was more of an Anne Tyler fan herself. Annie Proulx. Ann Patchett. She loved those American women. They had it over the men, was Laura's view, and after investigating them on her insistence, Seamus could not disagree. He found himself rereading them in search of the artistry they took such care not to reveal.

'Do you have to be called Ann?' he asked her.

'Not necessarily,' she said, citing Barbara Kingsolver, Alice McDermott, Lorrie Moore, Elizabeth Strout, in alphabetical order of course. 'You just have to make it look easy. The fellas are all hell-bent on showing us how *hard* it is to write a novel, what strength it takes, and courage. What superhuman endurance. But the hardest thing of all is to make it look easy, and the women get that. That's what I love about them.'

It was the delicacy of her that he liked. A delicacy that ran through her like the lettering in a stick of rock. From the white, papery skin of her fine-boned hands to her thin, wheaten hair. She had pale blue eyes that she set off by wearing willow-patterned dresses winter and summer. If it was cold or wet, she'd add a wool cardigan and a pair of lace-up leather boots.

'I made this cardigan myself,' she'd told him proudly, adding another small morsel to the growing pile of things he knew about her. For three months, they'd been having lunch together twice a week without ever seeing each other of an evening, allowing Seamus to fool himself into believing there was nothing between them, when he only had to look at her to know there was.

'So, are you going to marry this one?' Jim had asked him, only last week.

They were having a pint together at the bar, their backs turned to the huge picture window. The beach outside was slowly pooling with water as the tide turned. Jim had less than an hour to make it back to the island or he'd be stranded for the night.

'I hear you've been stepping out together.'

'Jesus,' said Seamus, 'what is this? Nineteen fifty?'

'You let that last girl get away. She was a good girl, but you let her get away.'

'It wasn't like that.'

'Was it not? It looked a lot like that to me. She would have married you in a heartbeat, but you didn't ask her. So, she went and married someone else.'

Seamus thought back to the day of Rhona's wedding. He'd been put at a ragbag table of old school friends and people from her office and, even then, Seamus was the odd man out. He slipped the waiter a few quid to leave an extra bottle of wine on the table and drank his way steadily to the bottom of it. After the meal, Rhona stood up to speak, as he knew she would. She went through the people who'd played a part in her life, but she did not mention him, which gave her speech a curious historical inaccuracy. The ten years they'd spent together had been conveniently disappeared. Watching Rhona and her new husband cut the cake under a barrage of camera flashes, Seamus felt like he was the baddie in a fairy tale. 'It's good to see her so happy,' he said to her bridesmaid, when they found themselves outside smoking beside a bonfire that had been lit in an oil drum. 'Do you know what?' she said to him. 'You're an awful gobshite.'

That was August, a year ago. By January, Rhona was on the phone telling him she was expecting twins. Seamus was happy for her – really and truly he was – but he couldn't help but feel he'd skipped a few pages in the life manual. It didn't help that Jim wasted no opportunity to fill him in.

'Sometimes you have to grab things,' said Jim, 'or they end up passing you by.'

'Like you did?' Seamus asked, with calculated calm, knowing this was as good as an invitation to a duel.

Jim paused, giving him a murderous stare.

'Yeah,' he says. 'Like I did. You know, for a smart fella, you can be awful thick. You might want to think about when you're going to start living your own life, instead of standing on the sidelines passing judgement on the rest of us.'

Seamus was so angry he could hardly breathe. An anger that grabbed him by the throat and choked him. The only thing that stopped him from retaliating was the treacherous voice in his head that was telling him Jim may not have been entirely wrong.

'Is there a charge for this?' he asked. 'Because I don't remember signing up for a head-shrinking session.'

He might as well have been trying to stop a train in its tracks.

'What are you so scared of, son? Are you afraid that someone might land a punch on you if you put your head above the parapet? That you'll be found out for the imperfect bloody human being that you are? Maybe you're worried that something good might happen to you for once, that some bit of happiness might come your way and you wouldn't know what to do with it, because you're so used to being miserable? Is that what you're so scared of?'

'Are you finished?'

But no, of course he wasn't. The ultimate performer, Jim was still only getting warmed up. He was ratcheting up the volume in preparation for the last verse, the one he knew would get the crowd clapping their hands over their heads and singing along.

'I've made mistakes, son, I won't deny that. But I'll say one thing in my defence. I was never afraid to love and be loved. To chicken out on love – that, to my mind, is the greatest sin of all.'

Seamus pushed his stool back from the bar and stood up, determined not to listen to another word. As far as Seamus was concerned, Jim had long ago lost the right to lecture him on life and how to live it.

28

Up close, it was clear that the caravan was in a state of dis-repair. It sat at an awkward angle, propped up by a stack of concrete breeze blocks. One of the windows was broken. Another was missing altogether, a piece of cardboard from a cereal box taped over the gap. Nettles grew in abundance around the base of the caravan. A rusted old Datsun Cherry was parked up nearby. Spare tyres lying around. Gas canisters. Oil drums to collect the rainwater. There were skeins of seaweed hanging along a barbed wire fence, giving it the appearance of a ghastly washing line.

'You are now entering paradise,' said Seamus, before climbing the breeze-block steps to the door of the caravan and banging on it. The door opened and a small black and white sheepdog peered out.

'Hiya, Gabriel,' said Seamus, bending to pet the dog.

Cassie hung back and watched as Seamus stepped into the caravan. From the doorway she had a partial view, over his shoulders, of the man sitting at the caravan's small, square table. A man with a shock of white hair, his face was heavily wrinkled, like the bark of an ancient tree. Only the blue, blue eyes were the same. If it weren't for the eyes Cassie would have had trouble believing it was him.

'Well, this is a surprise,' said Jim. 'To what do I owe the pleasure?'

'Just a social call,' said Seamus. 'We were in the area.'

When Cassie was a child, Jim had always seemed to her a big man, but she saw now that he was no more than average height. A stocky person once, he had shrivelled with age. The clothes he wore hung loose on him, like they belonged to someone bigger.

'You should have told me you were coming, son. I would have laid on some cake.'

'Wouldn't want to put you to any trouble,' said Seamus. The tone they struck between them was so sharp they might have been exchanging arrows rather than words. That's how it seemed to Cassie.

'And who is this lovely creature?' Jim asked, puzzled. 'Trust my son to find a beautiful woman in this God-forsaken place.'

'This is Cassie,' said Seamus, with both hands pushed deep into his jean pockets.

Cassie stepped forward, holding out her hand to him. Trapped by the table, Jim tried but failed to get to his feet. He hovered in a squat, moving Cassie's hand up and down as he stared at her.

'Cassie,' he said, with her hand still in his. 'Good God.'

He took his other hand and closed it over hers, making a sandwich of it as he sank back down onto the bench. 'Little Cassie, I don't believe it.'

He was feasting his eyes on her.

'I see it now,' he said, nodding in approval. 'You're your mother's daughter.'

Cassie tossed her head, like a horse, to shake off the compliment. All her life she had made the absence of vanity a central plank of her character, but despite all her efforts she could not conceal the desire to possess some small piece of her mother's unassailable beauty.

'I look nothing like her, if that's what you're thinking.'

'Your colouring is different, but you've something of her about you all the same.'

Christo stepped forwards, seizing that moment to make himself visible.

'Is it yourself, Christy?' said Jim, just as he always had. Whereas the child that Christo was would have blushed with pleasure, the man merely nodded.

'Jim,' he said. 'How good to see you.'

'Here. Sit yourselves down, for God's sake. Make yourselves comfortable.'

Jim shuffled round the table, making space for them to settle in either side of him. Seamus slouched at the edge, a belligerence in his attitude. They were all far too close for comfort.

'This calls for a drink,' said Jim. 'Let's see now, I can offer you whiskey or whiskey.'

'Jesus, Jim,' said Seamus. 'It's not even eleven o'clock.'

Ignoring him, Jim plucked a half-empty bottle of Paddy from its resting place on the windowsill. It sat among a clutch of tomato plants at various stages of ripening in recycled pot noodle containers.

'Seamus, reach behind you there, son, and grab some glasses.'

Twisting from the waist, Seamus did as he was told, and Jim splashed the whiskey out for them.

'Well, cheers,' he said, in a hurry to get the glass to his lips. 'Cheers.'

Cassie took a tiny sip and gasped as it passed from her mouth to the back of her throat. It burned all the way down, like she'd swallowed a hot coal. She could feel it smouldering down in her chest.

'I was very sorry to hear your mother had died,' Jim was saying, eyeballing them each in turn with his bloodshot blue eyes.

Cassie didn't know what to say, just as she had not known

what to say all those years ago at her mother's funeral when people offered her their condolences.

'It's alright,' she said, even though it was not and would never be in any way alright.

'I'd like to have been at the funeral,' said Jim, by way of apology.

'It was a long way to travel,' said Cassie, remembering nothing of the funeral itself, only the gathering of people in the incongruous sunshine outside the chapel when the service ended. A woman had handed her a white rose she'd plucked from one of the funeral wreaths. 'I thought you might like to keep this,' the woman said. 'To remember your mom's special day.' As soon as the woman moved away, Cassie threw the rose to the ground.

'All the same,' said Jim. 'I'd like to have been there to pay my respects.'

He raised a glass to them in a grim, silent toast, then drained what was left of his whiskey. Reaching forward to pick up the bottle, he offered a refill to each of them in turn, but they all refused. Jim helped himself to three fingers.

'Amateurs, the lot of you.'

There was a brief silence, then Cassie heard the sound of her own voice falling into it.

'Jim,' she said. 'Can I ask you a question?'

If she didn't ask it now, she never would.

'What was she like?'

Jim startled. 'What do you mean?'

'Well,' said Cassie, explaining herself with great precision. 'We were only children when she died. The memories we have are all from a child's point of view. We know nothing of the person she really was.'

In the moment that elapsed between Cassie's question and Jim's answer, another – deeper – silence fell over the table. Cassie watched nervously as Jim laboured to lift himself off the seat, patting his pockets in search of his cigarettes. Then he seemed to forget about them, dropping heavily back down.

'Jesus Christ,' he said, looking dazed. 'Where to start?'

He let out a noisy sigh that turned into a smoker's rattle. It ended in a coughing fit that took him a while to contain.

'You want to know what your mother was like?'

He was nodding rapidly to himself, like he was building up to something. A tongue protruding from his mouth and probing the dry reaches of his lips. His breath was slow and noisy.

'I'll tell you what your mother was like.'

There was in his delivery the long habit of carrying an audience. He paused, lifted the whiskey and drank from it, then carried on.

'She was a holy bloody mess.'

Cassie looked nervously across the table at her brother. He was working away at his fingers, like he was trying to solve a Rubik's cube.

'She was living her life as best she could, but she was terminally broken, like so many of us, by growing up in this blighted bloody country. This was no place for anybody with a bit of spirit, which was why your mother tried to escape it, but you can't escape what's inside you. It was always going to get her in the end.'

Cassie kept an eye on her brother's plaster-cast face, worried by the turn of the conversation, not for her own sake but for his.

'Your mother was a beautiful woman,' said Jim. 'But she couldn't see her beauty as a gift, so she used it as a weapon. She had oceans of talent but no self-belief, so nothing she did ever came to anything.'

He took a gulp of his whiskey, hardly pausing to swallow it before he went on.

'She was a work-in-progress, is what she was. She was like a human fucking building site. She was trying to make something of herself, only she didn't have the wherewithal.'

Cassie had forgotten, until that moment, her mother's repeated attempts at self-improvement. She was always embarking on some hopeful project – writing poetry or learning the guitar. Trying to become fluent in Spanish. Materials would arrive in the post – teach-yourself manuals or manuscript copies or collections of poems – and she would pore over them late into the night. Her ambitions would for a time soar, only to stall mid-air before crashing down to earth. She was like a little twin-engine plane, turning beautiful, brave circles in the sky only to spin out of control and fall, with tragic inevitability, into a fatal tailspin. Christo and Cassie had watched that pattern repeat itself, over and over again, throughout their childhood. Their house had been scattered with the wreckage.

'Your mother was doing her best, just like the rest of us. How far she succeeded is not for anyone to judge. It should be enough for you to know that she was doing her level fucking best.'

He threw back the last of his whiskey.

'Now,' he said, shuffling Cassie to the edge of the bench. 'If you'll excuse me, that's all you're getting from me. The rest of it is nobody's business.'

Cassie had to stand to let him out. She offered a hand to help him up, but he ignored it, struggling to his feet and making a desperate lunge for a fleece jacket that hung on a hook inside the door of the caravan. Patting the pockets to check his cigarettes were there, he ducked out the door and appeared a moment later outside the window in a puff of smoke, like a magician performing a trick on himself.

'Don't forget those library books,' he said to Seamus, poking his head back in the door and motioning to a pile of books that were stacked on the counter. They'd been bound in twine, with a looped knot as a handle.

'God forbid,' said Seamus, scooping them up and balancing them on his hip the way you might carry a sturdy baby. 'Now, are you right?'

The caravan was positioned to face west across the rocks to the open sea. The waves pounded the shore, sending fireworks of foam into the air. The only thing to break the skyline was a jagged piece of island.

'Cruagh Rock,' said Jim, indicating it with his cigarette hand. The rock had a small white house at one end. It was hard to imagine anyone living out there.

'It looks a little inhospitable,' said Cassie.

'Just a tad,' said Jim.

He was wearing nothing but a flimsy sweater on top. A pair of grey tracksuit bottoms had been tucked into his socks, as if he was about to go on a bicycle ride. On his feet were a battered pair of trainers.

'Aren't you cold?' Cassie asked him.

'Who, me? Never been cold in my life.'

He wrapped the fleece jacket about his waist instead of putting it on, knotting it like a climber's rope as he leaned into the elements.

'I'll walk you as far as the beach,' he said, holding the farm gate open for them to pass through. The dog spun off across the field, swallowed by the bumpy terrain. The last thing they saw was his white tail.

'That's rabbit city over there,' said Jim, as he closed the gate behind him. 'Gabriel lives in the hopes of catching one, but I wouldn't bet the house on it. Still, it gives him a purpose in life.'

Cassie hung back to wait for him while Christo and Seamus walked ahead. Together they crossed the field towards the beach, steering clear of a scattering of brooding cows. The cows all had triangular plastic tags stapled to their ears, like tribal decorations. They rotated their heads slowly to watch Cassie and Jim pass, their expressions disdainful.

'I've never felt easy around cows,' muttered Jim, with his head down. 'You get the feeling they're dying to attack you, only they can't be bothered.'

'You're a local,' said Cassie. 'I thought you'd be used to them.'

'Oh, that's where you're wrong,' said Jim. 'I am not and never will be a local here. I'm nothing but a gurrier from the city who came down to steal their women. I am tolerated because my son is one of their own, but I am still regarded by the natives with great suspicion.'

'And I thought it was just us,' she said, thinking of the harsh expression in Tilly Mannion's eyes when she'd looked at them. The fiddly little tasks that John Coyne had made a point of performing behind the bar the previous night before he came to take their dinner order. There was no escaping the measured nature of their welcome. 'I get the feeling that people round here don't like us very much.'

Jim didn't even try to deny it.

'John was Margo's cousin,' he said. 'Tilly was her best friend. Loyalty would be a big thing with them.'

They'd reached the beach, after a short scramble over lichen-speckled rocks. Sea campion grew on the fringes. There were big, bold sea daisies. A curious, cactus-like plant.

'Now,' said Jim, coming to a stop and laying his jacket down. 'This here is the greatest show on earth, and the auditorium is empty. We have the best seats in the house.'

He held his hand out in the manner of an usher.

'What about the others?' asked Cassie, watching them climb the path at the far side of the beach.

'Don't worry about them,' said Jim. 'They'll wait.'

She took a seat on his jacket, and he sat down beside her on the sand. Both of them facing out to sea as a wave gathered, rolling in from the deep in an impossible arc, until it rounded on itself and broke. When it did, there was a glimpse of an unearthly green within, a green more like molten glass than water. More hot than cold.

'Isn't that something?' said Jim, more to himself than to Cassie. 'Sometimes I sit here for hours and watch the waves and think. Other times I just sit here for hours and watch the waves.'

'I think that's called mindfulness, Jim.'

He spluttered a laugh. 'Is that what they call it?'

They watched as another wave gathered, and gathered, and gathered. Towering high, it trembled for a moment and then came crashing down. Cassie watched it, wondering how she would paint it. Would it be best captured in watercolours or oils? There was a time when she'd favoured watercolours, for the bleeding beauty of them. She later came to love the oily mess of acrylics. She'd worked with clay for a time, taking pleasure in the slippery offal feel of it. It was forgiving by nature, but there was something in Cassie that sought greater definition. The force of will that was required by stone. Stone was everything she needed it to be.

A cluster of small brown birds performed a ballet above the waves, whirling, rising, falling, before wheeling off to the right.

'What are those birds?'

'Oh, I'm the wrong man to ask. Margo knew the names of everything, of course. I don't know why I never thought to learn anything from her. One of the mysteries of life, I suppose. The endless fucking stupidity of mankind.'

Cassie watched the waves roll in, turning from darkest blue to glacial white as they travelled towards the shore.

'Now, young Cassie. Will we make tracks?'

He held out a hand to her. She was surprised by his strength as he hauled her up to standing.

'Okay,' she said, patting herself down for sand. She ran her hand through her hair. Took a gulp of air. 'Let's go.'

The wind had picked up while they'd been sitting there. The sand rushed in a fury along the ground. Cassie wound her scarf about her head for protection as she followed him. They caught up with the others on the headland, working their way in haphazard fashion around the mounds of tufted grass and the stray boulders and the rabbit holes until they'd reached them.

'Well?' said Seamus.

'This is where I leave you,' said Jim. He stooped to light a cigarette, making a wind-guard of one shoulder with surprising agility. He sparked up his lighter in a burst of small explosions. Only when he had the cigarette lit did he uncoil.

'Before you go, there's something I want to tell you.'

He stood with his feet planted firmly apart on the uneven ground, his mouth open in a ghastly gasp. Cassie felt a lurch of fear in her heart at what the thing might be. She looked nervously to Christo, then Seamus, before looking back at Jim.

'I want to tell you that your mother loved you.'

He jabbed the cigarette hand at them accusingly.

'I am a witness to the fact that your mother loved you,' he said. 'That's why you're here, isn't it? You're here because you need someone to tell you that. Well, I'll tell you. Your mother loved you, just as Seamus was loved by Margo. You were all three of you loved by your mothers.'

He stared fiercely at them for a moment, until he remembered the cigarette burning down in his hand. He held it to his mouth, taking a final ferocious pull before tossing it to one side.

'Now away with you,' he said. 'Let those poor girls rest in peace and, you lot, get on with your God-given lives.'

29

To get back to the car they took the same route they'd come, only in the opposite direction. The tide was coming in, so they were forced to climb up on the headland in places, descending a sandy path to cross each of the beaches before being forced up and over a headland again.

'Look,' said Seamus, pointing out where the island had at one time been joined to the mainland. He showed them the peat deposits that rose out of the sand, indicating where the land used to be. The granite that formed the backbone of the island was also a feature of the mainland. It was only when the sea rose, thousands of years ago, that the two were separated.

'Extraordinary,' said Christo, bending to touch the peaty ground.

'God, it's beautiful here,' said Cassie, whipping her head around to look at the sea that was coming in at a brisk clip over the beach. There was a silver sheen to the sand where an incoming wave had washed it wet, drying only briefly when the wave went out before being silvered again by the next one. 'When you're a kid, you don't notice how beautiful a place is. I had no clue how gorgeous it is here.'

'Yeah,' said Seamus. 'It's nice alright.'

The truth was that he seldom noticed the beauty of the place. All he saw in the landscape were its dark histories. He saw the serial drownings of fishermen in storms at sea, and the merciless damp that drove people to early graves in times past, and the bounty that was set on the heads of the poor borstal boys who ran away from the reform school into the hills above Letterfrack. It was a vicious history, known only to the locals, who had weathered these things and somehow survived. They had this over the holidaymakers who descended on the place in summertime, their cars loaded with surfboards and mountain bikes. They swarmed about the place with their wetsuits and their pedicures and their expensive sunglasses, before leaving their debris behind them and scurrying back to the city at the faintest hint of the long winter ahead.

Eight months of rain, you could count on. From October to May, it rained most days – if not for all of the day, then for a fair portion of it. Even in summer there were as many wet days as there were sunny ones, but Seamus didn't mind. The poor weather had protected the place in a way no preservation order could ever have done. It was a miracle to find somewhere of such natural beauty with no resort hotels, no high-rise apartment buildings, no oceanfront promenades lined with restaurants and nightclubs. Most days, you could walk the loop of Omey without ever encountering another soul, and if the weather was the price to pay for this miraculous solitude, then Seamus considered it a price well worth paying.

'I remember these!' said Cassie, bending down to photograph a branch of the thick sea-rods they'd once used as broomsticks. There were other varieties they'd pretended were snakes. A class of sea-bladder you could squeeze like bubble wrap to hear it pop.

'Here,' said Cassie. 'Look at this.'

She'd picked up something that had been washed in by the sea. It was the torn half-shell of a plastic water bottle, ridged along the spine and weathered by the water until it looked like the discarded exoskeleton of some transparent sea creature.

'It looks like some weird variety of lobster,' said Seamus.

'That's what I thought!' she said, lighting up with delight.

Seamus often saw lengths of orange rope that had taken on the appearance of a marine plant. The grills of those disposable barbecues could, in time, begin to look like an intricate piece of black coral. The same with the water bottle Cassie had found – it was almost as if the sea was trying to render native the rubbish it received from people.

'I'm going to keep it,' she said, sliding the bottle into her pocket. 'I think it's kind of cool.'

They came upon the remains of a sandcastle worn smooth by the sea. All that was left was a small mound where the castle had been. A moat around it, empty and waiting for the incoming tide. Seamus remembered how as kids they would form a chain to ferry buckets of water from the shallows to the moat of the castle they'd built. No matter how fast you worked, the moat always emptied itself faster.

'Wait a minute,' he said, as he realized that Christo wasn't with them. 'Where's your brother?'

They both turned and saw him standing several hundred yards behind them. He was holding his trousers up by a pinch of fabric in each hand, the way a woman holds the skirts of a long dress as she goes to climb a step. Hesitating as he negotiated the tidal puddles, he made a long leap, attempting to land ballet-style on his tiptoes to avoid wetting the whole foot. It was quite comical to watch.

'He'd be better off without his shoes and socks,' said Seamus.

'Hey, Christo!' Cassie was laughing so much she had difficulty getting the words out.

'Christo! Take your shoes off!'

Christo couldn't hear what she was saying, so the two of them tried it together, raising their voices in chorus against the wind.

'TAKE YOUR SHOES OFF!'

Christo couldn't, or wouldn't, hear them. He persisted in sidestepping the puddles in his shoes. They gave up on him and made their way back to the car. His face was grim when he joined them.

'Oh, that was funny,' said Cassie, with a sigh.

Christo didn't even smile. He took the car keys out of his pocket and bleeped the car open.

'I hope you didn't get too wet,' said Seamus, with as much solemnity as he could muster.

'I'm fine,' said Christo, but his face was like thunder.

'Are your socks wet?' asked Cassie.

'They're fine,' said Christo. 'Just leave it, okay?'

The air inside the car reverberated with silence after the roar of the wind. The pitch strained against itself, like the shudder of a sound system with the volume turned up too high. Christo lowered the driver's window, and it rebalanced.

'It was great to see your dad again,' said Cassie. 'He's absolutely wonderful.'

'Oh yeah,' said Seamus. 'He's wonderful, alright. A wonderful bloody pain in the arse.'

'Come on. You have to admit, he's a fantastic character.'

'In a novel, maybe. But he's a bit much in real life.'

'I think he's a sweetheart,' said Cassie.

She was in the back, with her head thrust into the gap between the two front seats, so she could look from side to side and see their faces.

'I wish you'd put on your seat belt,' said Christo, and Seamus saw he was still cross with them for laughing at his puddle-ballet performance. Seamus could see him struggling to regain his good humour.

'It must be lonely living out there,' Cassie was saying.

'Sure, he has the dog for company,' said Seamus. 'Nobody else would put up with him.'

Seamus was fond of the dog. Just as well, since his father had recently asked him to be the animal's guardian. 'Lest anything should happen to me,' said Jim. Like there was any chance that something *wouldn't* happen to him. The way Jim lived it was only a matter of time. The dog was a young dog. Someday soon, he'd be needing a home.

'Do they know what's wrong with him?'

Seamus counted the ailments off on his hand, thumb first.

'Diabetes. Emphysema. Deep vein thrombosis. If he doesn't stop smoking, they'll have to chop his legs off, one by one.'

'Jeez,' said Cassie, with a whistle.

'Couldn't he give up smoking?' asked Christo.

'Yes, but he won't. He figures what's the point. Reckons the heart attack will get him before the cancer does.'

'Doesn't that worry him?'

'His own father was dead at forty,' said Seamus, by way of an answer. 'He never expected to live this long. He sees himself in injury time, says he'd prefer to keel over on the pitch than die on the bench.'

'I suppose that's one way of looking at it,' said Christo.

'It is,' said Seamus, even though there was in the choices Jim had made a singularity that was hurtful to Seamus. The choice to live in the caravan, to eat out of the frying pan and piss out the door – the grass in summer smelled of whiskey and ammonia – and not care from day to day if you lived or died was an insult to his son, who wanted him to go on living, despite his many and obvious faults.

'Look,' said Seamus, as they rolled into town. 'You can drop me off here. I'll see you back at the house.'

They pulled in by the bookshop, where Seamus had left

his car. Cassie and Christo went up the street towards the supermarket. Seamus headed in the opposite direction, with the library books tucked under his arm. The dead weight of them was a comfort to him, as it had been all his life. He'd first taken refuge in fiction as a child, cut loose by his mother's death and trailing after his father on their annual circuit of the Irish bars of Blighty. In libraries all over England, Seamus threw himself on the mercy of kind ladies who could not refuse him the loan of a book, even though the only address he had was the address of a boarding house. Seamus would race to finish the books before they moved on to the next town, but all too often there was no time. 'Ah, just leave them there for the landlady to bring back,' his dad would say, as if there were a snowball's chance in hell that the landlady would bring them back. From time to time, even now, Seamus would wake in the night, troubled by the thought of all those unreturned library books.

'Hiya, Seamus,' said the postman, who was loading a mail bag into his van.

'Hiya, Martin,' said Seamus, raising a hand to wave.

'Seamus,' said the woman who owned the gift shop across the road. 'How's tricks?'

'Miriam,' said Seamus. 'How's it going?'

The building that housed the library was no more than a converted shop, with a lobby inside the door that was lined with community noticeboards. The boards were peppered with small ads that struck the fear of God into Seamus. There was Zumba in the church hall. Night courses in herbology. A listening service for older people. Seamus could see his whole life laid out in front of him in those small ads. His whole life if he stayed put.

Pushing the heavy fire door with the flat of his hand, he stepped into the hush of the reading room. There was a mother sitting on a low chair in the children's section, reading in a whisper to a little kid from a picture book. Otherwise, the place was empty.

'Well,' said Seamus as he approached the desk. 'I bear instructions from your most awkward customer.'

Laura had her head bent over the keyboard. When she looked up, he couldn't help but notice the change that came over her face, like the beat of a bird's wing, revealing the delicate plumage underneath. She was glad to see him.

'Hang on there,' she said. 'I'm just putting in an order.'

Seamus deposited the returned books on the counter and hovered as she punched away at the keys. He could hear his father's voice in his head as he waited.

'That girl's not getting any younger,' Jim had said, recently. 'She must be thirty-five, if she's a day. If you're going to do the right thing by her, you'd want to get a move on.'

Tilly Mannion had told him the same thing only the other day. 'I hope you're not wasting that girl's time. I'm sure she'd like to have a family. I hope you won't stand in her way.'

'What is this?' Seamus had asked Tilly. 'The valley of the squinting windows?'

It was the sense of being watched that he couldn't bear. The desire for a public spectacle, like the crowd at a bullfight roaring for blood. What they wanted to see, in this case, was a ring. They wanted a wedding, with the doors of the church open for anyone to come in and watch him walk Laura down the aisle. That was bad enough, but it was the thought of a baby that really put the fear across him. Not the baby so much as the buggy that would inevitably be required. He couldn't see himself wheeling a buggy down the street for everyone to see. You might as well walk naked through the village.

'Time was when someone would take a fella like you by

the scruff of the neck and tell him to piss or get off the pot,' Tilly had said.

Laura had no family around the place to perform that task. No father or brother to have a quiet word with Seamus, so Tilly had taken it upon herself. Seamus had received the message loud and clear, and while he wasn't about to marry Laura just because Tilly Mannion said he should, there was in his heart the sinking knowledge that she wasn't wrong. Laura liked kids – he'd heard her talk fondly of her nieces and nephews in Manchester. There was no reason to think she wouldn't like to have some of her own.

'They're looking for a substitute teacher up at the school,' she'd told him, the last time they had lunch. 'The history teacher they have has cancer. She'll be out until Christmas at the very earliest. She might not be back at all.'

'I don't have a HDip,' he said. It was an easy out.

'Oh, I don't think that would bother them. They'd hire you in a heartbeat.'

Seamus pictured himself standing in front of a class of lumpen teenagers. The smell of dope wafting off them in the heat of the classroom. The ammonia stink of fake tan. Seamus had seen those kids dragging themselves about the town. He knew what a good teacher could do for them. Knew that he could be that teacher. He just wasn't sure he wanted to be.

'I've this book to write,' he said, knowing full well as he said it that it was only an excuse. The writing of the book was hardly a job, even if it had expanded, like the foam builders use to fill cavities, to take over his entire day. It could easily be done in the evenings after a day's work, or at the weekend.

'So, will we get some lunch?' she asked him now. She was already slipping her arms into the sleeves of her cardigan.

'Do you know what?' he said to her, before he even knew what he was doing. 'I'm going to have to take a rain check on the lunch.'

He hardly recognized the sound of his own voice as he said it. The words he'd used were not his own. The use of the term 'rain check', in particular, was beneath him.

'Oh!' she said.

Her face was lifted towards his, her eyes shining as she waited for him to explain. He couldn't have felt worse if he'd kicked her.

'I have to get back,' he said. 'There's some friends of my mother's visiting. I said I'd eat with them later.'

She frowned, and he could see that she was struggling to weigh the excuse in her mind. Her inclination to be trusting competing with her intelligence. She was too smart not to know when she was being brushed off.

'No worries,' she said, drawing her dignity over her face like a veil. 'It's a movable feast if ever there was one.'

She had a pile of new books ready and waiting for him on the counter.

'The Bukowski arrived. I think he'll enjoy it.'

'Okay, great stuff,' he said, picking the books up. 'I'll have them back to you next week.'

Leaving the library, Seamus headed back down the hill towards Stanley's drapery shop, where he bought three new pairs of socks to replace his old ones with holes in them. He stopped at the delicatessen across the road to buy a tin of coffee. An expensive brand of coffee was one of the few luxuries he allowed himself, apart from the car. The car was a BMW, second-hand of course and purchased as a trade-in against the Nissan Micra he'd started out with. It was a vanity to buy a BMW, but God he loved that car. It had silvery-green paintwork and a walnut dash and tan leather seats.

Seamus liked to lean the driver's seat back as far as it would go and drive, astronaut-style, around the wilds of Connemara. He felt the romance of the open road, just as he had as a child, sitting in a car of sand on the beach with his mother.

'Where to today?' he heard her say. 'Ulan Bator? Kalamazoo?'

The radio came on with the ignition, the afternoon phone-in show fielding a row between some angry Dubliners over cycle lanes in the city. Seamus cruised the other stations until he found one that was playing music that agreed with him. To the sound of Talking Heads, he followed the one-way system of traffic that circumvented the town's three main streets, taking a left at the bottom to follow the wide bend in the road that led south, leaving the backside of the town behind him in the rear-view mirror. The car was full to bursting of warm sunshine, the sweep of the road smooth under the wheels of his beloved car as the radio segued into Van Morrison, which was alright by Seamus. He had everything he required for him to be happy, so why did he feel so unaccountably bad?

30

It was Cassie's idea to invite Seamus to dinner, but only after she'd issued the invitation did she remember that she couldn't cook. For the first time in her life, she found herself wishing she could. A primitive desire in her to nourish Seamus. He had the look of someone who lived on nothing but cigarette fumes. She thought of Eduardo's mother, who had weighed him as a child, paying the cook commission if he'd put on any weight. It occurred to her that maybe that was the problem between her and Eduardo. All that mothering had left him too rounded. She couldn't find anything to hold on to.

'I thought maybe you'd fallen off the edge of the earth,' he said, when she called him.

She was sitting in the car, which they'd parked near the supermarket. With all the windows shut, it had the closed-in feeling of a phone booth. Their conversation took on a radio-quality gravitas.

'It does feel a bit like that,' she said, peering through the windscreen at the three flags flying over the town's roundabout. One of the flags was Irish and one was American. The third she didn't recognize.

'Are you making progress?' he asked her.

'Yes,' she said. 'We found our friends. Some of them anyway. The mother's dead.'

'Naturally,' said Eduardo. 'Twenty-five years is a long time.'

'Tomorrow, we go to the school my mother attended,' said Cassie, speaking in English but using Spanish syntax. The effect of this was to make her conversation more

243

mechanical, less personal. 'How are things with you?' she asked, anxious to change the subject. 'Where are you now?'

'Stuck in traffic on Reforma,' he said. 'Where I spend half my life.'

Cassie saw him from above, as if she were watching him from a traffic helicopter. He was sitting at the wheel of his shiny new VW Bug, with the windows firmly rolled up to keep the thieves out and the air con in, the radio tuned to a classical music station. Eduardo had a sports utility vehicle that he used for his trips to the mountains, but he liked to use the Bug around the city. A clutch of loose change in the pocket of the car door to hand out to the kids who stepped forward to wash his windows at the traffic lights. Cassie was always struck by the patrician ease with which he distributed these alms.

'How's Mexico managing without me?'

'Badly,' he said. 'I am sorry to inform you that Mexico is not managing at all well without you. Mexico requires you to return with immediate effect.'

'Oh,' said Cassie. 'I'm not sure I can comply with that requirement.'

She twisted a little in her seat, looking out the side window of the car to where a row of brightly painted shops wound in a gentle arc down the hill. The vast, noisy spread of Mexico City seemed impossibly far away.

'What are you doing now?' asked Eduardo.

'I'm waiting in the car while my brother gets a haircut.'

'And what will you do then?'

'Go back to the house. Cook. Eat. Sleep.'

She noticed that she had avoided mentioning they were having Seamus to dinner. It was in her mind to mention it – she knew of no reason why she wouldn't – but still she didn't. Instead, she found herself engaging in a subterfuge that was entirely and absurdly unnecessary.

'I miss you,' he said.

'Yo también,' said Cassie, not sure if it was the truth she was telling or a lie. 'Me too.'

When the call had disconnected, she let the phone fall into her lap, leaning her forehead against the frame of the car door. In the wing mirror, she saw Christo coming around the back of the car. His hair was cut close to his head, and he was carrying several large paper bags, which he stowed on the back seat without a word of explanation. Despite her curiosity, Cassie didn't ask him what he'd bought, because to do so would rupture the shimmering soap bubble that separated her from the rest of the world. As Christo started the engine, she curled up in her seat, seeking a cold kind of comfort in her isolation.

Back at the house, they unpacked the shopping together, but Christo declined all her offers to help with the dinner. He'd found a battered old cookbook on the kitchen dresser and was sitting at the table happily perusing its index. How Christo loved an index!

Cassie poured herself a hot bath. The water that came out of the tap looked like weak tea. She heard ripples of her mother's voice, like an echo in a canyon.

'Sure, that's only bog water. Bog water does wonders for your skin.'

Cassie filled the bath as high as it would go. Her feet were cold to the point of numbness from the tiled floor. Her toes burned when they came into contact with the hot water, but she ignored the pain, stepping one leg in and then the other. She slid down into the bathwater, giving a shudder of pleasure as her shoulders dipped beneath the surface. Closing her eyes, she bent her knees, shunting her hips forwards so that her head disappeared under the water. When she came up again her hair was wet through and she began to shampoo it, her arms struggling to counter the torpor induced in her by the hot water. She dipped down again to rinse out her hair, twisting it into a knot above her head as soon as she was finished.

With the sense of someone preparing herself for a ritual sacrifice, she began to shave her legs. Careful not to nick herself, she shaved her bikini line and her underarms not once, but twice, to catch any stray stubble. Impatient now, she hauled herself up and stood for a moment, knee-deep in the bathwater, studying her reflection in the foggy mirror. She saw the shape of a woman, heavier than she would like to be, with large full breasts. She saw the figure curve in at the waist and out again over the hips. She turned slightly to one side and followed the line of her spine down to where it hollowed out at the small of her back, with two deep dimples showing above the cheeks of her bum. She stared at her reflection with interest and, for the first time in her life, she understood why men found women's bodies so attractive. From deep within her came a flash of vanity, something as unfamiliar to her as it was surprising. She wanted very much for someone to see that she was young and beautiful. She wanted someone to wallow in her beauty and understand the precious transitory nature of it. She wanted someone to remember it when it was gone. Shocked by the force of her own narcissism, she stepped out of the bath and reached for a towel.

She was standing at the sink doing her make-up when Christo appeared in the mirror.

'Wow!' she said, for want of anything else to say. She paused in applying her mascara, her eyes wide open and staring, as her brother displayed himself, arms out to the sides, for her to see.

'Well, what do you think?'

She turned, with her mascara wand held high, and saw

that he had performed a makeover on himself. He had exchanged his baggy corduroy trousers for a pair of dark blue jeans. The lambswool sweater was gone and, in its place, he was wearing a loose linen shirt. He had a wispy blue scarf looped twice around his neck and a new pair of Adidas sneakers on his feet. Cassie's shock at her brother's sudden transformation was matched only by a terrible tenderness for him. She didn't know what to say.

'I felt it was time for me to update my look,' he said, glancing down at his chest, as if to remind himself of what it was that he was wearing.

She nodded slowly, toying with what to say. She was aware that Christo was the one person in the world she was capable of being truly cruel to. Like a bear faced with the choice of eating a small animal or letting it get away, it was up to her how she used her power.

'It works,' she said. 'I like it.'

'Oh, good,' he said happily, and ducked out of the doorway. As Cassie resumed the job of applying mascara to her lashes, she couldn't escape the feeling that she and her brother were both preparing for a date with the same person. She, with all the practised artifice of womanhood. He with the fledgling awkwardness of a newly hatched chick.

She stared into the mirror, studying the face she saw there as if it belonged to someone else. She saw the efforts that had been made to soften its forbidding features, with the judicious use of blusher and a subtle eyeshadow that gave her eyelids the shimmer of the inside of a shell. By combing her thick eyebrows and carefully applying a line of black eyeliner to the insides of her lower eyelids, she had sunk her deep-set eyes even further into her face, making them dangerous and yet somehow alluring. Her hair had been carefully dried, and then mussed.

She made a last-minute adjustment to her plan, choosing a deep red shade of lipstick instead of her customary pale pink gloss. The lipstick went on like a scream, tracing the bow of her upper lip a fraction wider than it really was. The bottom lip took the stain of the lipstick in one long sweep. She checked herself in the mirror, noticing how the make-up had turned her into a different person – someone brave and bold and maybe even beautiful. She smacked her lips and went to join her brother in the kitchen.

Punctual to a fault, Seamus arrived two minutes late for dinner at eight. With his shirt freshly ironed and a bottle of red wine gripped by the neck, he stood at their door. The night was blustery behind him, swathes of cloud sweeping in from the south. The sea shifted with sinister intent. When the door opened a gust of wind forced it wide, throwing Seamus inside with it.

'Oops,' said Cassie with a laugh, as she was blown back with the door.

She was dressed like a cat burglar in a black polo neck, slim black trousers and black ballet shoes. Her hair was as glossy as seaweed. Her lips, as red as freshly spilled blood. Seamus brushed past her to go through to the kitchen and caught the decadent scent of jasmine, as surely as if he'd walked under an overhanging bough. Fighting a desire to turn towards the source of the scent, the way you would bend your face to a flower, he stepped into the kitchen.

Christo came to greet him, wearing someone else's clothes. The collarless shirt he had on was made of white linen. The blue jeans were so new and crisp that you could hear them crunch as he moved. The runners looked like those shoes that are sold for babies who are too small to walk. The scarf was a mysterious touch, too thin to provide any warmth, too plain to be decorative. Seamus could not imagine what it was for. He tried not to betray his surprise as he handed Christo the wine.

'That's most kind of you, thanks,' said Christo, taking the

bottle and turning it round in his hand to look at the label. He began to remove the foil from the neck, inexpertly, using a small knife.

'I've already opened some white,' said Cassie, reaching up to take two wine glasses down from the overhead cabinet. Seamus was reminded of the triangle they'd formed as children – the two of them always at odds with each other, and him in between.

'You've left me out,' said Christo, stretching up to fetch a third and placing it beside the others. Seamus noticed how Cassie paused momentarily in pouring out the wine to glance at her brother in surprise.

'Well!' she said, when they were standing in a circle facing each other, with their glasses in hand. 'To the long-overdue reunion of the Society of the Third Magnitude.'

Seamus raised his glass to theirs, remembering what he had up until that moment entirely forgotten. The secret society they'd formed as children. The membership cards they'd made. The den they'd carved out for themselves in the box room. A door had been opened that until now had remained stubbornly closed.

'We even had a secret language,' said Cassie. 'Do you remember? You had to swap the first and last letters of every word.'

Seamus smiled, but he was troubled by his own faulty recollection. How could he have forgotten all these things that Cassie seemed so effortlessly to recall? He looked over at Christo and saw that he too was struggling with the same question. Of the three of them, hers was by far the best memory. Seamus rested his eyes on her and waited, wondering what door she was going to throw open next.

'You guys were so mean to me!' she said, in a spurt of indignation. 'You used to lock yourselves in your room. You wouldn't let me in.'

Christo retrieved the bottle of white wine and went about refilling their glasses as Cassie was talking.

'You buried me on the beach one day and left me there!'

Seamus smiled, remembering how they'd worked up a frenzy with their plastic spades to pile her high with sand. The sand was slightly damp, and it split as you tamped it down. He recalled the intimacy of the task, how they used the palms of their hands to flatten the sand over her thighs, her belly, her chest, her shoulders. They left her head out, of course, so they could hear her shouting at them as they ran away. Their knees buckling under them, like soldiers running under heavy gunfire. It was hard to run when you were convulsing with laughter.

'Your mom had to dig me out,' said Cassie. 'I'd probably still be there if it wasn't for your mom.'

'You boys be kind to Cassie now,' Margo used to say. 'You're older than her, and you're both boys. Make sure you don't leave her out.'

As if there were any chance of that. Cassie was always more than a match for Christo and Seamus.

'Time to eat,' said Christo now, pulling on the dinner bell.

The vast square table in the kitchen was too large for the three of them. It was big enough to seat two people on each of its sides, or three at a squash, but instead they each of them occupied one side alone. The effect was to accentuate the formality of the occasion. If he wanted butter or salt, Seamus had to ask for it. To top up the wine, Christo had to stand and lean over the table like a waiter. To gather up the starter plates, Cassie had to move around the perimeter, clearing from the left like a waitress in a silver service restaurant. The same when she was serving the main course of hake baked in foil with herbs and lemon slices. There were roasted baby potatoes and buttered broccoli and green beans.

Seamus didn't usually eat greens, but he did so now out of politeness.

'This is delicious,' he told Cassie.

'Oh, don't look at me,' she said. 'It was Christo who did everything. I don't know how to boil an egg.'

'Good job, Christo,' said Seamus. He had to launch his words through the space, as if he was throwing a paper airplane across the table.

Christo hardly acknowledged the compliment, immersed as he was in the food. He was eating somewhat voraciously, it seemed to Seamus. He wondered could Christo be drunk, but it hardly seemed possible. They'd only been through the one bottle of white wine and a third of a bottle of red.

'So, you live in Mexico?' Seamus asked Cassie, with all the courtesy of a stranger. There was the curious duality of knowing her and not knowing her. One minute he saw in her the familiar features of the little girl she once was, with the same laugh and the same fizz in her black eyes. The next minute she was someone he barely recognized, a grown woman with a life he could not presume to know. Seamus watched her face flicker between the two.

'Yes,' she said. 'I've been there for nearly ten years.' She seemed surprised by the tally. 'I like it there. I like to be a foreigner in someone else's country. I like speaking a language other than my own. It makes me feel free.'

'You're the opposite to me, so.'

As Cassie waited for him to explain, Christo herded his knife and fork together on his empty plate and looked up, dazed.

'I always thought I'd live anywhere other than here,' continued Seamus, addressing Cassie, with one wary eye on Christo. 'As a kid, I was hell-bent on getting out of here. But as I get older, I've discovered a macabre fascination for the

familiar. I know the back story here. I know all the characters. I've a grisly interest in seeing how it all turns out.'

Something he had explained to Rhona only recently. They
were in the habit of speaking to each other regularly on the
phone. It was always her who called him, not the other way
around. She might ring him while she was waiting on the
platform for a train, or queuing to renew her driver's licence.
One time she called him while she was sitting in her obstetri-
cian's consulting room waiting for a scan.

'The home scar,' she'd said. 'That's what they call the mark
limpets make on the rock when they return.'

'Wait, they leave the rock?'

'Yes, of course. How else would they survive? They have
to move to feed on algae, and when they re-attach, they
return to the exact same spot. Their shells adapt to the shape
of the rock. They create their own dent in the stone. It's
known as the "home scar".'

It was Rhona's voice Seamus was hearing, but he could see
that Christo was speaking.

'Sorry, what did you say?'

Christo was staring at him with great intent, waiting for
the answer to a question Seamus hadn't heard him ask.

'Did you stay on here after your mother died?' he repeated,
lobbing the question across the table like a hand grenade. He
seemed to have no awareness of the careful line the conversation was taking before he entered it. It was clear to Seamus
now that Christo was drunk. His skin was mottled, the
expression in his eyes troubled with danger. He raised his
glass of wine to his lips and drank from it with great determination. For all the pleasure he took in it, he might as well
have been drinking poison.

Cassie reached out for the water jug and filled a glass,

sliding it towards her brother. He ignored it, refilling his wine glass instead.

'No,' said Seamus. 'No, we moved around a bit.'

With his mother gone and her steady teacher's salary gone with her, Jim had been the sole breadwinner in the family. There was some piecemeal demand for him as a session musician but not enough to make ends meet, so once a year he would hit the road to Dublin and take the boat to Holyhead with Seamus in tow. Never in one town for more than a day or two, they pounded the motorways of England, working the folk clubs and the Irish pubs and the college bars for a cash fee and a few free pints. Seamus would find a seat in a corner somewhere and wait out the gig with a book, his eyes straining to see the pages in the poor light. On the way back to the bed and breakfast they might stop off for fish and chips, eating as they walked, with his dad's raincoat draped over them to fend off the drizzle. The next morning Seamus would breakfast alone on multiple miniature boxes of Frosties, while his dad snored off the night before.

'It's a miracle I managed to complete my education,' Seamus said to him once. 'Considering I missed out on half my schooling.'

For years, he'd drifted on and off the school roll, going missing for months at a time before appearing again without warning. The teachers spoke to Jim about it, but he wouldn't hear of leaving Seamus behind.

'Christ, son,' said Jim. 'I did my best! The only other option was to leave you with the nuns, and I wouldn't have left a dog with those people. You have me to thank for that.'

Tilly Mannion would have taken him in. Tilly was only dying to mother him, but Jim was too proud to leave him with Tilly, so he took him on the road instead.

'Poor motherless chuck,' Cynthia used to say. Cynthia was

a girlfriend of his father's. These days you would probably describe her as a lover. She was a good person, Cynthia, with her painted-on eyebrows and her orange hair. She was kind to Seamus, making him tinned tomato soup and crinkle-cut chips that she cooked up in her rancid deep-fat fryer. 'Give us a love,' she would say to him. Reluctantly he would let her hug him, trying not to think about her big cushiony breasts and what his father might have been doing with them.

Cynthia lived in a little flat above the newsagent's shop that she owned in Liverpool. She used to let Seamus borrow the books from the shop so long as he was careful not to break the spine. Among her stock were paperbacks by Stephen King and Tom Clancy and Frederick Forsyth, and Seamus read them all. He read the Ian Fleming novels. He read Sidney Sheldon, on Cynthia's advice, and was thrilled by all the sex. The books still had to be sold after he was finished, so Seamus was terrified of making so much as a thumb mark on them. Even after all these years, Seamus would no more turn down the corner of a page, or leave an open book face down, than he would throw it on the fire.

'The way my dad worked, it was a bit of a gypsy life.'

He was aware that he was trying to cast it in a romantic light, when the truth of it was that they'd lived like vagrants.

'It sounds infinitely preferable to life with my grandma,' said Cassie. She was taking a breath to say more when Christo cut in. He was training all his attention on Seamus.

'I was stuck in boarding school,' he said. 'When the school holidays came around, the housemaster would ask for volunteers to take me home with them. If nobody put their hand up, I would have to stay at school.'

He gave a crumpled laugh and the glass he was holding wobbled, throwing a spray of red-wine droplets over his new shirt. When the glass listed the other way a wave of wine slopped over the side, casting a seeping red pool over the clean tablecloth.

'Christo,' said Cassie, reaching across and laying a hand on the table in front of him in an attempt to stay him. Whether he noticed the gesture or not, it had no effect. He kept on talking.

'The housemaster took me home to his place out of pity. I even spent Christmas there once. I had nowhere else to go.'

Christo was directing these confidences at Seamus with a deadly intensity. He did not so much as glance at his sister, keeping his eyes on Seamus the whole time. Seamus had the sense they were playing a game of cards. With every hand, Christo was raising the stakes.

'Sad,' he said to Seamus, laying the word down like an ace.

'Very sad,' said Seamus, thinking if this was a contest for the worst childhood, then he had a fair shot at winning. It wasn't a game he had any interest in playing.

'You'll have to excuse me,' he said. 'I'm going to nip outside for a smoke.'

Standing in the open doorway, Seamus took a pre-rolled joint from his breast pocket. He lit it and pulled the prickly smoke down into his lungs, holding it there for a moment until he could feel it do a lap of his body. Like the swirl a whiskey drinker gives his glass, Seamus liked to savour the feeling of the smoke inside him before he blew it out. His mind was momentarily stilled by it.

The night was closing in. A long, slow dusk settling over the landscape in greys and mauves. The sun had slid down behind the clouds, so that only their crimped edges were still alight, like the edges of a paper taper you might use to light a fire. Another moment and the fire had gone out. Seamus tossed the roach of his joint over the wall and turned his back on the falling night.

32

Back inside the house, the table had been cleared and Cassie was making coffee. Christo was leaning over the CD player on the kitchen counter, staring at the controls with drunken concentration. He hit a button and the room was filled with the sound of Patsy Cline. What is it about holiday houses and Patsy Cline? thought Seamus. No sooner had the first track started than Christo stopped it again. Seamus watched as he swayed precariously, trying to focus on the buttons. He weaved to the left and then far out to the right, moving his standing foot in a disastrous attempt to steady himself. Seamus just about caught him before he fell.

'Oops,' he said, as Seamus righted him. 'I was trying to put on some music. The occasion calls for dancing.'

'The occasion calls for coffee,' said Cassie, setting the pot down on the table as her brother grabbed her. He seemed not to have noticed there was no music playing. He took her hand and raised it high, steering her by the hip with the other hand as he shuffled her round in awkward circles between the fridge and the table. Over his shoulder, she threw a look of despair at Seamus. The despair turned to alarm as Christo attempted to bend her back on herself. She twisted out of his grasp, and he lurched forwards, missing the open stove door by inches as he hit the floor face first.

'Okay,' said Cassie. 'I think it's time you went to bed.'

He lay sprawled on the ground, trying to raise his head.

Seamus thought of a fish lying in the bottom of a boat. The helpless way he was flapping around.

'Can you help me?' asked Cassie, kneeling by her brother's side.

Together they flipped him over, and Seamus slid his arms under Christo's armpits, dragging him along the floor towards the kitchen door. Cassie cleared the way, moving obstacles aside and opening the door wide for them. Christo was surprisingly light, for a man of his height, and Seamus had no trouble dragging him along the corridor towards the bedroom. It took the two of them to raise him to his feet and topple him onto the bed.

'I'll take it from here,' said Seamus.

Once she was gone, he went around the base of the bed and slipped Christo's sneakers off his feet. He noticed there was a price sticker on the sole of one of them, and the sight of it made him feel very sorry for Christo. In a quick glance around the room, he saw the striped pyjamas neatly folded over the back of a chair. He saw the navy dressing gown hanging from the wardrobe door. There was a wastepaper bin by the bed, and in it he saw the discarded tags of the new clothes Christo had bought. Seamus was just about to creep out, leaving him fully clothed on the bed, when he saw that Christo's eyes were open and watching him.

'Do you know what I wish?' he asked, in a voice that was higher than his usual register, but surprisingly steady.

Seamus moved towards the door, followed by Christo's eyes.

'I wish we were children again,' said Christo, just as Seamus had feared he would.

'Ah, that's just the wine talking.'

Seamus slid behind the door and held it in front of him as a shield. He would have liked to retreat, but it seemed rude.

Instead, he remained where he was, powerless to stop the words that were pouring out of Christo.

'I wish we were back in our bunk beds, just the two of us. We were like Ernie and Bert.'

It was said without any hint of irony. Was it conceivable that Christo didn't know that Ernie and Bert were gay icons? The innocence of him was shocking.

'I don't like being an adult,' he was saying. 'The adult world is too complicated. It was much easier when we were kids.'

Seamus was struck by how fluent he was, despite his drunkenness. There was no slur to his words, no hesitation. The soliloquy he was embarked on was whimsical and vociferous and ferociously articulate. It reminded Seamus of the time he'd waited by Rhona's bed as she woke from surgery to remove her appendix. The anaesthetic they'd given her might as well have been a truth drug for the stream of consciousness she unleashed as she lay in recovery. Seamus learned more about her hopes and desires in that half-hour than he did in ten years of living with her. Enough to scare the life out of him.

'You should get some sleep,' said Seamus, desperate to be out the door.

'Yes,' said Christo, submissive as a child. 'I'll get some sleep now. But I just wanted you to know that I hate being a grown-up. I wish I could be a kid again.'

'Okay,' said Seamus, pausing for a moment to indicate that he'd given the revelation due thought, before adding, very gently, 'goodnight, Christo.'

Cassie was sitting by the window, with her feet propped up on the low radiator as she sipped her coffee. Seamus poured himself a cup before pulling a chair up to join her.

'Is he alright?'

'He's grand. He'll have a head on him tomorrow, but otherwise he'll be fine.'

'He doesn't usually drink.'

'Must be Jim's good example.'

'I suspect our parents' habits are precisely the reason why Christo *doesn't* generally touch alcohol. Or take drugs. Or date anyone.'

'Nobody at all?'

She dismissed that notion with a shake of her head.

'I'm not sure it would even occur to him.'

The way she said it, it sounded like a puzzle she was putting to herself.

'There was this fortune teller,' she said, wrapping her hands around her cup and staring into it, as if she was reading the coffee grounds. 'I think she was a friend of my mother's. She told Christo he would die alone. Wasn't that a terrible thing to tell someone? I've always wondered does he remember it? I hope he doesn't.'

Seamus was distracted for a moment by the perfectly round shape of her breasts under her black polo neck. The way the ribbed pattern of the wool swerved around them.

'So, what about you?' she asked him, just like that. 'Do you have somebody?'

In his mind he saw Rhona, with her red hair falling long across her face.

'I did have,' he said. 'She's married now, but we're still friends. She's asked me to be godfather to one of her twins when they're born.'

She laughed and, seeing that it was funny, he had to laugh himself.

'Oh dear.'

'Yeah, I know. It's tragic. What about you?'

'There is someone,' she said and stopped there, even though it sounded like the sentence wasn't finished.

'And?'

'He loves me,' she said, making that sound like a problem. Seamus understood only too well how that could be the case. 'He wants to marry me.'

Seamus was acutely conscious of his own voice as he answered her. Conscious of the tone of it. He was careful to sound impassive.

'And what about you? What do you want?'

'Eduardo doesn't really know me,' she said, tossing her head. 'The person he wants to marry is a figment of his imagination. When he says he loves me, it's not real, because the person he's talking about is not me.'

Seamus smiled, recognizing the feeling he'd had, all the years he lived with Rhona, of being at odds with her and the cheerful ease with which she occupied the world.

'It's not Eduardo's fault,' said Cassie. 'It's just that he doesn't know the person I was, before.'

Seamus was watching the reflection of her face in the window as she talked. Beyond her reflection was the wild, black night.

'You remember who I was,' she said, quietly.

'Yeah,' he said. 'I remember well how terrified I was of you.'

She laughed and kicked her shoes off, pulling her feet up onto the chair. Her lipstick had faded, and her mouth was stained in its place with red wine. She looked as if she'd been eating berries.

'Tell me what you remember.'

'I remember you jumping off the pier.'

The pier was high. Even at full tide, there was a drop of

ten feet to the water. Seamus had spent years working up the courage to do it.

'Come on, Seamus,' Jim would shout. 'Are you a man or a mouse?'

'Ah, Jim,' Margo would say. 'Would you give the child a chance. Look at the size of him.'

Seamus remembered walking all the way to the edge and looking down. There was a bulwark shoring up the pier that sloped out at an angle. Seamus was worried he wouldn't clear it as he jumped.

'There's plenty of room,' Jim would roar. 'Come on now. Go for it.'

It would occur to Seamus that a running jump might be better. A running jump would allow you to clear the wall for sure. But the problem then was that you couldn't see anything before you jumped. Seamus would find himself walking that plan back to the edge again, peering down dubiously at the surface of the water below. It felt like concrete when you hit it from a height. He'd heard that said at school.

'Get on with it, son,' said Jim. 'Jaysus.'

'I can't watch this,' said Margo, crossing her arms over her chest before turning to walk back to the house.

'You're not making it easy for yourself,' said his dad. 'You'd have it over and done with in a minute if only you'd stop thinking about it. I'll say one thing for you, you're a great man for torturing yourself. You poor sod.'

In the end Seamus had thrown himself off the pier. In the same way that he would, many years later, decide to cast off his virginity with a girl he hardly even fancied rather than live with the shame of it any longer, he chose to hurl himself off the high wall into the water with no expectation of pleasure, only the hope of releasing himself from the prison of his own cowardice. He chose a day no one was watching, repeating it three times in a row before he could believe he'd done it. He felt like a new person afterwards. Seamus Murphy, master pier-jumper.

Sometimes he would run and jump, other times he'd allow himself to fall off the edge like a statue toppling from a plinth. Most impressive of all was the backflip he mastered the summer Christo and Cassie came. He took great pleasure in showing that off. All the more so because Christo – despite being a year older – refused to jump. There was, in his failure to even consider it, a self-knowledge that Seamus found baffling but admirable. Of course, Cassie went straight up there and jumped without a moment's hesitation.

'I was very impressed by that,' Seamus told her now, which was no less than the truth.

'What else,' she asked.

'I remember you marking out a game of hopscotch on the beach and teaching us how to play. I remember, especially, how good you were at balancing on one leg. As I recall, you used to beat us every time.'

Her eyes glowed as she listened to him, and it seemed to Seamus that she was soaking up his words like a dry sponge.

'I remember you sitting on the floor playing solitaire. You had this long fringe that fell down over your eyes and you were wearing this little white skirt. When you crossed your legs I could see your Mickey Mouse pants.'

'I can't believe you were looking at my panties!'

He ignored her interruption.

'I remember how you hated to lose at Monopoly. You were always pestering us to play Monopoly, but you would get into a fierce huff if you lost.'

'Nonsense! You must be imagining that.'

She was pretending to be indignant, but he could tell that she was pleased. She stared through him, and in her black eyes there was something he couldn't read. He had a great desire to reach out and touch her, the way you might touch a statue, but then she turned to look out the window again and the moment was lost.

'It's funny,' she said. 'The past is so real to me here that I can almost imagine that the three of us are still out there somewhere, playing tip the can in the dark.'

They were out there in Seamus's mind too, the children they used to be, playing in the night and their two mothers still alive inside the lighted box of the house. From outside you could see them framed by the window, like people on a TV screen with the volume turned to mute. You could see they were talking to each other and moving about the room, but you couldn't hear what it was they were saying. Only now that Seamus was an adult could he imagine.

'Well,' he said, setting his coffee cup down. 'It's getting late.'

He stood up to leave and Cassie followed him out into the hallway, pulling her scarf around her shoulders as she went.

'Thanks for dinner,' he said, turning on the doorstep to face her.

'Thank you,' she said. 'For remembering me.'

He nodded, looking down at his feet for a second before raising his eyes again. His hands in his pockets, he felt a thrill of nerves rattle his blood. He hadn't felt like this since he was a teenager and he and his friends would dare each other to jump out the door of a moving car. The same rush of life, ready to receive you, if you could only find the courage to seize it.

'Well, goodnight,' he said to her, but neither of them moved.

'Goodnight, Seamus,' she said, hugging her arms to her chest and raising her black eyes to his. He saw flickers of light in them. A smile playing at the edges of her wine-stained lips.

'So, I'll see you tomorrow, I suppose.'

Instead of replying she leaned forwards, putting her hand on his shoulder to stop herself from falling. He put his hand on her waist, to steady her. The kiss that she so awkwardly offered him landed not on his cheek but in the hollow where his jawline met his ear. For all its awkwardness it was somehow more intimate. Seamus turned his face and buried his lips in her hair, breathing in the marzipan smell of her shampoo.

33

From the moment the door closed behind them, it was at best imperfect. Those breathless moments when they'd raced from her house to his – hand in hand like runaways – were already a thing of the past. From the awkward angle of her neck as she leaned up for the kiss to the smell of stale smoke from his clothes, none of it felt right. A shyness between them where only seconds before there had been conspiracy. They avoided looking each other in the eye.

Up in the bedroom, Seamus divested himself of his underpants and trousers in one move and hopped into the bed like a Victorian newlywed. Cassie stripped and slipped in beside him, registering the nubbly quality of his sheets that might not be quite clean. She was determined to ignore her misgivings. Thoughts of that parachute jump again as she drew her body alongside his. There was no way she was backing out now.

His skin was salty and surprisingly smooth. The shock of the new – Cassie had forgotten how different one man was from another. Eduardo's body was almost as familiar to her as her own, but this man was a stranger at every touch. She was relieved he made no attempt to explore her. There was no pretence of foreplay. Instead, they went at it like a steep mountain climb, each of them impatient to get on with it, so they could see what the view was like on the other side. When it was over, they lay side by side but not touching, looking up at the ceiling.

'Well,' she said. 'It was worth a try.'

He laughed a spluttery, smoker's laugh. 'Lucky I'm not sensitive.'

'Seriously,' she said, rolling over onto her hip to look at him. 'Are you okay?'

'Yeah,' he said. 'Same as I was before, no different.'

He held his arm out and she curled into him, hand on his chest, cheek to his heart.

'Me too,' she said. 'No different.'

They might have been two scientists discussing an experiment. The experiment was one to see if they could solve a problem they both knew to exist in themselves. If there was a way for two half-people to come together and somehow make a whole. If their jagged edges would by some miraculous equation fit together and create a smooth surface, and what they discovered was that they couldn't. There wasn't. They wouldn't. So now, at least, they knew.

All her life Cassie had been aware of this jagged edge in herself. During her schooldays she had tried – unsuccessfully – to smooth it out with beer and dope. She had a lot of boyfriends in high school, hoping to achieve by sheer force of numbers the intimacy she so badly craved. She made an extrovert of herself in college, driving her personality over the bumps in her life with such force that she hit a brick wall one night at a party in the desert. Cassie was about to tell a joke, but when she opened her mouth she found she could not speak. The girl she had created with such pathetic determination had, suddenly and without warning, abandoned her. While her friends smoked weed around the campfire and laughed at things that made no sense, Cassie spent the night wrapped in her own silence, with her knees hugged into her chest and her face staring up at the stars. Her mind had emptied itself of everything but the need to start again.

Mexico was where she reinvented herself, building a new life with all the careful deliberation of a bird building a nest. She was twenty-five when she went back there, travelling in the company of a guy called Mike, who she'd been seeing for a year or so. Their intention was to travel down through Central and South America, going all the way to the tip of the continent at Ushuaia.

'I've been to Ushuaia!' said Seamus, when she told him that bit of her story. 'I went there with an old girlfriend of mine.' He was very taken by the notion that their lives might have converged there, all those years ago.

'Except that they couldn't have,' said Cassie. 'I never made it to Ushuaia. Mike and I had an argument in Mexico City, so he went on alone.'

The argument started out as a minor one – over how much of a tip to leave after dinner one night – but in the years that followed it had occurred to Cassie that she might even have engineered it deliberately. She spent the next three months living in the guesthouse in Mexico City where she and Mike had planned to stay for only three days. The people who owned the guesthouse came to treat her like a visiting relation, inviting her to join them in the evenings to watch the telenovelas. Their children brought her their artwork to admire. The cat liked to sit in her lap.

The air in Mexico City agreed with her. She liked the food and the people. She liked the distance she had managed to put between the present day and everything she had up until then known. She found a small house for herself that would double as a studio. She established a relationship with a gallery that was interested in her work. She also dated, in the years that followed, a succession of men who all wanted to marry her. Cassie even went so far as to get engaged to one of them – momentarily suspending disbelief in her own ability to behave like a normal human being – but she broke off the engagement after his father very sweetly made a speech welcoming her to the family. It seemed obvious to Cassie that she was not and never would be a member of anyone else's family. It had been a mistake to think for a moment that she could be.

By the time she met Eduardo she had long ago given up on the idea of fitting her life neatly alongside another's. She had resigned herself to a relationship that would instead observe the gaps. It was only with Seamus that the hope had sparked in her again that there was in the world a person who could know all of her. Cassie saw the chance and grabbed it, allowing herself to imagine that their two souls would move across each other and perfectly eclipse the loneliness that had surrounded her for as long as she could remember. That was the hope she'd had, in sleeping with him, but it had come to nothing. She was left, as she had been before, in the circle of her own isolation.

'Here.'

He lit a cigarette for her and passed it to her before lighting his own. The two of them sitting wrapped in bedsheets on the window seat in his bedroom. They might have been a pair of Roman senators.

'It's just as well it didn't work,' said Cassie. 'I couldn't live with a smoker. I wouldn't have the will to resist.'

'There is also the fact that neither of us can cook.'

'We'd probably die of malnutrition.'

'If the lung cancer didn't get us first.'

She smiled and closed her eyes, luxuriating in the sensation of exhaling the smoke from her lungs, safe in the knowledge that this was her last. She had lost the taste for it, but she smoked it to the end anyway, tossing the butt out the window after his.

269

'It's a beautiful morning out there,' she said, gathering the folds of her sheet around her and standing up. 'I'm going to get dressed and walk the beach.'

'Do you want me to come with you?'

'No. If you don't mind, I'm happier alone.'

It was only when she said it that she realized it was true. She did not need him to fill the lonely spaces inside her. All the things she'd once wanted to share with someone were safe in the privacy of her heart. A campfire in the desert under a canopy of stars. A hammock, strung tree to tree, with a view of the sea. A child's scream – her scream – echoing through the wooden rafters of a Mexican guesthouse. Those were the key moments of her life, but they had settled in her, like stones on a riverbed. There was no need to disturb them now.

She let herself out the door and closed it behind her. She was wearing last night's clothes, and her skin bore the sting of the cheap soap she'd used to clean her face. Her hair was thick with the smell of the cigarette she'd smoked with Seamus before she left. Walking out the road, Cassie was conscious of the firm ground beneath her feet. She could feel her cheeks warming in the thin autumn sunshine. Her eyes watering from the shock of all the fresh air. She climbed the hill, enjoying the stretch at the front of her thighs and the shudder in her lungs. She tripped down the far side, allowing her legs to pick up speed until she found herself tumbling all the way to the bottom.

A solitary gull flew in black silhouette against the bruised sky. In the distance, Cassie saw the bright spots of a car's headlights moving along the low road on the far side of the bay. It alleviated the emptiness of the morning.

Crossing the headland towards the beach, Cassie watched the sheep scurrying away from her with comical haste. A horse stared at her as she passed. She looked down, observing the spongy grass beneath her feet. Every step she took she was trampling on sea pinks. Mayweed. Bird's-foot trefoil. It was amazing to Cassie to find their names still in her head. She noticed the tiny shells nestled among the wildflowers. As a child, she had once collected some of those shells and taken them home in a sling she'd made of her skirt. She'd been horrified to find miniature snails crawling out of them later.

'What did you expect?' said Margo. 'Those shells are their houses.'

Walking the shoreline, Cassie noticed shapes in the water. For a moment she thought it was a shoal of rays, but then she looked up and saw a flock of birds flying overhead. What she'd seen was the shoal formed by their shadows. It swept across the surface of the sea and disappeared, as the birds scattered over the headland.

She bent down and examined the seaweed that littered the sand. There were strands of some sea plant she could not identify, a kind of magenta arugula. There was a black, branched weed with the appearance of stiffened lace – it reminded Cassie of those intricate headdresses worn by flamenco dancers. Another weed lay in thick ribbons on the ground, like squid-ink fettucine heaped in a bowl, ready for a sprinkling of Parmesan.

Cassie studied the splatter marks made on the sand by the overnight rain. The footprints of the seabirds were so numerous they formed a repeat pattern, like a screen print. A desire formed in her mind to cut these patterns into stone, making something permanent of them and, by extension, of herself. She had the sense of a circuit completing itself in her mind. A settling feeling, like a throw of dice coming to rest with all the sixes facing up. Like a poker hand that forms itself into a perfect straight flush. For the first time in a long time, she felt connected to the grid.

On the way back to the house she put a call through to Eduardo. Even though it was barely five in the morning where he was, she wanted to hear his voice. He must have had the phone beside him as he slept because he answered right away.

'Que hay?'

What's up. She could hear the alarm in his voice, and she was touched by it.

'No, no,' she said. 'Tranquilo. Todo bien.' All is well.

She imagined him nestling back into the pillows. His default position was one of ease with the world, and he would revert to it immediately.

'Bueno,' he said. 'Now, tell me all your news. How have you been faring?'

It occurred to Cassie that it was not in her power to destroy Eduardo. He had been wired for survival from the moment he was conceived, and nothing that ever happened to him – no economic recession, no sudden insolvency, no protracted divorce – could scramble that wiring. He was like one of those earthquake-proof buildings he designed, with a sway built into them to withstand any tremors. No matter what came to pass in his life, Eduardo would still roll down the window of his car and hand out a few pesos to the street kids who mopped his windshield at the traffic lights. He would still stop to have his shoes shined every morning on the way from the car park to his office. Still spend his evenings happily chopping herbs for his signature salsas.

'Oh,' she said. 'We've been busy. Yesterday we met my mother's friends. Today we go see her old school. We hope to meet the nun who taught her.'

'That's wonderful,' said Eduardo. 'I'm very happy for you, Cassie. I'm pleased that your journey is bearing fruit.'

Cassie was struck, once again, by his unassailable good humour. All these years she had been afraid, not that Eduardo would be the ruin of her, but that she would ruin him. She saw now that this was not possible, that she had the power to make him happy or unhappy, depending on the day, but no more than that. It gave her a great feeling of freedom to understand this. For the first time in her life, she could see how she might be free to love without fear.

'So, mi amor. Are you ready to come home?'

'Yes,' she said. 'I'm ready to see some sunshine. It rains all the time here. Even the street signs are rusted. If I stay here much longer, I'm going to get webbed feet.'

'Webbed feet?' he asked, caught out for once.

Cassie could count on the fingers of one hand the mistakes she'd heard him make with his English. She'd once heard him speak of a man who walked with a 'lump'. He sometimes struggled to find the word for a flower or a fish. Otherwise, his vocabulary was equal to hers.

'Yes, webbed feet. You know, like the man from Atlantis.'

'Ah,' he said. 'Pies palmeados.'

'Pies palmeados,' she repeated, closing the gap that separated her from Eduardo by this one tiny increment. This was how it would be between them, she realized. There would be no great coming together, but inch by inch, moment by moment, they would close the spaces that separated them until they understood each other, perhaps not entirely, but well enough.

34

Christo woke late, with an acute feeling of unwellness. His first thought was that he was coming down with something, until it occurred to him that this might be what other people described as a hangover. He cast his mind back to what had happened after dinner but quickly reeled the line back in, unwilling to face up to what he might find. That didn't stop a vague, retrospective fear from sloshing around his brain. He felt like a sodden paper bag that might at any moment burst, releasing all the emotions that were churning around inside him.

He climbed out of the bed and made his way to the bathroom, moving with all the care of someone carrying a basket of eggs on their head. Blocks of memory from the previous night dropped like Tetris shapes inside his brain. Christo had played Tetris compulsively as an undergraduate, sitting up into the small hours to swivel those geometric shapes and steer them into place before they landed, but there was no turning the thoughts in his head now. They were dropping too fast.

He lifted the toilet lid and began to pee, hearing as he did so a voice in his head – it took him a minute to realize it was his own – fishing for sympathy. He heard himself whining about school. About his abandonment. About his father. Closing his eyes, as if that could block out the sound, he caught the unfamiliar smell of fermented grapes from his own urine and winced with shame. He remembered the red wine he'd spilled on the white tablecloth, and it seemed to him in that moment that his whole life amounted to nothing but a series of spills that had left stains that could never be removed.

Staring at himself in the bathroom mirror, Christo saw a deceptively normal-looking human being, someone who might have been expected to move with ease through the world. What nobody could see was the invisible suit of armour he wore, made up of all the clanging instances of shame and embarrassment that had punctuated his life. It was only the eyes that revealed what was inside. A look of desperation in them, like eyes behind an iron mask pleading to be released. Christo gripped the sides of the sink with his hands as if it were a lectern, allowing his head to fall forward so that his chin was almost resting on his chest.

He was tired of being with people. Tired of constantly trying to find a place for himself in their conversations. Tired of struggling to understand their cultural references – only yesterday Cassie and Seamus had been batting the names of TV shows back and forth between them while Christo sat there like the ball boy, powerless to do anything but watch. They'd fought over the dial on the radio in the car, objecting to each other's choice of music and only occasionally agreeing. There was a song of Rihanna's on the radio – a duet with Paul McCartney, of all people – and Christo had barely heard of Rihanna, let alone the song, but they both seemed to know it. They were on a straight, wide stretch of freshly laid asphalt, candy-floss sheep leaping out of their way in every direction as Christo ploughed the car along the unmarked road. Cassie was dancing with her arms and singing away in the back seat, while Seamus mouthed the words to the song and kept time to the beat with his hands on the legs of his jeans. Christo had never in his life felt lonelier. All he wanted in that moment was to be back in Cambridge.

Oh, it was no accident that it was Cambridge Christo had chosen as his home. A place of low and carefully calibrated voices, where history was stored reverentially in great mausoleums of paper and wood and stone. The distant past was more alive there than the recent past. More alive, in many ways, than the present. Christo had colleagues who hardly knew what century they were living in. There were people who spent their days studying the mating habits of a particular toad on a particular stretch of river, or trying to prove instances of infanticide in ancient Carthage. One of Christo's colleagues had been unaware of the attack on the World Trade Center in New York until eight months after it happened, so immersed was he in the book he was writing about the Black Death. The body count in New York seemed underwhelming to him by comparison, as he told a mildly amused audience at formal hall one night.

Some of Christo's colleagues had lived their lives with barely any awareness of the existence of Elvis, or the Beatles, much less of Rihanna. Christo was not an oddity among them – on the contrary, he was considered by his students to be among the most normal of the academic staff. 'Kris Kristofferson', they called him fondly, eagerly laughing at his jokes and partaking of his shortbread. He missed his students, he realized with a pang! He missed the deep silence of his study and the cold glow of the bricks of the courtyard outside as the sun fell on them. He missed his attic flat, with his books and his tea and his fingers of KitKat. Cambridge was his place in the world – a place he had found for himself – and what he wanted now more than anything was to be safely back there.

Passing out of the bathroom, he looked into Cassie's bedroom but found it empty – her bed undisturbed – as he knew it would be. He recognized the feeling of being alone by the curious hum to the space when there was no one else in it. He stood in the open doorway and looked at her black clothes, strewn across the chair and bed. Her voluminous scarves draped over the wardrobe doors. Her biker boots sitting side by side on the floor beneath the chair. He imagined her asleep in Seamus's bed, with her long black hair thrown across his pillow like a feathered wing. He pictured Seamus curled in behind her, and it was not jealousy he felt but humiliation at being excluded.

'Three's a crowd,' he remembered Jim saying to him, all those years ago.

Christo had been sitting alone on the beach when Jim found him. Cassie and Seamus were playing in the waves, using kitchen trays as bodyboards. Christo didn't want to join them – afraid of those waves that loved to gobble you up and spit you out again, half-drowned – but he was miserable at being left out of the game.

It was the same feeling he had now. Forgotten were all the nights when he and Seamus had whispered to each other, bunk to bunk. All the times they gave Cassie the slip, hiding behind the stone wall while she went about calling their names. All that was real to him now was the memory of himself sitting alone on the beach, while they splashed about together in the surf.

'Poor Christo,' Jim had said, then. 'You're the third wheel.'

It was always thus. As a child, his mother would make a friend of him only to throw him aside whenever a new man came into her life. At boarding school, Christo had time and time again become close to someone only to find his place usurped by another. There was a guy called David who had invited Christo to go skiing with him at his parents' chalet in Switzerland, only to rescind the offer at the last minute in favour of a girl he'd met at a school social.

Christo was fifteen when he was sent on a French exchange to Cannes. The host family were people his father knew from the record business. The boy was only a year older than Christo, but he looked twenty-five. He had long beach-blond hair with a goatee to match. He smoked dope from morning to night. Christo had only just arrived when the boy – whose name was Jean-Luc – announced they were going camping for the weekend. He packed Christo into the back of his small jeep, reserving the front seat for his girlfriend, who they picked up on the way. Jean-Luc was too young to have a licence, but that didn't seem to worry anybody except Christo. The weekend seemed to last a week – Jean-Luc and the girlfriend smoked and laughed all day and engaged in noisy sex all night in the shared tent, while Christo rammed his fingers desperately in his ears and tried to sleep.

Most recently, there was Aki. An economist on a year's leave from the Department of Finance in Tokyo, Aki was the clumsiest person Christo had ever met. He couldn't open a door but the doorknob would come off in his hand. Couldn't pick up a book without dropping it, couldn't make a mug of tea without knocking it over himself. It was this shambolic demeanour that had endeared him to Christo.

It was January of the previous year when he'd arrived, apologizing for himself from the outset. He was sorry to disturb Christo's peace, sorry to take up so much space in the room, sorry to make so much noise. This diffidence on his part was perhaps the reason why Christo took such pains to make him welcome. Normally Christo didn't like to take the initiative with people, but Aki didn't know anyone in Cambridge, so Christo assumed the role of host. He suggested they have dinner together at his favourite Thai restaurant. He even insisted on paying the bill.

When Aki reciprocated by inviting Christo to his home

the following week, Christo saw a future where they might dine together regularly. They might even holiday together – Christo had been thinking for some time of going walking in the Peak District, and it occurred to him that Aki might like to come with him. He decided to ask him that night over dinner and brought a walking guide with him, which he imagined them perusing together as they chose their itinerary. But when Aki opened the door of his flat, there was a small Japanese woman standing behind him, dressed in a pink silk kimono. Aki introduced the woman to Christo as his wife and Christo stepped forward to shake her hand, when what he really wanted was to turn and run. He spent the evening in a state of abject mortification, as Aki's wife offered him plate after plate of the delicious food she'd prepared, and Aki boasted of her skill at flower arranging, which she'd studied at home in Japan. Christo survived that meal somehow, but his heart had shrivelled into a hard little walnut of humiliation at the misapprehension he had so foolishly allowed himself to entertain. He had come to think of himself and Aki as kindred spirits – two gentle souls alone in the world – but it turned out that Aki already had his own kindred spirit. Yet again, three was a crowd. Yet again, Christo was the third wheel.

'Hello, Christo?'

He heard the front door slam shut as Cassie came in. Her ballet shoes made a flapping sound on the tiles as she made her way to the kitchen. As a child she'd slept in a rabbit suit with plastic pads under the feet that had made a similar sound as she moved around the house.

'Hey,' she said, when she saw him.

Her cheeks were scuffed pink, her eyes bright and shining with unashamed happiness. Christo's worst fears were confirmed.

'It's a beautiful day out there,' she said, walking across to the sink. She filled the kettle and turned it on. Opened up the bread bin and retrieved a slice of bread, which she started buttering without even bothering to get a plate out of the cupboard. She ate it standing up.

'Did you not have breakfast?'

In the movies, people who spent the night together always had breakfast together the next morning.

'No, just coffee. I'm starving.'

She opened the fridge.

'I might make some eggs. Do you want some?'

'Lord no,' he said, registering the roll of nausea in his belly at the thought of it. 'Maybe just some tea?'

Even that was a challenge. He could feel the blood pooling at his temples. The sound of the boiling kettle was deafening to him. The buzz of the toaster as it popped. The racket she made beating the eggs. He felt like he was sitting on a noisy factory floor.

'Couldn't you do that a bit more quietly?'

She laughed. 'Are we maybe a bit hungover?'

He did not dignify that with an answer.

'So,' he asked her, once she was sitting down in front of him with her eggs. 'Are you going to stay?'

He had it all mapped out in his mind. How she would stay and marry Seamus. How they would have children together – two or three of them – naming their daughter after Margo, naturally. Christo would visit them regularly, coming to know every landmark on the road like the back of his hand. The children would come running out of the house when he arrived, a sheepdog whirling about their feet. Seamus would step out the door and turn to call Cassie.

'Stay where?' she asked, pausing with her fork in the air. Eyebrows raised. Incredulous. 'Here?'

'I thought maybe . . .'

'What would I do with myself here?'

She was looking at him as if he were a simpleton.

'I don't know. I just thought, you know. You and Seamus . . .'

'That was nothing,' she said, shaking her head dismissively. 'I'll be leaving with you the day after tomorrow. I'm going back to Mexico. Of course.'

'Of course,' he said, feeling all at sea. 'Silly me.'

35

The last thing on their itinerary was a visit to the Abbey. It was early afternoon by the time they got there, and the place was awash with tourists. There were cameras slung from every neck. Guidebooks in every hand. Christo parked the car among all the other hire cars in the car park, and together he and Cassie made their way towards the visitors' centre.

'My mother was at school here,' Cassie told the young woman behind the desk at the entrance.

'Yes, we get a lot of people coming back for that reason,' said the woman. 'Is it a day ticket you want?'

'Oh no,' said Cassie. 'We're hoping to visit Sister Joseph, if she's here.'

Expecting to be sent on up to the Abbey, they were directed instead back through the car park towards the farm. They followed a path through a thicket of rhododendrons to where a big white farmhouse lay in a field of uncut grass. A black and white sheepdog came out and barked as they approached.

'Oh, would you shut up,' said the old nun who came around the side of the house, carrying a bucket that she set down at the base of the wall. She was wearing a full habit and, over it, a belted gingham smock. Under her skirts she had on a pair of black wellington boots. She stopped in her tracks, eyes on Cassie as she approached. Ignoring Christo, she reached out and took a hold of Cassie's fingers.

'I've often wondered when you'd come,' she said, staring hard at her. One of her eyes was fierce and sparkling, the other milky and still.

Cassie didn't know what to say.

'You look nothing like your mother,' said the old nun. She was about the same height as Cassie, when stooped. Straightened out, she must have been over six foot tall.

'No,' said Cassie. 'I look like my dad.'

The nun continued to stare at her with disarming intensity.

'This is Christo,' said Cassie, and the old nun turned her attention on him.

'I never met you,' she said, in an accusatory tone.

'No,' said Christo, apologetically.

They followed the nun into the farmhouse kitchen, a large square room heated by an old enamel range. A pair of huge windows looked out on the farmyard. Empty egg boxes were stacked on the windowsill. A small crucifix hung on the wall. A calendar featuring the local hurling team.

'I loved your mother dearly,' said Sister Joseph, with her back turned as she filled a stainless-steel kettle and placed it on the range. 'She was one of our bold girls, and I always loved the bold girls the best.'

Not sure where to sit, Christo and Cassie waited to be told.

'There,' said the nun, pointing Cassie to a wooden chair with a battered, tapestry seat. 'I'm blind in one eye so I need you on the right side of me.'

She moved aside some books and a sugar bowl and a ball of twine to make room for three mugs of tea on the cluttered tabletop. Then she set an oversized milk jug on top of the stack of books.

'You sit there,' she said to Christo, directing him to her blind side. 'I hope you eat fruitcake.'

The implication was that this was a test of character.

'Oh yes. We love fruitcake,' said Cassie.

'I made it myself,' said Sister Joseph, her old fingers fumbling to remove the greaseproof paper the cake was wrapped in. It took her a long time to release the cake, longer still to cut slices of it and find a plate for them. Then she had to warm the teapot and spoon the tea leaves into it and fill it with boiling water. Only when the teapot was on the table did she finally lower herself into her chair.

'You don't take sugar, do you?'

'No,' they said, in unison. 'No sugar.'

'Good.'

She leaned over the table to pluck at the jewel-studded cake with her fingertips. Her veil was fastened to her hair by a single pearl-headed pin. She wore a slim gold wedding band on the ring finger of her right hand.

'It's delicious,' said Cassie, taking a long drink of the hot, milky tea. In an armchair by the window, the sheepdog was dozing in a slab of sunlight.

'I was only a young nun when your mother came here first. It must be hard for you to imagine that.'

But Cassie could easily imagine her as a young woman. With her long, strong face, she would have been handsome. There was something manly about her features and she had aged the way a man would, with none of the blurring that befalls old women.

'We shared a birthday,' she said, speaking with a burst of renewed vigour. 'Your mother and I were born on the same day, twenty years apart. We were twins, she and I.'

'The thirtieth of September,' said Christo.

'That's this month,' said the old nun, with a flash of surprise. 'I'm going to be eighty-two. You have no idea how strange that is.'

'She'd be sixty-two,' said Christo, but Sister Joseph didn't respond. She sat staring into her lap, and Cassie wondered

284

had she heard? She caught her brother's eye across the table, wondering what to say or do, but then the nun sparked up again.

'I'm getting old,' she said. 'And I don't like it one little bit. I don't like not being able to do things.'

Sensing that platitudes would be unwelcome to this woman, Cassie said nothing.

'Would you like to see the school?' Sister Joseph asked, abruptly. 'It's closed down now, of course, but if you'd like to see it, I could take you up there.'

Abandoning their tea things on the table, they walked the rhododendron path together, emerging into the car park where tour buses were belching out fresh clouds of tourists. The nun cut a swathe through them, parting the hordes by the authority of her habit. She swept in the great Gothic door and beyond the public space of the parquet-floored hall, into the dark recesses of the school, where the walls were lined with pictures of girls long since grown and gone.

They stopped on the grand, sweeping staircase in front of an old framed black-and-white shot of five girls sitting on a wall with the lake behind them. Cassie had no trouble picking out her mother, with her hair clipped to one side by a bobby pin and her face raised to flirt boldly with the camera. Nobody could have traced that picture forwards to produce an image of the woman she would one day turn out to be. But it was possible to trace her backwards, and find in that pale, uniformed girl all the ingredients of the beauty she had later become.

In the empty classrooms the desks were still lined up in rows as if a class was about to start. There was a large sash window, with a hooked pole leaning against its casing waiting for a girl to be asked to open it. Bound books lined the shelves of the library waiting to be plucked and read. In the dormitories, the bunk beds stood ready for a new term to start. The mattresses had been stripped of sheets and stacked one on top of the other. The rows of toilet stalls lay vacant, their doors ajar. The shower cubicles were hushed and silent.

'They weren't all happy here,' said Sister Joseph, leaning heavily on the wooden banister as she led them up a narrow staircase, where pale blue lino had replaced the dark, waxed wood of the lower stairs. They followed her through a series of fire doors onto another long corridor. Keys with hand-written labels hung from the keyholes, each room identified by a saint's name. There was a sweet, institutional smell in the air.

'A lot of them were a long way from home,' Sister Joseph said, opening a door onto another empty dormitory. A small window provided a view not of sky but of the voracious rhododendron only inches away. Even three floors up, the Abbey leaned into the mountain. If you opened the window, you could reach out and touch it. Cassie imagined the cold comfort of damp linen sheets. The sound of rainwater gushing down towards the lake. She imagined February, as bleak as can be.

'I don't think your mother was unhappy here,' the old nun was saying.

Cassie tried to imagine her mother in this place. A young girl in a belted wool dress and a starched white collar running down the stairs with her feet barely touching the floor. A lightness to her that would be lost in adulthood. Cassie was overcome by the certainty that the nun was right. Her mother had been happy here.

'Of course, she ran away in the end,' said Sister Joseph. 'But I don't think it was this place she was running from. I think she was running towards something, or so she thought.'

The nun could not have known about the pregnancy, but perhaps she'd guessed.

'Girls had a hard time in this country,' she said. 'They were told from the moment they were born that they were good for nothing but marriage and motherhood. We tried to show them another path. We encouraged them to pursue careers. Not to be dependent on a man for the rest of their lives. I'm afraid there wasn't much romance in it, and romance is what girls that age are looking for. If I saw it once I saw it a hundred times.'

'You're a feminist,' said Cassie, with surprise, as they followed the nun down another narrow stairwell, where pipes lined the walls, all painted the same oily white. The place had the air of an old ship, below the waterline.

'Of course I am,' said Sister Joseph. 'I've worked with girls all my life. How could I not be?'

She paused for a moment on the stairs, a rabbity alertness to her as she turned to look back at them.

'Of course, it's all changed since your mother's day. Girls like her didn't stand a chance back then. They had to leave if they were going to survive.'

Head down, she continued her descent. As they went, the lino gave way to parquet again. The smell now was of wax polish. A window facing outwards revealed a slab of glistening lake, with trees dipping their branches to scoop the water from it.

'Your mother came back here in the hope of making a fresh start.'

'Did she say that?' asked Christo, his voice tumbling down the stairwell after her.

The nun ignored the question, following her own train of thought.

'I think she was looking for where she went wrong. She

287

was lost, and she wanted to go back and find the right path. She was looking for someone she could trust to point her in the right direction.'

Sister Joseph stopped on the first-floor return, where a waterfall of light tumbled down on her from a tall, narrow window.

'She talked about sending me to school here,' said Cassie.

The old nun pounced on this.

'That was my idea. I tried to persuade her to leave you with us.'

'But she didn't.'

'No,' she said, turning the word over as if to study it from the other side. 'She did not. And yet here you are now, come back to us.'

Cassie felt suddenly trapped. The air inside the school was so thick with second-hand memory it was like breathing soup. Every step Cassie took, she felt like she was treading on her mother's shadow. It was a relief to her when they reached the Abbey's great hall door and stepped outside.

'There's something I'd like to know,' Sister Joseph said, once they were standing on the parapet overlooking the lake. She had spun around to confront them. Her face appeared ancient in the harsh light of day. Her hairline was seagull-white where it met the rim of her veil. There was nonetheless something youthful – innocent, even – in the way she looked from one to the other of them, searching for answers. 'What happened to her?'

They both hesitated. It was hard to know what to say.

'She was so talented,' said the old nun, her one good eye shining as she said it. 'She could have been a singer. Or a writer. A poet, perhaps.'

Cassie remembered then, how her mother did once write some poems. Cassie's dad brought her on stage to recite one of them at a concert of his. People made fun of her for it, so she never did it again. That was the end of the poetry.

'She had a beautiful singing voice,' said Sister Joseph. 'When she was here, she sometimes sang solos with the choir.'

Another time, she tried acting. She auditioned for a bit part in a movie – it was Marty Legge who had arranged the audition for her – but the director said she was no good. Lovely as she was, she had no capacity for pretending. She could never not be herself.

'You may think this strange, but I often thought your mother would have made a good nun. She was a very spiritual person, but she was looking for meaning in all the wrong places. I think she could have found it here.'

Cassie smiled at the thought of her mother living out her life here, in a nun's habit.

'If it wasn't for her weakness for men,' she said.

'If it wasn't for her beauty,' said Sister Joseph, correcting her with the sharp rap of a teacher. 'It was her beauty that drew men to her, and the men were her downfall. I've always thought she was one of those women who would have been better off without a man, but she had a great need to be loved. She couldn't resist taking it wherever she could find it.'

A burst of birdsong was heard from the trees, so clear as to sound almost mechanical.

'Even if it was from someone else's husband,' she added, stating plainly what they already knew. It was a shock all the same to hear it so boldly spoken.

Cassie turned to look at the lake. The waves on the surface were tiered and grey as roof slates. The parapets that framed the view, a paler, pigeon grey.

'He comes to pray for her, you know.'

'Who does?'

'Jimmy Murphy,' said Sister Joseph. 'A couple of times a year. He goes down to the Gothic chapel to pray for her.'

'How do you know?' asked Cassie.

'Because the first time he came he asked to see me. He wanted my permission to pray for her, which is not something a person needs to ask, but I was impressed all the same that he would ask it. That was just after your mother died, and he's been coming ever since. I arranged for him to have a visitor's pass, so he doesn't have to pay.'

Cassie was touched beyond measure to think there was someone who still took the time to pray for her mother, more than a quarter of a century since she'd departed the earth.

'I'd like to see the chapel,' she said, hearing from the outside the shaky sound of her own voice.

'Follow that path,' said Sister Joseph, pointing towards the lake. 'You can't miss it.'

Following the old nun's instructions, Cassie took the path by the lake. Before she'd gone a hundred yards, she began to feel weak and made for a wooden bench that sat facing the water. Tourists passed her by – she closed her eyes and listened to the scuff and drag of their shoes on the path. The sound of a stick dragging a line in the gravel. The sound of someone biting into an apple. She heard snatches of language, some of which she understood, some she didn't. 'Their granddaughter is four years old,' said a woman, in an American accent. '*La touffe est chouffe,*' she heard someone else say, or something to that effect. From far away, Cassie heard the sound of women singing, a sound that came and went with the wind. She could almost imagine it was her mother's voice she was hearing.

Watching the water ripple the surface of the lake, she thought of all the times her mother must have cast her eyes out over this same view, seeing the same old knotted trees that rose along its fringes and the same gossiping reeds. Cassie raised her face to gaze at the same old mountains her mother would have faced as a girl. She must have sat on this same bench, watching the shadows of the clouds crawl across their vast, bleak surface. A motherless girl, as her own daughter would be. History repeating itself, like the endlessly overlapping waves of the lake.

'*I was only ten when I lost my mum,*' she'd told them. The word 'lost' a conundrum that Cassie would only later come to understand. There was no word more appropriate. It was the loss of a mother that had precipitated everything that came afterwards. Starting with the decision to send her to boarding school, and her subsequent escape. The estrangement from her father. The refuge sought in other men. It was a turbulent life, but by tracing it back to the little girl who once sat on this very same bench with her whole life ahead of her, it occurred to Cassie for the first time that her mother's tragedy was nobody's so much as her own.

36

A barrage of rain fell on them as they drove home. It had an insidious quality, so that even inside the car you didn't feel dry. Cassie sat staring out the windscreen at it. She'd hardly spoken since she came out of the chapel.

'Are you okay?' Christo asked her, leaning in low over the steering wheel as he tried to make out the road. He activated the wipers and the windscreen cleared momentarily, only to mist up again straight away. Christo turned the dial on the heater to its highest setting to clear the thick fog on the windows. If only he could have done the same to himself. His hangover had solidified, losing its sharp edges but acquiring instead a deep malaise that was almost worse. He longed for the comfort of his bed, longed for the oblivion of sleep and the hangover-free onset of a new day. He was determined never to drink again as long as he lived.

'Why do you think we never talk about her, Christo?'

The rain was falling so hard that the wipers couldn't keep up with it. Rain like the interference on a TV set. Mountains, fields and hedgerows all suspended in the same substance. They might have been driving along the seabed in a submarine.

'We never talk about what happened to her.'

'What do you want to talk about?' asked Christo, feeling very weary.

'Her *death*,' said Cassie. 'We never talk about that.'

Christo wasn't there when it happened. He'd left a month earlier for school in England. He could hang the date of his departure on his mother's birthday. Cassie had made her a pasta necklace as a birthday present, painting some rigatoni and stringing them along a length of dental floss. Christo had saved up to buy her a jar of lurid pink bath salts. From Marty she got an enormous parcel, as wide as the span of his arms and wrapped in brown paper and twine. He could barely get a grip on it as he carried it, sideways, through the door.

'Happy birthday to you,' sang Marty, as he leaned the parcel up against the wall of the living room. He struck up the second verse as they all stood and watched, continuing gamely even though neither Cassie nor Christo joined in. 'Happy Birthday' is not a long song, but it can seem that way when nobody else is singing.

'What is it?' asked Cassie.

'It's a painting,' said Marty, turning to their mother with a wink. 'But don't open it yet. Let's wait until our little friends are in bed.'

Christo came down the next morning to find the painting propped against the living room couch, with the wrapping lying on the floor like the pelt of a skinned animal. The empty bottle of bourbon by the fireplace was a relic of their evening, along with the overflowing ashtray on the coffee table. The discarded clothing and shoes.

Christo stood in his pyjamas staring at the painting. A six-by-four oil on canvas, it depicted a reclining woman with one arm bent at the elbow to support her head. The other arm snaked along her waist to hover over her hip. Her belly was swollen with pregnancy, her breasts dominated by the dark circles formed by her large, flat nipples. Her thighs met in a triangle of black hair that thinned in the centre to reveal a ripple of pink flesh, like a glimpse of oyster through an open shell. The woman's knees were open wide, but her ankles were crossed. Her mouth was closed but her eyes were open, holding you in a knowing stare.

'I see you,' said Marty, coming into the room from the far side. 'I *see* you,' he said, wagging his finger.

Christo felt his face heat up, not with shame but indignation, and he moved to leave the room by the other door, but Marty pursued him.

'You dirty lad,' whispered Marty, into his ear. 'Ogling a pregnant mother, whatever next?'

There was a riff in his voice to suggest complicity. A raise to his eyebrows indicating this was a joke they could share. Christo jerked his shoulder to throw off Marty's hand, running through the hallway to his bedroom, where he sat on the floor against the wall with his head in his hands and Marty's laughter sounding in his ears. The misery of being misunderstood made a storm in his head. He hated that painting – he found it disgusting – and he did not want to live in a house where it was hanging on the wall.

Christo would always connect that painting, and Marty's wagging finger, with his decision to go to boarding school in England. Something his father had been advocating for some time, not out of any desire to have Christo close by, but to satisfy his own perverse need to be part of the aristocracy he had for so long railed against. Christo had so far resisted, but he did an about-turn that day on a phone call to his dad in Devon. He presented it to his mother as a foregone conclusion. He'd be starting straight away.

On the night he left for school she drove him to the airport, but he hardly spoke a word to her in the car. He turned down her offer to accompany him to the gate, choosing instead to say goodbye to her at the security barrier. He surrendered himself to her hug but did not return it. He refused to meet her eye as they said goodbye. Walking through security he concentrated on not looking behind him. In his mind's eye he could see her standing there watching his back as he walked away. It would be the last image he had of her and the memory of it would haunt him forever, along with the thought of the sister he had so ruthlessly left behind.

'I should never have left you alone with her.'

'What do you mean?'

'You were only a little girl.'

He remembered the meadow-flowered nightgown she was wearing the evening he left. The pitiful way she clung to him, her face sticky with tears.

'I left you to witness her death on your own.'

This was something that had never not been in his head. A weight he had carried around with him ever since. A regret, of maddening proportion. Christo would give anything to be able to go back and do it differently.

'I've thought of it every day. How you had to go through that all by yourself.'

Cassie screwed her face up, as if she were staring into a bright sun.

'But that's crazy talk, Christo. You didn't know she was going to die.'

In Christo's mind, it had never been that simple. The chronology of it was all jumbled up, the rules of cause and effect warped by guilt and regret. In Christo's mind he'd left his sister to witness their mother's death alone.

It was the headmaster who broke the news to him. He had come in person to the classroom door, as ominous a signal as Christo had ever seen. He reached out tentatively to touch Christo on the elbow as he guided him down the corridor. 'I'm very sorry to be the one to inform you,' he said. Christo had never forgotten that. The precise phrasing of it. 'I'm very sorry to inform you that your mother has suffered an accident,' said the headmaster, and Christo took this to mean a car accident. Too shy to ask any questions – too shocked, too young – he remembered nothing of the journey to the airport. The only memory he had was of sitting alone in a hushed, carpeted lounge, waiting for the next flight back to LA. Could that be right? Would he have been left alone? In Christo's memory, there was nobody there but himself. A strange whooshing sensation in his head as his brain struggled to process the news the headmaster had delivered. It was not until Marty Legge picked him up on the other side – for once his pinstriped suit was appropriate to the occasion – that Christo learned that his mother had not died in a car accident.

'But you couldn't have known what was going to happen,' said Cassie.

'All the same,' he said, unable to let go of the story he had constructed. A story without any context or other actors. He had omitted his father's determination to send him to school in England and his mother's behaviour in driving him away. All that was left was his own dereliction of duty towards his sister. 'The fact is that I shouldn't have left you.'

'Please don't say that,' she said, shaking her head at him in what could almost be interpreted as annoyance. 'That's against the rules. It happened just the way it happened. It happened in a straight line, and there was no way of bending it. There was no way of knowing beforehand that it was going to happen. Surely you know that, Christo. You're the one who's supposed to understand these things. There's a formula, and you can't go playing around with it afterwards just to make yourself feel bad.'

He found himself face to face with that old certainty of hers. She had her jaw set, her eyes narrowed and glinting, and Christo knew better than to argue with her.

37

As a child, Cassie was never frightened while her brother was in the house, but without him she was suddenly afraid. On the first morning after he left for school she'd woken while it was still dark to the sound of a car engine starting. She looked out the window and saw Marty's car turning a circle on the gravel in front of the house. She saw the car pause, engine humming, as the electric gates opened in a wash of white light from Marty's headlights. The hedge on the far side of the road was illuminated for a moment as Marty's car made the turn out onto the road. Cassie watched his rear lights swing wide to the right before turning left and plunging into the darkness. The electric gates closed again, leaving the black morning outside.

Cassie's bedroom was brightened by a seep of yellow light that came in from the hallway outside through the gap under her bedroom door. She lay back down on her bed and surveyed her room, identifying one by one all the things that by daylight would need no identification. She saw the robe on the back of the door, a robe she knew to be pink even though in this light it looked grey. She saw the doll's house she knew to be built of lilac clapboard on the outside, with each room papered a different pretty pattern on the inside; in the darkness the house took on a sinister aspect. The Barbie dolls that were friends to Cassie by daylight seemed to taunt her with their lifelessness now. They lay on her floor in a plastic pile of naked limbs and tangled hair, like the victims of a serial killer.

It was upsetting how everything that was familiar to you in daylight could, in a different light, seem so horribly unfamiliar. She knew she could have climbed out of bed to turn on the overhead light, but she didn't. Not because she was too scared to move, but because she wanted to see how long she could stay scared. She pulled the covers over her head and hid inside the space that was noisy with her own breath, her head reeling with half-imagined horrors.

When the sun came up, Cassie made a lap of the house. Patrolling the place like a bereaved dog, she was conscious of a need to scope out her brother's absence. Each room felt wrong without him, the atmosphere somehow different without him in it. Cassie had learned Archimedes' principle in school, and it seemed to her that it applied to air just as well as to water. When Christo had left home, a space the size of him had emptied out of the house.

Without her brother there, Cassie was free to wander at will in and out of his bedroom. She opened up the drawers of his desk and found the collection of Star Wars figures she had once coveted. She was surprised to discover they no longer held the appeal they once had. She found the certificates he'd earned in elementary school for math, proudly gathered in a transparent folder. As a little kid she had once stolen them and stowed them in her own locker. She found a picture of him with his dad, and it created a pool of sadness in her, but she couldn't have said whether she was sad that Christo had such a lousy dad or sad that she didn't have one at all. She lay on the bed and looked at his ceiling, wondering what it was like to be him, but the thought of being another person and not herself was so confusing to Cassie that she abandoned it and went in search of breakfast.

Downstairs, there was no sound. No smell of coffee brewing, no half-drunk cups on the counter. Instead, there were only two wine glasses in the sink. Someone had filled them up with water that had turned pink with the dregs of the wine. Looking out the window, Cassie saw that the pool was perfectly still, and Christo's lilo had drifted to the far corner. The sight of it languishing there was very lonely.

Cassie helped herself to a bowl of Cheerios, which she carried over to the TV and ate while she watched *The Pink Panther*. She had a second bowl of cereal watching *Muppet Babies*, and after that she watched *The Smurfs*, and when *The Smurfs* was finished she switched over to *Alvin and the Chipmunks*, which she would never have been allowed to do if Christo was there. Christo hated *Alvin and the Chipmunks*. He preferred *Scooby-Doo*. She was sitting upside down on the couch, with her legs draped over the back of it and her head resting on the ground, when her mother appeared. It was interesting to watch TV upside down sometimes, for a change. It was a nice feeling, with all the blood flowing down to your brain and your legs up in the air.

'*How can you watch TV like that?*' asked her mother.

Her mother's feet were flat and bare on the white rug. Her robe hung open to a short satin nightie. From this angle Cassie could see that she wasn't wearing any panties. Cassie swung her legs down and pulled herself up to sitting, and her mother upended herself like an hourglass. Her eyes were black with the make-up she never bothered to remove before she went to bed. Her voice was blurry when she spoke.

'*Jesus, I'm wrecked,*' she said, pushing the heels of her two hands against her eyes, like a bear. '*Did you have any breakfast?*'

Without waiting for an answer, she drifted across to the kitchen island, opening the overhead cupboard where the liquor was kept. She took out a glass bottle – it was one of those gallon bottles with a handle – and filled a Slim Jim with the transparent liquid. She topped the last inch up with tomato juice from the fridge and poured it into herself with all the commitment of a boxer drinking a glassful of raw eggs.

It was either that same day, or another day, that her mother announced they were going to Mexico. There had been an argument with Marty. There had been some shouting and slamming of doors. The next thing, her mother was throwing things into a suitcase.

'But I have school,' said Cassie. There was also the approach of her birthday. She was hoping to invite her classmates to a pool party.

'*Come on, Miss Cass, where's your sense of adventure?*'

'How long are we going for? Where are we going to stay?'

'*Questions, questions,*' said her mother, batting them away with her hand. '*Never in my whole life have I met anyone who asks so many questions.*'

'But wait, who's going to feed the fish?'

The fish were a present from Rigo. He'd presented them to Cassie in a transparent plastic bag. They'd had to put them in the bath until they got a fishbowl for them.

'*Oh, don't worry about that, I'll ask Marty to feed them. They'll be fine.*'

Cassie was only ten at the time, but she was old enough to know that Marty Legge could not be trusted to feed the fish. When Cassie and Christo were little, Marty would arrive at their house and start pulling things out of the pockets of his suit like a magician at a children's birthday party. Marty pulled sweets out of his pockets, and paper money, and toy trinkets, but he never produced anything that succeeded in making them like him more. It was because of Marty that Christo had been sent away. Cassie knew this, from some things she'd overheard, without ever understanding it. All she knew was that it was Marty's fault.

'*Oh, Marty's not the worst,*' her mother said, which seemed to

Cassie, even at the time, like a low bar to set for a boyfriend. '*Don't look at me like that,*' she said. '*I will not be judged by a ten-year-old.*'

'I'm nearly eleven,' said Cassie.

'*Nearly never killed a fly,*' said her mother.

They set out, just the two of them, with their cases tossed on the empty back seat. Blowing into sleepy Mexican towns after dark, they ate tamales they bought from street vendors. They drank warm cream soda from fat glass bottles. They slept in cheap guesthouses under ceiling fans that turned slowly through the night, bringing a chill to the room by dawn, when Cassie would wake hungry for breakfast. Leaving her mother asleep, she would venture in search of food, finding a nearby café where she could buy a guanabana juice and some pastries. The taste of the guanabana was like stolen apples in a dream. The dense little cups of black coffee she carried back to her mother in the room had to be handled with care. Only when her mother had drunk the coffee could they hit the road again.

They listened to Simon and Garfunkel as they drove. Singing along until they knew every word of every song. Forever after, Cassie would dive to turn off the radio the moment she heard the opening bars of 'Kathy's Song' or 'Homeward Bound'. 'American Tune' was unbearable to her. 'Mother and Child Reunion' worse still. Those songs seemed to have been written with no other purpose than to preserve in a jar the last weeks Cassie had spent with her mother. She only had to hear any one of them to relive all the feelings she'd kept bottled up ever since.

The towns they'd passed through were often no more than a single street. Stalls by the side of the road selling brightly striped ponchos and patchwork tablecloths and joyful piñatas. They celebrated Cassie's eleventh birthday by staying at a fancy hotel in Acapulco, where they ate hamburgers and huge ice-cream sundaes. It was a special treat after all the Mexican food they'd been eating. All the crummy guesthouses.

Every time they reached a large town, they had to find the post office. They were expecting some kind of communication from the solicitor in Ireland. Something to do with the grandfather's will. 'Poste restante,' her mother said hopefully, every time, spelling out her name for the clerk and asking him to check and recheck. She used all her charm, but no letter was ever produced, so they picked themselves up again and moved on.

There was a sense of dwindling resources. A dead-end feeling as they finally came to a stop on the Caribbean coast. The guesthouse they made their home was a colonial mansion that had seen better times. It was full of backpackers – Cassie remembered Israelis and Norwegians and French-speaking Canadians and a lone Finn – who sat around the tables in the courtyard drinking bottled beer and smoking cigarettes and speaking English in stilted accents. Cassie's mother often joined them of an evening, while Cassie played solitaire or tried to teach the parrot to say curse words. She never succeeded in getting him to say anything, but whenever it rained, he would pluck the washing from the line and laugh a manic, cackling laugh as the towels and sheets fell on the wet tiled floor.

It rained the night her mother died. Rain so heavy that it drowned out every other sound. The quiet that followed seemed unnatural to Cassie after the tremendous roar of the downpour. She had a ringing in her ears from it, which was perhaps why she didn't notice that her mother had stopped breathing. It was only when she came back into the room the next morning with the coffee that she found she couldn't wake her. Cassie heard the sound of screaming, but it took her a moment to work out that the screams were her own. A sound that was all mixed up in her mind with the parrot's laughter and the pounding rain, even though these things may not have happened at the same time. They had merged in her mind, and it was not possible to disentangle them from each other now. The shock of it, as fresh after twenty-six years as it was then. Shock was not a thing that ever dissipated, as Cassie had learned. The memory of that day had never receded.

'Is that why you came to live in Mexico?' a therapist asked her, once. 'I'm wondering if you found the need to go back to the place where your mother died.'

'No,' said Cassie immediately. 'I don't believe so.'

If anything, it was the exact opposite. Cassie liked being in Mexico because that was the place her mother was last alive. She liked to think she was breathing the same air her mother had breathed before she died.

The post-mortem that was eventually carried out when they got her back to the States recorded a cocaine overdose as the cause of death. The coroner noted, as a contributory factor, the presence of a high dose of amobarbital in her bloodstream in addition to the benzodiazepines she was in the habit of swallowing, along with the antidepressants she had been prescribed for anxiety and the antihistamines she needed for her hay fever. Cassie had always been touched by the presence of an innocent antihistamine on the list, which was habitually described by the media as 'a lethal cocktail of drugs'.

'I just wish we knew, for sure, that it was an accident,' she said to Christo, as they drove the final stretch of road past the beach and the YOU ARE NOW ENTERING PARADISE sign.

'We do know,' he said, making no attempt to conceal the weariness in his voice. 'We know that she would never have abandoned you. She would not have left you alone in a guest-house in Mexico. There's no way on this earth she would have done that. So, it must have been an accident.'

'Maybe,' she said, and lapsed into silence again.

What Christo didn't know was that their mother had been pregnant when she died. Marty knew, because he was the father of the baby, and Cassie knew because her mother had told her. Swearing her to secrecy as they drove, the two of them had amused themselves by thinking up names for the baby as they passed through one-street towns festooned with skulls for the Day of the Dead celebrations. Cassie had carried the secret of that baby with her ever since, keeping it from Christo because she knew it would hurt him to know it. There was only so far she would go to diminish their mother in his eyes.

'*I'm going to need your help,*' she'd told Cassie, as they made plans for the baby's arrival. He was due in April the following year. For some reason, she seemed certain it was a boy.

'*This is going to be a very lucky baby,*' she said. '*He'll have two mums looking after him instead of one.*'

'Jesus!' said Christo, breaking into Cassie's thoughts with a shout as he yanked the steering wheel sharply round. The car swerved to the right, brushing the hedgerow on the far side of the road, before Christo pulled it back into the left-hand lane.

'What the fuck!' said Cassie, bracing herself against the dashboard as they slowed.

'There was a dog,' he said, looking into the rear-view mirror. 'I thought we were going to hit him.'

'Did we?' she asked, turning to look back down the road.

'No,' he said. 'I don't think so. Thankfully.'

His face was drained of colour, his expression weary as they drove the last few miles. Back at the house, he headed straight to his bedroom to take a nap, while Cassie changed into her leggings to do some yoga. She pushed the sofa to the edge of the living room and the coffee table to the other edge, fetching the threadbare rug from the hallway to use as a makeshift mat. It had been five days since she'd so much as touched her toes, and she was starting to feel out of kilter.

She started with a few sun salutations, moving impatiently towards the core of her practice. The more painful the pose, the better Cassie liked it. She was a master of the pigeon pose, capable of holding it for ten minutes or more. Tree pose, chair pose and eagle pose all offered her the opportunity to test her stamina. The ones she didn't like were the balance poses – she found them tiresome – but she loved the corpse pose at the end. The idea was to close your eyes and empty your mind of all your thoughts, but Cassie never could do that. Instead, she lay on the flat of her back with her eyes blind-open, searching out her own mind the way you might search out stars in the night sky.

The old rug she was lying on smelled musty. The ceiling she was staring up at was stained in places, patches of damp appearing as blooms of mould on the white paint. The rain came down relentlessly, falling like tiny pebbles on the sky-light in the hallway. Cassie could hear the sound of it sloshing on the flagstones by the door. The gush of water flowing from the drainpipes out front. The rain made a curtain of sound around the house, cutting it off from the outdoors and creating a make-believe feel to it. Sequestered from the world, you could easily imagine you were hurtling through outer space or braving a storm on the high seas. Those were all games they'd played as kids on rainy days, pushing the couches together to make a spaceship of them. They stripped the blankets off the beds and turned the bunk beds into a den. They flipped the kitchen table upside down and sailed it to America.

'*Somebody should build a roof over this bloody country,*' their mother said. '*Then it might actually be habitable.*'

There was this one rainy day when they all climbed into the car and went to a waterpark. Jim was driving, and Cassie's mother was sitting up front. Seamus was sitting in the back by the window, looking out at the passing fields. Christo was riding high in the middle, with his hands gripping the front seats for dear life, as if it were a speedboat he was riding and not a car on a quiet country road. Margo was wedged in by the other window with Cassie on her lap. Every time a tyre hit a hole in the road, Cassie's head hit the roof. 'Bloody potholes,' said Jim, every time. It became a chant, all of them shouting 'bloody potholes' every time the car hit a bump in the road.

'Bloody potholes, bloody potholes, bloody potholes.'

The waterpark was indoors, rainwater coursing down the outsides of the windows, so you felt like you were in Atlantis. Cassie raced Seamus to the top of the water slide and made sure to go down first, not caring in that moment whether she lived or died. The only thing that mattered was to show him she wasn't scared. The slide had ridges in it where the sections had been fastened together, and they hurt the bones of her bum when she went over them, but she was going so fast there was no time to think about it. The next thing, she was crashing into the pool at the bottom. Her knee smashed against the tiled floor of the pool, her hair was thrown over her face, chlorinated water up her nose. She was gasping for air when Seamus came tumbling down after her, his eyes wide open as he shot out the spout of the slide. Together, they went straight back up and did it again.

For lunch they had chips from the chipper. The chips were fat and salty and soggy with malt vinegar. Cassie loved how the vinegar did a dance on your tongue. She washed her mouth out with some fizzy orange straight from the bottle. If you kept the lid halfway closed on the bottle you could suck the orange out in a trickle, which was a nice feeling, like being a baby. Afterwards the sun came out and Jim treated them all to 99s from the van on the seafront. The ice creams came with chocolate flakes stuck into them like straws. Cassie ate her flake right away, but Christo used his as a spoon to scoop the ice cream. Seamus pushed his down deep into the cone, so that he could eat his way to it like buried treasure. Jim devoured his ice cream like a dog, in three great bites, while Margo twirled hers round in her hand as she licked it to keep it from dripping. Cassie's mother ate hers with her head tilted to one side and her eyes closed to savour the pleasure of it.

'*The 99 may be the best thing about this poxy country*,' she pronounced.

They were sitting on a bench on the promenade. Jim was at one end of the bench, and he started pushing his way towards the centre, knocking Seamus off the other end, as he sang 'six in the bed'. Seamus scrambled back onto the bench, and everyone pushed the other way until Jim tumbled off, and then Christo, and they all sang 'five in the bed'. Then it was 'four in the bed', as Jim and Christo climbed back on and shoved Seamus and the girls off. Cassie and her mother and Margo joined forces and pushed the other way, driving Christo and Jim off the bench onto the ground in a tumble of shouts. But then the boys went round the other side, the dirty cheats, and Cassie found herself on the edge with them all pushing her off. Her mother cried out for her – *Cass-eeeee* – and clung to her so hard that her fingernails cut into the flesh of Cassie's arms. That was how Cassie wanted to remember her mother — all wind-blown hair and grappling fingernails and ice-cream-spiked laughter. It was not the memory she had hoped for, but it occurred to her now that it was enough.

38

There was only one thing left for them to do and that was to climb the mountain. Their last day was clear and bright, as the weather forecast had predicted. There were light easterly winds, which wouldn't give them any trouble. They parked the car at the NO DOGS sign that was painted on the face of a rock and set off up the mountain in single file. Seamus had a backpack with him loaded with bottled water and oranges. Christo was kitted out in a North Face anorak and hiking boots that had the curious look of a costume. Cassie was, as always, dressed as herself.

The first stretch was the hardest. Seamus knew this from experience, how your breath struggled to adjust to the gradient. How you found yourself regretting every cigarette you'd ever smoked, fighting to clear your lungs to make way for the mountain air. The only thing for it was to dig in, head down like a goat, and press on. The terrain was damp and boggy, dotted everywhere with small clusters of sheep droppings. Jim had tricked Seamus into eating them once.

'You see these things,' he'd said to Seamus, picking up a few and displaying them in the palm of his hand. 'Do you know what these are?'

Seamus was six, maybe seven.

'I don't know,' he said, afraid of being caught out.

'These here are get-smart pills,' Jim told him. 'All you have to do is eat one of them and you get really smart straight away.'

Seamus took one and put it in his mouth. He moved it

around with his tongue, trying to avoid chewing on it. Jim watched and waited until he'd swallowed it.

'I thought they were sheep poo,' said Seamus.

'You see?' said Jim. 'You're getting smart already!'

Jim loved to tell that story, weeping with laughter every time. It almost gave Seamus pleasure to see him laugh like that. Old bastard that he was.

'How long to the top?' Cassie asked, stopping to take a gulp of the water Seamus handed her.

Seamus looked up the face of the mountain.

'Longer than you'd think.'

The gradient of the climb was steep but, step by step, they gained purchase on it. Every so often a conversation would strike up between them, only to drop off unfinished as they concentrated on the climb. Looking out for the next foothold on the ground, the rise of the mountain was their only perspective. After two false peaks and a strange boggy valley they had to traverse with care, they reached the summit, where a large standing rock acted as a gathering point. They rested with their hands on their hips, a burning feeling in their lungs, as they surveyed the view they'd won.

'Wow,' said Cassie, looking down on the beaches below.

'That's quite something,' said Christo, as he took in the view.

Seamus retrieved an orange from his backpack and peeled it, passing the segments around.

'Thanks,' said Cassie. 'That's delicious.'

'A feast,' said Christo, 'thank you.'

'Everything tastes better on top of a mountain,' said Seamus. 'I once had a flask of chicken soup up here on a wet day. I think it was the best meal of my life.'

Buffeted by the breeze that at sea level was barely noticeable, they stood sucking on the sweet orange segments as their eyes drank in the view. The twin beaches directly below them shone white as the surface of the moon, the sea they circled an impossibly beautiful blue. Turning to the right, the Twelve Bens stood clearly outlined against a sky busy with clouds. Turning again, they faced an expanse of bog that was lumpy and dimpled in places by black pools of water. There was barely a tree in sight.

'Okay?' said Seamus, once they'd had their fill of the view. 'Are we right?'

There was a lightness to their step as they picked their way carefully back down the mountain. The sense that in summiting they had gained something and then chosen to leave it behind. The backpack Seamus wore was weightless without the oranges they'd consumed at the top.

They had a late lunch in the village pub, shouting to be heard over the noise of a bunch of rowdy Dubliners down for the weekend. Seamus passed up on the offer of the usual lift back from the uncles, travelling instead with Christo and Cassie. They stopped off at the bridge, at Cassie's suggestion, abandoning the car and climbing over the headland to nestle in the dunes above the surfing beach. They sat close but not touching, as they would have as children, and watched the waves roll in. There were half a dozen surfers out to make the most of the last few hours of daylight. They loitered on the surface of the water, waiting for the next wave. Paddling along with it for a few strokes to take the measure of it, before abandoning it to wait for the next one. It was lovely to see them leap to their feet when they found a wave that was worthy of them. Christo and Cassie and Seamus sat and watched them for what seemed like hours. Only when the last streak of light was gone from the sky, and the surfers had packed up their boards and driven away in their vans, did they shake out their legs and trudge back across the headland, their voices like torches as they guided each other through the darkness to the car. They took their time driving the last stretch of road and lingered at the gate with the engine idling, reluctant to say goodnight. They knew the parting would be hurried in the morning.

Seamus woke early and watched, from his kitchen window, as they prepared for departure. He saw but did not hear the doors of the house slamming shut. He watched the car boot closing on their suitcases, the wheels dragging on the gravel driveway. He saw Christo swing the arse of the car out into the road and stop it there. Saw Cassie jump out and race back up towards the house, leaving the passenger door open. The brake lights dropped out as Christo cut the engine and walked down the road to say a last goodbye. Seamus went to open the door for him.

'So, you're ready for the off.'

'I'll see you in Cambridge,' said Christo.

Seamus had mentioned a conference he'd like to attend there the following spring, and Christo had lit up with enthusiasm at the prospect of hosting him.

'Don't even think about booking a hotel,' he'd said. 'I have a perfectly good sofa-bed. You'd be very welcome to stay.'

'I might take you up on that,' said Seamus. 'Thanks.'

'I'll even treat you to spicy prawns at my favourite Thai restaurant.'

'You're on. I'll look forward to it.'

'Well, take care,' said Christo, stepping forwards with his hand out to say goodbye. Seamus had an urge to hug him, but there was in Christo something that forbade it. Instead, Seamus put all the warmth he could into their handshake.

'Safe trip, now.'

Seamus was standing in his bare feet, his toes gripping the cold bar of aluminium that marked the threshold. He had no jumper on, only a short-sleeved t-shirt. He could feel the hairs rising on his arms.

'You must say goodbye to your dad for us.'

'Of course I will.'

'And you might give our regards to Tilly, in case we don't see her on the way out.'

Over Christo's shoulder, Seamus could see Cassie coming down the road. She had her hair pulled off her face in a high ponytail. She was wearing her usual uniform of black jumper, black leggings, black boots. The heavy swing to her walk made every step she took her own.

'I'll wait in the car,' said Christo, so they could take their leave of each other in peace.

'God, I hate goodbyes,' she said, turning to look out across the pier. Her eyes roamed the view from right to left, as if she was trying to engrave it on her mind. Seamus watched her take a deep breath in through her nose and, closing her eyes, hold it there. She might have been trapping the air in her lungs to take it with her. He stepped forwards and wrapped his arms around her from behind, exhaling with her as together they stood and memorized the world as it was in that moment, with the sun rising behind them and the water glistening like fish skin in the morning light and the mountains barely a whisper against the quiet sky.

After they'd gone, Seamus drove over to Omey, taking care to check the tides first. The last thing he wanted was to get stuck out there.

'Anyone home?' he shouted, knocking on the caravan door.

There was no answer.

Seamus swung the door open, expecting – as he did every time – to find his father dead in the bed, but it was empty and unmade. The coffee pot was sitting, still hot, on the hob. The frying pan next to it bore traces of Jim's cooked breakfast. A knife and fork rested in the pan, evidence that Jim had dispensed with the use of a plate. From behind the closed bathroom door Seamus could hear the sound of his coughing. Seamus poured himself a mug of coffee and slid onto the bench seat to wait for him.

The sound effects were terrible. It sounded like Jim was drowning in his own phlegm. Seamus could hear his efforts to dredge it up with each cough, hocking globs of it into his throat with unbearable patience and spitting them out. Just when Seamus couldn't stand listening to any more there came the sound of the toilet flushing and his father emerged, red-faced and battle-weary.

'Don't say it.'

Seamus took his fags out of his pocket.

'I was only going to offer you one of mine,' he said. 'I find it does wonders for clearing out the airwaves in the morning.'

'Ah don't worry. I have me own, son.'

Together they went to stand in the open doorway of the caravan to smoke. The weather was closing in. Dark clouds advancing from the north-west with sinister intent. The sea was the colour of molten lead.

'Sure, who wants to live forever anyway,' said Seamus, tossing the end of his cigarette into the field.

'Now you have it,' said Jim, drawing the door closed behind them as they stepped back inside.

They sat down, with their hands wrapped around their mugs of coffee, like an old married couple. Jim was wearing a diamond-patterned sleeveless jumper over the tracksuit bottoms. On his forearms were deep purple blotches. At first Seamus wondered were they bruises, until it occurred to him they might be age spots. Jim had the same marks on the backs of his hands, like the black spot you see on rose bushes in summer. Old age was eating away at him like a fungus. Again, it occurred to Seamus that there would be no conflagration, no bolt from the blue, and that this would be worse. The indignity of a slow death.

'So, they left this morning,' said Seamus.

'Right,' said Jim. 'And how do we feel about that?'

'What do you mean?'

'Well, I thought there might be something cooking between you and young Cassie.'

Seamus paused, tempted to cut him off at the pass, but for whatever reason he didn't.

'Yeah,' he said, 'so did I. For a minute there. But it turned out it was nothing.'

'Better off,' said Jim. 'No good could come of it. You'd want to hitch your wagon to something more hopeful, son. That's your only chance.'

'You missed your vocation,' said Seamus. 'You should have been a psychiatrist. You seem to see it all so fucking clearly.'

Jim shucked, acknowledging the truth of this, like it was said without irony.

'You should know that I wrote to her.'

Seamus had the feeling that he'd missed something, like he was listening to the radio and the sound had dropped out for a second. Jim's narrative had jumped forward without warning.

'Hang on. Wrote to who?'

'That girl. Rhona.'

'What do you mean you wrote to her?'

'I wanted to explain it to her. That it wasn't your fault.'

Seamus waited for the anger that would surely bubble up in him at hearing this, but to his surprise it didn't. Instead, all he felt was a huge, hollow sadness.

'It was because of my actions that you couldn't marry her. It was because of things that I did. The damage I caused. I didn't want her going through her whole life blaming you.'

'Right,' said Seamus, stunned.

'I accept that, and I'm sorry for it, but there's no undoing it now.'

Was that an apology? If so, Seamus didn't know what to make of it. All his life, he had blamed his father not just for his mother's death but for every little thing that had happened to him since. The practice of blaming Jim for everything was a part of him, unhealthy but immensely comforting, like the long habit of smoking. As a student, Seamus once even went along to a gig of his dad's – in a decrepit venue on Dublin's Francis Street which had long since been demolished – and shouted 'asshole' from the safety of the mosh pit. 'Asshole,' he shouted, to his heart's content, safe in the knowledge that Jim couldn't hear him behind the wall of sound. That was the only chance he ever had to fully vent his rage, but it was in every word he ever uttered towards his father, every enquiry he ever fielded from others about him. 'How's your dad keeping?' people would ask, and Seamus would always pause before he answered, as a hint at the heavy burden of bitterness he carried. Something that had never not been with him, it weighed him down like a sack of rocks. To have it lifted off him now was a strange feeling, and by no other person than Jim himself. It would take some time to adjust to life without it.

'What you have to understand,' said Jim, 'is that we thought we were the goodies. All the shit going on in this country with the priests and the nuns. We thought we were the opposite of all that. We never thought we were doing any harm.'

It was as close to an apology as he was going to get, Seamus realized. It was not proportional to the anger he'd nursed all his life, but it would have to do.

He drove back along the road with the rain clouds chasing him from behind, stopping at the petrol station on the edge of town to buy a bunch of flowers for Laura. He knew he had amends to make, knew this was the traditional way of doing so, but he felt awkward buying them, more awkward still at the thought of presenting them to her. Never in his whole life had he bought a woman a bunch of flowers, wary not so much of the sentimentality of the gesture as the public nature of it. Even as a child, Seamus hated to be made a show of in public. He'd lived in fear of getting a medal at the school sports day, because he'd have to stand up in front of everyone to receive it. Hated anyone singing 'Happy Birthday' to him, so his mother never put candles on his cake.

'Don't mind him,' she'd say. 'He's as odd as two left shoes.'

It became a point of pride with him. For nearly forty years, he had made it his business to avoid all such ceremonies, which was why the purchase of a ten-euro bunch of filling-station flowers was so difficult for him. He took his place in the queue for the till with grim determination, steeling himself against his own imminent mortification. His face was funereal as he paid for them, daring the girl at the till under pain of death to smile. But then something unexpected happened to him as he left the filling station, with the bunch of flowers held upside down by his side with one hand like a shotgun. Something strangely lightening – he found himself smiling at the thought of the pleasure they would so soon bring.

39

Christo had checked the tides before they left, timing their journey for low water so they would be sure to find the drowned forest. The wind was behind them as they drove, the grasses and reeds all blowing in their direction as if to speed them on their way. The sloping ground on either side of the car was the texture of rough animal hide. The mountains in the distance as soft and smooth as brown velvet.

They passed a plethora of FOR SALE signs on the route, but instead of imagining that his mother might still be out there somewhere hunting for a place to live out her life, Christo saw that the world had moved on without her in it, and that any possibilities that once existed for her had long since been left behind. For the first time he found peace in the knowledge that her churning, restless life was over, and that it could not now be altered for better or worse.

The sky lightened as they drove. The landscape brightened, leaving behind the strange dreamlike state of the western reaches and assuming something like normality. Trees began to make an appearance, at first only as aberrations, but then they began to see regular swathes of newly planted pines tucked into the folds of the hills. On the bend of a gushing brown river, a fisherman in waders was coaxing his line out of the water. They passed through towns with bookshops and chemists and solicitor's offices, all with their doors closed for the Sunday. The county's chequered flags fluttered hopefully from the lamp posts.

They found the turn for Séan Flynn's farm and parked in

the lane beside the farmhouse gate. There was a black and white dog roaming the yard but no sign of any human presence. They crossed the field and found the beach fully exposed by a low tide, with grey shingle as far as the eye could see. Christo had not been expecting the beach to be so wide, and his heart sank. The task of finding anything seemed all but impossible. He walked to the right first, stumbling over the stones in his leather shoes. Among them he saw nothing but debris: frayed orange rope and plastic water drums and a single blue rubber glove. There were big brutish daisies growing on the high ground and yellow lichen on the larger rocks. There were necklaces of gleaming black seaweed with swollen pustules that burst open when he stepped on them, but nowhere were there trees.

Christo turned and walked back the way he'd come, resigned now to not finding anything. He picked his way over the stones, looking up every so often at the sidelong rolling waves that swept in from the Atlantic. He saw four white birds shuffle across the sky, as awkward together as a pantomime horse. He was close to the shore now and the going was springy like a carpet. He looked down and saw bog water, dark as urine, gathering round his shoes. He saw brown peat where there should have been sand, and then he saw a network of roots embedded in the peat. He followed this miracle tenderly, taking great care not to step on the delicately preserved roots. What he'd found seemed to him enough to make the trip more than worthwhile, but then he caught sight of a tree stump.

It was a foot high and perhaps two feet in diameter. Wood with the appearance of old buried bones, it was soft and damp from being soaked through with salt water. The grain of the wood was clearly visible in rippling circles. The place where the rest of the tree should have been was nothing but an amputated trunk. The wound was as smooth in places as the knuckles of a hand. Christo hunkered down to be closer to it, closing his palm over a rounded stump. He felt the rare honour of touching something so very old. Peering into the trunk of the tree, he saw that the sea had hollowed out a space, and in the space there rested a single white stone, like an egg in its nest. Looking round him, Christo saw there were other tree stumps rising out of the sand. Trees surrounded by the incoming shallows, he counted ten, twenty, and then lost count. As far as the eye could see there were trees, rising out of the sea.

'Cassie,' Christo shouted, straightening up and looking around for her. 'I've found them.'

Acknowledgements

This book is the result of a long love affair with Connemara. People familiar with the area around Clifden will recognize some of the places I describe. People very familiar with the area will know that I've used poetic licence to play around with the topography.

I'm grateful to Alison Walsh for her work on an early incarnation of this novel. Meg MacMahon, Hilary McGouran and Valerie Bistany were valuable first readers. Patrick Scott was a great help with later drafts. Cormac Kinsella is a stalwart friend and adviser. My agent Marianne Gunn O'Connor has been a kind and loyal supporter from the start.

I'm fortunate to have the wonderful Patricia Deevy as my editor. Her intelligence and sound judgement helped improve this novel no end. Gemma Wain was a supremely patient and scrupulous copyeditor. I have Julia Connolly to thank for the gorgeous cover design. It's always a pleasure to work with Cliona Lewis on publicity, and I count myself very lucky to have Michael McLoughlin and the rest of the team at Penguin Sandycove on my side. Many thanks to all of them for their efforts on my behalf.

Finally, I want to thank my family and friends for their kindness and understanding of my work life. I can always rely on Des and Meg for support and encouragement, for which I'm endlessly grateful. To Lucy, Clara and Mark, much love always.

The hearts invisible fury
John Boyne

Shuggie Bain